Praise fo

The Pursuit of Ordinary

Original and compelling, *The Pursuit of Ordinary* is perfectly paced and beautifully written.
Colette McBeth, author, *Precious Thing, The Life I Left Behind, An Act of Silence*

This novel has a very striking premise which Nigel Cooper executes with great skill. He gets under the skin of his characters and gradually reveals the psychological wheels within wheels of his two main characters, Daniel and Natalie. A fascinating read.
Jane Lythell, author, *The Lie of You, After The Storm, Woman of the Hour, Behind Her Back*

An author with a truly compelling insight into the human condition.
Siobhan Kennedy, *Channel 4 News*

Cooper has a rare knack for presenting flawed characters in a way that makes the reader care about them.
Love Reading UK

Nigel Jay Cooper has the ability to grip the reader in a fashion I have never before experienced.
Lisa Doherty, *Book Blogger*

Nigel's works have a knack of grabbing me and pulling me in so that I can't put them down.
Nikki Murphy, *Book Blogger*

A new voice. Fresh and different.
Maha Diwan, *Book Blogger*

What readers are saying about

The Pursuit of Ordinary

Where to start about this lovely book? First of all, I've been a fan of Nigel Cooper after reading his debut novel, *Beat the Rain* which I absolutely loved! Dare I say this one is even better? The plot is so incredibly unique and yet all parts of it work to create a beautiful and heartfelt story that weaves in social commentary without becoming preachy... With marvellously flawed characters and poignant, lovely writing, Cooper speaks to the themes of passion, guilt, redemption, depression, mental illness, and homelessness. The book will make you laugh and make you cry as the storyline is slowly revealed in voices of Joe, Dan, and Natalie. It will also keep you guessing until the very end; quite simply put, it is superb!
Anne F, *Netgalley Review*

Twisting, hypnotic trip into the disconnect from ordinary. The book will not let the reader go, even after the last word has been read.
Mollie G, *Netgalley Review*

A very simple cover that encases a wonderful book ... one cannot judge THIS book by its dust jacket for sure. If you loved *Before I Go to Sleep, Gone Girl* or *The Girl on the Train*, this book is right up your alley and full of twists and shocking turns. Wonderfully written, it kept me guessing right until the end when I found myself saddened that the book was over. READ THIS BOOK! MAKE YOUR BOOKCLUB READ THIS BOOK! ... You won't be sorry.
Janet C, *Netgalley Review*

The Pursuit of Ordinary is an extraordinary novel. I had to sit back and think about what I thought about the book once I'd finished it. It is a compelling read with complex, emotional, real and challenged characters. My views towards the characters changed dramatically as the story unfolded and their true characters and agendas were laid bare. Nothing was as it first seemed. A gripping and intense read – don't expect to put it down until you've turned the last page, even then you'll still be trying to decide if the characters were truly justified in their actions!

Clare S, *Goodreads Review*

Beautifully written book that pulls you in from the start. What stood out for me is how well-crafted it is. *The Pursuit of Ordinary* is a wonderful piece of modern fiction. Thought-provoking from start to end, the characters and narrative are compelling with twists I didn't expect. And at its core are themes of love and mental health. Cooper has created characters so tenderly drawn that you ache for them as their story unfolds. Highly recommend this book to both new readers and those who loved his first novel.

Janet C, *Netgalley Review*

What an emotional read this was! Nigel's portrayal of the characters, and his analysis of homelessness and mental health issues is compelling and at the same time caring. The book keeps you guessing from start to finish and you cannot help but feel for the characters and get involved in their lives as their relationships unfold. One of those books you can't put down.

Sara M, *Goodreads Review*

Another brilliant book from Nigel Jay Cooper, one you won't forget for good reasons... a wonderfully creative story with all the depth of character Cooper writes with ease. A tale of the unexpected, a tale of hope and despair and life. Of smiles and tears, ups and downs. Friends, lovers and relations. A brilliant concept, beautifully written and a highly enjoyable read.

Nicki M, *Goodreads Review*

As with Nigel's debut *Beat The Rain*, this was beautifully written and very clever... just when I thought I knew what was what, the rug was pulled from under me. This novel was 'human' - it has a real heart. It raises so many issues and somehow made me think differently about them... A great read.

Andrew S, *Goodreads Review*

This is Nigel Jay Cooper's sophomore novel and he does not disappoint. This is a captivating Contemporary Fiction novel, both powerful and plausible. I think one of Nigel's biggest qualities as an author is his ability to write about the common fellow and see beyond the surface. His characters are real people, just like any of us. His talent is presenting these people as whole individuals. Neither good or bad. He leaves the judgment to us. In *The Pursuit of Ordinary*, he explores the themes of grief, mental health and love. How far are we willing to go to avoid the pain? What risks will we take? The storyline is compelling and exciting. His narrative beautifully flows and it unfolds chapter by chapter with the right amount of twists and turns...There is pain and grief between the pages, but also tenderness and understanding. As someone who works in the mental health field, I thoroughly appreciated how Nigel presented the subject with dignity and respect. It's refreshing to find a story where a person can struggle with mental health but still be worthy of self-agency and love. We need more books like this!

Michelle D, *Netgalley Review*

Beautifully crafted and so very unusual. My first impressions of the book as a kind of ghost story were quickly dispelled and I was kept guessing where the story would go... it was thought provoking and deliciously intriguing. Highly recommended.

Janet C, *Netgalley Review*

This book is original and thought-provoking and, essentially, a love story. It is beautifully written with believable characters. I love reading books set in Brighton, and I loved Nigel's first book *Beat the Rain* - very clever how he subtly linked the two. I thoroughly recommend you read this wonderful and intriguing story - especially if you liked 'Beat the Rain'.

Kate R, *Goodreads Review*

The Pursuit of Ordinary. Ordinary? I don't think so. This book, like Coopers debut novel, *Beat the Rain*, (which I loved) is extraordinary. His well and sensitively drawn characters engage the reader from the onset. The originality of the plot line with its tantalising twists and turns and the way the narrative unfolds from the seemingly similar, but differing points of view of the three principle characters, has the reader hooked wanting to know if these damaged souls will succeed in their pursuit of becoming ordinary.

Veryann W, *Netgalley Review*

Nigel Jay Cooper has given us another great novel! This was an intriguing story from page one... and what happens in the next 300 pages was completely unexpected and interesting. I wanted to know more about each character and it was deliciously delivered with a perfect pace. The characters are well-developed and multi-dimensional. The author paints a vivid picture of the situation. I can't wait for another novel by this fantastic author.

Becky N, *Netgalley Review*

The Pursuit
of Ordinary

The Pursuit
of Ordinary

Nigel Jay Cooper

Winchester, UK
Washington, USA

First published by Roundfire Books, 2018
Roundfire Books is an imprint of John Hunt Publishing Ltd., No. 3 East St., Alresford,
Hampshire SO24 9EE, UK
office1@jhpbooks.net
www.johnhuntpublishing.com
www.roundfire-books.com

For distributor details and how to order please visit the 'Ordering' section on our website.

Text copyright: Nigel Jay Cooper 2017

ISBN: 978 1 78535 806 7
978 1 78535 807 4 (ebook)
Library of Congress Control Number: 2017951462

All rights reserved. Except for brief quotations in critical articles or reviews, no part of this book
may be reproduced in any manner without prior written permission from the publishers.

The rights of Nigel Jay Cooper as author have been asserted in accordance with the Copyright,
Designs and Patents Act 1988.

A CIP catalogue record for this book is available from the British Library.

Design: Stuart Davies

Printed and bound by CPI Group (UK) Ltd, Croydon, CR0 4YY, UK

We operate a distinctive and ethical publishing philosophy in
all areas of our business, from our global network of authors to
production and worldwide distribution.

Contents

For Florence and Louis, who make my ordinary life extraordinary.

Acknowledgments

To Andy, Florence and Louis, thanks for your continued support—I couldn't do any of this without you. Also, thanks for putting up with me when I'm writing and 'not in the room' mentally. Thanks also to Luka dog, who obviously can't read this, for being the best dog in the world.

Thanks also to Amanda, Caroline, Sam, Emily, Kate, Michelle and Marc—your insight and feedback on the early drafts was incredibly valuable and *The Pursuit of Ordinary* is a better book because of you.

To everyone who has endorsed me and/or this novel, thank you so much—it makes such a difference. This crazy world of publishing is filled with self-doubt and your words and endorsements lifted me up when I needed it.

To all of the book bloggers who reviewed and shared my debut novel *Beat The Rain*, thank you so much, you were invaluable.

Thanks again to my parents for their ongoing support and last, but not least, thanks to Roundfire Books and JHP Fiction for believing in me and my novels—I'm incredibly grateful for your support.

PART I: JOE

'I think I'm losing myself.'

CHAPTER 1

Dan smiles at my wife again. He has such a beguiling smile; I wish mine were like his. When I smile at people, even if I'm happy, it comes across apologetically, like I'm embarrassed to be there, like I wish something dark would rise out of the ground and grab me, dragging me under and obscuring me from view. But, despite his problems, when Dan smiles, the room takes notice.

'What do you remember, Dan?' Natalie asks. She's not slurring. I would be after four glasses of wine, but I don't drink much anymore. Dan has never been a big drinker. I'd like to drink a little more than he lets me, but I must concede to his rules. After all, he's in charge now. Sometimes that's the hardest thing to adjust to: my lack of choices. Free will is something you take for granted until it's knocked out of you by a fast-moving vehicle.

'Dan? What do you remember about...?' she says again, trailing off without finishing the sentence, like she can't bring herself to say, 'the accident'. We never discuss it, and we don't tell her what we remember, what we know. She thinks the details are foggy, but that's not true, at least not for me. I know Dan doesn't like to think about it, but the whole thing is crystal clear in my mind, a moment frozen in time, chrome-filtered and shining.

* * *

At first, it was like a silent movie, everything moving too fast, a burst-eardrum vacuum in the aftermath of an explosion. Except there hadn't been an explosion, there had been a car crash. Was it two cars or three? Then came the screaming and shouting. It was horrific, intrusive. Other sounds; someone must have called an ambulance, sirens were approaching, weaving their way through traffic, jumping red lights, wailing and crying in distorted blue grief. Cars were pulling over onto wet, puddled curbs to let them pass. Dan was there, standing gobsmacked in the road, but even he didn't know how life-changing it would be, not yet. He could feel the buzz of electricity filling the air. His breathing was synchronised with the lungs of the other witnesses littering the pavement behind him, inhaling deeper and deeper and deeper, forgetting to exhale until it became painful. Lightheaded, like he might pass out.

Life, in the form of death, had arrived on the streets of Brighton. Everyone was staring past Dan toward the cars that had collided and the pedestrian they'd hit. People were speaking in loud whispers, fumbling for their phones, for their Facebook and Twitter and Instagram apps, at once horrified and exhilarated by the carnage before them, desperate to share it, to validate it, to become a street journalist, just for a moment.

OMG there's been a crash on Western Road #carnage

A woman, maybe in her early thirties, was in the road as well, cradling a man in her arms. He was bleeding badly from his head and there was blood on her hands and jeans. She was screaming, shouting for the help nobody was offering, because everybody was frozen, silently acknowledging the thing she clearly couldn't. He was already dead.

Dan pushed past someone so he could see more of the scene. As he moved closer, he could see the woman more clearly. She must have been the man's wife. There was a gold band on her wedding finger matching one on the man's own. For a moment, Dan got lost in the detail of the guy's fingers, thin brown hairs, smooth knuckle wrinkles and pale pink flesh with a couple of freckles on his index finger. Slowly, he moved his gaze upward, careful to avoid the man's broken head nestling in the woman's lap. When his eyes found her face, he was shocked to see she was looking directly at him, making eye contact. That was strange.

Nobody ever made eye contact with the homeless.

'Did you see?' She shouted, desperate, pleading, like she was scared, like she needed something from him. She was so beautiful. He knew it was wrong to even notice, given the mangled body on her lap, but he couldn't help it. He was lost in her.

'I'm sorry,' he mumbled, but there was so much commotion around her, he couldn't be sure she'd heard him. Maybe she hadn't been talking to him at all. The police and an ambulance arrived, pairs of rough hands pushed him backward, away from the roadside and back onto the pavement, where he could hear people shuffling away from him, muttering something about the smell — his smell.

'Madam?' an officer said gently. 'Madam? What's your name?'

'Natalie,' she answered quietly.

'And is this your husband?'

There were too many people pushing and shoving and he was being thrown backward, away from the scene, away from Natalie and...

'Joe,' she said.

Dan didn't understand why, but he already felt connected to her. Every part of him felt needle sharp, focused and alive.

'His name's Joe,' Natalie reiterated to the policeman.

For a second, Dan couldn't tell if she was talking about him or the body on the ground, but why would she be talking about him? She didn't even know him and his name wasn't Joe.

But mine is.

I'm piecing things together. I must have been dead on the street that day, for a little while, at least. The car hit me and I hurtled through darkness, memories rushing past me, black-and-white Polaroids caught in the wake of a massive storm. I couldn't catch them or feel them. They were on the edge of reality, taunting me, offering answers to questions I didn't remember asking. I don't know how long I was dead. Seconds? Minutes?

Either way, there were no tunnels with white lights at the end. There were no feelings of well-being or calm euphoria. There was nothing but a thick void, endless, timeless, emotionless. Then, a jolt. A painful explosion of heat rushed in as my body closed back around me. But it felt alien, uncomfortable, nothing like before. Not like my body at all, in fact. But I'd been hit by a car, I remembered that. I could still smell it, the burning rubber, the scorched metal and paint.

There was a commotion on the street around me. Pushing myself up, I leant back against a large black bin, rubbing the smooth plastic surface with my palm over and over again, shielding my eyes from the light with the other hand. It was weird, because despite being right handed, I was using my left hand to block the sun.

'Somebody, please?' I tried to speak, but couldn't make my voice sound like I wanted it to. Nobody was listening to me anyway; they were all too busy watching the drama unfold before them—the dead body being lifted from Natalie's lap, being carried to an ambulance.

'Somebody,' I whimpered again, fear and panic setting it. I wanted someone to tell me it was okay, that it was all going to be all right. Then came the blazing sirens, commotion and...

'Help me...' I croaked. The voice that came out of my mouth wasn't one I recognised. It wasn't my voice; it was deeper, much deeper. My head ached, like I had a hangover. No, not a hangover. It was like I was drunk, that kind of continuous, all-day-drinking drunk, part hungover, part paralytic. I couldn't work out why nobody was helping me, why they were all concentrating on Natalie and the other guy who'd been hit.

My body didn't feel right, it was like a scratchy knitted jumper I couldn't shake off. My feet were clad in stale, moist socks and I had a painful, persistent itching between the toes on both feet. Athlete's foot? My body didn't feel like an athlete's; it didn't feel fit or healthy at all, not like it used to. Painful molars ached in the back of my mouth, so much so that I immediately wanted to claw at them and rip them from my sweaty, bearded mouth.

Bearded? I was clean-shaven, I'd always been clean-shaven. But this face was itchy, covered in hair. My nostrils were running and sore, the snot so acidic it stung the flesh of my upper lip. I gagged slightly on the stench of half-eaten burgers and rotting fish coming from the black bin beside me. But there was another smell, like dried, day-old alcohol piss.

The body they were carrying to the ambulance... It couldn't be. It wasn't possible. I squeezed my eyes shut again and concentrated on the red glow coming through my eyelids. For a moment, a hazy image flitted into my head; a small child on an orange space hopper wearing denim shorts and a chequered blue shirt. An old woman standing in an open doorway before the boy, wiping floured hands onto her apron. I didn't recognise her. I'd never met her but somehow, I knew who she was.

This couldn't have happened. I never believed in the supernatural, anyway. Natalie was the one who visited psychics and read her horoscope every day like it meant something. *Gemini, you may tune in more strongly than usual to the thoughts and feelings of others, today. It's a good day to connect with lovers, friends and family.* That had never been me. Natalie was the one who thought homeopathy was a science and acupuncture worked and *Most Haunted* was a documentary.

There had to be an explanation, but everything was a jumble of thoughts and feelings and it was hard to tell which were my own and which were... Whose?

I squinted, allowing the light into my eyes as the street before me came into focus. Grey paving slabs, tarmac road with no cars parked on it, tower block walls on either side of me, grimy, charcoal smears. Taking a few steps, I saw I was now by some sort of alley, connecting one road with another. In the back corner was a row of large black wheelie bins, alongside a couple of green recycling bins. I think he'd slept behind these before, maybe even last night.

He.

I glanced down at his clothes – jeans, a jumper over a T-shirt, dirty black trainers. The stains and sick and piss seemed relatively recent, but by the same token, the feel of the clothes on his skin suggested they'd been on him for a few days at least. They were part of him, an itchy and constant reminder of hard times.

'I don't know what to do, gran,' I heard a frightened voice say from inside my mind, a memory that wasn't mine, playing internally. He was sitting opposite an old woman. She was in a nursing home or hospital. She was important to him; I could feel it in the pit of his stomach. This memory was strong, at the surface, waiting to pounce and overwhelm me. She was quiet, staring silently at the wall, letting the warm light from the window penetrate her translucent, screwed-up paper skin. He'd have done anything to hear her speak to him, to say his name.

'Dan.'

That wasn't my name. Who was I before I arrived in this body? It was already difficult to remember, to maintain any clarity. I was terrified I was going to lose myself to his memories forever.

Joe, my name was Joe.

I scoured the street, pushing past pedestrians and making my way along the pavement as the ambulance with Natalie and my real body inside pulled away. As it cleared my view, I realised I was in Hove; I recognised the Waitrose and the Mad Hatter Café opposite me. Brighton and Hove. I lived here with Natalie. I had to focus, to keep hold of her face, her dark brown eyes, anything, I needed to stop his memories invading and taking over and consuming me...

'You're putting a bit of weight on, Grandma,' came his voice. The memory was surfacing again, playing over and over in his head: Dan visiting the nursing home. 'You need to lay off the hospital puddings.' He smiled, leaning in to affectionately squeeze the roll of fat around his gran's midriff...and, oh my

God, no…I was laughing. For a bizarre moment, I found myself standing on the street, wrecked cars and police all around me, and I was chuckling, making Dan's body shake with a deep-throated laugh.

'Shit,' Dan said in the memory, retracting his hand as if his grandmother had stung him. The roll of fat he had gently pressed between his thumb and forefinger hadn't been a roll of fat at all, it had been her drooping breast.

'Sorry,' he said desperately, trying to make her understand he hadn't meant it. But her small, dark eyes told him she was scared. They pierced him through wrinkled folds, scouring him, trying to work out who he was, why he wanted to hurt her.

'It's okay. It's me, Dan,' he said in a calmer, quieter tone. 'Bob's boy.'

Her shoulders relaxed a little at this and, gradually, her thin, pale arms rested back on her lap. Pursing her lips, she turned away, staring once more at her brown cream wallpaper. She'd died that night. Accidentally squeezing her breast had been his last interaction with her.

As soon as it arrived, my laughter disappeared. Her death had been the catalyst for everything; it's how he'd ended up living like this, on the streets and alone. She'd been more than a grandmother to him, she'd been like a mother. I staggered and leant against a wall, rubbing tears from my eyes—his eyes—as waves of fresh emotion coursed through his body.

* * *

Focus. I didn't have a grandmother with dementia. I didn't live on the streets, I lived with my wife. My parents lived…somewhere. I tried to picture my mum, and saw her long red hair…no, her brown hair. Short brown hair, flower print dresses. I needed to keep hold of *my* thoughts, *my* feelings. He was trying to get the memory of the car crash out of his head, trying to forget my mangled body, the beautiful woman, screaming and crying and looking right at him, like she was desperate for something from him. And he *could* give her something, I realised. He could give her exactly what she wanted, he just didn't know it yet, because I was inside him, if only he'd look for me. But he was scared. No, not scared, unsettled. Edgy, like there was something he was trying to forget. He thought of the way Natalie had stared at him, filled with fear and desperation. He wasn't used to people looking at him at all. Most people looked away, assuming he was a drug addict or a drunk or a criminal. He had to be something *other*, something removed from their daily lives, from their hopes and dreams and fears. If they were good people, they created a version of him to pity. If they weren't good, they saw him as something that needed to be removed from polite society, hidden away, forgotten or ignored. But most people? Most people didn't see him, a homeless man, at all—and that kind of invisibility hurt. It etched away at his soul. Some days, he wondered whether they were right. Maybe he didn't exist. Maybe he was just some phantom wandering the streets, begging for acknowledgment, for existence, for a self. He'd spent a long time feeling like that. Like he didn't exist. That's why they'd medicated him.

Medicated?

'What?'

Did you hear me?

Nothing. He'd drifted off again, leaving me alone in his body. I was shivering; it was freezing. I could tell that part of him was comforted by the anonymity of life on the streets, but he was scared, too.

I don't know how long I drifted in and out of awareness. Sometimes it was dark, like I was sleeping, other times I felt fully conscious and part of him. At some point, I became aware he needed to find somewhere to sleep, anywhere that was warm and safe. Maybe he could sleep by the bus and coach station near the seafront, except he no longer had a sleeping bag and it was freezing at night near the sea. No, he was going to head for the park and sleep on a bench there because they weren't homeless-proofed yet. It would only be for a night, and then he'd have to find a hostel or something. He couldn't stand hostels, they made him feel anxious and there were too many people in a small space, damaged people, depressed people, people on brown or methadone. Unless it was absolutely freezing or pissing it down, he would rather be outside on his own. Better that than risk falling asleep in one of those places.

I wasn't used to sleeping rough, so I would have preferred him to go inside somewhere, because nowhere was clean outside and it was autumn and his arms, legs, and feet were all covered in insect bites. And the hostels might have given him food; they might even have given him a shower and cleaned his clothes. But going somewhere for help would have meant dealing with other people, and I could see why he wouldn't want to do that.

Everything was utter confusion, a bombardment of memories and thoughts and feelings that weren't my own. Darkness, light, awareness, sleep. Making sense of any of it was difficult.

'Did you see?' Natalie had asked him at the scene of the accident. She must have been devastated, watching me die like that. Natalie. My wife. I needed a pen and paper, quickly, while I still remembered. Scanning the street, I saw a café on the opposite side. I bolted across the road, dodging cars as I went, ignoring the beeping horns, slapping one car and terrifying the woman behind the wheel before bolting onward. In Pâtisserie Valerie, I ran up to the counter, where a teenage waitress was already wondering how to get rid of me, thinking that if she looked at the floor, I might disappear, taking my stink with me so she wouldn't have to deal with it.

'Give me a pen and paper,' I said. I was getting used to Dan's voice by this point, and was even starting to quite enjoy using it.

She looked up at me, a wide-eyed child.

'Now,' I said, firmly.

'Um.'

She pushed her dark hair back behind her ear and clicked her tongue piercing against the back of her teeth, staring at the cakes and quiches in the glass case in front of her, still hoping I was going to disappear.

'There,' I said urgently, pointing toward a small pad jutting out of the waitress pouch around her waist.

'Oh no, sorry, I can't, that's my...'

I leant over and snatched the pad and pen, running from the café as fast as I could. Rounding the corner, I crouched down, leaning the pad on my leg, using his left hand to write, which felt weird although his handwriting was quite neat, neater than mine ever was.

Natalie. Find her, tell her I'm still alive. She'll help you. She'll help us both.

Clutching the paper in my fist, I leant my head back against the wall and closed my eyes. I didn't understand what was happening to me, but I did know one thing. We had to find Natalie, for both our sakes.

* * *

At some point, Dan made his way up the steep hill from Western Road, weaving his way through familiar streets, past Brunswick School and toward the park. He barely noticed any of the people he passed because he kept his head bowed. If he didn't look at them, they wouldn't have to see him and he wouldn't impact on their well-constructed lives. Somehow, this comforted him, like he was doing something nice for them, even if they didn't realise it.

St. Ann's Well Gardens was a good place to sleep. The natives were pretty friendly and in the morning it was only dog walkers and families on the school run. People mostly left him alone, especially if he was in his little tent, tucked away around the back, behind the pond. If he was in a sleeping bag in the doorway of the Bowls Club area, he had to be careful that dogs didn't try and piss on him. There weren't many worse ways to be woken in the morning than a fat Labrador spraying urine into your face. It wasn't too scary at night there, either. He didn't feel worried someone was going to attack him or rob him while he slept there. Not that he had anything left to rob, since his tent, rucksack and sleeping bag had been taken by those dicks coming out of a nightclub near the seafront the other week. They'd been laughing their heads off like it had been the funniest thing in the world, like it hadn't been important. In fact, Dan suspected that when they'd woken up with hangovers the next day, they probably hadn't even remembered at all, it had probably been another pissed-up night, a laugh, no harm done. Loads of people had been passing by, watching as they pushed him to the ground, goading and egging each other on as if it were a game, grabbing his stuff and chucking it to one another – just a laugh and not his life, his warmth, his survival they'd been messing with. Nobody watching had tried to help. That was fine; Dan got it. He wasn't their responsibility, it wasn't their fault he was homeless. Nobody owed him anything. But if you see two drunken douchebags hitting a stranger in the street, stealing his things, the only things that keep him warm at night, surely you acknowledge that it's happening? You don't walk on by and let things like that happen to another human being, do you?

Another human being.

I think that's the point. He wasn't another human being, not to them. He was feral, forgettable, an oubliette of a man. They walked on and did everything they could not to notice, not to care. Not their problem.

Dan arrived at St. Ann's Well Gardens while it was still light. It was a while before dusk, and he shouldn't have been there so early. He didn't like being in the park while the families and happy couples were still active. Children were running around in the muddy grass and climbing on the massive carved wooden squirrel nestling in the bushes. Older kids were playing table tennis on the stone table on the green and couples were sitting outside the café, drinking coffee and laughing, unaware of other people's problems.

Being alone was better. He was safer alone. He needed to find somewhere to hole up until dark, when he could grab the spot in the Bowls clubhouse doorway for the night. As he walked along the side of the bowling green, heading out of the park toward Nizells Avenue, he heard a car wheel spin, screeching away down the road.

A car accident, he'd witnessed a car accident. When? Today? Yesterday? Last week? He couldn't remember. But a man had died; he'd seen it. And there was more to it than that. It was like there was something else niggling away inside his mind, something going on under the surface that he couldn't quite grasp. This was my chance. When he was thinking about me, I had an opportunity to be heard, I had to find a way to make him understand I was there, suppressed inside him. But he was too strong, I couldn't express myself, and I didn't know how to make my mind talk to his. There was no self-help book for this type of thing. Even if there had been, I wouldn't have known how to make him read it. Every now and then, he got flashes of my face and I knew he felt connected to me, but he was dismissing it because it made no sense to him. His memory of Natalie was stronger; he could picture her clearly, as if she was standing in front of him. Glancing down, Dan saw he was clutching a piece of paper tightly. Frowning, he opened his palm and spread the paper out:

Natalie. Find her, tell her I'm still alive. She'll help you. She'll help us both.

It was his handwriting, but he didn't remember writing it. He couldn't trust his own mind, his own actions, anymore. Maybe he should have started taking his pills again? But deep down, he didn't believe that. Leaning against the low railing between the table tennis table and the bowling green where the pensioners played, Dan squeezed the note, looking up at the tables and chairs on the grass in front of him.

Natalie.

His heart stopped for a moment, missing beat after beat after beat. He was looking right at her, but hadn't yet registered who she was. But I had. It was my wife. She was sitting alone, drinking a coffee on one of the small, dented silver tables set on the grass outside the café. She had a letter in front of her, its envelope ripped open and discarded alongside an empty hazelnut wafer wrapper. She always loved those hazelnut wafers, they were her 'fuck the diet' go-to treat. Her dark hair was loose, tucked behind her ear on the left side and hanging down on the right. I wanted to run over to her and grab her and kiss her and tell her that I was still here, that I was alive and okay. But I couldn't, because she wouldn't even recognise the body I was in and besides, I didn't have control of it anyway. I couldn't make him move or do anything, I was a passenger, helpless. A prisoner of sorts.

'That's her.'

Speak to her. You have to speak to her, I shouted internally.

He stepped toward her, slowly and tentatively. Steam was rising from her takeaway coffee cup as she lifted it to her lips. As he drew closer, she glanced up.

'Hi,' he said, nervously, his heart still jabbing, bobbing and weaving in his chest. He was standing a few feet away from her, feet sinking into the soft muddy grass, conscious not to step too close for fear of terrifying her.

'You were there,' she said, a slight tremble in her voice. 'At the accident. You were there.'

'Yes,' he said.

'I'm here!' I shouted, and she flinched like she was scared. 'Nat, I'm here.' I was making him speak. It was his mouth forming the words, his voice, but I had to tell her everything while I had the chance, before he took control of his body again, before he suppressed me and put me down and...

'My name is Dan,' he said, like he was unaware I'd even been speaking. Then he held his hand up, with the note scrawled and screwed up in his fist. 'I've got this, I wrote this.' He leant forward to hand her the note, but she was scared and didn't want to take it. She was looking over her shoulder anxiously, looking for someone else in the park, anyone else to whom she could signal, because a homeless man had come up to her and started shouting, started acting like he was mad. But he wasn't. How could he possibly make her understand what was going on when he didn't understand it himself?

'I'm sorry,' he said, dropping the note in front of her on the table. 'I didn't mean to scare you, I just...' his voice trailed off. He had no idea what to say or how to say it. Gingerly, she reached forward and picked up the note.

Natalie. Find her, tell her I'm still alive. She'll help you. She'll help us both.

A long pause.

'I know it doesn't make any sense,' I said, more quietly this time, in a more measured tone, aware this might be my only chance, 'but it's me, Nat. Somehow, it's me. In here, in him. You've got to believe me. I always said I'd find my way back to you.'

She inhaled deeply and held her breath, as if someone had a hand clamped tightly over her nose and mouth, squeezing tightly, tighter still, a tiny bit longer... Dan watched and waited. I watched and waited. Then, after what seemed like minutes, when I thought she was going to pass out, she exhaled, as if the hand had been removed at the very last moment, allowing the air to rush out of her lungs.

'Why are you saying this?' she said, flicking a sideways glance across at the café again. 'Please, I don't have any money, I don't...'

'No, I don't want anything,' Dan said, holding his hands up in the air, as if to show he didn't mean any harm. 'I just... I don't know. I didn't mean to scare you.' He backed away, hands still up in the air. I wanted him to stop, to go back toward her, but instead he stopped moving and watched as she stood up, grabbed her bag and quickly moved away from him and the table, running out of the park and out of sight.

We've got to convince her, I said.

'Who are you?' he replied inside his mind.

You can hear me?

'No,' he said, a deep impulse snapping back at him. 'It's my meds, it's...'

You're not ill, you aren't sick. I'm Joe, you saw me die.

He walked over to her empty table, picking up the envelope from the letter she'd left behind, reading the address on it.

That's where we live. Please, you've got to go after her.

'Natalie,' he said, mumbling as he fingered the envelope and shut his eyes. Her road was only a couple of minutes away from the park, through the alleyway and across the zebra crossing; he'd be there in no time. He didn't believe the voice in his head was real, but he still felt drawn to her, like he was connected to her somehow. On autopilot, he left the park and crossed the small road into the alleyway that connected Nizells Avenue with Davigdor Road, glancing up at the massive painted Jesus hanging on the wall, bloody nailed hands and a crown of thorns exposed for children to see on their way to school and nursery. Staring down at the pebbledash ground, he shuffled along, clutching the envelope tightly in his hand. He'd love a shower, maybe she'd let him have a shower. He was itching all over and his feet felt like they were bleeding, rotting away with constant moistness where his trainers never dried out.

When he got to my road, his body relaxed a little.

Home.

Spikey plants filled the front garden, evenly placed with

precision a few yards apart from each other. He braced himself and walked past them, ringing the doorbell. It felt strange to me, because normally I'd get my key out of my pocket and open the door, but of course he didn't have a key; he didn't have my pockets. He stood, tense on the doorstep, nearly turning and running, certain that this was madness asserting itself. There probably wasn't even anyone called Natalie living there, he thought. Maybe he was hallucinating. Except he'd never hallucinated before, he'd never heard voices—that wasn't his problem. It didn't make any sense that he'd start now, did it? But then again, having someone else's dead spirit inside him didn't make much sense, either. He had to keep things in perspective. He should have gone and found a bench in the park to sleep under, like he'd been planning; he shouldn't have been scaring this poor woman. He turned his back on the door, deciding to get as far away from her as possible, but he was too late. He heard a click as it opened behind him and then her voice. Oh God, her voice. *Natalie.*

CHAPTER 2

'Leave me alone.' Natalie moved to slam the door, but Dan reached out and pushed back, stopping it from closing.

'My name is Daniel,' he said, not letting go of the door, not letting her fully close it. She leant into the crack, face pale, shadowy. 'Except, I'm not just Daniel,' he continued. 'Sorry, it's a bit confusing, but please listen. It's about Joe.'

'I'm calling the police,' she said, pushing against the door again, forcing Dan to apply more pressure to keep it open. He paused, holding eye contact with Natalie for a moment, waiting to see her nod, almost imperceptibly, before he continued.

'He keeps talking to me, you see. Inside my head. I know how that sounds. I know it seems crazy but...'

'Are you a clairvoyant?' Natalie said quietly, unexpectedly. It surprised me, although it shouldn't have; she always believed in the supernatural, always wanted to think there was something better waiting, something beyond everyday life.

'No, no, that's not it.' He stared down at his feet, letting his arm drop away from the door. I wanted him to look at her, I wanted to see her face again, to touch her and stroke her soft skin.

'Then what is it?' she whispered.

'I don't know.' He looked up and attempted a smile. 'But Joe's here, with me. At least, I think...' He shook his head and looked back at the floor. 'Fuck, I don't know...it's just...'

'I don't know what you want...' Despite being free to slam the door shut, her grip seemed to be loosening a little, nudging it open a tiny bit wider.

'I know what this sounds like,' Dan replied.

'Tell me something *real*,' Natalie said, a tremble in her voice I'd never heard before.

I should have known. She was always visiting psychics,

believing in ghosts, but I never thought she took it seriously. Saying you're spiritual and believing a homeless stranger when he turns up on your doorstep telling you he's got your dead husband inside him are different things entirely.

'I'll tell you anything you want to know,' I said quickly. 'I'll tell you how we met, how we fell in love.'

'Things only I could know.' Her voice wavered slightly. Fear? Excitement? Maybe both, I couldn't tell, I'd never been good at reading other people's emotions.

'Yes,' I said. My heart was pounding, or rather Dan's heart was pounding, beating so loud and fast the whole street should have heard it. We stood impossibly still, the three of us.

Natalie, my wife, blocking the doorway, clearly battling inside her own mind, scared, terrified she was making a terrible mistake, but desperate to believe. Just like all those times she'd visited the psychic woman on London Road who told her someone beginning with an M—*Grandpa Michael!*—was talking to her, telling her he wanted her to be happy.

Then me, trapped inside Dan's body, holding my breath and, by extension, holding his breath too.

Finally, Dan, staring at her, drinking in her features, her shiny dark hair, her unblemished complexion and beautiful brown eyes. He was thinking she was the most perfect woman he'd ever seen, and I didn't know whether to feel jealous or proud.

'We met in a club near the seafront,' I spat out quickly, holding my hands up in the air, using the non-threatening 'no need to be scared' body language Dan had learnt on the streets.

'Do you remember? It had a multi-coloured dance floor.' The words poured quickly out of Dan's mouth as if it were my own. 'And I was wearing those Caterpillar boots and that red shirt. And you had that tight black dress on, you were the most beautiful girl in the room. I couldn't believe you weren't with anyone. It didn't make any sense to me at all that you could be single.'

Natalie didn't speak, didn't move, but I could tell her grip on the front door had loosened again, it had opened a fraction more.

* * *

'Look,' Dan said, 'I don't know what's going on any more than you do.' He could feel her stare burrowing into his head, burning him with desperation. 'But you're safe. I want you to know that. I won't hurt you.'

All was silent, not even a breeze rustled through the trees. Dan stood in our immaculate front garden, looking unkempt, a mess, out of place.

'And that's not a *don't think of elephants* thing, either,' he said. Oh God, he was a babbler, a nervous babbler. 'I mean, don't think because I've said, "I won't hurt you," that actually I am going to hurt you. It's not a double bluff or anything, it's...' he trailed off, snapping his teeth together as he shut his mouth. 'Sorry, I mean... Sorry.'

Natalie held our gaze for what felt like minutes before leaning back and pushing the front door open a little wider.

'You've got ten minutes,' she said, stepping back to let us in. For a moment, neither of us moved. Then, and I don't know which of us instigated the movement, we stepped forward, careful not to brush against her as we stepped inside my old home, which felt both familiar and unfamiliar at the same time.

She believes us, I said.

'Not yet she doesn't,' he replied internally. 'I'm not sure I do yet.'

You don't know her like I do. I was already feeling more relaxed as we stepped into my old hallway. *We've already got her.*

* * *

Dan, dirty and unkempt, stood in Natalie's living room, staring at her shelves and beautiful leather-bound books. I don't think he believed I was inhabiting him then, he suspected his mental health had taken a leap off the abyss, breaching hitherto uncharted territory. But he could see something in my story had resonated with her, how we met, the nightclub, the multi-coloured dance floor. He was beginning to doubt himself and so was she.

Part of him had expected she'd put him right. She'd realise he wasn't possessed, she'd send him on his way. He'd have had to think about his next step, whether he'd go back to the park or find somewhere else to sleep. That's if she hadn't called the police first, though at least that would have meant a warm cell for the night. But he could see she was being drawn in, that she was starting to believe.

'She shouldn't have invited me in,' he thought.

Us in. She shouldn't have invited us in.

'We're not an "us",' he snapped nervously, jabbing at his temple violently. 'You're not real, you're in my head.'

Am I?

* * *

Natalie's bookshelves were elegant, such a stark contrast to the bland, outdated books in…where? Dan's house? For a moment, I got a flash of his life before, he was leaning against the doorframe of his dad's living room, dressed in black. Funeral attire? His dad was manically stacking books on the shelves, the sofas around him filled with novels and plays and *Lonely Planet* guides and maps and travel books. The hotchpotch of books didn't seem to belong to one person; it was more like two entirely different personalities were vying for attention on his shelves.

'Dad,' Dan said, his voice low and gentle. 'You've lost your mum. It's okay to be upset.' Then, the memory was lost, like Dan had clamped down on it so I couldn't experience it. Despite not believing I was real, he was hiding things from me. There were things he didn't want me to know.

What are you hiding, Dan?

He ignored me, concentrating instead on the books before him. Blinking, I remembered we were in Natalie's living room. My old living room. Dan could feel Natalie standing in the doorway behind him, her gaze prickling his back. Little shivers and needle punctures at first, gaining in numbers as they Mexican-waved down his spine. Not daring to turn around, he leant over to pick up a book. He paid no attention to the title, it was more for something to hold, something to do with his hands, to grip and to stroke, like a child would twist and tease a comfort toy.

'What do you remember?' she asked.

'About what?'

'Anything. Us. Our life. The accident…' She wasn't moving from the doorway, keeping her distance, maybe because she was nervous, maybe because his clothes hadn't been washed since he got pissed on. 'How we met. I need to know this is real.'

Dan's heart—my heart—began to beat a little faster. It was so hard to get used to, his heart, my heart—the same thing but not the same at all. I'm sure I read somewhere that our heartbeats are as unique as our fingerprints. Nobody's heart beats the same way as anyone else's. Yet here we were. One heart, two different beats.

'How long has it been?' I asked, forming words with his mouth but using my own south-London accent. 'Since I died, I mean. It's hard to keep track.'

She paused for a second, clearly uncomfortable with the question.

'Nearly two months,' she said cautiously.

'Shit,' I said, as the sick rose up our throat, forcing us to swallow it back down, acidic, sharp. 'I thought it'd been a couple of days at most, not...two months?'

'The night we met,' she repeated sternly. 'Keep going or I'm calling the police.' I realised she was holding her mobile, she had it ready, one small thumb press and she'd have the police on the line.

Not so trusting after all, Natalie. That's my girl.

'You didn't notice me, not for ages. I followed you around, trying to catch your eye, looking at you and eventually your friend, what was her name? I can't remember her name. Anyway, she nudged you. You were drinking vodka and tonic through a straw, and she nudged you and pointed at me and you looked up and...' I trailed off. I was talking too quickly, I know I was, nervously babbling like Dan had done on the doorstep. Wait. Wasn't that Dan's trait? Why was I babbling like an idiot? I'd never been a babbler. A terrible fear hit me. I didn't know where Dan ended and I began. What if one day he engulfed me completely? I'd already disappeared for months since the accident, lost inside him, not even aware of time passing. I had to tell her things while he was still letting me speak.

'I won't supress you again,' he said in his head. 'I promise.'

How can I trust you? I've been inside you for two months...you must have known?

'I could feel you, sometimes I could even hear you...but I'm used to mental illness, Joe. What was I supposed to think?'

Mental illness?

'Leave it, will you? I'm listening now, aren't I? So is Natalie.'

* * *

Natalie. She was staring at us, not moving, breathing or speaking. I stared at her, devouring her features, her small nose, her stunning brown eyes with the lightest touch of makeup. I realised she was crying gently, not sobbing, nothing dramatic, a statue with a raindrop running down its cheek. I wanted to lean forward and wipe it away, maybe brush my moist finger against my lips to taste it, salty and sweet.

'Olyvia,' she whispered. 'My friend's name was Olyvia.'

I nodded, gripping the book Dan had taken from the shelf and transferring it from his left hand to my right so I could hold it more comfortably.

'So, we got talking, didn't we? Do you remember? In the club, I mean. And your mate Olyvia was there. Oh, and the other one...'

'Kelly,' she said slowly.

'Yes, yes and when you went to the loo, I took the chance to get the lowdown on you from them, didn't I?' I grinned as the memory started to solidify.

'Go on,' Natalie said cautiously.

'We got bottles of 20/20 to start us off, cheap and easy to get pissed on.'

'20/20, I'd forgotten all about that.' Natalie smiled, just a little. 'God it was rank. Do they still sell it?'

'No idea. Nowadays it's all Jägermeister and shit. Anyway, we drank, we chatted. Hours went by and we hadn't kissed yet, hadn't done anything but get to know each other. But I felt like I could talk to you about anything, you know? And you felt the same, I could feel it. It was something special, we both knew it straight away.' I nodded to myself and her, animated, excited even. 'It was this perfect connection, wasn't it? Right from the start.'

Natalie stared at me intently, slowly running her hand from her forehead back through her hair. I couldn't read her face, couldn't tell what she was thinking or how she was processing what I was telling her.

'When you went to the toilet, I cornered Kelly and Olyvia, asked them about you. "She's lovely, such a great girl," Olyvia said. And then Kelly was all like, "She's amazing, such a good friend, she'll do anything for anyone." Except... And I never told you this at the time... When Kelly said all that, she kind of stroked the collar of my shirt, like she was inviting me to find out if maybe I'd feel luckier if I tried her out instead.'

'Bitch,' Natalie said, an involuntary smile crossing her face. My heart began to beat a little faster because I could tell, could see from her expression that she was reminiscing too; she was living the memory like I was.

'Jesus, it's real,' Dan thought.

Of course, I'm real, I replied. *I keep telling you.*

'Anyway,' I continued to Natalie. 'There was this tacky rose seller, do you remember? He approached me and I thought, 'Fuck it, I'll get one.' So I did, I bought one, and you were mortified. You ran a mile, refused to accept it from me, said it was crass and embarrassing. But I could tell you were pleased I'd done it. You were just acting cool.'

'I am cool,' Natalie said quietly, almost sadly. I glanced down at her hand to see her thumb had dropped away from her mobile screen. There was no rulebook for this situation, no mores or social context to know how to behave. We stood awkwardly, two metres apart and unsure how to act. I gripped the book tightly in my right hand, feeling its cool, rough texture against my skin... Dan's skin. It was comforting, somehow. I understood then why he liked to rub things, to feel them, to experience them. There was something about concentrating on how things felt that centred him and kept him calm. I stared down at my new hands before lifting my gaze back up to Natalie. She was staring right at me and I didn't know what to do. I don't think she did either.

'She should kick us out,' Dan said internally.

Us.

'Even if she believes you're inside me...and that's a big if... she doesn't know me. I could be anyone.'

So?

'She's a single woman. I'm a homeless stranger.'

You keep talking like you're dangerous...

'No, no it's not that...'

Then what?

'How can she care so little about her safety?' Dan glanced down at the book in his hand, reading the title and nodding to himself.

I'm her husband, I spat.

'But I'm not, Joe. Something isn't right...'

I died, Dan, of course something isn't right.

'Maybe,' Dan said desperately, looking up from the book and making eye contact with her again. She looked nervous, but that wasn't the main thing. Dan wished he was better at reading emotions, at understanding what other people were thinking and feeling. He could tell she was beginning to believe what he — what I — had told her. But there was something else, something he couldn't put his finger on. Maybe it was simply desperation, a need to believe her husband had come back to her? But if that was the case, why did Dan feel there was something else going on under the surface?

'It's like she doesn't care if I want to hurt her or not.'

You're being ridiculous.

'Maybe. I've never been good at reading people's emotions.'

It's a lot to take in, Dan. What we're telling her.

'I know.'

Dan? I paused, feeling nervous myself. *I can tell you're hiding things from me. Be honest...you aren't dangerous, are you? You wouldn't hurt her?*

For the smallest moment, I saw an image in his mind, a woman, long brown hair — his ex-girlfriend Debbie. She was staring at him, eyes wide and scared. She was glancing over at their open living room door, edging away from Dan slightly. Then the memory was gone, Dan had clamped down on it, obscuring it from me.

'Trust me,' Dan said.

I'm trying. But you keep hiding things from me.

'They're my memories, Joe, not yours.'

And she's my wife.

* * *

Our minds fell into silence and we stood opposite Natalie, chewing Dan's bottom lip and waiting. Time dripped dryly by until finally:

'Have a shower, I'll make us a cup of tea,' Natalie said, as if she'd made a decision we weren't party to. 'There's a razor in the cabinet, and a toothbrush…' Natalie was awkward, gulping and licking her lips. 'Joe's razor, Joe's toothbrush. You can use them.'

I passed the book back to Dan's left hand and he clasped it in his palm so tightly it hurt. His back was straight, locked into position. His neck felt stiff, like he couldn't have turned even if he'd wanted to.

'Natalie.' I stepped toward her and grabbed her. 'I've missed you.'

She tensed up, turning her head and pushing me away slightly.

'Too fast. I'm not…look, just take a shower.' she scoured Dan's face, as if she was looking for a trace of my real self in it, as if his features would somehow morph into mine and she'd be sure, she'd know it was me. Then she turned and walked away. Not knowing what else to do, we followed her out of the living room and into the hallway.

I was halfway up the stairs when she said, 'The towels are…'

'In the airing cupboard,' I finished. 'It's okay, I remember.'

* * *

Upstairs, Dan turned the shower on to warm up and discarded his dirty clothes in a pile on the bathroom floor behind the locked door.

'You've got a lot of beige in your house,' Dan said, grabbing a beige towel from the airing cupboard in the bathroom and shutting the door again.

Beige seemed a safe colour to choose; it's neutral.

'It's boring,' Dan retorted, holding his hand underneath the shower water before stepping into it.

'Oh God, that feels amazing,' he said aloud, holding his face under the water and squeezing his eyes shut. I had to admit, it did feel good. It was the best shower I'd ever had. As he scrubbed and cleaned his feet and rubbed shower gel over his entire body again and again we chatted, getting to know one another a little bit.

What's wrong with beige? I asked. How quickly we'd learnt to communicate. It was strange how not strange it was, how we'd evolved and adapted.

'I told you, it's boring,' Dan said. 'Like you lack the confidence to have a personality.'

Lack confidence?

'Yeah, like you're scared to have an opinion. Nobody can object to beige, can they? But if you chose red or orange or yellow, you'd be making a statement. You'd be drawing attention to yourself.'

I felt a contented smile on Dan's face. Already, this new arrangement was working for him. Now he was starting to believe I wasn't some trick of his addled mind, he was embracing me. But there was something else. With me inside him, he didn't feel dislocated like he used to. It was like he was back in tune with the world, experiencing real, solid emotions for the first time in years.

You feel real again.

'Yeah,' he laughed. 'How fucked up is that? I feel more normal with you in me than I have done for years on my own.'

I felt content, too. I should have felt claustrophobic. My body was dead and I was trapped inside someone else with no real power or control.

Orange or yellow?

'What?'

You think I should have painted the house orange or yellow? It would have looked like a brothel.

'Are brothels yellow?'

No idea, never been in one.

'Nor have I. What about blue then? Or any colour?'

There's green in the hall, I said, not quite defensively. We chuckled and our chest rose and fell with gentle, content vibrations.

'You were never going to be an interior designer, were you, Dan?' I said aloud with his voice, once again enjoying its cadence mixed with my accent. Once we were out of the shower and dry, Dan walked over to the mirror to study his face before shaving. He had some shaggy beard growth and as he smiled back at us, I realised I hadn't seen what he looked like before now, not externally. I knew he was about the same age as me, in his thirties. I knew he was white from the skin on his arms and hands and I could tell he had fair hair because...

Ginger. Jesus, you're ginger.

'Shut up and pass me the razor,' he said.

I glanced down to see it sitting on the side next to the sink and picked it up.

'Right handed?' Dan said.

Yeah.

'Okay. That's going to be weird,' he said, picking up the shaving foam and beginning to prepare his face.

'It's good to meet you, Joe,' he said, sending a twinkling smile into the mirror.

You, too, Dan, I replied. *And I appreciate it.*

'What?'

You...putting me up like this.

It was the best analogy I could think of. He was letting me stay in him, after all. If he put his mind to it, I'm sure he could have turfed me out, but that hadn't even occurred to him. There was an advert, I can't remember what it was for. The strapline was: *Together, we are stronger.* And maybe we were. Maybe we were more than the sum of our parts. Maybe, despite the weirdness of it all, we would be able to make this work. He smiled back at me from the mirror, his teeth still intact, not rotten or damaged like I thought they might be.

'You're welcome,' he said aloud.

When you're done shaving, you can grab some of my clothes to put on. They're probably still in the wardrobe in our bedroom.

'Okay,' he said, opening his mouth to stretch the skin on his cheek and applying the razor with his left hand.

My clothes were soft and fragrant, gently kissing my skin in a way I didn't remember clothes doing before. Dan walked downstairs to the kitchen, clean-shaven and comfortable. As he stood awkwardly in the doorway, Natalie stopped mid-motion, a butter knife in her hand, staring at him.

'I hope you don't mind,' he said, holding his arms up, demonstrating the shirt and jeans he'd taken from my wardrobe. Natalie was standing beside the boiling kettle and I could tell from her expression she hadn't expected him to be so handsome underneath the beard and grime.

'No, it's fine,' she said, slightly flustered. Silence for a moment, then, 'You want to wash your other things?'

'Yeah, great.'

Awkward fidgeting, shifting feet, picked fingernails.

'Machine is over there,' she said, nodding toward the washer-dryer. It was a suspiciously everyday scene as Dan went back upstairs and got his clothes, then put them in the washing machine in the kitchen as Natalie handed him a gel tablet to put in with them along with the fabric conditioner from the cupboard under the sink. It was the same softener Dan's grandmother used to use, plain, no-frills with a spring-fresh odour.

Dan leant back against the kitchen counter, unsure what to do. He opted for looking at the floor. He was feeling a little embarrassed, a little naked without his facial hair.

'I thought you were older,' Natalie said eventually. 'Because of the beard, I mean.'

She was blushing slightly and fingering the skin at the base of her neck.

'I thought you were *a lot* older, actually.'

She walked over to the counter and picked up the freshly boiled kettle, pouring water into plain white mugs, then picking up two teabags from a silver jar and popping one in each mug. Silence hung in the air as she stirred and removed the teabags, pouring milk into both mugs.

'How did you end up like this?' Natalie handed Dan a mug of tea.

'Like this?' Dan glanced down at the cup. I take milk, he doesn't. She'd made a cup of tea for me, not for Dan—yet she was talking to him, not me.

'On the street, I mean.' she paused, clearly thinking she'd made a faux pas, that maybe she'd overstepped and shouldn't have asked.

'I mean, you are homeless, aren't you? I don't mean to presume, I just...'

'Yes,' Dan said gently.

He didn't want her to feel bad, he wanted her to feel at ease. I liked him. I'd spent a lot of my time around arsehole men having pissing contests when I'd been alive. He wasn't like that. He wanted people to feel happy; I could feel that it was a genuine motivation for him. He'd spent a lot of time having people analyse him, question him, make him feel abnormal in some way. Because of that, he made a point of not doing that to others. If anything, he did the opposite, trying to make sure people could be fully themselves, whoever that was.

'I didn't mean to...'

'You didn't, it's fine.' Dan took a sip of his tea and almost spat it back out. 'Sorry, can I have it black?' he asked.

'Yes, of course. I didn't think to ask. Sorry.'

'No, it's fine. I'll make it.'

Dan emptied his cup in the sink and rinsed it, glancing over his shoulder at Natalie and smiling. I could tell by her reaction that it soothed her. He was well practiced at trying to put people at ease. Weirdly, this was precisely because he'd spent so much time putting people on edge.

'This is all a bit weird, isn't it?'

'Just a bit.' She nodded, and returned his smile, albeit with a hint of nerves. As he put another teabag in his cup and waited for the kettle to re-boil, he stood with his back to her for a moment.

'It's a long story,' he said slowly, deliberately. 'And to be honest, it's hard to keep track of things. I think I've been sleeping rough for a couple of months, maybe? Definitely not a year, I haven't had a winter yet.'

'Why are you homeless?' She pulled a chair out from the small square table in the middle of the room and sat in it. 'Is it drugs?'

'No. God, no.'

'Sorry, I didn't mean…I…'

'No, it's okay. Drugs do keep a lot of people on the street. Maybe they put them there, too. They're a trap. If you learn anything sleeping rough, you learn that.'

'Is that what happened to you?' she asked. She was calm, measured. She wasn't looking at him, like she was still testing him out, trying to work out if he was dangerous or not.

'No,' Dan said, poured his water and swilled his teabag around. 'I'm not on anything, I promise. Not even for my condition.'

'Condition?' Natalie asked. She sounded nervous again, worried. So was Dan. The last time he mentioned his condition— to his ex-girlfriend Debbie—he was kicked out onto the street.

What is your condition? I asked.

'I don't have to tell her everything, yet.'

What about me?

'Be patient, will you?' he said internally. Then, aloud to Natalie, 'I'm not dangerous, I promise.'

'I didn't mean...' she started.

'You've every right to be scared,' Dan said.

'I'm not scared,' she said, looking directly at him. And he realised she was telling the truth. She wasn't scared, not really. If he had to describe it, he'd say she seemed defiant. Confident even. But was that all an act? As he studied her face, it was like her entire body was beating a little faster, like she'd come alive. Maybe defiant was the wrong word. Maybe she was excited?

'It's terrible,' she said, changing the subject. 'That people have to live like that. Why isn't the government doing something about it?'

'Oh, please.' Dan laughed. It was the first time I'd heard him laugh—I'd laughed for him before, but it was me laughing through him. His laugh had a different rhythm.

'I mean, people should be doing something about it, nobody should have to live like you do, like your friends do.'

'I didn't say I had friends,' Dan said, clearly uncomfortable.

'I meant...'

'Look, it's not your problem.'

'Something should be done. People...'

'People what?' Dan interrupted. It was the first time I'd heard him irritated. 'Post something righteous on Facebook as they step over the guy sleeping under the railway bridge?'

'People aren't all...' Natalie started.

'Yes, they are...' Dan said.

'Fuck you,' Natalie replied. Bizarrely, this made Dan smile.

'Sorry,' he said. 'It's just... People talk a lot, but they don't *do* anything. It's so rare that people actually *do* anything. So, you get tired of hearing them talk, you know?'

They stared at each other for a moment before, amazingly,

Natalie smiled back, nodding.

'Yeah,' she said quietly, her cheeks flushing a little.

What the fuck, Natalie? He's not me. I might be inside him, but you're not talking to me, you're talking to him. Flirting with him.

Jesus, they were flirting. He was handsome, I had to give him that, but I was surprised she liked him. I didn't think he'd be her type; he wasn't like me at all and she'd never been into ginger men.

'What about me?' I burst out, managing to form the words with his mouth while he was distracted enough not to stop me.

'Joe?' she said, her smile faltering, like she'd forgotten I was even there for a second.

'Yes,' I said. Dan was standing with his back to the kitchen work surface and I could feel him clutching the side with his hands, squeezing them tightly around the edge. Glancing down, I could see the tips of his fingernails—our fingernails—had turned white-purple. I could feel them pulsating.

'It's okay,' he said to me, internally. 'Go on, take control. I'll take the back seat. You've got a lot to talk about.'

'Okay, Joe,' Natalie said, leaning back, pushing a chair from the table toward Dan. 'Carry on. Tell me more. I need to know this is real.'

'Okay,' I said, moving toward the chair and sitting down opposite her. The feeling of being in control of his limbs, of walking and talking without having to make a gargantuan effort, was fantastic, I was lighter than air.

'But turn off the main light, will you?' I nodded toward the main light switch. 'Leave the table lamp on. You know I've always found it too bright in here.'

Natalie walked over and turned the main light off before moving back to the table and sitting down, sitting cross-legged on her kitchen chair, feet resting on top of her thighs, yoga-style. She stared right at me, into my face, even though I was wearing Dan's skin. I wished it was my face she was looking at and not his; I wished she was seeing me, the real me, not the façade. But I guessed that was the point, that was what I had to show her. I was alive, after a fashion. I took a deep breath, realising that while I'd already died once, I wasn't done yet. I was still fighting for my life.

'Your eyes are different colours,' Natalie said, sitting back in her seat.

Are they? I said internally. *I didn't notice.*

'You were too busy looking at my ginger hair.'

You are very ginger.

'Fuck off.' He laughed.

What colour are they?

'What?'

Your eyes.

'Oh, one blue, one green.'

Dan stared at Natalie, a tiny, almost imperceptible smirk on his face. He missed people being fascinated by his eyes. It had always been a conversation opener whenever people noticed it. Ordinarily, it made him bashful and he wanted to hide his face, get away from the attention, but with Natalie it was different, easy. She could ask anything or say anything and it wouldn't scare or unnerve him.

'What causes that, then? Latent genes?'

Dan and I both stared at her, externalising again and wondering if she'd noticed the fact we were having our own internal conversation. She hadn't. Dan was lost in her and only half concentrating. We both wanted to gently unbutton her shirt, just a little, enough to...

'Yeah. You know, like the ginger hair,' she continued.

'The ginger hair?' I could see a hint of her breastbone where the top buttons were undone and if I leant over and undid the third button...

'Recessive genes, like ginger hair or blue eyes? You need two copies to activate them. Is it something to do with that?'

'What?' he asked.

'Your eyes.'

'What about them?'

'Being different colours?'

'Oh. No, it's heterochromia.'

'That's a word,' she said, a playful smile crossing her face. 'A name, not a reason. Why does it happen?'

'What?'

'Your eyes,' Natalie said again, exasperated. 'And while we're at it, any chance of you using them to look at my face instead of my tits?'

Dan jerked his head up, meeting her gaze, terrified he'd overstepped until he saw her smile.

'Sorry,' he started. 'I just...'

That's my wife, remember.

'Sorry. I forgot. Shit.'

'It's all right.' Natalie picked up her mug of tea and took a sip. 'I'm kind of flattered, to be honest. It's been a while since anyone checked me out.'

Wasn't this conversation supposed to be about me? I should have been telling Natalie about our past, our life together but instead she seemed more interested in Dan and how he ended up homeless.

'Don't be like that.'

Like what?

'Jealous.'

The three of us drifted into silence until Natalie said, 'Want something to eat?'

'God, yeah. I'm starving, absolutely starving.'

'I can do you something. Want a sandwich?'

'Chips,' I said, realising how hungry I was. 'Let's go and get some chips.'

'I don't want to go out again,' Dan said internally. 'We've just...'

Chapter 2

'Okay,' Natalie said, standing up. 'Chips it is.'

See. You're not the only one with some control here, Dan. She was my wife, remember. Not yours.

CHAPTER 3

That first day with Natalie was a blur. Sometimes I was present, sometimes I wasn't. But as we left the house, Dan withdrew back into the shadows, giving me the spotlight. He knew he'd never be able to convince her I was real; he didn't know anything about us. We walked past the redbrick hospital and up Davigdor Road. I'd never been sure what type of hospital it was, to be honest. It specialised in something or other, it wasn't a regular hospital with an A&E. I'd lived down the road from it for years, you'd think I'd have known what it specialised in, but it was so hard to remember anything without my own body.

'Let's go to the pub. They do chips in there,' Natalie said, to herself more than to us. We didn't speak again until we walked into the pub and got a table. Natalie ordered at the bar and soon we were sitting, avoiding the conversation to come. I sipped a black coffee, realising I was already getting used to drinking it without milk. I'd always had lattes before, but somehow, I knew if I tried one with Dan's taste buds, I'd hate it. Natalie was drinking a tea because she'd already had coffee in the park and she only liked to have one coffee a day, something to do with limiting the amount of caffeine she drank. I stopped short of telling her tea was also full of caffeine. I always used to tease her about it, but somehow it didn't seem the right time to bring it up.

'Thanks for the coffee,' Dan said to Natalie, smiling. 'I don't have any cash...'

'It's fine,' she replied, inhaling deeply and glancing around the pub, filled with late afternoon drinkers. 'Now talk. You understand this all sounds pretty 'way out there,' don't you?'

'Of course,' we replied in unison.

That was weird.

'Yeah.'

'So?' Natalie probed.

'Your first date, then,' Dan said. 'Joe? You've got the floor, so to speak. Or the mouth. You know what I mean.'

'Jesus, this is fucked up,' Natalie said.

'You're telling me,' I tried to use Dan's mouth to smile and comfort her. I stared down at the pale hands resting on the chipped wooden table before me. My hair was dark; my skin was naturally a little more tanned than his. It was weird to look at my own body and know it was someone else's.

'You'll get used to it,' Dan said. 'Trust me.'

What do you mean? Has this happened to you before?

'You're drifting off again,' Natalie said, jolting us from our thoughts. 'You realise that, don't you?'

'Are we? Sorry.' I took a sip of Dan's coffee, letting the warmth sit on my tongue for a moment, focusing myself on the room, the sound of the bar staff chattering, the clattering of plates and cutlery being loaded into the dumbwaiter shaft at the back of the room to go down to the kitchen. For a second, I was struck by the other people in such proximity to us, all going about their business, suffering from their own worries and concerns, stresses and problems. They were also enjoying their own successes and joys, too, I supposed. There was a name for that feeling, I'd read it somewhere, although I can't remember where. *Sonder. The realisation that each random passer-by is living a life as vivid and complete as your own.*

'Yeah, you keep doing it. One minute we're talking, then you kind of... I don't know, zone out,' she said, as she reached over and gently touched my hand. *Dan's hand.*

'Sorry. It's a lot to get used to, that's all.'

'You haven't convinced me you're not a lunatic, yet.'

Natalie was almost joking, but not quite. She withdrew her hand as the waiter came and plonked a plate of chips down between us, next to the wooden box with ketchup, serviettes and cutlery.

'Okay. Our first date,' I said, grabbing a chip with my fingers. 'We arranged to meet at the train station, do you remember? The day after we met in the nightclub.'

Natalie nodded slowly but didn't speak, indicating that I should continue. I glanced over her shoulder at the woman sitting alone on the table next to us, directly behind Natalie. She was wearing a pair of enormous black sunglasses, despite the fact she was inside and it was autumn. She looked a bit like Jackie Onassis and she was staring right at me as I looked back at her. She didn't flinch, didn't look ashamed to be eavesdropping on us; she just nodded her head almost imperceptibly, as if she too were willing me to carry on. I looked away uncomfortably, staring at the plate of chips as I spoke.

'I was wearing those skin-tight beige jeans and that denim shirt, do you remember?' The memories were foggy, coming to me slowly, as if I had nowhere to pull them from because they didn't exist in Dan's brain, but in mine, six feet under somewhere, buried or...

'Did they bury me?' I asked. I couldn't believe I hadn't asked sooner, that it wasn't the first thing I thought of. 'What did they do with my body?'

Natalie looked uncomfortable and visibly shrank back from me in her chair.

'Sorry,' I said. 'I just...'

'No, no. It's fine,' she said quietly. 'We had you cremated.'

'Okay, good,' I said, nodding my head and squeezing my eyes shut. 'I always hated the idea of being buried. It never sat well with me. I kind of wanted to be scattered somewhere beautiful, over the Downs or something.'

Natalie nodded. 'I know you did.'

'It's okay.' I was lost in her large, sad eyes for a second. 'I'm still here, I didn't die. At least, not all of me did.'

'You always said you'd come back for me,' Natalie said. 'Do you remember, you used to say, "I'll always find you, Natalie".'

I grinned, squeezing her hand.

'And I did, didn't I?'

Everything was in slow motion around us, like the world was unreal and we were the only things that existed.

'We didn't scatter your ashes.' Natalie said.

'Why not?' I asked, letting go of her hand again as the pub came into sharp focus around us.

'Your mum wouldn't let me. She's got you in a pot on her mantelpiece.'

'You're joking,' I said. For some reason, it was the funniest thing I'd heard in ages and I began to laugh. 'Jesus Christ, the mantle?'

'Your dad tried to stop her.' Natalie started to laugh. 'To tell her to scatter you like I asked, but she wouldn't have any of it. And you know what she's like, Joe.'

My laughter subsided and I nodded.

'Yeah,' I said quietly. 'I know what she's like.'

I miss them. Mum and Dad.

'Yeah,' Dan said. 'You'll see them again.'

Like this? And say what? Hi Mum, Dad, I'm not dead. I've got a new body!

'Don't be a dick.'

Silence again. Natalie and I sat opposite each other, not speaking, until she finally said, 'Fuck it, you want a pint?'

'No thanks,' Dan said, answering for me.

'Seriously?' Natalie said.

'Yeah, I don't drink, not with my condition,' Dan said.

'But I bloody do,' I said. 'Can't we try it out? See how it works with me in you?'

Natalie was staring at us, as if she was waiting for an explanation.

'Sorry, I didn't mean to say that out loud,' I said.

'Joe?' she asked. 'Jesus...'

She stood up and walked to the bar, trying to get the attention of the bartender.

'I'll have a pint of pale ale,' she said. Then, without looking back at us, 'And he'll have the same.'

'No, seriously...' Dan started. 'It makes me feel more detached, I don't...'

'Detached from what?' Natalie asked. The bartender was standing, staring. I'm not sure if he was waiting for the order or waiting to hear Dan's response.

'My body,' Dan said.

'What?' Natalie said.

'Alcohol makes it worse, always has done. I don't drink.'

'Two pints,' Natalie repeated to the bartender.

When she arrived back at the table with the drinks and a couple of packets of crisps, Dan pleaded, 'Look, I can't.'

I realised then that I'd been wrong when I first arrived in him. I'd thought he was drunk or hungover, but that wasn't what he'd been feeling...that detachment was *normal* for him. He never felt quite part of his own body; life was always like that for him. Until now. With me in him, he was anchored, he was...

'How do you feel now?' Natalie said, sitting down next to us.

'I feel fine, but...'

'Then have a pint with me. I'm not drinking on my own.'

She's right. You don't feel like you did before.

'What do you mean?'

I know what you felt like when I arrived in you, like you were drunk. But you weren't, were you? But with me here, you're feeling everything. You're normal.

'You'd say anything to get a pint.'

Do you blame me? I'm dead. You're ginger.

'Fuck off.'

You fuck off. I'm not spending the rest of our lives not drinking.

'Hello?' Natalie said.

'Sorry,' we replied. Then, taking my chance I grabbed the pint and took a large gulp.

'Bastard.'

It's good though, right?

'No, it's bloody horrible. Who drinks pale ale? Why does she drink pale ale? I thought women drank wine and spritzers and...'

Jesus, what type of women have you been hanging around with?

'Debbie, mostly.'

Well, she wasn't the best benchmark...

'And again,' Natalie said. 'You're going to have to stop doing that.'

'Doing what?' I asked, taking another gulp of my pint, in case Dan took control and stopped me.

'Never mind.' She sat back in her chair and took a large sip of her own pint. 'So, talk to me. Convince me I'm not being ridiculous.'

'Ridiculous?' I said.

'Believing you're Joe.'

'Not just Joe,' I said. 'It's complicated. Hard to explain.'

'Try,' she said.

'We're both of us, I suppose. But he's in charge; he could suppress me if he wanted to.'

'I told you I won't,' Dan interjected. 'Not now I know you're there.'

'You've got to stop doing that, as well,' Natalie said. 'You can't both talk at once, even if you do have different accents. It's confusing to be around. You've got to develop a system.'

'Yeah,' I said.

'I suppose we do,' Dan finished.

We drank and quietly processed the enormity of what was going on. After a while, I said, 'You didn't tell me you hated them at the time.'

'Hated what?' Natalie frowned, the small lines on her forehead creating a cute little dent at the top of her nose between her eyes.

'Those skin-tight beige jeans. Do you remember? When we

moved in together, they mysteriously vanished... I reckon you threw them out, right?'

Natalie smiled a little.

'Anyway, I remember I was standing and waiting—it was summer, boiling hot and I was worried you weren't going to turn up. We'd met in the club the night before, but even though you'd kissed me, you'd refused to come home with me, so I wasn't sure you were interested, not really.'

'Wasn't that a good thing?' Natalie said, crossing her legs on her lap in her seat again, feet folded on top of her thighs like she was some sort of bendy escapologist. 'That I wouldn't go home with you the first night?'

I shrugged.

'It wasn't a good thing or a bad thing, if I'm honest. It was what you wanted. I'd have been happy either way.'

She smiled again, hands resting on top of her legs.

'Who can do that with their legs?' Dan wondered, staring at her lap.

Oh, you don't know the half of it...

'Don't.'

I'm just saying.

'I'm glad she didn't go home with you the night she met you.'

Why, what difference does it make?

'You wouldn't have respected her.'

What bollocks.

'You ended up marrying her. Do you think you would have if you'd slept together the first night?'

Of course. We were meant to be, me and Nat.

'Nat and I.'

I'm serious. Our love survived my death, didn't it?

'Are you from south London?' Dan asked, ignoring me. 'You get this cockney twang sometimes, it's like...'

'You've drifted off again,' Natalie said.

'Sorry,' I refocused on the pub around us. The Jackie Onassis tribute lady who had been staring at us was standing up and readying to leave. As she walked past us, she turned and put her hands on our tabletop, looking from Natalie to myself and smiling.

'You make a lovely couple,' she said lightly.

'We're not a couple,' Natalie said, a little too quickly, like the very idea made her ashamed. The woman didn't react, but simply smiled and nodded, turning and opening the pub door and bursting into loud song as she walked onto the street. Natalie and I sat staring at each other before bursting into laughter.

'Brighton,' I said, smirking. 'Full of lunatics.'

'I think I've seen her before,' Natalie said quietly. 'I dunno, coincidence probably.'

'No such thing as coincidence,' Dan said, shoving a handful of chips into his mouth. 'It's all part of something bigger. Most people shut themselves off from it, pretend it isn't happening. Or worse still...' he said. 'They put you on drugs to control it.'

I pushed Dan's index finger back and forth on the table, trailing grains of salt with his fingertip into an infinity symbol again, again, again.

'You were living in that house share when we met, I can't remember what road it was on. Doesn't matter. Still in Brighton, down from North Laine,' I said, trying to pull another memory from the ether, grabbing it and holding it to give it some clarity.

'Anyway, what matters is you came to meet me. You were late, of course. Always late. Some things never change. You never leave enough time to get anywhere, always leave five minutes to do a half-hour journey, then act surprised when you don't make it on time. I used to take the piss out of you, but secretly I loved you for it, you know. It was part of you. So many things were. I didn't notice when I was alive; I ploughed on through, letting the days escape, one by one. But death changes you. I see things differently now. The little things were so important, all those moments we shared, day in and day out. The ordinary stuff, that's what made us, not the big stuff. You know what I mean?'

Natalie didn't nod or move, but I could see from her expression that she knew what I meant. I could see the glimmer of something I used to see all the time there. Love. She was remembering us, she was letting the emotion back in.

'So, yeah,' I continued. 'You were late, always late. And you'd blame other people if they got pissed off about it as well, like it was them being anal about timekeeping, like they should chill out or something.'

I smiled.

'But it *is* annoying hanging around and wondering where you are for hours on end. And you never have your phone on, like you're some kind of granny, having your mobile switched off in your pocket all the time.'

'Is this supposed to make me feel good?' Natalie laughed, shoving me playfully. 'Because it isn't working, Joe.'

She called me Joe.

'Okay, okay.' I grinned, holding my hands up, palms facing outward. 'So, there you were.' I continued. 'Hurrying along, late, a bit sweaty...'

'Sweaty? You cheeky bastard...'

'A bit sweaty, but still stunning,' I said, still grinning. 'The most beautiful woman I'd ever seen, actually.'

'Better,' she said, smiling and uncrossing her legs from her lap. She leant back in her seat. 'Much, much better. No wonder we fell in love.'

'Who wouldn't fall in love with you, Natalie?' Dan said.

Admit it, you're enjoying this pint now.

'It's all right,' Dan replied. Then, 'You're lucky, Joe.'

Lucky? I'm dead, or did you miss that part?

'But look at you two... I've never had what you two have. Not even close.'

'And again,' Natalie said. 'One minute we're talking, the next you drift off. It's driving me mad.'

'Sorry, I'm sorry. I'll work on it,' Dan said.

'There's no manual for this, Nat. You're not the only one finding it difficult,' I said. It was the most awkward we'd all felt since Dan and I turned up on her doorstep earlier.

'You're right. Sorry. But it's two against one, right? I'm on my own here. You've got each other.' she leant back in her seat, a visible sadness sweeping over her.

* * *

Dan had never been a big believer in destiny, but his grandmother had been. She used to tell him there was more to the world than the eyes could see. Dan hadn't ever believed her, not even as a child. If there was an afterlife, he'd have felt his mother there. And he didn't feel her, not one little bit. But he'd liked his grandmother's conviction, he'd liked her belief. She hadn't been religious as such, she'd had no church affiliations. But she had been what he'd call 'spiritual.' She'd believed in predestination, that life would take you where you needed to go, even if it wasn't via a route you wanted to tread.

Dan had always thought that was rubbish, platitudes dreamed up by people whose lives were tough and needed to believe there was some purpose to them, some reason for the hardship they faced. But sitting drinking pints of ale he'd never have touched before and listening to Natalie's soft, lilting tones, he felt that perhaps his grandmother had been right about fate all along. He was consumed by an unfamiliar feeling that took a while to identify. Calm. All-encompassing calm. Maybe his illness, his condition, had predisposed him to all of this. Maybe he'd had to go through everything he'd been through in order to be on that street at the time when the car hit Joe and his spirit was flung out of his body. Maybe only someone like Dan, detached as he was, could have accommodated Joe's spirit. Before that day, Dan would never have believed any of this, but now? What else could he believe? What other options were there? That he was mad? If that were true, the stories he was telling would have been fake, made up. But they weren't, they were true. Natalie remembered everything, too.

Detached? I asked.

'What?'

You said 'detached'. That your condition made you detached. What did you mean?

'Not now, Joe,' Dan said.

Then when? What is your condition? Why won't you let me access it? You're blocking those memories off.

'I'm not blocking them, I just...'

'What else do you remember?' Natalie asked.

'I'm sorry, what?' Dan said, refocusing on the room around him, on Natalie. How many pints had they had? One? Two? Not three, surely not three. He didn't drink, he'd be off his head if he'd had three.

'The accident? How did Joe get inside you?'

She might as well have raised the palm of her hand and thrust it violently into his face. He recoiled in his seat, a darkness clouding his vision momentarily.

'I don't remember,' he said. 'One minute I was...then I was...'

'Has it happened to you before?' Natalie persevered.

'No, of course not,' Dan said, cautiously. 'One minute I was on the street, the next I heard brakes screeching...then...this.' He flapped his arms up and slapped them down by his side.

'Okay,' Natalie said eventually.

'Okay, what?' Dan said.

'Let's go home. We've got a lot to work out.'

'We can go back?' I said, smiling and leaning forward, unable to contain my excitement.

'Of course. But we've got to get our story straight, got to work things out.'

She leant back and put her legs down, planting each trainer-clad food onto the wooden floor of the pub. I wrapped my hand around my cold pint glass, feeling its cool moistness seep into my skin, Dan's skin. It was comforting, it made me feel more at home in him, at home with this whole messed-up scenario.

'Not least what we're going to tell my parents,' I said quietly, not looking at Natalie's face as I spoke.

* * *

As we walked home, we chatted, reminisced and laughed, as if it wasn't weird, as if I was in my own body and not someone else's. Internally, however, Dan was worrying.

'Something isn't right, Joe.'

'What do you mean?'

'She's letting us stay, just like that?'

'You're overthinking things...I'm her husband, remember?'

'And you're dead...remember?'

We drifted into silence then, both struck by the strangeness of our situation and worrying not just for ourselves, but for Natalie as well.

* * *

Back at the house, we grabbed another beer from the fridge and sat down next to each other on the sofa in our immaculate living room, chatting. At some point, we ordered a pizza to be delivered. I rubbed my hand along the soft cushions of the sofa, the same sofa Natalie and I chose from Sofa Warehouse when we'd moved into the house. How strange it was to experience these things second hand, through someone else's touch.

'And I woke up to find you vacuuming the curtains at four in the morning,' Natalie said. 'Do you remember? You never did like mess, everything had to be in order.'

'Is that why the house is so tidy?' Dan asked. 'I mean, seriously,

I've never seen anything like it. Nothing is out of place.'

'Yeah, I couldn't break Joe's programming.'

'Programming?' I said. 'Is that how I made you feel?'

'It wasn't like that,' she said, as if she was worried she'd offended me. 'I didn't mean you were...'

'Are you a tidy freak?' Dan asked out loud, smiling and widening his eyes.

'Fuck off, I wasn't that bad,' I said, shrinking back into the sofa a little.

'You were quite bad,' Natalie replied quietly.

Dan smiled at her, pleased they were agreeing on something. *Are you two ganging up on me?*

'Right then,' Dan said, grabbing Natalie's hand and standing up. 'Where shall we start?'

'What do you mean?' she said.

'Messing the place up a bit.' Dan grinned, grabbing a cushion from the sofa and throwing it onto the rug.

'No, Dan, you can't,' Natalie started.

'Come on, live a little.' Dan grinned again. He picked up another cushion and Frisbeed it across the room.

'Go on,' Dan said. 'Life's too short, Natalie.'

'But...'

Dan walked over to the bookcase and perused the shelves.

'Fuck me,' he said, grinning widely. 'He had it all in alphabetical order.'

'Are you for real, Joe?' he said internally. 'Alphabetical order?'

Not just alphabetical, I said, taking a book off the shelf. *Genre-specific groupings in alphabetical order. What's wrong with that?*

'Yeah, it was a bit...' Natalie paused, like she was being naughty even saying it. 'Anal. To be honest, I never understood the system.'

'Anal?' Dan retorted, grabbing a book himself, so we were holding two, one in each hand. 'It's like he had a pole up his arse.'

Dan started grabbing books and rearranging them, putting some upside down, some back to front and none in alphabetical order.

'Don't,' I said, laughing in spite on myself. I'd never have coped with this before I died, when I was in my own body, but somehow this felt right, like it was what Natalie needed. And that was important. I wanted her to heal, to move on.

'Come on, Natalie,' Dan said, chucking a book at her. 'Live life on the edge and put a literary fiction novel next to a biography. You know you want to.'

With that, she burst out laughing, catching the book and rushing over to the shelves, grabbing a whole row and simply dumping them on the floor.

* * *

Half an hour later, lying on the living room floor, our heads touching, both staring at the ceiling with books and cushions and remote controls and magazines all around us, we listened to our own breathing and enjoyed the smell of the pizza boxes by our heads.

'Thanks,' she said.

'Don't thank me,' I replied. 'Thank Dan.'

'Thank you both,' she said, rolling over and propping herself up on her elbows. 'I haven't laughed like that since Joe died. It feels good.'

'This should feel weirder than it does, shouldn't it?' Dan said quietly.

'Yes,' she replied.

Dan was staring at her face, her lips. No lipstick, full, moist and waiting. He leant in, slowly at first, checking whether she was going to retreat. Closer. The skin of his lips brushed hers and for a moment everything stopped, time was non-existent and the only thing I could feel was his heart smashing its way through his chest and the warm moistness of her mouth. Then she pulled back, pushed herself to her feet.

'No,' she said firmly. 'Just…no.'

'Shit, I'm sorry. I'm so sorry,' Dan started. 'I didn't mean, I…'

It's okay, I replied, surprised that I meant it. *I can feel everything you're feeling. I'd have done the same.*

'I wasn't talking to you.'

'Look,' Natalie walked toward the living room door. 'You can stay, of course you can, but there are some rules. We are not a couple, okay? You're not my husband, Dan. Joe might be…but…'

'Okay.'

'That's not your body, Joe.' She gestured toward Dan, toward me. 'Do you understand?'

'I do, but…' I started.

'Look, you have to let me process this, okay? Don't rush me.'

'We're still processing it ourselves,' Dan said. 'I shouldn't have tried to kiss you, I'm sorry.'

'Which one of you is that?' she asked, flapping her hands down by her sides. 'Do you see how difficult this is? How do I even know which one of you I'm speaking to?'

'Can't you tell by the accent? That was Dan,' I replied. 'He tried to kiss you, not me.'

'Thanks for that,' Dan replied.

'Oh, for fuck's sake. See? This isn't going to work…' Natalie looked over her shoulder at her living room door. 'I'm not sure I can do this.'

'He doesn't have anywhere else, Nat,' I said, pushing myself to Dan's feet and holding his hands in a prayer position in front of my mouth. 'Please. He'll be back on the street if you kick us out. And part of him won't mind that, part of him is already used to it; he even finds it a bit comforting. But I don't. I'm scared Nat. I'm really scared.'

'So am I. I don't know you, Dan. You're asking a lot of me.'

'You're my wife. Who else should I be asking?'

Silence. The last of the evening light flickered through the living room window. Dan was repressing himself, letting me take control of his body again, letting me implore my wife to help us. Deep down, I could feel part of him desperate to get out, to get away from her and be alone on the street again, to find somewhere to hole up and sleep, to hide. He wanted somewhere he could pretend none of this was happening, where he could forget me again.

I can't let that happen, Dan. You understand that, don't you?

'You have to get a job, earn some money. I'm not keeping you. Do you understand?' Natalie said.

'Yes,' I answered.

'That means Dan,' she said. 'Dan will have to get a job, get his life back on track. Dan has to sort himself out.'

'Okay,' I answered.

'Both of you?' she asked.

'I don't know,' Dan said. 'I don't know if I can...'

Try. You have to try. Please, for me. If not for me, then for Natalie.

'Well? They're my terms, Dan. It's no good if only Joe agrees.'

I'll help you. We'll get your life back together.

'Maybe.'

'Well?' Natalie asked again.

Dan refocused on her worried face, and without thinking, he started nodding.

'Okay, I'll do my best,' he said.

'No, that's not the deal. I'm not keeping you. I'm not caring for you. Sort yourself out and you can stay. I'm not fixing you, that's not who I am anymore.'

'But I don't know if...' Dan started.

'Yes, Dan, you do. Everyone does. Make a decision. Take your life back or don't. There are no in-betweens.'

'You sound like Yoda,' Dan said, adopting a Yoda accent. 'Do or do not, there is no try.'

'I'm serious,' Natalie said, but I could see a little smile

creeping into the corners of her lips. She liked him already.

'Okay,' Dan said, nodding again and putting on his best sombre face. 'Sorry.'

'You'll do it?'

Natalie reached her hand out and touched his arm. Her fingers were gentle, soft. I remembered kissing them, as we lay in bed together, not speaking, not fucking, just enjoying being next to one another. I wished I could kiss them again, for a moment.

'Yes, I'll do it. I promise,' Dan said.

'So, we can stay?' I asked.

'You can stay,' she replied. 'In the spare room, though. Not with me, I'm not ready for that. I might never be ready for that.'

PART II: NATALIE

'Joe's not the man you think he is.'

CHAPTER 4

Emotions don't arrive intact. If Natalie has learnt anything, it's that. Shards injure you incrementally, so small at first you don't notice them. Over time, the damage builds and one day you realise the nicks and cuts have become gaping wounds. Worse still, they've become the very thing that defines you.

She didn't mean to fall in love with him. But maybe that's the way of love. It doesn't wait to be invited in, and it won't be coerced. It gently creeps under your skin, a mild itch at first, not giving itself away in case you scratch it and cause an infection. But then it sinks in deeper, getting into your bloodstream. It travels. By the time it reaches your brain and you're aware of the infection, it's already taken over your heart. In Natalie's experience, love is anything but innocent. It's a captor, a guard, imprisoning you in the clutches of another, knitting the fabric of your own life to somebody else's, whether you like it or not. But that's the thing. With Dan, Natalie *does* like it, maybe more so because she *shouldn't*. Despite the surreptitious way it has imprisoned her, she can't help feeling that deep down, love is still beautiful, that its intentions are benign after all, despite her experience to date.

She can't help thinking there's a way for them to work, a way for them to cut through the impossibility of how they met. And she'll do anything she can to find a way to escape the lies and make a go of it with him. Her feelings don't make sense, she knows that. But since when have feelings listened to reason? The last thing she needs in her life is another complicated man. But how could she have known how he'd make her feel every time he looked at her? And the stories he tells, the memories he shares. She could listen to them forever.

But there's Joe to consider—a complication, certainly, but she refuses to believe he's an insurmountable one. None of this was meant to get so out of hand, she just needed to know what Dan had seen. But that's the thing about lies, once they're out in the world, they develop a life of their own. They keep on growing, spiralling and turning. Thorny vines, wrapping themselves around everything good, strangling the life from the most innocent of victims. And she thinks Dan is innocent, in the scheme of things. She'd like him to stay that way, uncorrupted by her or Joe, by their marriage.

Mostly, Natalie tries not to think about Joe at all, it's too painful, too difficult a problem. Instead, she tries to focus on Dan, on getting him back to health and happiness. If she can help him sort himself out, the Joe problem will sort itself out. As long as Dan never finds out the truth. As long as Joe doesn't either, she supposes.

Natalie doesn't dwell on Joe's accident too much. She pushes it to the back of her mind where the murky things live, shadow creatures, scrabbling in the dirt for scraps. But she can't help asking what Dan remembers from that day. The police came up with nothing, labelled it an accident. But someone is always to blame, somewhere, somehow. It's like an insect bite she can't help scratching. Even though she knows it'll make things worse, she finds herself bringing it up again and again, wanting to talk it through with them, over and over. Dan wants to forget about it, of course he does. And so should she, but she can't let it go. Can't stop waking in the night screaming, feeling the weight of Joe's head on her lap as she cradled him the road, covered in blood, listening to the sirens getting closer and closer as she tried to ignore the crowds of people taking pictures on their phones, like her husband was something titilating to be Tweeted, Facebooked or Instagrammed.

He was dying. She remembers seeing some of them realise this before she did, their phones dropping limply by their sides, their grips getting slightly weaker around their smash-proof cases, jaws slack, the reality that they were watching a life slipping away finally sinking in.

Then Dan appeared, in the road next to her, in front of the smashed-up cars, dirty, unshaven, stinking of piss. Staring at her, not at Joe, but at her, like she was the only thing in the world.

'Did you see?' Natalie shouted at him, desperately, her heart a kicking foetus in her chest. Then, all hell broke loose. A policeman was talking to her, asking her questions, and paramedics were loading Joe into the ambulance, bundling her in after him.

To this day, Dan has never answered the question, no matter how directly she poses it to him.

'Did you see what happened?' Over and over, she asks. 'Did you see the accident?'

She sees how uncomfortable it makes him, how he averts his gaze from her, kicking his feet on the floor like an awkward teenager. Except he's a grown man in his thirties. She understands things changed for him that day. She knows it's difficult, but it wasn't all bad for him. In fact, you could say things improved for him. You could say things improved for all of them...well, except for Joe. Things aren't better for him, of course.

'Joe says he feels like a deadheaded plant,' Dan said to her last week, a light smile on his face. 'Like his head has been chopped off and mine has grown back in its place.'

'Don't be ridiculous,' Natalie replied, turning her back on him and unpacking the shopping, emptying it onto the side in the kitchen rather than putting it in the cupboards and fridge, taking one item out after another after another.

'But is it ridiculous?' Dan said, coming up behind her and putting his hands on her waist. Strong hands, bigger than Joe's had been. 'Isn't that exactly what's happened?'

'I hate it when you talk like this, Dan,' Natalie said, stepping out of his embrace and carrying a bag of carrots over to the fridge.

'We can't pretend it's not happening, Nat.'

'Please,' she said, closing her eyes and letting the cool air from the refrigerator waft over her face, eyelids and cheeks. 'Joe calls me Nat. Can't you call me Natalie?'

* * *

What about Joe? She knows Dan would never accept it if she told him she wanted Joe gone, that it was only him she wanted. And even if he could accept it, what could he do about it? It's not like he could ask Joe to go and he'd disappear quietly into the night.

She's not sure when her life started unravelling to the degree it has. She knows it was long before the accident. Even before she met Joe, really. The seed was sown when she was a little girl, sitting on the bus, blinking back tears. All her decisions since then have somehow been built on top of that experience. Funny how Joe's accident has allowed her to see everything so clearly. But how did things get so insane? Nothing in her life is as she planned it. Plans are now something other people get to enjoy, they're nothing to do with the terrifying, breath-stealing madness of her life with Dan.

Madness. She shouldn't use words like that, she knows. But what else would be more appropriate? Their life seems ordinary. An onlooker wouldn't suspect a thing. She's sitting in her back garden, enjoying the early evening sunshine with a glass of wine, wondering where her boyfriend is. Nothing would seem untoward to anyone else. But usually, he's always in the house when she gets home. He's there waiting for her; he doesn't go out; he doesn't work or socialise. So, where is he? She can't work out if his absence is a good thing or a bad thing. She's spent the past two months trying to ease him back into the world, into behaviours other people would consider normal.

Normal. She shouldn't even think things like that, she knows she shouldn't. Dan is normal, in his way. *Normality* carries baggage, a judgment she doesn't mean and doesn't care for. She closes her eyes in the fading sunlight and wonders at the complexity of her feelings. In part, she's glad he's out. He doesn't go out often, so it shows progress. But she's also worried about him, because she's not sure he can cope, not yet. Then again, he survived on the streets alone all that time without her, so he's resilient, resourceful. Perhaps it's arrogance on her part that makes her think he's dependent on her. Maybe it's her own fear of entering into a co-dependent relationship that's causing her such angst. She can never have a partnership based on *need*. She's done that before, she'll never do it again. Because that's how things start: with *need*. It never leads to anything positive. Need and love aren't synonymous with each other, but so many people, including her, make the mistake of thinking that needing someone is the same as loving them, or vice versa. Perhaps in reality, need and love are each other's opposites.

Reality. It's such a strange word, one that used to be concrete. She doesn't even know what it means anymore. She downs her wine, staring at the ivy that's creeping over her back fence, even though Joe cut it back what seems like days ago. But the accident was months ago, so it must be at least that long since it was trimmed, probably longer. And how long has it been since Dan moved in? It's hard to tell. Time rolls into one long stream of questions without answers nowadays.

Madness. Normality. Reality. Concepts that used to feel real but which no longer make sense.

'I'm cooking dinner,' Dan's voice booms through the open window, making her jump. It's deep, vibrating some part of her core with every uttered syllable.

'You've been out on your own?' she calls back, masking her concern but not looking around. Instead, she continues to stare at the ivy climbing the fence, strangling anything in its wake, relentless, ruthless and unremitting.

'Yeah, we have news,' Dan beams. *We.* Her heart flutters

slightly. *News.* For a normal person, this wouldn't necessarily come with a sense of foreboding, but with Dan it could mean anything. Natalie doesn't know if it's exciting or terrifying. Probably a bit of both.

Natalie isn't sure what to do for the best, and it's a feeling she's had since the day she met Dan. She should have kept on running; she should have slammed the door in his face, but something about him drew her in and made her listen, made her fall in love, like she had no choice. Fate, crooking its bony finger and chuckling his dry chuckle.

Love. She's never known it before. Not like this. Maybe this is how Joe always felt about her, maybe that's why he...

No. There's no point in reflection, in introspection. She must move forward, concentrate on helping Dan sort himself out. She needs to make him visit his dad. Then, he needs to get a job. But how can she get him to take the first steps? Any time she tries, Joe gets angry about it, starts shouting at her that she's trying to marginalise him. But she wants to help Dan, or rather, she wants him to help himself.

Who is she trying to kid? Joe knows as well as she does that she's fallen in love with Dan. No wonder he's hurting. She still talks about Joe like he's the man she married, like he's still present in any real sense. And he's not; he's nothing like the man she married. Not physically, not emotionally. And yet...

The sex is different with Dan. It's much less aggressive than with Joe. One night, soon after they were married, Joe pulled out a clump of her hair at the point of orgasm. It was both terrifying and...well... But Dan is nothing like that. He's gentler, more tentative, like he doesn't know what he wants or how to get it. But the sex is good in its own way. It's unhurried, not urgent, not animal. And that's okay. If he's facing her, she has time to stroke his cheek, to kiss him before the pace builds up, before she digs her fingertips into the skin of his back.

'Why didn't you shout my name during sex?' Joe asked last

night, after her first time with Dan.

'What do you mean?' Natalie said, leaning over the bedside cabinet and reaching for a glass of slightly stale water.

'You didn't shout my name when you were coming, you shouted his,' Joe said in his brittle, south-London accent. She'd quickly grown to hate it. She took a sip of her water, not looking back at him, at his pale skin or the troubled frown she knew he would be wearing.

'Leave it, will you?' she said quietly. 'It would seem weird, okay?'

He rolled over at that, his back exposed with no covers on, glistening with sweat in the moonlight coming in from the window.

'I don't mean anything by it,' she said, gently touching his skin. He flinched a tiny bit, like he didn't believe her. She respected him for that. It gave her hope for the future. She *was* lying. She meant *everything* by it, and it was good that he recognised that. It meant that somewhere deep down, Dan could tell fact from fiction. That was progress.

* * *

Sitting in her garden, twirling an empty wineglass, teeth pressing into her bottom lip, Natalie breathes in deeply and stands, walking back through the open doors into the house where Dan is busy cooking. She paints on her biggest smile as she enters, bracing herself for what he has to tell her.

'News?' she asks, leaning against the doorframe.

'Joe says he can't cook,' Dan says, smiling over his shoulder as he dumps a handful of chopped onion into a wide-based pan. 'But I can, and I do. And I've had a good day. A great day, so I thought I'd make us a meal.'

His childish grin gives her goose bumps every time she sees him and her knees weaken a little. She's in her mid-thirties, but what is it about him that, despite everything, makes her feel like a teenage girl?

'What news?' she asks, walking over and putting her arms around his waist. Dan turns and kisses her on the lips, then busies himself opening cupboards and grabbing things like coconut milk and lime leaves.

'Go back in the garden and relax,' he says. 'I'll shout to you when it's ready. Green curry. Okay?'

'Yeah, my favourite,' she says, walking back out into the fading sunshine as her heart pummels her chest.

'I know it is,' Dan shouts gleefully. 'Joe told me.'

It's not her favourite. She only said that to make him feel better. But it's nice that he's cooking for her because Joe never did.

* * *

Natalie and Joe were married ten years ago in a simple registry office ceremony. No friends, no family, just her, Joe and two strangers as witnesses. It had been a whirlwind romance, the type she'd always sneered at. She'd always thought men and women who married quickly on a whim were either idiots or delusional. How could they know they wanted to spend the rest of their life with someone they had only just met? But then she met Joe, and instantly they connected. Nobody else existed, and he needed her in a way that made her feel *special*. It was the two of them against the world. It had been Joe's idea to run away and get married. He hadn't liked most of her friends, anyway, let alone her family, so it made sense. No politics, no drama, just the two of them. It had felt romantic at the time.

'I'll never leave you,' Joe used to say.

But no matter what Dan thinks, Natalie knows Joe would have wanted to stay with her like this.

Not like this.

* * *

Natalie forks the last of the green curry into her mouth and sighs. Dan is sitting opposite, wiping his plate with wholemeal roti bread and humming to themselves gently. He's in a good mood and seems more relaxed than she's seen him in ages.

'So?' Natalie says quietly, her elbows digging painfully into the wood of the table as she leans forward seductively. 'What do you remember?'

She's smiling softly, pretending it's a nonchalant question, that she's not desperate to hear the answer. She cups her wineglass firmly between her hands, meeting Dan's gaze, enjoying the way he devours her with every glance. She's never felt so wanted by a man—not objectified, but something more... loved, she supposes. Adored and desired. Wanted not for an invented version of herself but for being herself. He doesn't want her to be anything and she's surprised how liberating that is. How many people live an entire life without finding someone who is happy to be around them without wanting to fix them?

It makes her feel even more guilty, because she can't reciprocate that feeling. In fact, it would be wrong to. Dan does need fixing and she has to help him do it. Nothing in her life makes sense apart from that. Last night, as she'd watched him sleeping, she'd thought she should leave it alone. After all, they were weirdly happy. But by morning, her resolve had stiffened again. It was too dangerous to let things carry on as they were.

'I don't remember anything, love,' he says, and it takes her a moment to spot the accent, to realise it isn't Dan speaking, but Joe. Confirmation comes as she opens her eyes and sees a small smile creep along the edges of his mouth as he talks. It's not like Dan's smile. Dan has the type of smile that forces you to return it, even if you don't want to.

'We've told you before, Nat,' Joe continues, leaning over to take her hand and squeezing it. 'Why do you want to keep asking?'

'Okay, Joe,' she says, pulling her hand away. He doesn't speak, but leans back in his chair, handsome and pale in the flickering light. After a while, she realises he's checking her out, not even pretending he's not looking at the open buttons at the top of her blouse, at the gap between her breasts.

'What's for pudding?' she says quickly, feeling uncomfortable, like she always does when Joe's looking at her.

'I've got a job!' Dan says, excitedly.

'Seriously?' she bursts out, her heart skipping a beat. This is good news, a step toward independence, toward normality. There's that word again. Why does it rear its head so often, peaking around every corner, beckoning her? Nothing about this is normal, it never will be. Why is she starting to crave *normality*? That's not what she entered in to. She knew what she was doing; she knew exactly what she was signing up for when he turned up on her doorstep. Maybe normal isn't the right word, then. Perhaps the right word is ordinary; maybe she'd like the chance to be *ordinary*.

'Yeah,' Dan says excitedly, getting up and walking around the table toward her, grabbing her hand and pulling her up toward him into an embrace. 'My old firm, where I worked before...'

He twirls Natalie around and she laughs, clutching his face and studying it. This is Dan. This is the man she loves. And little by little, he's sorting himself out. Things are going to be okay, she knows there are.

'And they said they'd take you back on? Even after you ran out on them?'

'Yeah. Luckily, the person who replaced me is leaving and... Well, I told them I lost it a bit after my gran died, you know. They understood that. Grief does funny things. And it was only a half lie, wasn't it?'

'Not even half of one.' Natalie grabs him and pulls him close. 'You didn't mention Joe, did you?'

'Of course not,' Dan laughs. 'What do you take me for?'

* * *

Later, after the dinner plates are cleared away and Natalie has poured herself another glass of wine, she lies down on the sofa, resting her head in Dan's lap.

'I'm proud of you,' she says. And she means it, she *is* proud. In all honesty, there are days when she's wondered if she's lost her mind, taking up with Dan, as if her incessant need to fix things has gone into self-destructive overdrive. She's questioned whether anything good can ever come of the two of them; but he can always surprise her. He can always show her there's hope. Like today, going out and getting his job back against all odds.

'Don't be proud of me; be proud of Joe,' Dan says calmly, stroking her hair lightly and gently thrusting his crotch upward into her head on his lap. 'He's the one who convinced me I could do it. He's a good influence.'

Dan has tensed up slightly; Natalie can feel it. He's stopped stroking her head for a moment and is sitting rigid. He's drifting off again, like he's having some kind of internal conflict she's not party to. She's not sure which she likes less, when he and Joe argue externally or when she can tell they're doing it inside his head. In these moments, Natalie feels alone, a dimly lit island of sanity in a desolate twilight sea. She stares up at the dull glow of her living room ceiling.

I wish Joe would go, she thinks, but doesn't say. She knows she can't say it yet; Dan's not ready to hear it. But one day he will be. And that's the day she's dreaming of, when she can get rid of Joe once and for all.

'What's up?' Dan says, startling Natalie. He's staring down at her intently.

'It's nothing,' she says, sitting up and leaning away from him on the sofa. 'Don't worry about it.'

'You're worrying me now. Have I done something wrong? Have I—'

'Dan, stop apologising for everything. You haven't done anything wrong...'

'Me, then?' Joe starts.

'For fuck's sake, no,' she says. Then, seeing the hurt look on his face, she softens, leaning back over and stroking his arm.

Finally, Dan says, 'Time for bed, work in the morning. How mad is that?'

Natalie looks into his eyes and strokes his cheek.

'Pretty mad,' she mutters to herself. 'Pretty mad.'

CHAPTER 5

For a while after Joe's accident, things were okay. Far from grieving, for the first time in years Natalie felt like the world was full of possibility again. But the world also expected something from her. It expected tears and distress. It expected hysteria and mourning. But all she felt was relief, like his death had thrown her a lifeline, one she'd tied tightly around her waist.

She'd been getting by, sorting out the paperwork, trying her best to move on and ignore the feelings gnawing away at her. The hardest part of her daily life in those first months was the guilt. People would nod at her with big, sad, knowing eyes and she'd stare back at them, thinking, *I didn't love him. Stop pitying me. I don't feel how you think I feel.* But she played along, acted like she'd lost the love of her life and was being strong. That part was true, she supposes. She felt stronger than she had for years. She'd never let anyone else control her again.

Joe's funeral came and went. Days came and went. People moved on and she didn't have to pretend to grieve with such intensity; she could now be the brave woman piecing her life back together again. The only person who didn't buy it was Joe's mother, Valerie. She felt sure Natalie was bottling things up too much. She kept foisting bereavement leaflets on her, telling her she had to talk about it.

'You don't have to talk with me, Nat,' she said, leaning over and touching Natalie's hand gently. 'I'm seeing someone myself. A counsellor.'

'No, honestly, that's not for me, I...' Natalie started.

'I know. I know it's not. But how about a group? There's this bereavement group; I found a leaflet for it. It might help you, Nat.'

Valerie was using her most caring voice, her most desperate one, the one Natalie couldn't say no to. She took the leaflet from her mother-in-law's hands and nodded.

'Please?' Valerie said. 'Because whether you admit it or not, you need someone to talk to about him.'

'I'll give it a go,' Natalie said, quietly. 'But...'

'No buts,' Valerie said, finally leaning back and taking her hand away from Natalie's, her voice hardening a little. 'He wasn't all bad, you know. You can't blame everything on him.'

* * *

The signs were there even before she and Joe were married, if only she'd looked for them. One morning, quite early on in their relationship, Natalie had woken to find Joe staring at her.

'What are you looking at?' she'd asked, coy with pride. He'd been watching her sleep. She knew what that meant. It meant he loved her; she'd seen it in the American movies she'd grown up watching, snuggled up next to her mum on the sofa on a Sunday afternoon.

'You,' Joe had replied. For a moment, Natalie felt warm, content, happy. 'You were snoring and dribbling... You looked like you were retarded or something.'

As he'd laughed and pushed himself out of bed, Natalie had rolled over and closed her eyes. *He doesn't mean it*, she'd told herself.

Another time, when he'd told her how much he loved the *Star Wars* films, she'd thought she'd try something fun and sexy.

'Do you like the buns?' she'd asked, swishing into the kitchen as he ate breakfast, hair styled like Princess Leia and, more importantly, wearing a slave Leia costume delivered that morning from Amazon.

'You've got lovely hair,' he'd said, turning the page of his newspaper without looking up. 'But you look bloody ridiculous.'

She hadn't taken offence; it was just his way. After all, he had complimented her. He'd told her she had lovely hair. Okay, so he hadn't liked the Leia buns, but she could easily let them out. And that's what she'd done; she let the buns down immediately. Looking back, she can see how quickly she was changing, altering her behaviour to please him, to make him happy. At the time, she didn't see it; all she saw was her beautiful, damaged fiancé. He loved her. More than that, he needed her. She could fix him; she could help him to work through his emotions and find himself.

'You didn't have to get rid of them,' he'd said as she shook the buns loose.

'But it's better like this, isn't it?' she'd replied, flicking her locks over her shoulder and posing, half glamour girl, half awkward child.

'S'pose,' he'd said, shaking his paper out and leaning back into his chair. 'But the slave outfit is a bit slutty.'

* * *

Natalie isn't quite sure why she took her mother-in-law's advice and went to the bereavement group. It wasn't like she needed to talk. She knew what Joe had done, what he'd *taken* from her, and while her distance from it made her marvel that she'd ever allowed it to happen, she was able to move on without elaborating to strangers. The weakness people presumed of her, the idea that she couldn't cope without talking, never rang true for Natalie, but she was so caught up in pretending that she kept playing along. *Pretend to grieve,* she thought. *Pretend to need support. Hope nobody will notice the cracks beneath the surface and the rivers of lava bubbling beneath.*

Perhaps in the end it was the guilt that pushed her over the edge and made her jump onto the number seven bus into town. Clutching the flimsy leaflet from her mother-in-law, she stood nervously in the doorway of a run-down community centre and looked cautiously at the circle of plastic chairs before her, a few of them filled, but most of them empty. A woman with long grey hair was standing by the centremost chair, in a flowing flower-print dress and open-toe sandals. She looked like the human embodiment of an Afghan hound, a living, breathing stereotype and just the sort of person Natalie would have imagined would run a group like that. Natalie, rooted to the spot, almost turned her back and walked away, but the Afghan hound clearly had a sixth sense for such things.

'Welcome,' she said. Her voice fit the stereotype beautifully, all soft and flowing, gentle, with a hint of understanding. 'Please,' she motioned for Natalie to enter, 'come in. Sit down.' Her long, drawn-out syllables Pied-Pipered Natalie into the room, from which there was no escape, no quick exit.

'No, it's okay. I think...' Natalie started, but the Afghan hound walked toward her and took her arm gently, ushering her into the room.

'The first session is always hardest,' she said. 'You don't have to speak if you don't want to, but you can listen to some of the others in the group. It might help.'

* * *

A fidgety man with a shiny tracksuit stood up first. His face was flushed and blotchy, like he'd been drinking too much or doing something else to medicate himself.

'Did any of you used to fantasise about your partner dying before they actually died?'

The room was silent, uncomfortable, but he had Natalie's full attention. Her mouth was dry, her throat sore. The man, faced with no murmurs of agreement, fidgeted even more, but Natalie was captivated, she wanted to jump up and hug him.

'I don't mean I really wanted him to die or anything. I just mean...' He paused, sounding desperate.

Natalie's shoulders sagged.

'It's okay, Martin,' Afghan hound said, all soothing, soporific silk. 'We're listening. There's no judgement here.'

'I just mean sometimes I'd imagine what it would be like if something happened to him. Not because I wanted it but because I loved him so much. I'd make myself cry, thinking about what it would be like sometimes.' He paused, glancing around the room, clearly relieved to see a few others in the circle nodding, finally understanding what he meant. 'But it didn't come close. Nothing I imagined could have prepared me for him dying.'

Natalie sat back in her chair, shoulders stiffening again. He wasn't like her after all. He was another grieving widower, another partner left behind struggling with loss and loneliness. Was there nobody else who felt released like Natalie did?

'What did he die of?' an older woman asked. 'Was it the AIDS?' She whispered 'the AIDS' like it was a swear word, the way a *Daily Mail* reader would whisper 'black' or 'gay'.

'No, it was pancreatitis,' he snapped, and the room fell into silence, everyone uncomfortable again.

'Well done, Martin. I think we can all learn something from that,' Afghan hound said quickly. 'Does anyone else have anything to add?'

Natalie quickly looked at her feet, careful not to make eye contact or be drawn into the conversation.

'No?' Afghan Hound asked. 'Okay, thanks Martin.' She nodded, indicating Martin should sit down. His unloading was over for now and she clearly wanted to move on.

Natalie stayed for the entire session, sitting silently listening to tale of woe after tale of woe, thinking, *How can you do this? Sit here and air your feelings with total strangers like it will change anything? How can you think that will help?*

'Half the time, I want him prosecuted,' a woman said vehemently, standing up and dropping her shoulder bag onto the plastic seat behind her. 'What was he thinking? Driving Adam to Beachy Head, the state he was in? Adam was drunk, he had a head injury, for fuck's sake. And that taxi driver took him up there, dropped him off and took his money.'

'I'm sure he didn't mean...' Martin started to say.

'Let Louise finish,' the Afghan hound said quietly, compassionately. 'It's good for her to release the emotion, to *externalise* it.'

'No, he's right,' Louise said, deflating a little. 'It's no good *blaming* him all the time, is it? I want to lash out...to avoid the truth.' Her voice dropped to a whisper, so much so that Natalie had to lean forward, elbows on her knees, so she could hear what the woman was saying. 'It's my fault. He's dead because of me.'

To Natalie's horror, the circle began clapping at that. Every single last one of them started slapping their hands together, as if something good had happened. She frowned, looking from the woman, Louise, back to the Afghan hound, who was beaming as if some huge breakthrough had been achieved.

'Well done, Louise,' the Afghan hound said, holding her hands out in front of her. 'You're letting your emotions out...' She paused for effect. 'You're *externalising*.'

Natalie covered her mouth to stop a snigger escaping. One by one, people shared their stories, standing up and receiving rounds of applause for 'putting their emotions out' and 'externalising.' And then came the moment she'd been dreading.

'We have a new member today,' Afghan hound said, motioning toward Natalie. 'Can everyone welcome Natalie to the group?'

The introduction was met with a muted round of applause and a few mumbles of 'Hi, Natalie.'

'Would you like to share your story with the group, Natalie?'

Would I fuck, Natalie thought. For a moment, she pictured herself on the day of the accident, after the hospital, after the doctors and the police and the endless questions. She went back to the moment after the sympathy and mutual hugs with Valerie and Joe's dad, Harry. Home alone at last, she'd dropped her bag in the hall and made her way upstairs to the bathroom. She'd stood empty of emotion, staring at herself in the bathroom mirror, lipstick smeared across her face. Large, dark rings of mascara smudged around her eyes, and snot dripping out of her nose and into the sink. Then, she'd seen it: the relief. He was gone and she was free.

'Natalie?' Afghan hound had pushed.

'No, no, not today,' Natalie had said quietly, thinking, *Not ever, Ms. Hound. Not ever.*

Later, after a few more people had unloaded, the meeting mercifully ended.

'It's not for you, is it?' one of the women from the group said to her as they filed out the door. Natalie had shaken her head apologetically.

'It's okay. I understand,' the woman went on, pleasantly. 'I didn't think it would be my cup of tea at the beginning, either.'

'It's Louise, isn't it?' Natalie said, smiling through pursed lips.

The woman nodded, slipping her bag over her arm and walking out the door before Natalie.

'Mother-in-law make you come?' Louise asked, smiling.

'Yes,' Natalie replied, a genuine smile crossing her lips. 'How did you know?'

'Mine too,' Louise touched Natalie on the arm lightly and walked away down the street without another word.

* * *

Natalie never went back to the bereavement group; it wasn't her thing. She couldn't see how it could help her. Her situation was too complex. She had nobody to talk to, and never would have. Besides, she'd always been a 'straight down the line' kind of woman, like her mother. Things were as they were. Joe was dead and she didn't miss him. These facts would remain, whether she stood in a room full of strangers and invented stories or not.

A month passed, then another. Life began to normalise, and while people were still a little weird with her, unsure how they were supposed to react, things got easier. Work was a help. Her role entailed a lot of deep thinking, number crunching, and strategic thinking. It was a good distraction and meant she wasn't required to engage socially with people too much. It took her a while to adjust to the space at home, to the freedom of doing what she wanted, when she wanted it. One Saturday afternoon, she received a letter from the life insurance company, confirming they would pay out on Joe's accident. Clutching it in her hand, she left home and went to the café in the local park to get a coffee.

At first, she didn't notice him. She sat outside, eating wafers and drinking coffee, staring at the letter from the insurance company. At least money wasn't something she'd need to worry about. Not that she'd give up her job; she loved it and liked the sense of purpose. But she'd been supporting Joe for a while before he died and it had been putting a massive strain on her. While she sorted through his things in the weeks after his death, boxing things up for his parents, she'd been surprised to find that Joe had life insurance. She didn't have any herself; it had never occurred to her. Though, given Joe's control issues, it shouldn't have surprised her at all. She'd sipped her drink and stared at the letter, noticing but not registering something outside her field of vision. It wasn't quite in focus; it was just something blurred on the outside of her reality until he said:

'Hi.'

She looked up, recognising him instantly.

'You were there,' she said, her heart expanding and contracting with her breath, like it might overinflate and explode. 'At the accident. You were there.'

'Yes,' the man, dirty and unkempt, replied.

He looked down at a note squeezed into his hands, then

75

shouted in a terrifying growl, quite unlike the soft, gentle voice he'd used moments ago.

'I'm here! Nat, I'm here!'

Natalie scrambled for her bag, glancing over her shoulder to check if anyone else was in the park who could help her.

'My name is Dan,' he continued, the soft voice back again. 'I've got this. I wrote this.' He leant forward to hand her a note. She didn't take it and didn't move as he dropped the note on the table before her.

'I'm sorry,' he said. 'I didn't mean to scare you, I just...'

Glancing down at the note before her, she could make out her name. Tentatively, she reached forward and picked it up.

Natalie. Find her. Tell her I'm still alive. She'll help you. She'll help us both.

'I know it doesn't make any sense,' the homeless man said again, quiet and gentle, with the smallest trace of a south-London accent. 'But it's me, Nat. Somehow, it's me. In here. In him. You've got to believe me. I always said I'd find my way back to you.'

Natalie sat bolt upright, acid rising in her throat and burning the back of her mouth.

* * *

'She's not your friend,' Joe said, shortly after they'd moved to Brighton and Natalie had made friends with a woman who lived near them.

'What do you mean?' she asked.

'The other day, in the café in the park, I saw her taking the piss out of you. I didn't want to say anything; I know you thought you were becoming friends.'

'She wouldn't. Maybe she was joking around?' Natalie said, her back to Joe in the kitchen, fighting back the tears.

'No, love,' he said, coming up behind her and putting his

arms around her. 'She said you thought you were better than her since you got a new job.'

'Maybe she was feeling a bit insecure, you know?' Natalie turned to look at him, squeezing her eyes shut to stop the tears. 'She's been finding things tough and...'

'No,' he said. 'I think she's jealous. And look at her: single, shitty job in a supermarket, for Christ's sake. You *are* better than her.'

He grabbed her and hugged her tightly, holding her until she gave in and put her arms around him too.

'You've always got me,' he said. 'You'll never lose me, I promise.'

He broke their embrace, holding her at arm's length and staring into her eyes.

'I'll never leave you, never lose you. Even if I died, I'd find a way back. You never have to worry.'

She shuddered slightly as he leant in and held her again, cuddling her a little too strongly, compressing her lungs and squeezing the breath from her body.

'I'll always find my way back to you.'

* * *

'I always said I'd find my way back to you,' the homeless man repeated.

She knew it was madness, of course it wasn't him. She'd never believed in anything like that, not psychics, not religion, nothing. She was a rational person. She liked numbers and solid facts. In fact, she prided herself on not being 'spiritual,' whatever that was supposed to mean. She was a trained accountant, for God's sake, a finance director. She liked things to be solid and quantifiable. But this? She scrambled for her bag, standing up and putting it on her shoulder.

'Why are you saying this?' she said, flicking a sideways

glance across at the café again. 'Please. I don't have any money, I don't...'

'No, I don't want anything,' the homeless man held his hands up in the air, as if to show he didn't mean any harm. 'I just...I don't know. I didn't mean to scare you.' He backed away, hands still up in the air, like he was aware he was scaring her and didn't want to.

She turned on her heel and ran away, leaving her coffee, biscuits and the letter from her solicitor on the table where she sat. She ran all the way home, slamming the door behind her and standing pressed up against it, as if he was behind her, pushing and kicking at the door, trying to gain entry. That was ridiculous, she knew. It was an unbalanced stranger, down on his luck. He didn't know where she lived. He couldn't find her.

I'll always find you, Natalie, she remembered Joe saying as he cuddled her strongly from behind. *Always.*

Shuddering, she hung her jacket up on the end of the banister by the stairs, hanging her bag on top of it. He couldn't have been telling the truth, could he? That would be ridiculous. Walking into her kitchen, she filled the kettle, trying to shake off the unease. As she grabbed a cup from the cupboard and put a teabag in it, she heard the doorbell ring and her heart jumped in her chest.

'It's him. It's Joe,' she thought, before correcting herself. 'No. He's dead. Pull yourself together. He's dead. People don't come back.'

For a moment, she stood unmoving in her kitchen, leaning back onto the granite work surface, feeling its coolness on her skin, through her blouse. Maybe whoever it was would go away; they hadn't rung again. She ran her thumbnail over her teeth, weighing up whether or not to answer the door. After Joe, she'd promised herself she'd never let fear rule her again; she'd never let it stop her doing anything. Slowly, she braced herself and walked toward the door. It couldn't be the same man, anyway.

How would he know where she lived? Unless he was telling the truth and Joe was inside him, somehow. Then he'd know exactly where she lived.

She pushed the latch down and opened the door a fraction to peek through, sure that it would be her mother-in-law Valerie standing there. She was sure it wasn't going to be...

'Leave me alone,' she pleaded. 'I'm calling the police.'

The homeless madman had found her. He must have followed her; he must have...

'My name is Daniel,' the man said.

Instinctively, she went to slam the door but he jammed it open with one hand, leaving a dirty smudge on the light blue paint as he did so. She leant into the crack, her chest thumping. Joe's voice was inside her mind, saying the same phrase over and over again.

I'll never leave you.

'Except, I'm not just Daniel. Please, listen. It's about Joe,'

He stank. She could smell him through the gap in the door. His hair was matted and dirty, his beard unkempt. There was something strange about his eyes as well, although she couldn't put her finger on what it was at first. They were unsettling her, as if anything could unsettle her more. She tried to push the door shut again, but he pushed back, matching but not exceeding her own force.

'He keeps talking to me, you see. Inside my head. I know how that sounds, I know it seems crazy but...'

Natalie's entire body was flooded with hormones, with fear and anxiety. But there was something else as well, something deeper and more intrinsic. She would never let fear rule her again. She had to end this somehow; she had to know.

'Are you a clairvoyant?' Natalie asked. She didn't believe in clairvoyance. She didn't believe in anything, really. But she wanted to know why *he* believed he was Joe.

'No, no. That's not it,' he said, staring down at his feet and dropping his hand away from the door. Weirdly, she wanted him to look up again, to make eye contact. Through the grime on his face and the beard and the itchy red skin on his cheeks, there was something...his eyes. That was it. They didn't match. One was green; one was blue. They were compelling.

'Then, what is it?' she said, her foot pinned to the bottom of the door in case he shoved it again or lunged forward and tried to get in.

'I don't know,' he said, looking up and smiling. It was a safe smile, boyish, somehow. Innocent. She knew that was stupid, she knew people could manufacture any smile they wanted to fool you into believing them, but she couldn't help thinking: *He's kind. He's a kind man.*

'But Joe's here with me. At least I think...' Daniel shook his head and looked back at the floor.

'I don't know what you want...' Natalie said, letting go of the door with her hand, but being sure to keep her foot in place as she opened it a tiny bit wider.

'I know what this sounds like,' Dan went on.

Could it be him? Natalie found herself wondering. The universe was filled with inexplicable wonders; what if people could transcend death? Dan had been there at the accident, after all. He'd watched the whole thing; he'd been standing in the road next to them as Joe died. What if Joe's consciousness had migrated? Was that so impossible?

'Tell me something *real*,' Natalie said slowly, despite the fact her mind was turning everything over at superhuman speed.

'Anything you want to know,' Daniel said quickly, but his accent sounded different. A moment ago, he'd sounded like he was from Brighton, like he'd been brought up here. Now he had a bit of a cockney twang.

'I'll tell you how we met, how we fell in love,' he continued, sounding more like an *Eastender*'s extra with every syllable.

'Things only I could know,' Natalie said, her voice wavering slightly.

She was terrified. It took every ounce of willpower to stop herself from slamming the door and calling the police. But she had to know. If there was the slightest chance Joe had come back for her, she had to know and put a stop to it.

'We met in a club near the seafront,' he spat out quickly, holding his hands up in the air, as if he wanted her to know he wasn't a threat. 'Do you remember? It had a multi-coloured dance floor.'

Her heart sped up a little. She'd met Joe in the student union bar in Nottingham. Land-locked. Nowhere near the sea. As he continued, muttering about Caterpillar boots and tight black dresses, all fictitious, all imagined, her mind raced. He wasn't Joe, that much was clear. He didn't have her dead husband's consciousness nestling inside him. So, who was he? Why was he here? He'd seen the accident; he'd been there on the street that day. What had he seen? He wasn't here by mistake, was he? There was something...something he needed from her. She stared at him as he held his arms up, palms outward, nonthreatening.

'Look,' he said, flustered. 'I don't know what's going on any more than you do. But you're safe. I want you to know that. I won't hurt you.'

Natalie didn't respond; she just stared at him, this wreck of a man standing in her front garden trying to convince her of the impossible. But she wasn't picking up any malice from him; he seemed gentle. Confused, insane maybe, but still gentle. She believed him when he said he didn't want to hurt her. If Joe had been inside him, she knew it would have been another story entirely.

'And that's not a *don't think of elephants* thing, either,' Daniel said, the innocent smile creeping over his lips again. 'I mean, don't think because I've said, 'I won't hurt you,' that actually I am going to hurt you. It's not a double bluff or anything, it's...

Sorry, I mean...sorry.'

'You've got ten minutes,' Natalie said, bracing herself and taking her foot away from the bottom of the door, letting it swing open. She had to know what he'd seen the day of the accident, once and for all.

CHAPTER 6

Two months later, Natalie is resting on Dan's lap, chatting and listening to him tell beautiful stories about her life with Joe, as she'd done the day she met him. She wishes she could remember everything with such rose-tinted beauty. She's lightly stroking his arm, letting herself feel ordinary for a moment, pretending they're a couple like any other. That's all she wants; all she can dream of: a life with Dan, uncomplicated by Joe's ghost.

'I didn't always want to be an accountant,' she says quietly. 'I wanted to work with great apes when I was a teenager.'

'I love chimpanzees,' Dan says excitedly. 'You wanted to be a primatologist?'

'That's overstating it...' Natalie can feel him harden a little under the pressure from her head on his lap. 'I wanted to work with primates, in conservation or something. Got a load of books from Waterstones. It just seems more fulfilling than number crunching and cash flow management, you know?'

'Yes, yes of course. You should have pursued it, why didn't you?'

'Joe put a stop to it,' Natalie says quietly, pushing herself to her feet and walking over to the open French doors and out into the garden. The night is cool on her cheeks and she's only half listening as Dan begins to talk, flitting between his own voice and Joe's.

'What? Why? Why did you do that?' he starts. She knows they are having their own conversation now and not even addressing her. She tries to shut them out; it's spoiling her moment. She wants to sip her wine and enjoy the garden and night breeze as her boyfriend relaxes on the sofa behind her. It's such an everyday scene, one that's surely playing out in houses all over the country. But then he starts having a conversation with himself and any kind of façade is impossible.

* * *

The day Dan knocked on her door, she ushered him into the living room and made sure to take a position in the living room doorway, where she could run out of the house easily if needed. She tried not to inhale too deeply because of the smell, and watched him closely as he picked a book off her shelves. She had her mobile in her hand, unlocked with 999 already dialled in. All she had to do was press the green button and she'd be onto the emergency services. If he turned aggressive, she'd run out of the house, she'd have him carted away, locked up in a mental institution or worse.

'What do you remember?' she said slowly.

'About what?'

'Anything. Us. Our life. The accident...'

She kept her distance, finger millimetres from the dial button, questioning her sanity for letting him in. What did he want from her?

'How we met, you said you'd tell me how we met. I need to know this is real.'

'How long has it been?' he asked, turning around and looking directly at her again, the mild south-London accent back again. 'Since I died, I mean. It's hard for me to keep track.'

'Nearly two months,' Natalie replied. He was talking like he was Joe. *How long since I died?* Too weird.

'Shit. I thought it'd been a couple of days at most, not... Two months?'

'How we met,' Natalie said again, ignoring him. 'Keep going or I'm calling the police.'

'You didn't notice me, not for ages,' Dan continued. 'I followed you around, trying to catch your eye, looking at you and eventually your friend, what was her name? I can't remember her name. She nudged you., and she nudged you and pointed at me, and you looked up and...' he trailed off, stopping the fast flow of words spilling out of his mouth by snapping his jaw shut.

Natalie didn't move, breathe or speak. The smell was overpowering; it was making her living room smell as well. He was staring at her and those weird, mismatched eyes of his seemed...compassionate somehow. Gradually, she realised her thumb had dropped away from the dial button, as if her subconscious had made the decision for her, like it already knew what she didn't. She rubbed her cheek, surprised to find tears there. Why was she crying? Was it relief? Fear? She couldn't work out her own emotions; the hormones that had flooded her system since he'd arrived were overpowering. She stared at him, unmoving, overcome with a strange sensation. Wouldn't it be nice if his story was the real story, if her first meeting with Joe had been in this club, with her friends around her? Not one where she was covered in vomit and wanking him off in a taxi. She wanted to know how Dan's story ended. She hadn't seen her husband's true colours until after they were married, until it was too late. But this man, this stranger, was standing in her living room telling her such beautiful lies, lies that somehow emitted a truth, that showed her who *he* was and how *he* saw the world.

'Olyvia,' she found herself saying. 'My friend's name was Olyvia.' It wasn't a complete lie, she did have a friend called Olyvia. He nodded, smiling and gripping the book he'd taken from the shelf tightly.

'So we got talking, didn't we? Do you remember? In the club, I mean. And your mate Olyvia was there. Oh, and the other one...'

'Kelly,' she said slowly.

'Yes, yes. And when you went to the loo, I took the chance to get the lowdown on you from them, didn't I?'

'Go on.'

* * *

As Dan talked, telling her of sots and drunken friends making passes at him, of romantic roses and the heart-pounding first moments of love, Natalie listened, entranced and overwhelmed with feeling. Dan's story was intoxicating, and she'd have done anything to rewrite history, for her Joe to have been anything like Dan's Joe. She took a deep breath, still trying to calm her beating heart, but instead taking in a lungful of unwashed clothes and stale urine.

'Why don't you have a shower? I'll make us a cup of tea. There's a razor in the cabinet and a toothbrush...' She stopped, gulping and licking her lips. 'Joe's razor. Joe's toothbrush. You can use them.'

As Dan stepped toward her, arms out, she realised he meant to hug her, kiss her even. The smell was overpowering, turning her already somersaulting stomach. As he started to mumble something about missing her, she recoiled backward, snapping:

'Take a shower, the towels are in the air...'

'In the airing cupboard,' he finished. 'It's okay, I remember.'

Fuck. What are you thinking? She thought as she watched him mount the stairs. *You stupid, stupid bitch.*

She'd get rid of him. She'd let him have a shower, she'd wash his clothes and find out what he knew. She'd give him some food, then send him on his way. He wasn't her responsibility. She wasn't *shelter*.

* * *

Natalie had always had a penchant for fixing and mending. When she was ten, Natalie's mum picked her up from school. They were talking about lipstick and eyeliner, or rather, Natalie was imploring her mum to let her wear it to school even though it was clearly against school policy and her mum didn't even let her wear it at weekends unless she was playing 'makeup' at home.

'I'm ten, Mum. It's so embarrassing. Melissa wears eyeliner and the teachers don't even say anything. And Sally always has lipstick in her school bag.'

'I've told you, Natalie, you're too young for that,' her mother said gently. 'And too pretty. You don't need it.'

It was fine for her mother to say that; she was naturally beautiful, one of those women who didn't need makeup. She had smooth skin and eyes that radiated without the need for enhancement. But Natalie already knew she had too much of her father in her, that she'd never be able to go through life makeup-free like her mum did. Why couldn't her mother see that? Why wouldn't she accept her little girl was growing up and needed to experiment?

As they reached the car, Natalie was about to make another plea, when she saw it, flitting and shaking on its side by the curb.

'Poor little thing,' her mother said, crouching down by the injured squirrel. 'Must have got knocked by a car or something.'

All thought of makeup and how unfair her mother was being went out of the window immediately. The squirrel looked so helpless, so needy. All Natalie could think about was how she was going to save it, how she was going to make it better.

'We have to help it,' she said to her mum, crouching down next to her and reaching out to pick the squirrel up.

'No,' her mother almost shouted in shock, grabbing Natalie's hands and holding them so she couldn't pick the injured animal up.

'But, Mum...' Natalie started.

'Don't touch it. It might be carrying disease,' her mum said.

The squirrel carried on twitching and jerking on the pavement, letting out tiny, mournful squeaks as it did so.

'It's not a rat, Mum. We can't leave it here,' Natalie said sternly, looking her mum in the eye. She knew her mother. She knew she'd never forgive herself if they left it there. They were more alike than Natalie cared to admit. Her mum held her gaze for a moment before sighing heavily.

'All right,' she pointed down at Natalie. 'But don't you touch it. Let me get a blanket from the back of the car. I'll pick it up with that.'

As she walked over to the car and opened the boot, Natalie said, 'What are we going to do with it? Take it home?'

'Don't be silly, Natalie. How can *we* fix it? We'll have to take it to the vet.'

'Do people do that?' Natalie said, eyes fixed on the injured squirrel, tears welling up in her eyes.

'I don't know, but I can't see what else we are going to do,' her mum said, leaning down with the blanket to scoop the squirrel up.

'It's okay, little one,' Natalie whispered comfortingly. 'We're going to fix you up, don't you worry.'

Of course, the vet probably let the squirrel die. Natalie and her mother went rushing in with it, realising it was convulsing a little less than before, squeaking a little more quietly.

'Please, can you help?' Natalie's mother started, placing the blanket and squirrel down on the counter in front of the vet's receptionist. 'We found it by the road. I think it—'

'It's a squirrel,' the receptionist said.

'And it's hurt,' Natalie's mother said. 'Do you think one of your vets would be able to look at it?'

Natalie quietly studied the receptionist's overly made-up face, captivated by her eyeshadow-covered eyes, so lacking in empathy for the injured animal before her. What a strange job for someone who clearly didn't love animals.

'We normally only deal with household pets. I don't think there's anything we'll be able to do.'

'Please,' Natalie implored. 'Please.'

Silence. Large, heavy lids, scraping shut over empty, grey eyes. Scraping shut, scraping open. Scraping shut, scraping open.

'The vet is very busy and I don't think...' she started, before Natalie's mother, understanding the situation clearly, reached over and grabbed her by the hand, obscuring long pink nails with her own delicate, smooth hand.

'Help the squirrel,' her mother said firmly. 'I'll pay.'

'It's not... It's just, we can't prioritise a squirrel over people's pets.'

'Then we're leaving the squirrel,' her mum said assertively. 'You decide whether to save it or not.'

'You can't leave it here,' pink nails said, wide-eyed.

But Natalie's mum has already grabbed her hand and the two of them were walking out, leaving the squirrel convulsing on the side in their old picnic blanket.

'They're going to put it down, aren't they?' Natalie said as they reached the car. Her mother paused, as if weighing up whether to answer honestly or not.

'I doubt it,' she said. 'That would cost them too much money. They'll probably let it die.'

* * *

The day Dan arrived, Natalie stood in the kitchen waiting for him to finish his shower and shave. She'd changed her mind again and was bracing herself to tell him to leave. Now she knew there was no truth in it, that he wasn't somehow Joe returned from the grave, she felt foolish. More than that, she felt reckless. He was clearly mentally unstable. Just because he *seemed* like he wasn't dangerous didn't mean he wasn't. If anyone knew that, she did. She'd never put herself in a position where she wasn't in control again. It didn't make sense, what she was feeling. It wasn't like the fear she'd had with Joe. She felt in control of herself. Of him. But was that an illusion? Was he going to come downstairs and threaten her with a kitchen knife? What did he want from her? Shit, why had she let him in? Had *she* lost her mind? He could have been upstairs sniffing her underwear, for all she knew.

No, she needed him gone, out of her house. Except one thing kept niggling away. He'd been there the day Joe died. He'd been right there on the street next to her after the accident. What had he seen? Had the police even questioned him?

'I hope you don't mind?' Dan said, startling her. She spun around, one hand steadying herself on the kitchen work surface as he walked in, arms spread wide, wearing her dead husband's clothes. She remembered buying Joe that shirt, it had never fit him properly, it had always been a little tight but on Dan, who had a slighter frame, it seemed like it was made for him. She looked at his face, clean-shaven after his shower. Clean and pale. Jesus, he was young, much younger than she'd thought at first, probably only in his late twenties or early thirties. And he was handsome. She hadn't noticed before, apart from the eyes and the smile. He scrubbed up well.

'No, it's fine,' she said, slightly flustered. 'You want to wash your things?'

'Yeah, great,' he said, but didn't move. They stood still for a while, neither one moving or speaking, not awkward as such, but not comfortable.

'Machine is over there,' she said eventually, trying to break the tension, trying to normalise everything, to make it seem a little more ordinary. In some ways, it *was* normal, if only for a few minutes. Dan went back upstairs and got his clothes, then put them in the washing machine in the kitchen. She scrambled in the cupboard under the sink and handed him a gel tablet to put in the washing machine, impressed in spite of herself that he knew how to use one. Joe had never washed his own clothes. He'd never called it 'women's work' as such, but neither had it ever occurred to him that he could do it himself. She suspects even if he had done the laundry, he'd have washed his own clothes, not hers.

Once the machine was on, the sound of water filled the drum, creating background noise for their silence. Natalie watched Dan as he leant back against the kitchen counter. He looked a bit gangly, like a teenager whose limbs had grown overnight and wasn't sure how to use them properly. His cheeks looked a little flushed, not with warmth but with embarrassment.

'I thought you were older,' Natalie said, wanting to make him feel at ease, which was odd. Surely, it should have been the other way around; he should have been trying to make her feel comfortable and safe.

'Because of the beard, I mean,' she said.

She scratched the skin below her neck nervously, worried that she might be blushing. He was good-looking. She hadn't been prepared for that; that hadn't been on her agenda at all.

'I thought you were *a lot* older, actually.'

She walked over to the counter and picked up the freshly boiled kettle, pouring water into plain white mugs, then taking two teabags from a silver jar and popping one in each mug. Silence hung in the air as she stirred and removed the teabags, and poured in the milk.

'How did you end up like this?' she asked, handing him his tea. The face looking back at her was nothing like the homeless man she'd seen on the street the day Joe had died; she could barely even believe it was him.

'Like this?' Dan asked, glancing down at the cup, clearly uncomfortable with the question.

'On the street, I mean.'

She immediately wished she hadn't brought it up. She'd overstepped the mark; it was none of her business. Or maybe she'd been mistaken? *Shit, maybe he isn't homeless,* she thought. Maybe she'd presumed and now she was the rudest woman alive.

'I mean, you are homeless, aren't you? I don't mean to presume, I just…'

'Yes,' Dan smiled compassionately.

'I didn't mean to...'

'You didn't. It's fine.'

Dan took a sip of his tea before heaving slightly and spitting some back into his cup. 'Sorry. Can I have it black?'

It hadn't occurred to her to ask. How weird that she'd made him a cup of tea the way Joe used to like it, despite the fact she knew he wasn't Joe. Dan emptied his cup in the sink and rinsed it, glancing over his shoulder at Natalie and smiling again.

'This is all a bit weird, isn't it?'

'A bit.' Natalie nodded, returning his smile. It wasn't as genuine as his, though. She still felt nervous, but now it was coupled with something else. Butterflies. A hint of excitement.

'Why are you homeless?' she said, pulling a chair out from the small square table in the middle of the room and sitting in it. 'Is it drugs? Is that what happened to you?' she asked. Was it drugs? Was he fixable? She knew from experience that some people couldn't be fixed; they were screwed up, without the possibility of redemption. But if she let Joe take that from her, the belief she could make a difference...well, then, he'd won, hadn't he? He'd got what he always wanted.

'No,' Dan said, pouring his water and swilling his teabag around. 'I'm not on anything, I promise. Not even for my condition.'

'Condition?'

'I'm not dangerous. I promise.'

'I didn't mean...' she started, looking once again into his weird, mismatched eyes and seeing...nothing dark. Just concern. But he could just be good at hiding the darkness. The charm, the smile...they could be his weapon.

'You've every right to be scared,' Dan said. As she held his gaze, studying him, hoping for some inspiration or insight, she realised something. She'd been thinking he needed her somehow, like his note had said. But the feeling she got from him was the opposite. It felt genuine that he didn't want her to feel upset or afraid; she could see it in him, more clearly than anything she'd ever seen before.

'I'm not scared,' she said, and in that moment, she meant it. She felt brave, like her old self again. Strong and in control. She must have seemed convincing because he said, 'No. I can see that.'

Reminding herself what she wanted from him—answers as to what he saw the day of the accident—Natalie fumbled for conversation, trying to find a way back to the subject. She was babbling a bit, she realised, talking about being homeless, asking why the government wasn't doing more...anything to buy her time so she could work out her next steps.

'Something should be done. People...' she said.

'People what?' Dan interrupted, sounding a little irritated. 'Post something righteous on Facebook as they step over the sleeping guy under the railway bridge?'

'People aren't all...' Natalie started, refocusing on him. He was getting angry. Agitated. The safety she'd felt moments ago ebbed away and she realised she had to get him out of her house, somewhere public, somewhere she was more protected.

'Yes, they are...' Dan snapped.

His tone had activated something in her, something deep inside. She'd never let a man speak to her that way again. She'd never be backed into a corner again.

'Fuck you,' she spat, surprising herself. She looked up; he was smiling. More than that, he was grinning, as if he liked her honesty.

'Sorry,' he said quietly, a small smile still on his face. 'It's just... People talk a lot, but they don't *do* anything. It's so rare that people actually *do* anything. So, you get tired of hearing them talk, you know?'

'Yeah.' Natalie felt her cheeks flushing.

'What about me?' Dan shouted, the south-London accent back again. For a few precious moments, she'd almost managed to forget about Dan's alter ego.

'Joe?' she said, her heart lodging in her throat. He might not be her Joe, but that didn't mean he wasn't a problem. Something like hatred rose in her stomach. Did he expect her to fall to her knees, his widow, stricken with wonder that he'd come back to her, returned from the grave.

'Okay, Joe,' Natalie said, gritting her teeth and pushing a chair toward Dan. 'Tell me more.'

'Okay,' he said, moving toward the chair and sitting down opposite her. 'But turn off the main light, will you? Just leave the table lamp on; you know I've always found it too bright in here.'

Joe never gave a shit about the light, she thought.

It was like reality was closing in on her again. She was sitting in her kitchen with a mentally unstable homeless man. She was letting him think he was inhabited by the soul of her dead husband. She knew how wrong that was, but she had to find out what he knew about the accident. No witnesses had come forward and now here he was, on her doorstep. It had to mean something, didn't it?

She walked over and turned the main light off before sitting back down, crossing her legs on her lap, the way she always did when she needed to force a state of calm, when she knew the stress hormones were rising.

She stared at Dan again, searching for the goodness and compassion she'd been drawn to only moments earlier.

'Your eyes are different colours,' she said. 'What causes that? Latent genes?'

He didn't answer, instead staring at her quizzically.

'Yeah, you know, like the hair,' she continued, but she could see his attention was wandering, he was glancing at the open buttons at the top of her blouse, not even pretending that he wasn't looking.

'The hair?' he mumbled.

'Recessive genes, like blue eyes? You need two copies to

activate them. Is it to do with that?'

'What?' he said, lost in her cleavage, his elbows on the table.

'Your eyes,' she said, the feeling of excitement rising again. Somewhere deep inside, she already knew she wasn't going to kick him back out on the street, but she also knew she wasn't going to take any chances. She wasn't going to put herself in danger, not for a second time.

CHAPTER 7

After Joe died, Natalie had a lot of time to think, to be objective. Reality crept back in, slowly at first, like light twinkling through the corners of a dark box. She started to see what he'd taken from her—what she'd allowed him to take. She understands the events that led to her husband's control over her now—and it started long before she met him. She can see the first germ being planted when she was eight years old, getting the bus into town with her parents and brother, Simon. She and Simon both wanted the window seat, so she ended up sitting in the seat in front of her parents and Simon was in the seat in front of her. At the next stop, the bus began to fill up and a middle-aged woman sat next to Simon, which made Natalie smirk at him, teasing him as he shifted uncomfortably next to the stranger. Then, her heart dropped as an old man lowered himself unsteadily into the seat next to her.

'Hello, little one,' he said amiably. 'You're a pretty thing, aren't you?'

Natalie smiled and turned away to look out of the window. As the bus jolted and started moving again, she could hear her parents in the seat behind her, talking about grown-up things she didn't understand, involving mortgage payments and council tax. She could see the back of Simon's head in front of her as he bashfully looked away from the woman next to him. At first, Natalie thought it was an accident that the old man's hand was brushing against her leg. But as it moved into her inner thigh, and as one of his wrinkled fingers pushed itself in between her legs, upward, embedding in the fabric of her knickers and further into her, she yelped slightly—just slightly, not loud enough for her parents or brother to hear. She moved her leg, lifting it up and forcing his hand away. Turning away slightly and staring out the window, her heart was pounding. It was so shocking, she even questioned whether it could have happened at all. Not on a crowded bus. Not with her parents sitting behind her and her brother sitting in front of her. But it had happened. And somehow, it had changed her.

* * *

Natalie decided to take Dan out of the house. She knew she should get rid of him, tell him to go. But she needed to know what he'd seen, what he knew about Joe's death. So instead of kicking him out, she took him to the pub at the end of the road. He was hungry and she needed a drink to take the edge off the waves of panic that kept coursing through her, causing a burning sensation in her chest. She felt better in public. She could run away and call the police if she needed to.

They were silent for most of the walk there, perhaps both wanting to avoid the conversation to come. She wanted to get back to her conversation with Dan about his life on the streets. She wanted to know how he'd come to live like that. But she could also tell he needed to talk about Joe; he needed to continue convincing her of his validity. At the pub, their first round was coffee because Dan said he didn't like to drink.

'Now, talk. You understand this all sounds pretty way out there, don't you?'

'Of course.'

'So?' Natalie shrugged, maintaining eye contact.

'Your first date, then,' Dan said confusingly. Did he want her to tell him about her first date with Joe? About wanking him off in a taxicab?

'Joe?' Dan continued. 'You've got the floor, so to speak. Or the mouth. You know what I mean.'

'Jesus, this is fucked up,' Natalie said, to herself as much as him.

She knew she had to stop this, before it went too far. Not

just for her own safety, but for Dan's. It wasn't fair to let him think this was real. He was sitting there having a conversation with Joe because she'd validated him; she'd made him think it *was* real. How could he begin to get better if he thought Joe was genuinely possessing him?

'You're telling me,' Dan said, the south-London accent he used for Joe back in full twang. Then he cocked his head to one side and sat silently, not speaking.

'You're drifting off again,' Natalie said, a little irritated. 'You realise that, don't you?'

She'd call the police. She couldn't very well call an ambulance; it wasn't like he needed A&E. If she called the police, they'd know what to do with him. She'd given him a shower and clean clothes; she'd done her bit. He wasn't her responsibility. He had nothing to do with her, despite what he might have thought.

'Do we? Sorry,' Joe said.

How easily she could distinguish between the two. When Dan spoke, her heart relaxed and she was overcome with feelings of... Well, she liked him, she supposed. Then Joe's voice came out and she wanted to slap him, to get as far away from him as possible.

'Yeah, you keep doing it. One minute we're chatting, then you kind of... I don't know, zone out,' she said, reaching over and gently touching his hand. Could she help him to sort himself out? Was that even possible for someone with his type of problem?

As they chatted, Natalie relaxed a little. They were in public, in a pub half filled with local people, recognisable faces. She was safe for the moment. It was going to be okay. She shivered slightly, despite not feeling cold. As Dan spoke, she stared at his mouth, his teeth, the tiny razor nick about his top lip. Then he paused, as if something else had occurred to him.

'Did they bury me? What did they do with my body?' He seemed genuinely distressed and Natalie felt a huge pang of guilt.

'Sorry,' he went on. 'I just...'

'No, no. It's fine. We had you cremated,' Natalie said, piling lie upon lie. So many emotions had been flooding her system that she hadn't realised the guilt was there—but there it was. Strong, overpowering. She had to stop. She shouldn't have been doing this to him.

'Okay, good,' Joe said, nodding his head and squeezing his eyes shut. 'I always hated the idea of being buried; it never sat well with me. I kind of wanted to be scattered somewhere beautiful, over the Downs or something.'

Natalie nodded, saying, 'I know you did,' before she could stop herself. It was true in a way. Joe *had* hated the idea of being buried, which is exactly why she'd told his mother it was what he'd wanted. Valerie had ignored her and cremated her son anyway, of course. Valerie always ignored anything Natalie said.

Coffees turned into beer and the conversation flowed. Dan's stories were lovely. Comforting, even. As the hours drifted by, she relaxed into them, wondering what her marriage would have been like if his version of reality had been true.

'Anyway, I remember I was standing and waiting. It was summer, boiling hot and I was worried you weren't going to turn up. We'd met in the club the night before, but even though you'd kissed me—eventually—you'd refused to come home with me, so I wasn't sure you were interested, not really.'

'Wasn't that a good thing?' Natalie said, enthralled by his story, and a little drunk. 'That I wouldn't go home with you the first night?'

He shrugged, a cheeky smile on his face.

'It wasn't a good thing or a bad thing, if I'm honest. It was what you wanted to do. I'd have been happy either way.'

He went silent again, almost in a daze.

'You've drifted off again,' Natalie said, reality invading her bubble again.

'Sorry,' Dan said.

'You make a lovely couple,' a weird woman said as she walked past their table. Despite being inside a pub, she was wearing massive sunglasses, like the ones Jackie Onassis used to wear in the Sixties.

'We're not a couple,' Natalie snapped.

The woman didn't react, she simply smiled and nodded, turning and opening the pub door and bursting into loud song as she walked onto the street.

'I think I've seen her before,' Natalie said quietly. 'I dunno. Coincidence, probably.'

'Fucking Brighton,' Dan laughed. 'Full of lunatics.'

Natalie smiled back and sipped her drink, listening as Dan continued to tell her stories of their made-up life together. Natalie could almost picture it, this life she'd had with him. She could almost taste it. But none of it was real. Her real life with Joe had been quite different.

She stared at Dan's open, smiling face and realised something terrifying. She didn't know why he was there. Joe wasn't inside him, that much was certain. So, how had he known who she was? How had he found her?

It had to be the accident; everything came back to the accident. He'd been there on the street that day; he'd seen Joe die. He must have known something.

'What else do you remember?' she blurted out.

'I'm sorry, what?' Dan said.

'The accident? How did Joe get inside you?'

He sat back in his seat, almost like she'd slapped him.

'I don't remember,' he said. 'One minute I was…then I was…'

'Has it happened to you before?' Natalie prodded. People didn't develop mental illness like this; they all had histories. Maybe this had happened to him before? Were there other voices? Oh, God. Maybe Joe wasn't the only voice he heard, maybe there were others. What if the others wanted to kill her in her sleep? No, no. Dan had found her for a reason. How had he found her? He had that note with her name on it. How had he even known her name?

'No, of course not,' Dan said. 'One minute I was on the street, and the next I heard brakes screeching...then...this.' He flapped his arms up and slapped them down by his side.

'Okay,' Natalie said slowly. She'd have to keep him close, at least for the time being. She needed to know what he knew. '"Okay" what?' Dan said.

'Let's go home. We've got a lot to work out.'

'We can come back?'

'Of course,' she said, as if 'of course' was a reasonable response, as if any of this was reasonable.

* * *

After the incident on the bus as a child, it was like Natalie developed two versions of herself. The confident, happy little girl she'd been, and the insecure, confused little girl on a bus with the pain of an old man's hand pushing between her legs. If it had been an isolated incident, perhaps she'd have been able to file it away and forget about it, but as she reached puberty, she noticed how things changed. How men were with her. The 'accidental' brushing of her behind as she passed them, the friend's dad whose eyes followed her inappropriately.

When she turned fifteen, she went to a house party with Olyvia and a few others from school. She'd fancied a boy from her class, Gavin, for ages, but had never had the guts to say anything. But that night, he was there. As the drink flowed and the weed was passed around, Natalie found herself in the back corner of the kitchen, kissing him. She was so excited she almost wanted to stop so she could find Olyvia and say, 'Gavin kissed me!'

Naïve, young and virginal. She knew other girls who had already had sex, but she didn't want her first time to be in the back bathroom behind the kitchen in a stranger's house. Gavin, on the other hand, had other ideas. As they kissed, he shuffled them back, shutting the bathroom door behind them as they entered, his tongue never leaving her mouth. Then, his hands were all over her, stronger than before, more urgent. In fact, she was struck by the notion that he wasn't in the toilet with her at all, she was nothing more than a receptacle, a thing, something to put his tongue and dick into.

'No, I don't want to,' she managed, pushing him back a little. Everything she had been told suggested this should be enough, that he should listen to her and respect her. But what she'd been told and the reality were two different things. Reality encompassed dirty old men trying to finger little girls on buses and teenage boys not taking no for an answer. Gavin didn't respond, didn't seem to be listening at all. He carried on, octopus arms writhing; his hand moving up her skirt, finger jamming itself inside her. He didn't ask, didn't pause and didn't listen as she said no, as she struggled and pushed him back.

'Gavin, no,' she said again, ashamed that she was crying.

With one hand, he pinned her arm back and carried on exploring with his other hand. With her free hand, she pushed him harder still, finally prising him off her and shoving him back against the opposite wall of the small bathroom.

'What's your problem?' he asked gruffly.

Sobbing, she straightened her skirt and left, rejoining the party to find Olyvia talking to a group of school friends, a bottle of wine in her hand, swigging from it.

'Hey, Nat. You okay?' she said, noticing the tears.

Natalie lied. She wiped her eyes and said that yes, of course she was okay. After all, it wasn't like anything had happened. He hadn't raped her or anything. He'd been drunk and gone a bit too far. But blokes were like that, weren't they? They couldn't control themselves. Besides, she'd probably led him on.

'Give me some of that,' Natalie said, grabbing the wine and

swigging it back.

In the background, she could hear Gavin and his mates laughing. She could hear the word 'frigid' being bandied about like it meant something, like it was the explanation for what had happened.

In school, a week after the party, she told a teacher about what had happened. Somewhere deep inside, she knew that it hadn't been okay, that Gavin had gone beyond 'trying it on', and that if she hadn't been stronger, he'd have carried on further, taking what he wanted, whether she liked it or not. But that feeling was internal. As these thoughts made it further toward the surface, she began to question them. Was she being oversensitive? Maybe she was frigid like he'd said? Maybe that's how guys were and she had to learn to deal with it?

'Had you been drinking?' her teacher said, furrowing her brow. Natalie nodded, feeling the shame rising, the blush coming to her cheeks. It had taken everything she had to talk to the teacher, to actually spit out the words. She was hoping to get some clarification, some advice on whether it had been okay or not, whether she was being silly. Now she had her answer.

'You have to understand how teenage boys are, Natalie. You can't let yourself get into situations like that.'

Deep inside, Natalie knew what her teacher was saying was bullshit. Someone should have been having this conversation with Gavin, not her. Someone should have been telling him that nobody has the right to treat another person's body like it's their plaything, teenager or adult, drunk or sober. But the problem with 'deep inside' was that it was wrapped in layer upon layer of conscious thought, tied up with a bow of reasoning and societal pressure.

The issue was finished off with the words of a teacher who should have helped her but instead dismissed her, making Natalie confirm the things her outer layers were suspecting: she was frigid and oversensitive. The message was clear. She hadn't been wronged. What Gavin did to her had been okay. What the old man had done on the bus had been okay. It was simply 'guys being guys'. She'd have to learn to deal with it. This was the world of women. This was what she had to learn to accept.

* * *

Natalie brought Dan home from the pub and ordered takeaway pizza for dinner. Loosened up by drink, she'd forgotten her fear and was even enjoying his stories.

'Do you remember that time we went to Capri on holiday?' Dan said in his Joe voice, his south-London accent almost perfect.

'Remind me,' she said, cautiously. She wanted to hear it, this invented reality. She loved the idea that she and Joe could have an alternate history, one of love and laughter, nightclubs and roses and holidays in Capri.

'You must remember!' he said, grinning, and for one crazy moment Natalie wanted to grab him and kiss him, this mad, fucked-up, beautiful man before her.

'We'd done Pompeii, but you hated Naples, so we decided to get a ferry to Capri. When we got there, we didn't have anywhere to stay, but we thought "fuck it, let's go for a swim."' He paused, looking up at the ceiling for a moment, as if he was genuinely remembering it, as if it had really happened.

'We found this little cove. There was this old guy there, a hermit. Looked like he lived in one of the caves.'

'I remember,' she said, urging him on, wanting to reach out and touch his skin, just lightly, for the human contact.

'And there were these steps leading down into the sea. We got our costumes on and dove in. The sea was a bit rough, but it was hot…' He drifted off for a moment, lost in the memory. 'But that little fucker,' he continued. Dan was instantly animated. He leant over and grabbed her arm gently. 'As the sun started to set, the hermit ran up and pulled the steps up. He pulled them up and ran off with them, and we realised there wasn't a way back on shore. We were surrounded by sharp rocks and the sea was getting rougher.'

'Oh, God,' Natalie said.

'What a prick.' Dan smiled. 'He could have killed us, couldn't he?'

'So, how did you get out?' Natalie asked earnestly, before the doorbell interrupted the story.

How had they escaped after the hermit left them stranded?

She paid the pizza guy—it was always guys, she noticed. She couldn't remember every seeing a pizza delivery girl. Why didn't girls get pizza delivery jobs? Sitting back down on the sofa, she and Dan ate the pizza straight from the box, something Joe would never have allowed or approved of.

'How did we get out of the sea?' Natalie said eventually. 'After the hermit took the ladder?'

'You remember,' Dan answered, taking a bite of his pepperoni pizza. 'Joe still had the scars on his hips and legs.'

Natalie sensed that this was it, the story was over. He expected her to remember the rest, to know the details. Perhaps she'd never know how she and Joe escaped the dark and stormy Capri water after the hermit stole the ladder. Perhaps it didn't matter. What mattered was that she was laughing and joking. She was enjoying herself with this man, this weird, mentally unstable guy who'd arrived on her doorstep claiming to be possessed by her dead husband.

She hadn't had any male company since Joe died, not unless you classed her work colleagues, which she didn't.

She liked it. It was nice to feel someone looking at her the way Dan did. The conversation drifted in and out, some of it real, some of it his invented history, but all of it easy.

* * *

'And I woke up to find Joe vacuuming the curtains at four in the morning.' She laughed. The pizza was long gone, and now they were simply sitting and chatting. 'Joe never did like mess, everything had to be in order.'

'Is that why the house is so tidy?' Dan asked. 'I mean, seriously, I've never seen anything like it. Literally nothing is out of place.'

'Yeah, I couldn't break Joe's programming.'

'Programming?' Joe said, all cockney geezer. 'Is that how I made you feel?'

Yes, you prick. You did, she thought.

'It wasn't like that. I didn't mean...' Natalie said instead.

'Are you a tidy freak?' Dan asked, smiling and widening his eyes. He had no idea what Joe had been like. Why would he?

'Right, then,' Dan said, grabbing Natalie's hand and standing up. 'Where shall we start?'

'What do you mean?' she said.

'Messing the place up a bit.' Dan grinned, grabbing a cushion from the sofa and throwing it onto the rug.

Natalie's heart was thrashing around in her chest. Despite the fact that he'd died months ago, she'd still been keeping the house how Joe liked it. As Dan flew around the room, mixing books up, throwing cushions around, she stood still, a lone figure in the eye of a hurricane. Then, the anger came, the full flush of hatred at the fact that, despite everything, she still wasn't free of him. In something like a mania, she joined in with Dan, throwing things off the shelves, her anger turning to laughter. It felt good; it felt cathartic. So much so, she couldn't believe she hadn't done it sooner.

Half an hour later, lying on the living room floor, her head touching Dan's as she stared at the ceiling, she realised she felt happy, perhaps the first genuine happiness she'd felt since she'd married Joe. Cushions and books and magazines were strewn all around her and she knew Joe's books wouldn't even make it back onto the shelf; she'd take them to the charity shop in the morning. She was rid of him, once and for all.

'Thanks,' she said quietly, listening to the sound of her own breathing.

'Don't thank me,' he said. 'Thank Dan.'

'Thank you,' she said again, rolling over and propping herself up on her elbows. 'I haven't laughed like that since Joe died, it feels good.'

'This should feel weirder than it does, shouldn't it?' Dan said quietly.

'Yes,' she replied, realising again that she didn't feel scared, even as he leant in, the skin of his lips brushing hers. For the tiniest second, she considered kissing him back, then reality asserted itself and she pulled back, pushing herself to her feet.

'No,' she said firmly. 'Just...no.'

'Shit, I'm sorry. I'm so sorry,' Dan started. 'I didn't mean, I...'

'Look,' she said, walking toward the living room door. 'You can stay, of course you can, but there are some rules. We are not a couple, okay. You're not my husband, Dan.'

Her heart, which had been beating slowly moments earlier, was racing again.

Dan stood silently, staring at her, and she could see his confusion. She'd let him believe her husband was inside him. That was on her. She could have put him straight, told him he was ill, that it wasn't true. But she hadn't. She'd wanted to find out what he knew.

'Look,' she said again. 'You have to let me process this, okay? Don't rush me.'

She had locks on all the doors upstairs. She could lock her bedroom door when she went to sleep. She could even lock his if she wanted, but she wouldn't do that; he wasn't a prisoner.

'We're still processing it ourselves,' Dan said. 'I shouldn't have tried to kiss you, I'm sorry.'

'Which one of you is that?' she snapped, stress hormones

flooding her body. 'Do you see how fucked up this is? How do I even know which one of you I'm speaking to?'

'Can't you tell by the accent? That was Dan,' he replied in his south-London accent. 'He tried to kiss you, not me.' Then, in his own accent, he followed up with, 'Thanks for that.'

'Oh for fuck's sake. See? This isn't going to work.'

'He doesn't have anywhere else, Nat,' he said. 'Please. He'll be back on the street if you kick us out. And part of him won't mind that, part of him is already used to it. He even finds it a bit comforting. But I don't. I'm scared, Nat. I'm really scared.'

'So am I. I don't know you, Dan. You're asking a lot of me.'

'You're my wife. Who else should I be asking?'

I'm not your wife, she thought.

Silence.

The last of the evening light flickered through the living room window as they stood opposite each other, at an impasse.

'You have to get a job, earn some money. I'm not keeping you. Do you understand?' Natalie said finally.

'Yes,' Joe replied.

'That means Dan,' she said. 'Dan will have to get a job, get his life back on track. For you to have a chance, Dan has to sort himself out.'

'Okay,' Joe answered.

'Both of you?' Natalie said, fidgeting with her hands as she studied his face.

'I don't know,' Dan said. 'I don't know if I can...'

'Well?' she tried to sound strong, to maintain a strength that she was no longer feeling. If he didn't agree soon, she'd show him the door, send him back out into the night. So what if he'd seen the accident? It was done and dusted now. Joe was dead. Why did she care so much?

'They're my terms, Dan,' she continued. 'It's no good if only Joe agrees. You're the one in charge. You could switch him off if you wanted to, right?'

'Thanks a lot, Nat,' Dan says in his Joe voice. 'Remind him, why don't you?'

'Well?' Natalie asked again.

'Okay, I'll do my best,' Dan said, nodding.

'No, that's not the deal. I'm not keeping you. I'm not caring for you. Sort yourself out and you can stay. I'm not fixing you. That's not who I am anymore.'

'But I don't know if...' Dan started.

'Yes you do, Dan. Everyone does. Make a decision. Take your life back, or don't. There are no in-betweens.'

'You sound like Yoda,' Dan said, adopting a Yoda accent. 'Do or do not, there is no try.'

'I'm serious,' Natalie said, a smile spontaneously bursting out.

'Okay,' Dan said, faking a serious face, a twinkle in his eye. 'Sorry.'

'You'll do it?' She reached her hand out to touch his arm, feeling like she wanted to lean in and kiss him this time, but stopping herself. It wouldn't have been appropriate.

'Yes, I'll do it. I promise. So, we can stay?'

'You can stay. In the spare room, though. Not with me. I'm not ready for that. I might never be ready for that.'

* * *

Natalie locked her bedroom door securely that first night, and while it took her a little while, she finally drifted off to sleep, only to be woken by the sound of Dan screaming. At first, she sat up in bed, not sure what to do. Perhaps it was a trick. Maybe he was luring her out of her room. But no, he wasn't like that, she could tell he wasn't.

Grabbing her dressing gown, she unlocked her door and made her way along the dark landing to the spare bedroom where he was sleeping.

He jumped as she knocked on the door and walked in without waiting for a response. He was sweating and shivering, whimpering lightly to himself.

'Are you okay?' She rushed over to the bedside and sat down, putting her hand on his naked shoulder. She loved how pale his skin was, loved the way her touch gave him goose pimples.

'Nasty dreams,' he whispered, putting his arms around her and nestling into her chest. She hesitated for a moment before hugging him back, stroking his neck as she did so.

'It was a dream,' Natalie said, still stroking.

Calming him was also calming her; it was as if they were breathing as one in the darkened room.

'It was the accident,' Dan said, releasing her to meet her gaze. 'I was watching Joe die again.'

Her heart stopped, and the synchronicity she'd felt a moment ago was lost.

'What happened?' she snapped.

'I don't remember, not in detail. I was dreaming,' Dan said, shaking his head.

'What did you see?' she wanted to scream. Instead, she sat silently, staring at him for what seemed like minutes.

Eventually, she said, 'I'd better get back to bed. You all right?'

'Yeah,' Dan said, and before she could say another word, he leant forward and kissed her, and this time she didn't pull away, she didn't stop him.

'Goodnight, Natalie,' Dan said. She withdrew, gently touching her lips, eyes down, avoiding his gaze as she walked back out of the bedroom, shutting the door behind her.

PART III: JOE

'What if Dan decides he wants Natalie
all to himself?'

CHAPTER 8

The day he arrived at Natalie's and she told him he could stay, Dan was surprised. But I wasn't. Her love for me had always been overwhelming, she couldn't bear to be parted from me again, even if I was inside somebody else's body.

* * *

After the pub and pizza, after messing up the living room, Dan headed up to the bathroom and used my toothbrush to brush his teeth. Our teeth. My things were still there; Natalie hadn't got rid of anything even though I'd died months earlier. In some ways, it was nice that she wanted to hold onto them, that she couldn't bring herself to get rid of my stuff; but in other ways it made me sad. I wished she'd been able to move on, I hated to think of her sitting in the house, lonely and crying, hugging my old jumpers to her nose, inhaling me as if my scent could somehow bring me back to her.

Maybe now I was back she'd get the closure she needed. I'd only had a couple of pints at the pub, but I felt a bit woozy and a bit full. After not eating for a while on the streets, we'd pigged out on crisps and chips and peanuts in the pub, then on pizza at home. Dan could feel it all sitting in his stomach and I could tell it was troubling him in some weird way, like it was making him edgy. It didn't feel like he needed a piss, but as we got to the bathroom instead of heading toward the sink, he'd headed over to the toilet and crouched down and before I realised what he was about to do his fingers were reaching into his mouth to make himself sick.

What the fuck are you doing?

'I have to,' Dan said desperately, but I wasn't letting his hand move any farther, I was not letting him do it. I was controlling him, stopping his fingers from pushing farther into his throat. I concentrated all my efforts and gradually managed to force his hand back out of his mouth until finally he gave up and grabbed the side of the toilet, head hanging over the bowl.

How long have you been doing that? I started.

'It's none of...'

Everything is my business now, I said. *Do you understand? Everything.*

I pushed our body to its feet and walked over to the sink, staring at his reflection.

Whatever your reasons, you don't need that anymore.

'You don't understand,' he started weakly, staring at his face in the mirror and trying to focus on his breathing, trying to calm himself down. It was as if all the fight had left him, as if his body was limp and he needed me to move it, to keep it upright.

Dr Alabi.

'What? How did you...'

Who was he? What happened to you? Stop shutting me out.

'I don't mean to,' he said, maintaining eye contact with himself in the mirror. I stared at the reflection before me, feeling overwhelmingly disjointed. This wasn't my face. It wasn't my body and he had...behaviours...ones I'd never understand.

'You'll learn to live with it,' Dan said. 'I did.'

I don't want to.

Dan reached his hand up to touch the mirror in front of us.

We've got Natalie now. You've got something to fight for.

That made him smile a full, uncontrollable smile.

'We're going to be all right, aren't we?' he asked.

Yeah, I said, nodding. I wasn't sure whether I was only saying it to make him feel better. For the first time since I arrived in his body, I was scared. There was stuff going on with him I didn't know about and couldn't access. I felt powerless. Alone.

Eventually, we started to brush our teeth, a once-simple operation that now seemed weird at best, horrific at worst. Not because he'd been homeless and without a toothbrush for a while and I'd been…well, dead. Not even because his teeth weren't my teeth—although that was super strange, like I imagined it must have been for people who had a whole new set of porcelain teeth that felt nothing like their old set. It was because he brushed weirdly, a random scrubbing with no method. When I brushed, I started at the top back left and methodically worked my way across the top set, front and back, making sure I hadn't left any gaps. Once I was sure the top set had been thoroughly cleaned, I moved onto the bottom set and did the same thing again. But Dan randomly rubbed the toothbrush around for a bit and rinsed. His mouth—my mouth now—must still have been full of bacteria, feasting on the sugar in his saliva and shitting out enamel-rotting faeces all over his mouth. As he put the toothbrush back in the holder, I felt like screaming and grabbing it, asking him what the fuck he was thinking of.

'What?' he asked, a slight frown on his face.

Nothing, I said.

'It's not nothing. What's your problem?'

He was smiling gently into the mirror before us, like he was teasing me or something.

It's just…can you let me brush our teeth?

He started to chuckle lightly, making a comforting vibration I wasn't expecting.

'If you like, Joe,' he replied aloud, picking up the toothbrush with his left hand and handing it to me in my right. I smiled back at him, turning the tap on to rinse the toothbrush before applying a fresh load of toothpaste.

Cheers.

'You're welcome,' he said. Then, more quietly, 'Thanks for stopping me.'

I nodded my head, glancing at the toilet bowl before starting to brush.

* * *

As we walked back on to the landing, we saw Natalie standing there, still fully dressed and nervously fumbling with the base of her blouse.

'You okay in the spare room?' she said, as if there was another option, which she'd already made clear there wasn't.

'Of course. I'm exhausted,' Dan said. 'It'll be good to sleep in a real bed again; it's been a while.'

Dan leant toward her, and when she didn't shy away, gave her a peck on the cheek. 'Thanks for letting us stay, Natalie.'

She paused, holding his gaze for a moment, unconsciously biting her bottom lip.

'I could hardly kick you back out on the street, could I? But I meant what I said. If you're going to stay, you've got to sort yourself out.'

'I know, for both our sakes,' I said.

'And I'll be locking my bedroom door tonight,' she said, turning around and walking toward her own bedroom—the one we used to share. 'Just in case.'

* * *

Walking into our spare room, I realised I'd never actually slept in it. It was where friends and family stayed when they came to visit. In fact, I'd barely ever gone in there at all, so it felt almost unfamiliar to me. Dan was tired, I could tell, but I wasn't, which was strange as we shared the same body, I should have been feeling the same thing as him, shouldn't I? But maybe he was more directly connected to his body's mechanisms than I was? He was tired, but I was buzzing and excited to be home again, with my wife.

Thank you, Dan.

'Nothing to thank me for,' Dan said, pulling his shirt over his head and taking his jeans off, leaving them on top of the dresser. He sat on the edge of the bed to take his socks off as I thought of Natalie, her face, her hair, her smell. My Natalie.

I can't believe I've found my way back to her.

'Yeah, impressive for a dead man,' Dan said. We both chuckled, walking over and sitting back comfortably in the armchair by the window in the dim light of my spare room, breathing easily.

Both our minds were quiet for a while and we sat, listening to our breath, not moving, not feeling. Dan's mind was wandering, thinking of Natalie, of her open blouse, her soft skin. He'd started to absently rub his cock and balls through his boxer shorts, making himself semi-hard.

You know you're not on your own, right? I said, drawing attention to it.

'Shit, sorry, I...' He jerked his hand away, the embarrassment making our cheeks flush, I could feel the warmth.

No, no it's all right. It's not like you're ever going to be alone again, is it?

We both sat silently, letting that thought sink in for a moment. Neither of us was ever going to be alone again. A few more moments of silence and I gently moved his hand back to where it was before.

It's okay. I could do with one too. You sit back and relax. I'll take care of it.

* * *

Later, lying in bed with the duvet pulled up under our neck and our feet tucked in, Dan said, 'Night, Joe.'

Night, Dan.

I stared at the ceiling and watched glimmering specks of light floating toward me through the crack in the curtains opposite. I think Dan was starting to dream. In his mind, I could see wings where his arms used to be and he was flying over a busy road and then the screaming started, the screeching of brakes, the smell of burning rubber, the impact of a car. Then I saw me, the old me, the real me and there was blood all over my face. I wanted to make Dan feel better, so I tried to smile at him, but it was his dream and he wouldn't let me and besides, my gums were bleeding, staining my teeth with pink-white froth so I was probably scaring the shit out of him. I didn't want that body, my old body, all broken and bruised and bleeding, I wanted Dan's, I needed to get to him, to hide in him, to possess him.

'What am I?' I whispered aloud into the darkness.

Nobody answered.

Dan didn't wake up and I felt scared and alone. I didn't want to go to sleep. If I did, I might never wake up again. Nevertheless, I could feel myself drifting off, as if Dan's bodily functions were catching up with me ten minutes after they'd already sent him to sleep. Darkness engulfed me and I couldn't swim against it, couldn't stop it as it dragged me down and down, further underwater until I couldn't breathe, I couldn't feel, I couldn't see, *oh God,* I thought, *I'm dying all over again...*

The screaming that woke me was my own, or Dan's. Same thing, I suppose. I was sweating and shivering. I jumped as the bedroom door burst open. Natalie was standing in the doorway in a white dressing gown that fluttered against her in the darkness.

'Are you okay?' she asked, rushing over to the bedside and sitting down, putting her hand on my naked shoulder. Her fingers, pale and ethereal in the dim light of the bedroom, gave me gooseflesh down my back and torso.

'Nasty dreams,' I whispered, my hands scrabbling for Natalie to hold her in an embrace. She hesitated for a moment before hugging me back tightly, her fingers finding my hair to stroke as she did so. I tried to concentrate my mind for a moment, to stay on the surface, but I could feel that Dan was present now, too, and it was like I was being buried again, pushed back down to the edge of reality.

'It was just a dream,' Natalie said.

'It was the accident,' Dan said, releasing her from the hug to find her face with his. 'I was watching Joe die again.'

I'm here, I said, terrified for a moment that I was alone again, that he couldn't hear me anymore, that he was losing me, that I was losing myself.

'Yes, you're here. It's okay,' he said internally, almost as if he was soothing himself rather than me. 'You're still here, don't worry.'

'What happened?' Natalie asked intently.

Dan paused, putting his hand to his temple and shaking his head.

'I don't remember, not in detail. I was just dreaming,' he said. His breathing was calmer now, and the dream was escaping him. Natalie sat, holding his hand for a few moments until she was sure he was okay.

'I'd better get back to bed,' she said. 'You all right?'

'Yeah,' Dan said, and before she could say other word, he leant forward and kissed her. This time she didn't pull away, she didn't stop him. He tingled at the feel of her skin, the softness of her lips.

'Goodnight, Natalie,' he said.

She withdrew, gently touching her lips, eyes down, avoiding his gaze. Then, snapping out of it, as if she felt embarrassed, she walked back out of the bedroom, shutting the door behind her.

'Goodnight,' Dan said again, quietly.

He lay back in the darkness, a small smile crossing his face.

But I didn't feel like smiling. I didn't feel like smiling at all. As he closed his eyes to go to sleep again, I had no option but to close mine along with him. But I was terrified of the darkness, terrified he was going to bury me until I no longer existed at all. What if one day he decided he wanted Natalie all to himself and he didn't want me anymore? What would happen to me then?

Chapter 8

* * *

Time drifted on. Dan and I learnt how to give each other space, how to alternate our speech and when to step back and let the other one take the floor. Dan's eating disorder was still present, but I could help him manage it, focusing him and stopping him from making himself sick. It got to the point where we could even have the conversation about it before we ate something.

Can you eat this without running to the loo to throw it up?

'Would you let me even if I wanted to?' Dan would reply, at first accusingly. His shoulders would tense, like they'd been injected with cement, incapable of any kind of flexibility or movement. But over time the tone changed, the reaction softened. And after a while, I could tell without asking that he wasn't even going to try to make himself sick. It was always a decision he had to make, an ever-present demon, but I was helping him control it.

* * *

Days turned into weeks turned into months and life felt...natural. Comfortable, even. Natalie's home had become our home, like it was meant to be. For ages, Dan wouldn't go out alone, wouldn't see the outside world. I tried to convince him to go to the gym or work out, like I used to. I thought if I could get him exercising a little bit more often, it would be good for his physical and mental health. I was starting to go stir-crazy sitting around in his body, not knowing when he was going to let me out. I needed to run, to pump some iron, to feel my body ache a little. I needed to feel my blood rush. How else was I supposed to feel alive?

Alive. Such a small word, weighted with all the significance in the universe, and yet it tripped off people's tongues like it was incidental, a word like many others: 'toast' or 'chips' or 'table' or some other five-letter mundanity. But it means so much more, or it should. *Alive*. It should be synonymous with blood-bursting *life*, but for so many it's nothing of the sort. It's synonymous with existence—just getting through the day. I didn't want that for Dan. I didn't want it for myself or for Natalie. But what's the old phrase? Be careful what you wish for?

* * *

'Dan? What do you remember about...?' Natalie asks, swigging back her wine. I worry about her drinking sometimes. I think she uses it to cope, to manage her emotions. I don't blame her for finding it hard, of course. It *is* hard, for all of us. It's been two months since we arrived on her doorstep and we're still living with her. Two men, one body. It's still difficult to make sense of things and I wish Dan could be more open about his past. I feel if he told us more we'd have a chance at understanding what was going on. But he's a closed book and I know he deliberately hides things.

'I'll tell you anything you want to know,' he often says when he senses me feeling anxious. Except when it comes down to it, he doesn't. When it relates to my accident, he locks down completely.

'What more do you want from me, Joe? I'm looking after you, aren't I? Like I promised. Why else would I be here with Natalie?'

Because you're in love with her, I think but don't say. But of course, Dan hears me anyway. He can hide his thoughts from me, but it seems I can't hide mine from him. One more downside to losing my own body.

Despite his silence, his unwillingness to tell me or Natalie anything of value, he's doing his best. We both are. We're trying to make Natalie happy. She took us in, after all. She believed when most wouldn't.

Earlier today, when we arrived home, Natalie was sitting in

the back garden, staring at the ivy on the wall, humming gently to herself. Dan was desperate to run out and tell her his good news, but I told him to hold off until we'd eaten dinner. Good news. For him at least. I'm not sure what it means for me. As Dan regains more control of his life, I feel mine slipping further away. I'm happy for him; I am. I can never thank him enough for what he's done for me. But that doesn't mean I'm not scared. Of course I am. Who wouldn't be in my position?

Dan cooked for Natalie tonight. Earning more brownie points, I suppose. Wheedling his way into her affections. At first, I thought it was a bit lazy, a bit of a generic thing to cook. It's the new spaghetti Bolognese, isn't it? Green curry. It's the thing blokes these days learn to cook to impress a woman. But, hats off to him, Dan can cook. He made it from scratch, not from a jar. I can't even boil an egg, although I suppose I've never tried. I never needed to; I always had someone to do it for me. People used to look after me a bit too much, I think. That happens to a lot of men. They move from their mothers to their girlfriends to their wives, never realising they're not actually looking after themselves at all, never acknowledging they've never taken responsibility for their own lives. It's a terrible thing, I think, to mindlessly empower another person, making them responsible for your well-being without even realising it. Especially if you kid yourself into thinking you're the one in control, like I did.

No wonder Natalie fell out of love with me. No wonder she's falling in love with Dan: chef, lover, all-round Peter Perfect.

'That's not fair,' Dan says. 'Relax, will you? It's been a good day.'

For you, maybe.

I stare at my wife through Dan's eyes. Her smooth skin, her dark hair tucked behind her ears, the way I've always loved it. The candlelight is flickering over her features, making her seem otherworldly. Dan and I share many things, but our love for her is the strongest. We'd both die for her; sometimes I wonder if one of us will. We can't keep sharing a body like this indefinitely.

This morning, as Dan watched Natalie pull on her tight grey skirt and tuck in her blouse, he felt a contentment he hadn't thought possible. As she started to put on her shoes, he exhaled, deliberately pushing every ounce of breath out of his lungs and holding it, holding it, holding it, until it was painful. When his senses went into panic, he finally gave in and inhaled again, making a decision. He'd get his job back. If not for him, then for her. He had to stop relying on Natalie and take control of his life again.

I don't think that's a good idea, I said.

'What are you talking about? You're always going on about me taking charge of my own destiny.'

I'm not sure you're ready, that's all.

* * *

After seeing Natalie off to work, Dan grabbed his jacket from the banister and headed into town. What did he have to lose by asking?

It's been months. I said nervously. *You job isn't going to be sitting there waiting for you.*

'You're so negative, Joe. You're a positivity vampire.'

I'm just saying...

'You're always just saying.' Dan waved his arm in the road to stop the number 7 bus into town. 'How about a little self-belief?'

Self?

'You know what I mean.'

* * *

Now, eight hours later, Dan is leaning back in his chair and smiling. He's gearing up to tell Natalie his news, a glint in his eye. We're both ignoring her question about the accident, like we always do, but I can see from the look on her face, she isn't done with it yet. She's going to keep asking until Dan or I swat her away.

'And you don't remember anything else, nothing new?' Natalie presses, leaning over and grasping Dan's hand across the dinner table. I refocus on her, feeling guilty again that I've never told her any of it, I've never told her what it felt like that day, never told her the detail. I haven't discussed the confusion with her, how scary it was. But how can I? How would I even begin to describe something so removed from everyday reality? Except, that's exactly what it is, my everyday reality.

'Why do you want to keep going over and over this?' Dan asks Natalie. 'It must be painful for you.'

'And what about you, Joe? What do you remember?'

Me? She almost never addresses me directly. Her tone of voice has changed now she is. It's almost stern, she spits the words out, like she hates me, like she can't stand the idea of me, her husband. Why should I explain what I remember when she treats me like this? I never thought I could feel this way about her but I'm starting to mistrust her. Something is off, I can feel it. She's not acting like my wife, like the woman I remember. I know what's happened is difficult to accept or understand, but she's had two months to process it. Besides, she doesn't have the same problem with Dan. She treats him like the new messiah.

'Joe, stop it,' Dan says internally.

Well it's true.

'No it's not, you know it's not. Just answer her question, will you?'

What question?

'Well?' Natalie says quietly, hands cupping another glass of wine. I stare at her over the dinner table, at the remains of the green curry smeared on the plate before her.

The accident. Always the accident, like there's something she wants me to remember. But I was a little preoccupied, what with being hit by a speeding car and all.

'Nothing new. We've told you before, Nat,' I say aloud, trying not to sound stroppy and leaning over to take her hand. 'Why do you keep asking us?'

'Okay, Joe,' she says, rejecting my hand and sitting back. She does this more and more nowadays. She prefers speaking to Dan. I notice the change in her, the frostiness. I was her husband — I am her husband. But I see the way she looks at him. He sees it too. Maybe that's why he's retreated again, letting me do the talking. Does he feel guilty?

'It's not like that, Joe,' he says.

What is it like, then?

I stare across at Natalie in the candlelight, at her open neckline and barely visible gap between her breasts.

'What's for pudding?' Natalie says breezily, trying to move on and change the subject at last. But we both know she doesn't feel breezy; we both know she's troubled about something.

'Time to tell her our news? Cheer her up?'

Your news.

'I've got a job,' Dan blurts out.

Natalie is speechless for a moment, before a wide grin crosses her lips.

'Seriously?' she says, eventually.

'Yeah,' Dan says excitedly, getting up and walking around the table toward her. He grabs her hand and pulls her up into an embrace. 'I went to see my old firm, where I worked before my gran died, before I... Well. Before.'

He twirls Natalie around and she laughs, clutching his face with her hand and studying it.

'And they said they'd take you back on? Even after you ran out on them?'

'Yeah. Luckily, the person who replaced me is leaving and... Well, I told them I lost it a bit after my gran died, you know. They understood that. Grief does funny things. And it was only a half lie, wasn't it?'

'Not even half of one.'

Natalie grabs him and pulls him close, resting her head on his shoulder and holding him in a way she never holds me anymore.

'You didn't mention Joe, did you?' she says quietly, as if I'm not even in the room, as if I can't hear her.

'Of course not,' he laughs. 'What do you take me for?'

A fucking lunatic, Dan. What do you think she takes you for? What do you think everyone takes you for?

* * *

Later, sitting on the sofa in our living room... Natalie's living room now, I suppose. Everything I own is now hers. That's a weird thought. I don't own anything anymore, not the sofa we are sitting on or the radio that's playing in the background or the house we're sitting in. Not that I begrudge her anything, of course I don't. She's letting Dan stay here, after all. But that doesn't make my situation easier to cope with. I don't have anything anymore, no freedom, no possessions, nothing.

'Are you feeling sorry for yourself again?' Dan says internally as Natalie lies down, legs up and over the arm of the two-seater, resting her head in his lap.

'I'm so proud of you,' she says to Dan.

'Don't be proud of me. Be proud of Joe,' Dan says, trying to appease me. 'He's the one who convinced me I could do it. He's a good influence.'

'You're such a liar. I tried to stop you,' I snap out loud. 'You were calling me a positivity vampire this morning.'

'Don't be like that...' Dan replies, but trails off.

Feeling left out, I start stroking Natalie's hair lightly, thrusting my crotch gently upward as I do so. Like flicking a switch, we both feel she's tensed up, that something is wrong. Shadows are dancing beneath the surface of her skin.

'What's up?' I start.

Within a second, she's recomposed, brushing her dark hair behind her ear and sitting up. But it's too late, Dan and I have noticed something is wrong.

'It's nothing,' she says, leaning away from us on the sofa. 'Don't worry about it.'

'You're worrying me now. Have I done something wrong, have I...' Dan says.

'Dan, stop apologising for everything. You haven't done anything wrong...'

'Me, then? Have I done something?' I start.

'For fuck's sake, no,' she snaps, cutting me off.

It is me, then.

'Maybe it's both of us?' Dan says, trying to make me feel better.

We both know that's not true. Look at how she spoke to me. She can't stand to be near me, Dan. It's you she wants.

* * *

I don't blame Dan. It's not his fault. With each passing day, he is more in control and that's a good thing. Except...I should have thought things through properly. At first, I could only think of myself, of getting back to Natalie, of saving our marriage whatever the cost. And I couldn't do that without Dan. It never even occurred to me they'd fall in love.

'Time for bed,' Dan says. 'I've got work in the morning. How mad is that?'

'Pretty mad,' Natalie says quietly to herself. 'Pretty mad.' She lightly strokes his arm, all traces of her earlier irritation gone. Part of me wonders if she's going to creep into the bedroom again later, like she did last night, even though she swore she'd never sleep with him, that she'd find it too weird. To be fair, she held out for a long time before she slipped under the covers, fingers gently spidering their way down his body. Afterward, Dan lay there, stroking her warm skin and lifting her hand to his mouth to kiss it.

'You didn't run, Natalie. When I arrived on your doorstep. Why not?' He leant up on his elbow, leaning in and kissing her on the lips.

'Because I'm her husband, Dan,' I said out loud before Natalie could answer. 'We made a promise to each other, didn't we, Natalie?'

Natalie recoiled at my voice, like she'd forgotten I was in the room.

'Till death us do part, Joe,' she said quietly, rolling over in bed, exposing her back to me. Dan lay back down and stared at the ceiling, a small smile creeping over his face. I wasn't smiling. What did she mean? What was she trying to tell me? Was that a threat?

'I'm sorry if it wasn't very good,' Dan said, not realising it was me she was angry with, worrying it was something he'd done.

'What do you mean?' Natalie said, rolling back over and nestling her head into his chest, fingers stroking his stomach.

'The sex. I'm not very experienced, that's all,' Dan said. 'I've only slept with one person before.'

'You're shitting me,' Natalie said, sitting upright, her hair dangling over his face slightly, tickling his nose. 'One person? But you're thirty...'

'All right...' Dan squirmed, brushing her hair off him and looking over her shoulder rather than directly at her.

'Sorry, I didn't mean... I just. Wow. One person.'

'Debbie. I lived with her before...'

'It was good...I mean, you know it was good,' Natalie said, but Dan couldn't tell whether she was just trying to make him feel better or if she really meant it.

'When we first got together, me and Debbie I mean, I didn't know anything. She taught me.'

'She did a pretty good job,' Natalie smiled. 'But I don't believe that. You must have known *something*...'

Dan smiled, wriggling and grabbing her lightly, tickling her.

'Well, some things...but nothing much.'

'Did you love her?'

'Debbie?' Dan said quietly, trying and failing to picture her face, her features. 'No,' he said simply, 'I'm not sure I even liked her. Don't get me wrong, I mean...we lived together, I was with her for years. But I was never *with* her, if you know what I mean. We kept moving on to the next stage. We got together at uni, we moved in together, we graduated. One thing followed the next. But she was barely even real for me.'

'Why did you stay with her?'

'I didn't think anyone else would want me, I suppose. Or I was scared to be without her. I mean, look what happened when...'

I'm still here, you know, I said quietly. But Dan was too busy with Natalie to hear me. So, I sat there in the darkness, listening to him chatting intimately with my wife, powerless to stop them from breaking my heart.

'What *did* happen after she finished with you?' Natalie asked. 'You've never told me what happened...how you ended up living on the streets.'

'No,' Dan said, putting his arm around her and letting her snuggle into the nook of his arm and chest. 'I didn't.'

CHAPTER 9

I don't know what he said to convince her to sleep with him, I don't know how he convinced her to creep into his room that night, because he supressed me. *I didn't sleep with my wife, he didn't let me. He took her for himself.* I've started to wonder if he wishes I wasn't here at all—I don't think he's as comfortable with me as he used to be. It's funny how relaxed Dan can feel with some people and how tense with others. Some—like me—bring out his neuroses, his ticks and the mannerisms, the bowed head and chewed fingernails. Others, like Natalie, bring about a wonderful calm. He doesn't feel the need to be something for these people, to paint on an exhausting 'external' version of himself to be deemed acceptable.

'I want to tell you everything,' he said, making eye contact with Natalie. 'My past and my condition.'

'Okay,' Natalie replied, sounding a bit nervous. 'You don't have to, only if you want to.'

'I do want to. I hid everything from Debbie and that was wrong. Well, not wrong, because she was... Well, she wasn't you. But you need to understand how this happened to me, how Joe...'

'It's okay.' Natalie leant over, tactile as ever, touching his wrist lightly.

'Am I babbling again?'

'Little bit.' Natalie held her hand up and pinched her fingers together, a small smile crossing her lips.

'Okay,' Dan said, taking a deep breath and nodding. Finally, he was going to tell us the things he'd been hiding from me. Except, it was getting cloudy for me. Like a dark mist swirling around, pushing me down, into the tar-like waters below. If he'd known what was down there, Dan wouldn't have done it. There was something terrible I couldn't quite describe down there with me. I was scared for both of us. Did it want me or Dan? If he'd known, he'd have dragged me up into the light and held me there for all to see. If I'd had lungs, I'd have been choking, thrashing and struggling, desperately swimming to the surface.

But I didn't have lungs of my own. I didn't have a body of my own. All I could do was fade into unconsciousness and hope at some point I'd wash up on some shadowy, cavernous floor where he could find me again.

Eventually, I came around. Dan and Natalie were lying cuddling on the sofa, spooning and breathing easily. I must have been out for hours because it was dark outside.

Why did you do that? I asked.

'You don't need to know everything, Joe,' Dan replied curtly.

* * *

Like the flick of a switch, everything has changed. Dan and Natalie are a couple. He's got a job and a home. Now I'm nothing more than an inconvenience, something in the way of their happiness. And I have to sit in an office, bored, from nine to six five days a week, going out of my mind.

Natalie is closer to Dan every day, but farther away from me. It's like she can't stand the sound of my voice anymore. And Dan continues to hide things from me, keeping things locked away so I can't access them. He's got no idea how this feels for me, imprisoned in his body, only allowed out when he says it's okay.

Dan does his best to stop me from accessing his memories, but he doesn't always succeed. I get flashes. His grandmother features a lot. His father. Sometimes I see bits of his ex-girlfriend Debbie, but not very often. What happened between them? What happened to her? The only good thing about him getting his job back is that when he's concentrating at work, he has no choice but to hide me. And while I'm down there in the darkness, I've learnt how to delve a little deeper. Does he expect me to sit here, languishing blind for eight hours, doing nothing else? I get it, he can't have me popping out and saying 'hi' to his work colleagues. He can't have me scaring the shit out of everyone. I don't blame him, but he's never once asked me how I feel about it or whether I want to do this shitty job. He's never asked me if I mind.

In retaliation, I've developed a new skill set of my own, one Dan isn't aware of: memory plundering. If he's distracted, I can have a little wander, see what he's trying to hide from me. Some things are clear and easy to access. I remember them as if they were my own memories. But others are murky, like scared insects, scuttling under a rock when I focus my attention on them. His mother, for instance. She's a blank space, a shadow I can't see. But Dan feels her absence, like something gnawing away in his stomach, a constant orbiting vacuum, delivering empty space where substance should be. His dad and grandmother wanted to keep her memory alive for him, of course. They did everything they could, but in the end, they failed. You can't bring a memory back if you don't own it in the first place. She is nothing but a story for Dan, a void. His entire childhood was spent looking through photos of her, stroking her glossy red hair, billowing in the wind, watching her running and laughing on Brighton beachfront or holding his father's hand walking in the Lanes. The photos he found most difficult to look at were the ones where she was pregnant with him, smiling and heaving with the expectation of his arrival, not yet aware he was going to kill her as he entered the world.

How could Dan tell his father he didn't want to see her pictures all the time? How could he explain to him that they reinforced his guilt? Seeing his mother, so happy and full of life, laughing and existing so vibrantly, made Dan's own heart stop beating. Because he was the reason she was no longer there. No matter how much his dad or gran told him it wasn't his fault, that it was a terrible, rare condition, he couldn't believe them. If she hadn't been pregnant, she'd never have had an embolism in her amniotic fluid. It only existed because he existed. It was his foetal cells that entered her bloodstream and caused the allergic reaction that killed her. His own mother had been allergic to him, so what chance did he have with anyone else?

From the youngest age, his father's efforts to keep his mother's memory alive had been destined to fail because Dan never *had* any memories of her. The photos he was relentlessly shown were just stories, no more real to him than the *Famous Five* or the *Mr Men*. They wore no flesh. If he was honest, he didn't want them to, either. He didn't want them anywhere near him.

He never told his father any of this, of course. He didn't want to break his heart. He could see the little smile at the edge of his dad's lips as he talked about his wife, Bridget. And Dan loved the softness in his dad's voice as her name rolled off his tongue. *Bridget.* He could feel the love vibrating out of every pore in his father's body as he flicked through the old photo albums, telling his son story after story after story of how they met, their first holidays, what it had been like when she'd found out she was pregnant. Despite how Dan felt, he grew to love how telling the stories *made his dad feel*. He could see how important it was to his father, and in the end, maybe that was enough. Dan didn't feel the things his father wanted him to about his mother, but perhaps that didn't matter. What mattered was that it gave his dad some happiness.

Dan didn't want for anything as a child. For all intents and purposes, he had two parents, his father and his grandmother. The way his dad told it, he never had a choice about that; Dan's gran moved in with them after Bridget died.

She'd simply said, 'A man can't bring up a child alone; I'm moving in,' and that had been that.

Adult Dan suspects there was more to it, that she was lonely after losing her own husband two years earlier. Whatever the reason, she moved in with them almost immediately.

When he was about eight, he had been playing in the street

on his scooter with Jamie, one of the kids who lived up the road. They'd been racing, both sitting down on the base of the scooter, legs in the air, screaming and laughing, when a car had come around the corner. They'd both swerved out of the way, but Dan had fallen off the scooter, scraping along the pavement and taking the skin off his leg from knee to thigh. He'd run home crying and his gran had quietly washed the wound and applied Savlon to it, gently soothing him by stroking his hair and cuddling him. In those moments, as he sat in her embrace, he understood something the world didn't: his gran was his constant, a mother by another name. All of which made it more horrifying for him when she started forgetting things—not overnight, but gradually over months and years. At first, she became a little more forgetful, a little vague, and Dan and his father hadn't thought much of it. They'd even laughed about it.

'I'd forget my head if it wasn't screwed on, wouldn't I, Dan?' she'd laugh when she'd forgotten what she came in the room for. But as time passed, things progressed. One day, Dan's dad, Bob, was vacuuming and his gran was following him around, from room to room, frowning, looking scared and confused.

'What you doing, Gran?' Dan asked. 'Do you want a cup of tea or something?'

She didn't answer him. Instead, she flinched, staring at him like she wasn't sure who he was before scuttling away.

'Who's that boy, Bob?' she said, grabbing hold of her son's arm. 'Why is he in our house? Your dad won't like it, inviting your friends home without asking.'

Another time, she put a pan filled with water on the stove and forgot about it until it boiled dry and the pan turned black, setting off the smoke alarms. When Dan and his father found her, she was outside in her nightgown, wandering the streets, crying, not sure why she was there. Eventually, Dan's dad did the only thing he could do: he got help. Not that Dan understood at the time.

'Why?' Dan screamed as his father and a male nurse each took one of his grandmother's arms. Dan would never forget the moment she glanced back at him over her shoulder, a terrified darkness in her eyes.

'She's scared!' Dan yelled, running after them, trying to grab the back of his gran's dress, trying to stop them getting her out of the open front door. 'Let go of her!'

'Daniel, enough,' his dad shouted, physically pushing him backward. 'Don't you think this is hard enough?'

'I hate you.'

'Danny. You'll understand when you get a little older, I promise. I'm doing what's best for grandma.'

'What's best for you, more like,' Dan spat.

'You can visit her every week.'

Dan's father reached out to touch his arm, and Dan stepped back, not allowing the contact.

For weeks, it felt like the anger was going to consume him, the grief, the emptiness he felt without her at home was overwhelming, like the double vacuum of mother and grandmother had combined to create a black hole in his stomach, sucking everything into it, with no hope of escape.

After she'd moved in with them, she'd insisted on redecorating her bedroom, despite his father's protestations that it wasn't her house. Her style could kindly have been described as old-fashioned. In the end, her room had ended up coated in flowery wallpaper—burgundy and cream, raised and furry—pink flock carpet, plump in the first year or two after she'd moved in, but over the years becoming thin and threadbare, uncomfortable to look at. Her mustard lampshade sat on the white plastic-coated chipboard bedside table and was always tilted to one side, tassels dangling limply at an angle so they cast dancing shadows on the wall behind her headboard. Nothing in her room had matched anything else. There had been no style, no reason, no plan. There were things she had picked up from car boot sales and charity shops. Fashion and style didn't interest her and she'd never dreamed of being rich, never cared much about anything but her family and their happiness. And now she'd been removed from the very thing she loved most. Dan learnt to love her bedroom and its eccentricities. It felt safe, somehow. It was the essence of her. After she went into the nursing home, Dan spent a lot of time in there, sat on her bed, clutching her knitted blanket to his chest and crying.

Years passed and Dan would find himself questioning everything, wondering if he could have done anything to keep his grandmother with them, to stop his father sending her away. If only he'd looked after her better, kept an eye on her properly. But he'd had school, he couldn't have been with her all the time. Still, somehow, he felt like it was *his* fault, like he was to blame. His mother had died; his grandmother had been taken away. His only constant was his father. Even back then, Dan knew that his dad was doing his best, but the teenage Dan still couldn't help *blaming* him.

The hurt and anger didn't last forever. Gradually, it was replaced by something else, an emptiness, which was comforting at first, then unsettling. Sometimes, he'd find himself contemplating his face in the mirror in the morning, staring at his reflection like it was that of a stranger, like it didn't belong to him at all. He didn't think much of it to begin with, but over time he became increasingly convinced that the reflection he was looking at wasn't his at all. Some days, it felt like he was watching himself from afar, like he'd been separated from his own limbs, breath and emotions. To the outside observer, he went about his daily business like normal. But for him, it was like he wasn't *there* anymore. School, swimming practice, having a kick about with his friends, even visiting his grandma in the home—none of it seemed 'real' anymore, whatever 'real' was. His body was on automatic pilot and he was a bystander, watching his life through a misty, bevelled glass window. It felt like his 'self' and his 'body' had become separate entities. Feelings were something distant, something happening to a body he could see but not touch. Reality had shifted away from him, sidestepped out of the room, leaving him a shadow, still stitched to the real world, pulled along by it, but separate and unable to partake in it. He could only watch, a prisoner of physics, of time, and of cause and effect.

Dan kept how he felt—or didn't feel—to himself for a long, long time. Years passed. He developed coping strategies, things that helped, like rubbing his hands together when he was talking to people. If he created friction between his palms, warmth and movement, he could grab a few moments where he felt anchored, where he felt like himself again, attached and complete. Exercise was grounding. For a good five or ten minutes after a run, he could feel like he lived in his own skin, but it never lasted. Other things made it worse. Alcohol, weed, coffee—any kind of stimulant or depressant—seemed to have an extreme effect on him, as if he might never anchor back in his body again.

This detachment meant he could get lost in a mental loop for hours some days, wondering, 'If I'm not me, who am I?' Some days, he felt the people around him were actors, people playing parts in a *Truman*-style show. Other days, it felt like he was the actor. He knew that was ridiculous, but couldn't help feeling it was true nonetheless. *Nothing was real. There was no reality, only people playing parts.*

It wasn't constant; it went in cycles and some days were better than others. Then, at age seventeen, he discovered something that grounded him and made him feel part of his own body like nothing else, albeit only for a short while. The day that it happened, he hadn't bothered with dinner. His dad was a terrible cook and although he had been trying his best because it was only the two of them, there was only so much chicken in breadcrumbs or spaghetti Bolognese with lumps of carrot that Dan could take. He'd pushed the plate away and gone straight for a bowl of chocolate chip ice cream. After his dad had gone to the sitting room to watch TV, Dan had followed it up with a chocolate bar, a packet of sweets, a packet of crisps, a glass or two of Coke and some Jelly Babies. Then, feeling disgustingly full, he'd gone upstairs to the bathroom and dropped to his knees, put his fingers down his throat and thrown up.

Afterward... Oh God, after. He'd felt relaxed, he'd felt calm, he'd *felt*. Standing, staring at his bloodshot eyes in the bathroom mirror, he'd been himself again, normalised, inside his own body. The reflection staring back had been unequivocally Dan Garrison. As the cycle of binging and vomiting became ingrained into his daily routine, he realised that he could at least snatch some moments of normality if he did it more regularly. But he also began to worry about his health. What if some of the junk he'd eaten sat in his stomach too long? He'd get fat. The quicker he could eat it, the quicker he could get it all back out—but if it lingered, he worried it would start being processed, that his stomach acid would start digesting the sugars and fats and it would start entering his bloodstream. So, he had to be quick to purge it because he didn't want the shit he'd eaten to enter his bloodstream.

He hated the fingers-down-the-throat moment. He hated himself as he walked upstairs to do it. He hated kneeling down in front of the toilet, hated the fact he had to check that his dad couldn't hear him before he started. Sometimes, his fingernails would scratch the back of his throat as he forced them down over and over until the heaving started. Sometimes it was harder than others. Sometimes it came up easily. And when it was done, when he was completely sure he'd got as much out as he possibly could, he'd wash his hands, brush his teeth and gargle. And then the calm would descend. His body would be clamped around him again and he'd be locked back in. Secure. Everything would be okay; he was going to be okay. For a little while, at least.

When he thinks about it now, he is sure that he never would

have told anyone what was going on if his dad hadn't caught him. At first, he'd managed to talk his way out of it, saying he felt ill, and just wanted to be sick to make himself feel better. But his dad wasn't stupid, he started noticing the patterns, when Dan would go upstairs, when he'd lock himself away in his room. Then, one day, Dan came home and his father was sitting on the side of Dan's bed, the wardrobe doors open. He'd found Dan's stash of crisps and biscuits and chocolate and sweets, hidden under a pile of clothes.

'You've got no right,' Dan shouted, but the damage was done. His father knew and he wasn't going to let it go. But how could Dan tell his dad the bulimia was only the tip of the iceberg? How could he explain that it was a symptom of something bigger and even more troubling? As Dan's father grappled with his son's bulimia, Dan played along, trying to find a solution without revealing the full extent of the problem. Eventually, after months of getting nowhere, Dan knew that it was time to confide in his father.

They were both sitting on different sofas in the living room, surrounded by bookshelves filled with Dan's grandmother's books. Dan was on the small two-seater sofa next to the fire; his father was on the three-seater against the wall, watching the television.

'Dad,' he said, eventually.

'Hold on, I want to watch the news,' his dad replied, flapping a hand at him, as if to shoo him away.

'Dad, I'm serious,' Dan said, picking at the skin around his thumbnail—pick, pick, pick—until little spots of blood appeared, gradually growing, bulbous, full of life, scarlet bubbles of reality nestling on top of his skin, taunting him with their realness, a visual anchor to a life he could no longer attach to.

'I think I'm going mad.'

The sounds of the house magnified, creaking wood, wind on windows, water churning somewhere, in the dishwasher or the washing machine.

'Sometimes, when I look in the mirror, it doesn't feel like me staring back. I stare and stare at my face and it doesn't feel like my face at all. It doesn't even look like me.'

Dan paused. His dad wasn't looking at him, but Dan could tell he wasn't listening to the news any more, he was frozen, unsure what to do or say.

'I don't think I exist, Dad.'

His father finally looked away from the television and toward him. On his face was a look of concern, even fear.

'Are you being serious?' he asked quietly.

'Yes,' Dan said. 'That's why I make myself sick. It makes me feel something. Anything, for a little while.'

* * *

A diagnosis hadn't been easy. His GP hadn't had any real ideas, and several referrals and therapists, each with their own approaches and labels and treatments, had proved equally ineffective. Eventually, one month shy of his eighteenth birthday, his father had found the Babalaway Clinic, a small private centre near Portslade. The consultant there, Dr Alabi, smiled a lot, twirled his biros, nodded. He understood. He said that a lot, 'I understand.'

'He shows all the signs of chronic, refractory and obsessional self-observation,' Dr Alabi said, without looking up from his notepad. Dan shifted uncomfortably in his seat, glancing over at his father, who refused to look at him, despite the fact that he could clearly sense Dan staring at him.

'And what does that mean?' his father asked.

Dan turned his gaze away from both his dad and the doctor, choosing instead to stare at the bookshelves at the side of the room, filled with medical textbooks and psychology tomes. No fictional or recreational reading for Dr Alabi, it seemed, only books to make his patients and their families feel confident about his expertise.

'Often, like Daniel, patients have symptoms for many years before consulting a doctor,' Dr Alabi continued, still scribbling notes to himself. Finally, after what seemed like an age, he looked up—but not at Dan.

'Depersonalisation disorder is rare, especially in someone so young, Mr Garrison,' Dr Alabi said, leaning back in his chair, arms spread widely. 'But it's not unheard of. People suffering from the condition often feel they're not real, that they're watching themselves from afar, like in a film.'

'Yes,' Dan's father said, animated and excited to have a name to put to his son's condition. 'Yes, that's what it's like, isn't it Dan?'

He grabbed his son's arm, smiling, as if something good was happening. Dan didn't answer; he just stared at Dr Alabi, wondering why he wouldn't look back at him.

'It's a neurological disorder mainly, and we aren't sure of the trigger. What we do know is that sufferers often develop other psychological disorders, like self-harming or...' Dr Alabi trailed off.

Dan picked at the cracked leather arm of his chair, dark brown leather, with grey weave underneath, like a cotton lattice was holding everything in place.

'There's no *proven* treatment, I'm afraid, Mr Garrison,' Dr Alabi continued, maintaining eye contact with Dan's father. 'But there's some evidence that a combination of Lamotrigine and some kind of serotonin reuptake inhibitor might benefit your son.'

Dr Alabi leant back in his enormous black chair, grinning widely with advert-ready white teeth.

'We'd like to combine this with an experimental new drug that shows some early promise. And maybe some Fluoxetine,' he continued, his voice deep and reassuring, so much so that it seemed impossible to Dan that anyone could disagree with him about anything at all, let alone what experimental medications to prescribe to a mentally ill son.

'And is it safe?' Dan's father asked, barely masking the excitement in his voice. 'Are there any side effects?'

'I think we need to consider psychological approaches alongside pharmaceutical treatments,' Dr Alabi said, as if that answered the question. 'Especially with the additional problem of the bulimia. He'll have to be admitted to the clinic.'

Dan's father nodded, as if he agreed his question had been answered.

'Dr Alabi,' Dan blurted out, shocking both his father and his doctor with his presence. 'The experimental drug. Is it safe?'

'Dan,' Dr Alabi said in his deepest, most reassuring tone. 'I've told you, call me Babatunde.'

Dan sat watching from afar, wondering, not for the first time, why none of the doctors he'd seen had ever entertained the idea that he was simply telling the truth, that he was living outside of his own body, no longer connected to it in the conventional way.

'Rest assured, Mr Garrison,' Dr Alabi said, once more addressing Dan's father. 'We can help your son. But we'll have to admit him for a few weeks, maybe even months.'

'And if *I* don't agree, Dr Alabi?' Dan asked quietly.

'We need your father's consent, Dan,' he replied.

Dan turned to his dad, who reached out and grabbed his hand, squeezing it.

'You aren't eighteen yet.'

His father let go of his hand and leant forward to sign the forms on the doctor's desk.

'We're going to get you well, son.'

'We'll get your medication sorted, Dan,' Dr Alabi said. 'You'll have to have an injection first, to get you started, but it will be oral medication after that.'

'What, *now*? You're admitting me *now*?' Dan said, panic rising.

'I'm here,' his dad said. 'It's all going to be okay, I promise, Dan. They're going to make you better.'

Dan doesn't remember much about his first days in the clinic. At some point during admission, he fought back and strangers restrained him. Dr Alabi's apple breath stung his eyes as a needle penetrated his skin.

'Please,' Dan tried to say, licking his lips, disoriented as blurred images fussed around him.

'Your dad's outside,' Dr Alabi said. 'He'll visit every day.'

'Dad!' Dan wanted to scream, but his throat was too dry.

'The injection I'm giving you now has shown some initial promise,' Dr Alabi's voice was soft and low, a vibrating bass, a reassuring melody.

'Then we'll start you on a course of Lamotrigine,' he continued. 'The combination can sometimes be unpredictable, but we're having some good initial results.'

A calming, deep, soothing voice, so soothing it was like he was reciting a nursery rhyme to a dozing child, not listing the drugs he was pumping into Dan's body to fix him.

Dan felt weird, like was on a treadmill and someone had changed the speed without telling him. For a moment, he couldn't keep up, couldn't find a new stride. He was navigating a tightrope as it snapped beneath him, plunging him into an impenetrable fog.

This wasn't progress; it wasn't going to make him better. How could his father have done this to him? How could he have left him thrashing and screaming and pounding at the walls, head aching, like screws were tightening into his temples? Deep breaths, His body was cold and it didn't feel right. He had to stop it, had to make them stop, to get them off him, to get the needles out of him, anything to make it stop. Visions of doctors and nurses in doorways, white gowns and masks, and everything felt different as they wrestled him back down onto the clinic trolley. Different, yet somehow real. Time had slowed and all he could concentrate on were his hands, which felt heavy, as if they'd been injected with cement—a little tingly, a little cold. Was that a side effect? Would they always feel like that now, or would it pass?

'We're going to have to sedate him,' he heard a voice say, maybe Dr Alabi's, maybe someone else's, it was difficult to tell. 'He's injuring himself.'

'Make him comfortable,' his father replied. 'You're sure this will help?'

Cold, wet lips, like ice. Or maybe the drugs were making him feel like that. Experimental drugs? What did that even mean? If Dr Alabi had given him a name, he'd have felt better about it. He'd told him the name of the other drug, so why wouldn't he name this one? Was it even legal? What were they doing to him? It was a private clinic, not NHS, so maybe it wasn't even regulated. What were they doing to him? He thrashed about again, fighting and hitting out at the blurred figures who were trying to restrain him. Screaming, someone was screaming, maybe him. The blood was pumping through his ears, drowning everything else out. For a second, blackness filled his view, and then he saw a glaring white light and felt tingling through his body and then—darkness. No movement. No convulsing. He saw a silver bubble in the darkness. It felt like he had been propelled along an enormous tunnel inside a shadowy train. On the edge of his vision he saw the haunted glimpses of other passengers, none of them any more aware of what was happening than he was.

'Is it safe?' Dan's father asked again, sounding concerned as his son slipped away into darkness. Dan didn't hear the answer.

* * *

Once Dan woke from sedation, once he calmed down and accepted his fate, things got better. The drugs weren't so bad when he wasn't fighting, and after a few weeks he noticed a difference. He noticed he felt more *normal,* like they'd told him he would feel. It wasn't only the medication, of course. Endless counselling followed, talking about his *feelings*, his mother's death, his grandmother's dementia. Did he feel abandoned? Did he feel this or that or the other? Dan learnt to say what they wanted to hear. It got to the point where he wasn't even sure if what he was saying was true or not. Did he feel the things he professed to or not? It didn't matter; the result was the same. Everyone believed he was progressing. They wanted the pretty lies, so he produced them with ease. He couldn't tell if he was better or worse. All he knew is that he wanted to get out and go home.

It was months before Dan was deemed functional again. He was discharged from the Babalaway Clinic, albeit on a high dose of medication and with regularly scheduled therapy sessions to continually track his progress.

'Perhaps over time we can try to gradually reduce your dosage,' Dr Alabi said. 'But I think you'll need to stay on them for a while yet.'

'How long is a while, Dr Alabi?' Dan asked, picking at his fingernails and not looking his consultant in the eyes.

'Babatunde, Dan,' Dr Alabi said, as if he'd been answering the question. 'Please, you can call always call me Babatunde.'

CHAPTER 10

I've been lost in Dan's memories all day, deep in the recesses of his brain. As I refocus on the world around me, I can see Dan's office, hear one of his colleagues talking to him.

'I need your new details, Dan, or I won't be able to add you to payroll. And did you ever ask your dad about your P45? I posted it there when you did a runner last time.'

'Yeah. Sorry, Steve,' Dan says, smiling back as Steve smirks, proud of his 'did a runner' comment and unaware that Dan had been living rough.

'Monday, I promise.'

'Okay, mate. I haven't put you on the system yet, that's all. Can't pay you if you're not legal.'

'Okay,' Dan replies, slipping his laptop into his bag and rummaging around in one of the front pockets to make sure his door keys are in there. 'Have a good weekend.'

'You too, mate.'

* * *

As we walk from the building, I can tell Dan is irritable, looking for a fight.

'You been rummaging around in my memories again?' he asks internally.

Sorry, I didn't mean to, but it's so boring here. How can you stand it?

'It's helping me, Joe. Can't you see it's helping me?'

Yeah, well, you need it. I know all about Dr Alabi, now. About...

'It's none of your business, Joe,' he says angrily, slinging his laptop bag on his back, then wrestling the other arm in.

How is it not my business? It's not just your body anymore. In case you hadn't noticed, I live in here, too.

'Oh I've noticed, Joe. Trust me, I've noticed.'

We walk silently through North Laine, both feeling the anger and resentment rising in Dan's body chemistry. Stress hormones and cortisol flooding his system, forcing him to concentrate on his breathing to calm down, to balance himself.

I'm sorry, all right? But what do you expect me to do?

Dan is silent, trudging up the hill, head bowed. Everywhere in Brighton and Hove is on a hill, everywhere. You can't walk anywhere without going up or downhill. It's tiring, so very tiring.

'Natalie's cooking us dinner tonight,' Dan says eventually, his way of offering an olive branch.

Yeah, I reply, a little sulkily.

'She wants us to pop into the Co-op and get something for dessert.'

She wants you *to get something for dessert, not us.*

'Come on, don't start that again. Let's not fight.'

* * *

It's a ten-minute walk up the hill to the mini supermarket at the end of our road. We don't speak as we walk, bunched up against the cold. It's no warmer inside the Co-op, and as we stare blankly at the poor array of mousse-type desserts, we hear a silken voice, one that stops our breath.

'It's Daniel, isn't it? Daniel, it *is* you.'

It's a low voice, so low that it vibrates our chest slightly. I don't want to hear it, don't want to remember the things Dan remembers. All at once, I wish I hadn't gone into those memories earlier, because if I hadn't, maybe I wouldn't be so scared. Dan's heart speeds up, faster and faster. Our vision gets slightly blurred and when Dan refocuses, I see a handsome, smiling man, reaching out to shake Dan's hand. He looks friendly; he looks like he did in Dan's memories, like he hasn't even aged.

'Dr Alabi,' Dan mutters under his breath, taking the hand he's been offered into a strong handshake. For a moment, Dr Alabi holds our gaze, then he pulls us toward him and hugs us tightly, which both surprises and disturbs us.

'It's so good to see you looking so well, Daniel.'

Dan's heart is pounding so fast, I think he might be sick.

'Your father is worried sick about you,' Dr Alabi continues.

'I'll call him,' Dan stutters. 'I should have called him ages ago. I know I should have.'

'I heard about your grandmother. I'm so sorry.' Dr Alabi reaches his arm out again and brushes our arm lightly, a reassuring smile on his face.

'Thanks,' Dan says.

'Why don't you give me your address, so I can tell your dad where you are living now?'

A gentle enough request, but Dan knows what's behind it. Dr Alabi suspects that Dan has stopped taking his medication. He knows something isn't right with him; he is trained to notice such things. He wants to fix it, to fix me.

'No, really, I'll call him. Let him know I'm safe.'

'And *are* you safe, Daniel?' he continues, his hand still on our arm, clutching it a little tighter than before.

'Quite safe, Dr Alabi,' Dan says quietly, making eye contact and holding it. For a moment, there is an impasse, no movement, only silence.

'Babatunde,' the doctor says, his broad grin returning as he lets go of our arm. 'I'm always Babatunde to you, Daniel.'

Dan backs away slightly, leaving our basket on the floor and walking backward away from the doctor. Once he is out of the aisle, he's running. Out of the supermarket, down the street. He doesn't stop until we are back at Natalie's house, safely leaning our back against the closed and bolted front door, panting for breath.

'You're home,' Natalie shouts from the kitchen. 'Did you

remember to get pudding?'

Deep breaths, slow it down. It's okay. It's okay, don't let Natalie see you're rattled.

'How did he find me?' Dan says internally.

Coincidence?

'Don't be fucking stupid.'

All right. Does it matter? I mean, is he dangerous?

'I don't know.'

It was just a coincidence. Try not to...

'I don't want to go back in that place, Joe,' he snaps. 'You'd never survive it.'

Now it's my turn to be shocked into silence. He's not worried about himself, he's worried about me.

'They'd cure me of you. It's the first thing they'd do.'

You don't think it was a coincidence? Him being there?

'No such thing as coincidence. Someone called him, maybe someone from work?'

Why would someone at work have your old doctor's number?

'I don't know,' he snaps again. 'Unless...'

Silence. We both process the thought that's popped into his mind.

She wouldn't have. She'd never do that to us, would she?

'Who else, then?'

She wouldn't, I reply without conviction. She's so different from how I remember her. Hiding things. I wonder if I even know her at all.

'Hey?' Natalie has walked into the hallway, drying her hands on a tea towel, frowning quizzically. 'What's up?'

'Hey,' Dan says, pushing himself away from the door and walking over to give her a hug, doing his best to pretend everything is fine. 'Nothing, love. Tough day, that's all.'

'Want to talk about it?' she asks.

'No, no, it's fine. Just work stuff, you know.' Dan manufactures his best fake smile, which, irritatingly, is still more endearing than my most natural one. She holds his gaze for a second, and I can see she's deciding whether to push it or let it go. She obviously decides on the latter, turning on her heel.

'Come and chat with me while I finish dinner.'

You okay? I ask.

'Yeah, yeah, I'm okay,' he replies, following her into the kitchen.

It couldn't have been her, could it? I ask desperately.

'I don't know,' he says unconvincingly.

* * *

After the Babalaway Clinic, life moved on for teenage Dan. He went home to his father, took his medication and visited his therapist. He learnt to cook and took his A Levels. They turned into a degree, which turned into a job. He met a girl and moved in with her.

Okay, so he didn't love Debbie, she wasn't 'the one,' but he wasn't sure he believed in that kind of thing, anyway. He wasn't sure love existed, not really. Emotions were still a slightly alien concept for him. But he was functioning, at least, and no longer making himself sick to feel alive or connected to his own body. He felt *normal*. He didn't know if that equated to the normal that other people felt, but he figured that nobody else knew that either. Everyone was locked inside their own bodies, constrained by their own biology, unable to experience anyone else in any true fashion. He comforted himself with the fact that, at least once, he'd been free. Sometimes, he longed for that again. It was as if the very skin around him was a straightjacket. But he was okay. He was acceptable now. Life was moving on.

He visited his grandmother twice a week, and some days, she made his soul sing. He'd live for the days when she was present, when she remembered who he was. On those days, they chatted and laughed and it seemed impossible that she could be the same woman who, on other days, didn't even remember she had a grandson. Over time, he reduced his medication slightly and his therapist sessions dropped in frequency. Life continued, day by day. Then, just as he turned thirty, his grandmother died in her sleep, and his world—so carefully constructed—came tumbling down all over again.

Over the years, he'd imagined several scenarios for his last moments with her—he'd had more than enough time to contemplate it. He'd pictured her using her last breath to lean in close to him and tell him a secret that explained his mental condition. Perhaps it was hereditary, passed down from his mother. Maybe there was a hidden compartment at the bottom of his grandmother's wardrobe where a small decorative box lay hidden, fastened shut with a tarnished green copper hook. Maybe it was filled with clippings documenting family members, going back into history, all suffering the same affliction. He'd enjoyed these fantasies, where she'd waited until the last possible moment to tell him his condition wasn't something terrible, but the beginnings of something wonderful, something magical that his entire lineage had been blessed with.

'It's nothing to be ashamed of, Dan,' she'd say, squeezing him hard in one final emotional embrace. 'You're special; you just never realised it.'

In reality, there had been no revelations or hidden boxes or declarations of love. There had been no family secrets offering insight into his mental health. Just death, bland and ordinary and gut wrenching.

After her funeral, Dan told his girlfriend Debbie he wanted to stay with his dad for a few days, to make sure he was all right. Despite their differences, his father had lost a parent and Dan knew he needed someone to be there for him. Debbie had asked if she should come with him, but that was exactly how she'd phrased it.

'Should I come with you?'

Dan had known she hadn't meant it by the way she'd hidden her face behind her long hair as she'd asked. If he was honest, he hadn't wanted her there. She'd been part of a new life, a fake life with painted smiles and the overpowering stench of acceptability. She'd had nothing to do with his family, his condition or his past. She'd been part of a lie, a manufactured version of himself, medicated and mundane and presentable. Maybe she'd only existed to help him more effectively hide the *real* version of himself, the one the world found too objectionable to exist. Whatever the truth, he'd known she had no part in his grieving process or his family.

Dan went to his father's house straight from the funeral. He stared at the bookshelves, no longer filled with his grandmother's novels, but instead half full of maps and guidebooks and manuals of bland design. His father was already re-stacking the shelves and there were piles of books on the sofa as he carefully decided which would go where, which would be most prominent and which would be at eye level. Dan wondered why his father had waited until his mother died to remove her books—she hadn't lived at home with them for years. Why hadn't he done it before? As he watched, it occurred to Dan that his father wasn't stacking bookshelves at all. He was removing his mother and replacing her with himself. He was deciding which image to project to others now she was gone. He was moving on, in a sense. Taking the final steps, liberated by the loss he'd already dealt with years ago.

'You okay?' Dan asked eventually, leaning on the doorframe, still wearing his black funeral attire.

'I know it's hard,' his father said, without turning around. 'But you have to stay focused, Dan. Keep on the straight and narrow.'

He was talking faster than normal, a continuous stream, so unlike him. He was normally a man of such few words.

'You've been stable for years and I don't want grandma's

death to set you back. You've got a degree, a good job, a lovely flat and girlfriend. I mean, she's not who I'd have chosen for you, you know that. But you're happy, that's the main thing. You're living a normal life. And when I think back to how things were for you...' He paused, like he was trying not to shudder. 'And Dr Alabi is so pleased with your progress. We don't want any relapses.'

'Dad,' Dan said, his voice low and gentle. 'You've lost your mum. It's okay to be upset.'

'Do you talk to Debbie about things?' his father carried on. 'I know you haven't told her about your condition or your medication. And that's good, she doesn't need to know everything. But what about the bulimia? You're looking skinny again. You're not...'

'No, Dad,' Dan said, wincing slightly, trying to remain calm. He had come home for his father, to support him, not to argue.

'Dr Alabi has been so happy with your progress,' his dad said again, picking up a battered copy of a Rough Guide from the late 1990s. 'So you can't let this set you back, you hear me?'

'Dad...'

Finally, his father turned around, fixing him with worried eyes.

'Don't let grandma's death drag you back down. Please, she wouldn't want that.'

Then Dan decided to do something extraordinary, something he hadn't done for years. He moved toward his father with outstretched arms, and for the first time in their adult lives, he embraced him. His father was stiff at first, uncomfortable with the contact, but he finally let go of the emotions he'd been holding in and his entire body began to shake.

That evening, after his father had stopped sobbing, Dan made himself sick again. He didn't even know why. Things weren't like they had been when he was a teenager, when being sick had made him feel connected. The meds kept him balanced and there was no reason to return to being sick. Except...that it made him feel safe somehow. Being back in his father's house, listening to his father quietly trying not to weep in the living room, he'd needed to feel safe again, in control of something. He'd gone to the cupboard and started with some healthy food, still in denial about what he was doing. A stick of celery, a carrot and some hummus. Then, a slice of bread, a yoghurt, a packet of organic crisps, a whole sticky toffee pudding for four with double cream. Then, he'd gone calmly upstairs to throw it all up. And as he'd stared at his bloodshot eyes in the mirror once again, he'd felt happy, like his best friend had come to stay with him in troubled times, telling him everything would be okay. Things were going to improve. He was going to get through losing his grandmother. He was going to stay on track and thrive.

The next day, he did it again, crouching over the toilet in his father's house. It made no sense to him that the chocolate biscuits and liquorice allsorts wouldn't come up, because he'd eaten those last. They must have been on top, so how could the garlic bread and pasta come out but not the sweets, biscuits and chocolate? He'd have to have another go, even though he'd already washed his hands and gargled. He couldn't leave them in there, he'd only eaten them because he knew he was going to throw them back up. He wouldn't have touched them if he'd thought they were going to be stubborn and stay in there. It was the biscuits, the bloody biscuits. He knew from experience that they created a big, gloopy, cement-like deposit that was hard to shift. The biscuits always struggled to travel back up his throat. He shouldn't have eaten the bloody things.

Then he realised what else he'd thrown up and he began to panic. *His pills.* No matter what he was feeling, he didn't want to go back to being that man; he didn't want to be the teenage boy dislocated from his body again. His dad was right, he'd come such a long way. But the next day, he couldn't stop himself from doing it again, couldn't escape it. It was something to hold onto, something positive to grab hold of and clutch with scratched and bleeding palms. At first, he tried to make sure he took his pills long before he purged, but they had to be taken with food, and it quickly made him too jittery to leave it in there, so he ended up throwing them up again in a panic.

The next day, standing in the supermarket, choosing the sweets and chocolate and crisps and fizzy drinks he was going to buy for lunch, Dan realised something fundamental, something that would change his life forever. The pills weren't helping him; they were hindering him. They were suppressing him. How could he have believed Dr Alabi's lies so readily? Did he have to be the same? Did he have to experience the world the way other people did? The next day, he stood in the bathroom and opened his hand, glancing at his pills. There was no point taking them if he was only going to throw them up again. Besides, detaching from himself wasn't a bad thing. It meant he didn't have to feel the pain of losing his grandmother; it meant he could have some respite. And it wasn't like he was a teenager anymore. He could cope with it now. Staring at the smiling face in the bathroom mirror, he began to chuckle—the low, comforting sounds of freedom. Whatever he was, he would be that. He would not be some chemically induced version of Dan that the world found more acceptable. He'd be himself, whatever that was and wherever that took him.

* * *

Dan knew if he was to travel this path, he needed to be honest. Not with his dad, who'd just try and commit him to a clinic again, but with Debbie. She was his girlfriend, after all. He should be able to tell her everything. If he kept it to himself, things would spiral and he'd be lost. His life with Debbie wasn't complete because he wasn't allowing it to be. He'd been living a lie with her, hiding his medication, hiding his past. It was his fault their relationship was so grey, so lifeless. He'd never let her in; he'd hidden so much from her. In that moment, filling his basket with the food he knew he'd throw up again within the hour, Dan felt an overwhelming clarity. Ever since he'd left the Babalaway Clinic, he'd manufactured a life where he kept everyone at arm's length. He'd felt more protected that way. But it meant he'd shut down, he had no outlets. He took pills to moderate his body chemistry and avoided intimacy in order to limit his social interactions—and he was going to stop doing both of those things. It was the only way he could move forward.

Walking back to his flat, preparing to speak to Debbie, he started to notice things again, things he'd been too dull to see when the pills were still in his system. The extra looks people on the street would give him, the second glances, like there was something *about* him they couldn't quite reconcile. The street lamps shone a little more brightly. People's smiles spread a little wider, as did their scowls. Then, people started to make him feel uneasy, like they knew something he didn't. Then came the old habits, old coping mechanisms. Rubbing his hands together, gently at first, then a little more furiously. Friction, warmth, feeling. *Feeling*. The emotions he'd never trusted started to slip a little further away, taking the hurt and loss with them.

CHAPTER 11

'What are you cooking?' Dan asks Natalie, nonchalantly. He's sitting at the kitchen table, watching Natalie roll pieces of chicken in breadcrumbs, trying to forget his meeting with Dr Alabi in the supermarket.

'Chicken in breadcrumbs,' she says. 'You said you liked it the other day, so I thought I'd cook it for you.'

'I said my dad cooked it for me a lot,' Dan says. 'I never said I *liked* it.'

Natalie doesn't answer, turning her back on us as the doorbell rings. She pauses for a second longer, staring at us before wiping her hands again and walking toward the kitchen door.

'Watch that while I go and see who this is, will you?' she says, nodding her head towards the pan on the stove.

'You're not even cooking it yet,' I reply grumpily. Dan's stress is allowing me an outlet, as always. 'What's to watch?'

She frowns again, looking more worried and scared than she has since the day we arrived on her doorstep.

'It's her. She called Alabi, she must have. She's been on at me to visit my dad for days and now Dr Alabi turns up in the Co-op at the end of the road?'

You might be right.

Dan chews his nails and we watch the second hand of the silver and white clock on the kitchen wall tick by. We listen to the clicks and turns of the front door catch opening as Natalie answers it, fully expecting it to be Alabi again, following us, coming to have us committed.

'Natalie!' a woman's voice says shrilly. 'I've been trying to get hold of you for weeks! Have you been avoiding me?'

'Valerie,' Natalie says, the air escaping her like's she's been winded.

'Who's Valerie?' Dan whispers. Before I can answer, he

finds the answer himself, remembering Natalie mentioning a bereavement group she'd been to after I died, a group her mother-in-law Valerie sent her to.

'Not your *mum*?' Dan hisses, standing up and walking over to the kitchen doorway so he can peek down the hall toward the open front door. As we lean on the kitchen doorframe, the tears start coming and our legs buckle underneath us as we collapse headfirst into the hallway.

I'm used to the darkness, but this time it feels different, like I'm being deliberately supressed again, like when he told Natalie about his past. I can't tell where I am, it's dark and I can feel something soft under my head. A pillow? Am I in bed? My mum was at the door, I wanted to speak to her, to see her. But I can't hold on to my thoughts. Am I unconscious? Is Dan?

In the darkness, I see more of Dan's memories floating past me. If I grab one, I can dive into it, immerse myself, see and feel everything.

After his grandmother's death, Dan left his father's house and went back to Debbie, determined to stay off his medication indefinitely. When he thought of his grandmother in the home, taking pills and staring at walls, no longer herself, living out her final years as nothing more than an automaton, he knew he was making the right decision. He wouldn't live and die like he had been, unfeeling. If he had to be a shadow, outside of normal connection, then that's what he'd be. At least it would be real. He was what he was, abnormal or not. He wasn't hurting anyone. He didn't need fixing.

'We have to be honest with each other if we're going to have a future together,' he said to Debbie, desperately grabbing her by the arms. 'I mean, we're all supposed to think we're overweight, right? Drinking SlimFast and counting the calories in Big Macs as we wash them down with Diet Cokes.'

He thought the bulimia would be an easier place to start than the depersonalisation disorder.

'Like, everyone is supposed to think…'

He paused, aware he wasn't making any sense, aware he was losing her attention.

'I've stopped taking my meds,' he spluttered, not sure what else to say but knowing he needed to say it quickly or he wouldn't get it out at all.

'Your meds?' Debbie replied, terror creeping into her eyes, wriggling her arms free from him. 'What do you mean, meds?'

He told her everything, all the things he'd been keeping from her, his history, being institutionalised. When he finally finished, laying himself bare before her, she stared at him silently, back straight, arms resting on her lap rigidly.

'Why didn't you tell me before?' she asked.

Because I didn't want to see you looking at me like this, he thought, but didn't say.

'Are you still getting help?' she said eventually, and he knew there and then that it was over. Immediately and without question she'd assumed he was dangerous.

'Yes,' he said quietly. 'I've been seeing therapists for years. I'm stable, I'm fine. I just…you know, with my gran dying and stuff, it's a trigger point, you know. I don't want to live my life pumped full of drugs to keep me *normal*, you know?'

'I'll stand by you,' she said, but her eyes flitted toward the open living room door, making sure she was safe and had an exit in case her mad, soon-to-be-ex-boyfriend flipped out and decided she needed to live in a box with no arms and legs. 'But I think you'd better go back to your dad's tonight, okay?'

Dan couldn't go back to his dad's house after Debbie kicked him out, though. He couldn't bear to see the look of disappointment on his father's face. He didn't want to sit on the sofa watching TV with him, infected by the sadness seeping out of his father's body, its gelatinous tendrils making their way toward him, curling around his arms and legs and neck and face until he was suffocating, unable to see anything else.

So, he went to Stu and Karen's house. They were friends from university, now a couple and living together nearby. They were more Debbie's friends than his, but he and Stu got on well, so he was sure they wouldn't kick him out. They'd give him a place to stay while he sorted himself out.

He'd been there a couple of nights before Karen came home from meeting Debbie—who had clearly told her everything. Dan heard hushed arguments in the bedroom as he lay on their sofa, feet sticking out from underneath the green knitted blanket Stu had given him because they didn't have a spare duvet. He knew Karen would ask him to leave in the morning, or she'd get Stu to.

Sleep didn't come easily to him that night. Drifting off, he felt a sudden jolt, and for a moment it was as if he were crouched, doggy-style, with his face pressed into a soft, white feather pillow, and long hair flowing on either side as someone quickly, without warning, pushed himself urgently into his arse. Dan screamed, shocked and horrified, flipping over, kicking the man—Stu—backward across the bedroom.

'What the fuck, Stu?' Danny screamed, but it wasn't his voice, it was Karen's.

Dan was inside her body; it wasn't him lying there, it was Karen.

He woke up on the sofa, screaming, as Stu came running out of his bedroom, naked and cupping himself, looking urgently in Dan's direction.

'What's going on? You okay?' he said, frowning.

'Sorry. Bad dream,' Dan replied, getting his breath back, confused and giddy. Stu nodded, turning around, still cupping himself and walking back into his bedroom, where Karen was hush-shouting in a loud whisper:

'What the fuck are you doing?'

'Didn't you hear him screaming?' Stu said.

'I told you what Debbie said, Stu. We aren't safe,' Karen whispered as the bedroom door closed behind them.

Dan lay awake on the sofa, trying to forget his nightmare, worrying about going cold turkey from his medication and listening to the heart beating in his chest, wondering why it felt like someone else's.

Sure enough, when he woke up the next morning, Stu was standing in front of him nervously.

'Look, Dan. I'd love to let you stay a bit longer, you know I would, but Karen has some friends coming to stay and we need the sofa back...'

'Don't be silly. Of course,' Dan had replied, glancing at the redundant CD rack against the wall of their flat, filled with CDs that would never again leave the shelf because Stu and Karen used Spotify, like everybody else. Dan could understand people who put their vinyl on display, but CDs? It was like a declaration of blandness, like they wanted to scream to the world that they were only planning on existing until they died, nothing more, nothing less.

'Can't you go home to your dad?' Stu had offered, hopefully.

Dan had shaken his head and looked at the floor.

'Do you have anywhere else to go?' he probed, desperate to hear an affirmative, something that would make him feel less guilty, like he'd done his Good Samaritan bit and could now be let off the hook.

'Yeah, don't worry. I'll sort something.' Dan grinned, his eyes dead. 'Everything will be fine.'

Of course, everything had been far from fine. He hadn't ended up on the street that first night. He'd spent a few days in a Travelodge until his money ran out and his credit card stopped working. Even then, he hadn't planned on sleeping rough. Nobody *plans* on sleeping rough.

One evening, as the light faded, he found himself wandering, not sure what to do. That's when the fear set in, a dread and vulnerability like nothing he'd ever felt before. At first, he walked, and walked. The movement helped him to quash the panic; it helped him force it down. If he put one foot in front of the other, marching, head down, bag on his back, he could pretend this wasn't happening, that he had somewhere to go, anywhere to go. As the night drew on, his feet began to hurt. The seafront was too exposed and the drinkers and clubbers seemed scarier than before. It was as if everything and everyone was now a threat. Queen's Park didn't feel safe, nowhere felt secure. Finally, at around 3 a.m., he found himself stumbling into St. Ann's Well Gardens. He remembered playing there as a child and somehow it made him feel safer than anywhere else he'd been. Exhausted by his own anxiety, he curled up by a bush around the back of the park and fell into a deep sleep.

As the days passed, he grew used to being the thing in the corner of people's eyes, the thing they'd do anything not to acknowledge. He learnt where he could sleep, where he couldn't, who to avoid, where to get food, how to keep warm. He tried shelters, but they scared him more than the streets, somehow making him feel more exposed and vulnerable. He started to enjoy his own company, keeping to himself.

Homelessness wasn't his only problem, though. He knew that he wasn't thinking straight, that something was deeply wrong. He'd been warned about stopping his medication without withdrawing properly, but he hadn't expected it to as bad as it was.

The morning I died, Dan was around the corner from the clock tower in Brighton, trying to get through the crowd, but there had been a hen party in front of him, blocking his way. He'd reached out to ease past one of the women, who was wearing ill-fitting leggings and a pink *Grease* top and carrying a massive wobbly dildo in her hand. As he touched the flesh of her arm, he felt a weird sensation, like his disconnection was connecting to her somehow. Blackness engulfed him and he thought he was going to pass out, but then he was upright again, feeling things, feeling everything. Blood pumping, heat between his legs, wind on his face. He staggered a little, like he was pissed, then looked down because he could feel something in his hand, something rubbery and… It was the dildo, he was clutching the hen party woman's dildo, but more than that, his hand wasn't his own, it was white with red painted nails. The other women were shouting and crowding around someone on the street – a man, lying on the ground, twitching, eyes rolling. Not having a fit, not jerking around, just…

Him. It was his own body convulsing on the ground.

'You okay?' a man said. His voice was deep and sturdy, so reassuring that Dan could have listened to him forever. Then, darkness again, a moment of nothing. He felt the ground beneath him, the concrete on his back. He could hear the hen party girls again.

'Are you okay, mate?' the man's voice came again, except nobody was near him, nobody was helping him up, probably because of the smell.

'Yeah, I think I passed out…'

'You collapsed, mate. You sure you're okay?' the man asked again, taking a step backward, away from Dan.

'Yeah, I'm fine,' he replied, leaning on one elbow and glancing at the hen party, searching out the one whose body he'd been in. She showed no signs of alarm that he'd been inside her head, inside her body. Maybe he'd passed out and imagined it. He stared for a moment, thinking that she'd remember, that she'd realise, but she didn't seem to know.

'Come on, girls!' one of the women said looking past him, already bored with the drama. As he pushed himself to his feet, the hen party moved on. It was the first time since he'd stopped taking his medication that he wondered whether it had been the wrong decision.

Jesus, Dan. Why didn't you tell me this had happened to you before? This body-jumping shit?

But Dan is asleep. We passed out earlier, when my mum

arrived at the door. He's dreaming, remembering things from his past as his eyes dart back and forth in his head.

My mum was at the door.

I force our eyes open, bringing the spare room into focus. It's dark. I don't know how late it is or how long we've been sleeping for. Natalie must have carried us up here, but she couldn't have done that all on her own, could she? Surely mum didn't help her? I can't imagine them both carting our body up the stairs, it doesn't seem...

'They didn't carry us,' Dan says. 'I walked.'

You're awake.

'Yeah.'

And mum? Where is she? I have to talk to her.

'Don't be an idiot, of course you can't.' Dan pulls the cover up closer around us, keeping the chill out.

I have to.

'And say what, Joe? You're dead. You can't ever tell her, it wouldn't be fair.'

I fail to see how...

'You fail to see a lot of things,' Dan says quietly.

She'd want to know, so would my dad.

'I'm sorry, Joe. It can't happen. Not now, not ever.'

What is wrong with you? Just because you're too scared to visit your own dad, I've got to stay away from mine?

'That's not fair.'

There you go again. Fair. Who said anything was fair, Dan? What's fair got to do with anything?

We lie in silence for an age, before I realise something is missing. Someone.

Where's Natalie?

'She took Valerie for a coffee to talk.'

How do you know that?

'Just be quiet and rest, will you Joe?' Dan says wearily. He's always keeping things from me, holding things back, hiding things. It's like he doesn't trust me.

* * *

As the evening draws on, Dan and I don't move from our bed, even after we hear Natalie come back from the café. She's alone, she's managed to offload mum and I feel tired, too tired for explanations, for lies and half-truths. I don't matter anymore. Losing my body lost me my rights as well.

'It's not like that, Joe.'

What is it like then?

We slip out from under the covers to undress. We've been lying fully clothed this whole time. Once we've taken everything off, we sit naked and cold on the edge of the bed, no dressing gown, no duvet over us. We stare at the wall, or at least I do. There is a towel on the back of the chair, from John Lewis, last year's January sales, beige. Natalie has a green one with the same design, I remember. Dan strokes his nipples for comfort as I listen to Natalie turning on the television downstairs. Eventually, I pull the duvet over us and curl up into a foetal position, with a terrible sense of foreboding creeping over me.

Don't do this to me, I whisper.

Dan doesn't answer. He's hiding. Retreating into himself, into the darkness of sleep, where reality can't find him. Periodically, I hear Natalie move between the kitchen and living room, getting a glass of sparkling water, grabbing a packet of those cardboard baked crisps she's fond of. At some point, she laughs lightly at the television, as if everything in her life is totally normal. I stare at the closed wooden bedroom door in the dim twilight.

I don't want to say hidden forever, Dan. I want to see my mum.

Deep down, I already know that's never going to happen. Dan and Natalie will never allow it. Somehow, they've been colluding without me, I can feel it.

I don't want to die again, Dan.

He doesn't answer. I sit in silence, listening to our heartbeat, knees pushing into our chin. I want my mum. I want to hug her and hold her. I want to hear her tell me everything is going to be okay like she used to when I was a little boy. As I start to sob, Dan wraps his arms around us, rubbing his hands up and down our arms and whispering, 'It's okay, it'll be okay,' over and over as we rock back and forth. I can't tell if he's trying to comfort me or himself.

* * *

The next morning, after we've showered and dressed, we go downstairs to find Natalie already up and drinking coconut water.

'Hey,' she says softly. 'How you feeling? You were asleep when I got back. I didn't want to wake you.'

I nod, not sure how she expects me to answer.

'You must be starving,' she says, waving her arm over to the chicken in breadcrumbs, still sitting raw on the side. 'I never even cooked.'

'How do you know I was asleep?' I ask quietly.

'Joe, don't,' Dan starts. 'It's not easy for her either you know, don't be...'

'I don't...what do you mean?' she stutters.

'You didn't come and check on me when you got back. I was awake but you didn't come to see how I was. You watched telly.'

I walk over to the kettle and pick it up and shake it, checking whether there's water in it before I click the switch to boil.

'Don't, Joe,' she says. 'I thought you wanted some space. I can't imagine how hard that was for you.'

'Or for you,' Dan says, walking over to her and crouching down next to her seat, putting his hand on her knee. 'Did it go okay?'

I'm still here, you know. She was my mother. And have you

forgotten about Dr Alabi?

'It wasn't Natalie. She wouldn't,' Dan snaps.

'She was upset,' Natalie says, squeezing Dan's hand. 'Of course she was. She thinks I've shacked up with another man so soon after Joe's death. She thinks I've moved on.'

Haven't you? I'd say that's exactly what you've done.

'For fuck's sake, Joe, will you shut up?' Dan shouts. Natalie flinches, scared.

'Oh, shit. Sorry, Natalie. I didn't mean to say that out loud, it's just Joe won't shut up, moaning and...'

Natalie is holding her head in her hands. For want of something else to do, Dan walks back over the kettle and takes a mug out of the cupboard. He's about to get a teabag, when he turns.

'Fuck this. I'm starving. Let's go to the café and get breakfast, shall we?'

Natalie doesn't answer straight away. She stares at Dan, like she's weighing something up in her mind.

'Okay,' she says eventually.

Silently, we put our jackets and shoes on and walk up the road. Dan doesn't know what to say; he's waiting for Natalie to make the first move. I don't know what's going on in her mind anymore. It's like I don't even know her. The claustrophobia I'm starting to feel inside Dan is crippling; I'm a scream trapped in a vacuum chamber. They're keeping me from my mum, my dad. I'm a prisoner and neither of them even seem to notice. Or maybe they do. Maybe they don't care because everything is all about them nowadays. Dan and Natalie, Natalie and Dan. The perfect couple.

* * *

'I know the woman who runs this place,' Natalie says as we push the café door half open, not quite tinkling the bell yet.

'You said,' Dan replies, giving her a tiny smile. Not too wide, not a happy smile, but a pleasant one. Through the door, I see two women chatting at the counter, one behind it serving, the other on the customers' side, leaning on the counter and pushing spilled sugar around and around with one long, painted fingernail.

'And you're seriously considering it?' I hear one woman saying.

'Imogen, I have to at least think about it...' the woman behind the counter replies.

'No, you don't. Look at all the grief he caused you. I can't believe you're even...'

'It's complicated. You don't know the full story.'

'And besides, how are you ever going to meet someone new if you...'

The woman, Imogen, trails off, hearing the bell above the café door tinkle as Natalie pushes it open wider, signifying our presence.

'Natalie, hi,' the woman behind the counter says breathily, glancing at Imogen with a 'shut up now' face and painting on a false grin.

'Imogen, you remember Natalie, don't you? I met her at the bereavement group after Adam...' She trails off, aware she doesn't need to finish the sentence.

Bereavement groups only exist for one reason.

We walk toward the two women and I wish Natalie hadn't brought us here. I feel uncomfortable and disjointed anyway, without having to talk to her friends, people I don't know. They are people from her life *after* me. Her life hadn't been on pause, after all. She hadn't been sitting grey and alone at home sniffing my jumpers, she'd been coping, going to support groups and meeting other widows. She's been *talking* to other people about her feelings.

'Of course I remember Natalie,' Imogen, the posh one, says,

reaching out and not quite hugging Natalie, while air kissing the space near her cheeks.

'I'm Louise,' the woman behind the counter says, making eye contact with me and smiling.

'Hi,' I say, pausing uncomfortably.

'I'm Dan,' Dan says, taking over, extending his hand to shake hers and then nodding towards Imogen.

'Latte?' Louise asks Natalie.

'Yes, please,' Natalie answers. 'And a black Americano?' she asks, glancing toward us. He nods and we head over to one of the tables by the window, far enough away from the women to signify we aren't here to socialise, that we want to talk to each other. They look like they feel the same, like they were also in the middle of a conversation they don't want eavesdroppers to hear. For a while, we don't speak at all. The sun is cascading through the window and warming my cheeks. Natalie is relaxing back in her seat, kicking her trainers off and crossing her legs in her lap, the only way she seems to feel comfortable.

'You have to visit your dad,' she says as Louise brings our coffees over, giving a pursed-lip smile and taking her leave, her café owner instincts recognizing we need privacy.

'Are you serious?' I say, my heart skipping slightly. 'You've stopped me from speaking to my mum and you want him to patch it up with daddy?'

'Joe, please...'

What, you're okay with this?

'I didn't say that.'

Well what are you saying?

'I need to get my P45, anyway.'

Oh, it's that easy, you're just going waltz back in after everything.

'No, it's not that easy, Joe. Nothing is that easy. Doesn't mean we shouldn't do it, though, does it. Life is hard, in case you hadn't noticed. But what good does running away do?'

'Dan?' Natalie says, reaching over and grabbing his hand.

'I'm talking to you, not to Joe. If you're going to move forward, you have to patch things up with your dad.'

Our heart jolts, like it's moved in our chest and is now sitting in the wrong place, unable to beat, unable to pump the blood to the area of our body that needs it most.

I'm nothing to her.

'I don't think I can, Natalie,' Dan says, leaning over to gently brush her arm. 'And it wouldn't be fair on Joe, either. We stopped him talking to his mum. Do know how that felt? He's gutted.'

'He'll be fine, Dan,' Natalie says, moving her arm away. 'It's you I'm worried about.'

'Don't say that...'

'You need to get your own life together. You've got a job and that's great. But it's time you started sorting yourself out. You can't keep running from him. He'll be worried about you.'

I'd forgotten she was like this. Not hard, not even harsh, but pragmatic, unwilling to accept anyone's bullshit.

'What would you know?' I spit.

'I'm talking to Dan,' she says firmly. 'I'm sorry about your mum, Joe, I am. But you know why you can't see her. Deep down, you know.'

The bell above the café door tinkles and a man walks in carrying a rucksack on his back. He seems to know the owner, saying, 'Hey, Louise,' as he walks up the counter.

'Okay?' Natalie says, redirecting Dan's attention back to her.

Silence.

'Dan, you've got to move forward,' she continues. 'You've done the running away thing. Now you've got to stand up and face things.' She's stern, almost angry. 'Nobody else is going to fix you. Not me, and not Joe.'

'I don't need—'

'Yes!'

Now Natalie's almost shouting and we both flinch slightly.

'If we're going to make this work, you can't keep running.

You've got to meet things head on.'

'Make this work?' Dan says quietly.

She doesn't answer, but breathes out, uncrossing her legs and planting them back on the floor before slipping them back into her trainers.

'Yes, maybe. But I've got to know I can trust you. I've got to know you mean it when you say you're going to sort yourself out.'

Dan's heart is beating faster, his mind racing with the possibility.

'Yes, yes, okay. We can make this work. I know we can.'

'And your dad?' she presses, one hand grasping her mug tightly.

'Okay,' Dan says, surprising himself and scaring me.

It's no longer seeing my own parents that's concerning me. It's not even seeing Dan's dad. It's their conversation. I'd thought it would be impossible to ever feel lonely again, now I have a constant companion in Dan, now we've found Natalie again. But listening to them talk, it's like they've both forgotten I'm here. Or they are deliberately trying to push me out. What Dan doesn't seem to realise is that he doesn't need Natalie. He doesn't need his dad. He'll never be alone. I'm here. I'm always here. And Natalie is telling Dan to get his shit together, telling him she likes him, that they can make a go of it, that he needs to visit his father, but neither of them have mentioned me at all. I'm slipping out of reality and neither of them even notice or care.

'I'm sorry, Joe,' Dan says. 'I didn't mean to leave you out. We're in this together, you know we are.'

It doesn't feel like it.

'I know. I'm sorry, okay?'

Do you know what this is like for me? Not being me anymore, not being in control?

'I'm doing my best, Joe.'

I want to see my mum and dad, I say quietly, but he's already talking to Natalie again, telling her about his father's house where he grew up, explaining to her about his mother dying and how important his grandmother was to him. And she's nodding and smiling, giving him reassuring strokes, tucking her hair behind her ear and blushing ever so slightly when he looks directly at her, like her heart is fluttering a little too quickly, like it's flirtation rather than conversation.

I'm her husband, Dan, not you, I say, but Dan isn't listening. I don't have access to his mouth to form the words. I'm floating in darkness, watching them chat in the café as if I'm at the other end of a forever-long periscope. I'm trying to claw my way toward them, but the insides of the periscope are all greasy and slippery, and I can't make any headway at all. I get exhausted quickly, so in the end I settle down into the darkness, watching them through the circle of light beyond, hoping Dan will help me back up when he remembers me, when he stops flirting with my wife.

CHAPTER 12

I wake to find that Dan is already up. He's leaning against the side in the kitchen, watching Natalie eat melon from a three-pronged fork, feeling both content to be with her but nervous of the day ahead. This is happening to me more and more now. I zone in and he's already up and about, doing things without me. Time was, I'd have woken up with him, we'd have been a team, experiencing the world together. But now he's leaving me behind.

'Are we still going today?' Dan is asking breezily, trying not to show how desperate he is for her to find a reason they don't have to.

'Yes. You promised, right?' Natalie says, forking the last of the melon into her mouth. A wide smile crosses her face. It's reassuring, loving, even. 'I'll be with you. It'll be fine. Honestly.'

Dan had never felt like this with Debbie. When I access his memories of her, all I can feel is him constantly trying to convince himself of something, that his feelings, his life, mean something. His life with Natalie is altogether different.

Do you trust her? I ask. None of this adds up but he seems oblivious, blinded by his feelings for her. I'm worried, it feels like something dark is heading our way, something just out of sight.

Dan nods his head in response, but Natalie thinks he's nodding in acquiescence to her.

'Great,' she says, walking toward us and putting her arms around our waist, kissing us on the lips. For a second, she even looks surprised, like she hadn't meant to do it. It had seemed so natural, it caught her off guard.

'This is insane,' I say. I mean it as a rebuke, but neither of them take it that way.

'Yeah, I'll second that,' she says, resting her head on my

shoulder.

'I'll third that,' Dan says quietly and I feel her embrace pause, as if she's questioning herself, questioning everything. Then her head burrows into our chest and we are one again. A trinity, for now at least.

* * *

As we enter his father's street, Dan tenses up and simultaneously the darkness around me lifts. It's hard for me to understand his feelings toward his father or why it's making him so stressed out. It's not like they fell out... Scouring his memories, I can't find any time where his dad mistreated him; he's always tried to do the best for him, but Dan's still terrified of seeing him. Maybe it all stems back to how his father had him committed. Or maybe it was the fact that he put Dan's grandmother into the home—except Dan's an adult now, he should understand it was the best thing for her. Maybe life isn't like that, though. Maybe logic never marries fully with emotion—echoes of injustice have a long emotional shelf life. I still feel angry at Debashish from primary school for hitting me in the face with a cricket bat, even though it was an accident and it was my own fault for standing too close to him as backstop. Or was that Dan? We didn't even play cricket in my primary school, did we? God, it's so hard to separate him from me, sometimes.

As we walk toward his father's home, Dan shoves his hands into his pockets, squeezing an old tissue with his right hand and rubbing it between his fingers, finding some comfort in the texture and the repeated action. He glances at Natalie beside him, her hair blowing slightly in the wind. She smiles and squeezes his arm as they arrive at the front gate.

'You okay?' she asks, pushing the gate open.

'I don't think I can do this,' he says, and takes a step backward.

'Of course you can. If you want to move forward, you

have to.'

* * *

We've done a lot of nervous standing on doorsteps since I entered Dan's body. First Natalie's and now his dad's. If anything, Dan feels more nervous now than last time.

'You'll be fine, Dan,' Natalie says, grabbing his hand and squeezing it tightly. 'I'm right here with you. You're not alone.'

He nods faintly and reaches out to push the doorbell. Time slows to a halt around us, even the breeze freezes mid-gust, like it's snapped its mouth shut and is holding its breath like the rest of us, waiting. Until—

'Danny!' His father, who had only opened the door a crack to begin with, flings it wide open as soon as he sees his son. Slowly, the street starts breathing again, cold and fresh on our skin. He looks thinner than before, a lot thinner. It's not like he was ever fat, but he's become gaunt and a little bit greyer.

'Oh, my God.'

His dad steps forward and grabs us—no, not us, Dan. He holds him tight for longer than Dan ever remembers him doing before and when he finally releases him, he takes him by the shoulders and stares into his eyes, making me feel a little uncomfortable. I try and look away, staring at his shoulder instead of his face.

'Where have you been, Danny?'

Danny. The name his father had used with his little boy when he'd ruffled the blond-ginger hair on his head as they walked to football practice. The name he'd used as they'd cuddled in bed reading *We're Going on a Bear Hunt*. It belongs in the past, to a time before depersonalisation disorders and bulimia and homelessness.

'Don't call me that,' Dan says simply.

'Dan,' Natalie starts, her fingers reaching out to find his hand again, to try and steady him.

'Please, Daniel,' his father says, stepping back slightly and dropping his arms by his sides. 'Let's not fight.'

'I...I need my things, Dad. My P45, some of my clothes. I'm trying to sort myself out, trying to...' He trails off, gulping down the rising panic he's feeling as he shoves his hands back into his pockets, desperately searching for the scratchy kitchen tissue paper he's secreted away in there, fingers searching for its pattern, its rough, not-quite-sandpaper-not-quite-soft texture.

'But where have you been, Daniel?' his father implores. 'You've been gone for months, and I've been *worried*.'

Dan makes eye contact with his father for the first time. His dad looks older than before, like life has been landing him body blows, each one draining a tiny bit more of his life force away, aging him and robbing him of colour. Dan concentrates on his heart, slowing it down a tiny bit. It had never occurred to him that his father would worry. He hadn't even considered it when he'd decided not to go home after Debbie, then Stu and Karen, kicked him out.

'I'm sorry, Dad,' he says. 'I didn't think. I didn't...'

They drift into silence again until, eventually, Natalie holds out her hand.

'I'm Natalie, by the way,' she says, and Dan's father shakes her hand. 'And I'm dying for a wee.'

Dan's dad smiles at that, a broad, charming grin. I can see Dan in him now; the grin is like the one in my reflection.

Your dad seems nice.

'He is nice,' Dan answers. 'He's not the problem. It's me. It's always me.'

* * *

Inside the house, Dan's dad shuts the door behind us and indicates the staircase on the left of the hall to Natalie.

'First on the right.'

'Thanks.'

Natalie slips her trainers off and heads upstairs to the toilet. Dan and I follow his father into the kitchen and lean against the side as he begins the time-honoured British ritual deemed to solve any problem: making tea.

'She seems nice,' Dan's dad says, his back turned to us as he fills the kettle and flips the switch on.

'She is,' Dan says, unconsciously taking mugs out of the cupboard. There's a 'world's greatest dad' mug, the one Dan had bought for Father's Day; his 'Mr Messy' cup, the one he's had since his tenth birthday. He pauses for a moment, surveying the cups in the cupboard, skimming over his gran's thin, dainty china cup with the roses on it. He isn't sure which cup to pick for Natalie and eventually he plumps for a plain white one, a cup that belonged to nobody. The spare. The guest mug with no emotional baggage.

'You kept gran's cup, I see.'

'Of course,' Dan's father replies, staring from the kitchen window into the garden rather than looking at his son.

'Is she your girlfriend?' he continues.

'It's complicated,' Dan replies, dropping a teabag into each of the cups in front of him.

'Everything is complicated with you, Daniel,' his father says.

It's not an accusation, he isn't being spiteful. It's a statement of fact. Dan chuckles slightly, relaxing into his dad's company almost immediately.

'She knows everything, Dad,' Dan says.

His dad puts his hand against the kettle to check if it's getting warm, then turns to look out of the window.

'Everything?' his voice is scratchy, older than before, less sure of itself.

'She knows I'm not right in the head, if that's what you're worried about...'

'Don't speak like that, Danny,' his dad says, turning around, looking him in the eye. 'You've got a condition, that's all.'

'And you never let me forget it, do you?'

'Christ, Danny.'

His dad turns away again, focusing on the overgrown lawn in the back garden, where a wheelbarrow and pair of sheers sit, as if he'd been planning some gardening months ago, then decided against it. The grass is coming up around the wheelbarrow, reclaiming it, trying to bury it as if it had never been there.

'Are you looking for an argument?'

'It's suffocating, Dad. I can't breathe when I'm around you. I did everything you wanted. I went to university. I got a girlfriend. I took my medication.'

'You could have *talked* to me, Daniel. I'm your dad.'

'You didn't want to *talk*, Dad. You wanted to *fix me*!' Dan raises his voice.

'Of course, I wanted to fix you. What did you expect?' Dan's dad doesn't raise his voice in return, instead turning his attention back to the kettle, as if he can make it boil faster by staring at it.

'You've been terrified I'm not *normal* for years. It's there all the time, in every conversation we have. When Dr Alabi wanted to commit me, you jumped at the chance, signing any form you could get your hands on...'

'Babatunde said...'

'For fuck's sake dad, call him Dr Alabi. He's not our friend.'

'He did a lot for us, Daniel. For you. Don't forget that.'

The room descends into silence as Dan's dad pours the boiling water into the cups. Dan stirs and fishes the teabags out before pouring milk into Natalie's and his father's teacups.

'You've lost weight,' he says, handing his father a cup.

'Yeah,' his dad mumbles, looking at the kitchen floor. 'I've been having lots of tests.'

'Shit,' Dan says urgently. 'What for?'

His dad shifts uncomfortably, refusing to look up.

'It's nothing. At first they thought it was stomach cancer,

pumped me full of dye and gave me a scan, but they couldn't find anything wrong.'

'Oh, Dad. I'm...' Dan starts, holding his cup tightly, letting the heat burn his skin slightly, enough to hurt, to make him feel the pain.

'It's okay, Danny,' his dad waves him off. 'It wasn't cancer. But I couldn't eat, see. Couldn't face the thought of food at all. And it got so I couldn't concentrate on anything for very long, couldn't hold any coherent thoughts together.'

'So, what is it?' Dan asks. His heart rate has doubled and sickness has risen in his stomach. 'What's wrong with you?'

'They couldn't work it out at first, the GP thought I had all sorts...'

'Dad, for fuck's sake, what's wrong with you?'

'I'm depressed, Daniel,' his father snaps, slamming his cup down on the side. 'They think I'm depressed. It's affecting my appetite, causing my weight loss. The anxiety and inability to think. All of it.'

'What? It's mental, not physical?'

'Oh, Dan, you know it's not that straightforward. It's both, I guess. But the depression is causing it, that's all. They've given me some pills. I don't know if they'll help me...'

'Pills? That's all they want to prescribe. They never want to fix the problem...'

'How could they fix it, Daniel? My wife is dead. My mother is dead and my mentally ill son went missing. How could they *fix* that?'

Shocked, Dan flicks a glance at Natalie, who arrives in the doorway as Dan's dad shouts. She smiles nervously as he continues, to her, 'I haven't seen him in months. Does he care how worried I've been? Does he care he's made me ill? I've had the police out looking for him!' Then he turns his attention back to Dan. 'You're a *missing person*, Danny.'

Dan is genuinely taken aback. It hadn't occurred to him. He's been so busy dealing with his own emotions he hasn't thought about his dad or what he's been going through. He'd only come because of work—well, that and the fact Natalie had wanted him to.

'What the fuck did you think, Daniel? That I'd forget about you and move on? You're my *son*.'

His father hardly ever swears. Dan leans back against the side, looking to Natalie for support.

'He's been dealing with some things, Mr Garrison,' she says. 'I'm sure he didn't mean to...'

'I *know* my own son,' Dan's father snaps. 'I'm aware how self-absorbed he can be.'

'Jesus, Dad. Come on...'

'I lost my mother, Daniel. Then I lost my son. You disappeared.'

'I didn't think...' Dan says. And it's true, he didn't. He'd barely given his dad a second thought, freezing him in time, stacking his living room bookshelves with his own books instead of his dead mother's. He hasn't once thought about how his absence has affected his dad.

'I'm sorry. I'm an arsehole, I'm...'

'Don't, Daniel,' his father rounds on him angrily, walking toward him, finger in the air, pointing. 'Don't do the self-pity thing. I'm not going to make you feel better, not this time. You *are* an arsehole, is that what you want to hear? You're selfish. You're a prick. All of those things.'

He comes so close that he's pushing up against us and Dan feels scared and upset, like a little boy being told off for doing something naughty, something he shouldn't have done, like the time he'd drawn all four Ninja Turtles on his wallpaper with felt-tip pens.

'But you're my *son*, Daniel,' his father says, tone softening again.

Dan exhales, exhales, exhales and holds it there.

'I'm glad you're safe,' his dad says, grabbing Dan and holding him tightly. 'I'm glad you're home.'

'I'm not home, Dad,' Dan says, taking a deep inward breath. 'I can't come home. But it's not you. I need to sort myself out, okay? I can't rely on you.'

'You can always rely on me...' his dad starts.

'No, no. I didn't mean that. I mean, I have to do this by myself.'

His dad extracts himself from the embrace, smoothing his shirt down awkwardly and nodding sadly.

'Okay. But whatever you do, I'll have to ring the police in a minute, tell them you're not missing. They'll probably want a statement.'

* * *

It was a long afternoon. The police came and Dan answered their questions. He apologised, told them he'd gone off the rails after his gran's death but that he was fine now, getting back on his feet, and that he had somewhere to live.

'You're really not coming home?' his dad said at one point, desperately.

'No, Dad,' Dan said, smiling apologetically at the policeman sitting on the sofa opposite him, pencil and pad poised. 'I'm living with Natalie now, I told you.'

'No, son, you didn't tell me,' his father said.

'Why don't you come in the other room with me, Mr Garrison. Let the police finish up with Dan,' Natalie said, touching Dan's father's arm gently. She's a real toucher, constantly touching people. It's affectionate, and she means well, but she also doesn't understand personal space sometimes. Not everyone likes to be touched. Some people actively dislike it. I can tell Dan's dad is one of those because he shrinks away from her as she brushes his arm hair. Instead of building a bond, creating a closeness, her unsolicited touching has the opposite effect on Bob, it makes him more hesitant to go with her, less sure of her motivations. But she's sensitive, too, she notices him withdraw from the contact and she retracts her hand.

'Come on, I'll make more tea.'

He nods lightly.

'It's Bob,' he mutters. 'Call me Bob.'

He lets her lead him out of the room, seeming a little smaller than before, less like a grown man and a father and more like a child in need of looking after.

The statement takes longer than Dan thinks it should — Really, what was there to tell? He'd been living on the streets, and now he wasn't. What business was it of theirs, anyway? By the time he closes the door on the police officers again, it's late afternoon. Dan stands leaning with his back to the front door, closing his eyes and concentrating on his breathing, trying to regulate it, to get back in control.

That was intense.

'Look, Joe, give me a minute, will you?' Dan says.

Whatever you need.

'Thanks.'

I feel alone. Dan's moving on, I can sense it. He doesn't need me anymore. He's stolen my wife and my life and now I'm an inconvenience, a bump in the road to be smoothed out, like his relationship with his father.

'No, Joe. It's not like that. Just let me deal with my dad, okay?'

Sorry, I just...I'm so powerless in here. You've got no idea how it feels. I'm terrified all the time, scared you're going to forget me or bury me or medicate me away.

Dan doesn't answer. He squeezes his eyes shut, leaning back against the front door and rubbing both hands against the wood behind him, over and over. The grain feels good against his palms. It feels textured, real, rooted in the world of everyday. He doesn't know how long he stands there, but by the time he walks into the back room to find his father and Natalie, his heart is beating slowly again, rhythmically.

'They're gone,' Dan says, walking in to find his dad laughing, an open photo album on the dining table. He's showing Natalie pictures of Dan's mother, Bridget. Natalie looks up, with an almost guilty expression on her face.

'Your dad was showing me some pictures of your mum. She's beautiful.'

'And some of you as a baby. Couldn't help myself,' his dad says, smiling his 'memory lane' smile, the one he can only manage when he remembers his late wife.

* * *

'Why didn't you ever remarry?' Dan had asked his father once. His father had been crouched in the back garden, pulling weeds out from in between the paving slabs where they were beginning to push through, threatening the balance and status quo.

'What made you ask that?' he'd asked, standing up and wiping muddy gardening-gloved fingers on his trousers. Dan was awkwardly shifting his weight from one foot to the other, kicking at the edges of paving slabs, already wishing he hadn't asked.

'She died years ago, but you've never dated anyone.' Dan had paused, his mouth drying slightly. 'I just... Was it me?'

'You?' his dad had frowned, like he was genuinely confused.

'Being a single dad, I mean. Was it my fault nobody wanted you?'

His dad had laughed at that, a deep, healthy laugh.

'Cheeky sod. I'm a catch, I'll have you know. The ladies love a widower.' He'd winked, then turned around and started rummaging around in his wheelbarrow, looking for some gardening tool or other that he'd thrown in there earlier.

'So, why are you still alone?' Dan had asked, not sure if he believed him.

'I loved your mother, Danny. Love like that doesn't come

around twice. I was lucky to have it at all. I don't want anyone else, never have done, never will.'

And with that, he'd picked up a trowel and moved over to the flower beds. Dan had stood and watched him, leaning against the wall and wondering if he'd ever meet anyone who made him feel the way his mother had made his father feel.

* * *

'You were a weird-looking baby,' Natalie says, smiling. Dan blinks, refocusing on the scene before him, his father and girlfr— Natalie. His father and Natalie, looking at old family photos, something he had never done with Debbie. He'd barely even liked Debbie, let alone loved her. How weird that he'd assumed what he felt for her was okay, that it was *enough*. It was a hollow, ghostly feeling. Being with her was like loneliness, but her terrible trick had been that she'd made him feel he needed her. But now that he has Natalie, he can see their entire relationship clearly. With Debbie, there was no relationship at all. It was two people play acting, each one trying to make the other person into something they weren't, telling one another they were something they never could be. That's why she'd run for the hills as soon as she'd learnt of his condition. Why would she stay with him when he'd so effectively shattered the illusion she'd created of him? That wasn't real love. That wasn't true.

But Natalie? She was taking it all on: the madness, the possession, everything. She didn't want him to be anything. She wanted him to sort himself out, to be the best version of himself he could be. And standing, staring at her chatting to his father he is filled with overwhelming love. He wants to get better for her. He wants his life back, his real life, not the chemically induced one he had before, not the homeless life of a man who couldn't cope, but this life, the one he's starting to build with her.

'Yeah, he was an ugly thing, wasn't he?' his dad says to

Natalie, grinning. 'But look how cute he got...' He pauses, flicking through the album, jabbing his finger toward a picture. 'There, look at him at four. Cutest little boy that ever lived.'

'Oh, my God. You were adorable,' Natalie says, smiling broadly and beckoning Dan over to see the picture. He moves toward them, heartbeat calming, smiling inside and out. He pulls a chair up beside Natalie and looks at the photo of himself as a boy in the family album. She grins at him and puts her hand gently on his thigh as his father says:

'Oh, you wait until you see him on his fifth birthday. Do you remember, Danny? You found the poster paints before me and gran woke up. You were covered head to foot in blue paint, and so was the carpet...'

'Oh, God, yeah. I remember. You were livid. I thought that vein in your forehead was going to burst. Even grandma lost her temper and shouted at me...'

'That's because you'd painted her jewellery box and engagement ring with royal blue poster paint.'

'You didn't!' Natalie exclaims, laughing lightly.

As they sit and giggle and chat, I float here in the darkness. Voiceless. He's pushing me further and further down, marginalising me in a way he promised he'd never do.

It's gone five when we finally leave. Dan promises he'll call his father every day, to let him know he's okay.

'Yeah, well. I know you, son,' Bob says, turning to Natalie. 'Make sure he calls me, will you?'

'Will do,' Natalie says, giving him a warm hug.

'Thanks for bringing him back to me.'

'I didn't bring him, Mr Garrison. He wanted to come.'

He smiles at that, hugging Dan and whispering in his ear, 'She's a keeper, that one.'

As we walk away, Dan and Natalie absently grasp one another's hands. It's relaxed and easy for them, so much so that I don't think either even planned to do it. Maybe they're not even conscious they are holding hands. They're clasped together, their sweat mingling, one unit, unifying more and more with every step. They're so content in each other's company that it doesn't make sense, not given the circumstances, not given the fact he's hosting me. How could she have fallen out of love with me so quickly? I've only been dead a few months. How can she move on like this, like it's nothing? Like we were nothing?

'I managed to keep Joe in check,' Dan says, leaning in to kiss her on the cheek as we walk out of his father's road.

'Fuck you,' I say out loud. Time was, Dan would have cared what I was thinking or feeling, but nowadays he pays so little attention to me, I don't think he's bothered at all.

'Oh, lighten up, Joe.'

Fuck you, I repeat internally.

'Don't you miss me at all, Nat?' I blurt out.

'Joe,' she says, but she doesn't sound pleased to hear me, doesn't sound like she's happy I'm here at all. I bet she wishes I'd disappear and leave her and Dan together to laugh and fuck and...

'Enough, Joe,' Dan snaps internally. 'Don't get paranoid, it's not like that.'

What's it like then? I ask.

'Do you remember our first argument, Joe?' Natalie asks. Her question is so unexpected that I stop dead in the street. 'You keep telling me about all of our good times,' she continues, 'but what about our first row? It wasn't all good, you and me. Don't you remember?'

'We never had any proper arguments, though, did we Nat? Just silly stuff,' I say, putting on my best fake grin and linking arms with her to continue walking.

'That's not how I remember it, Joe,' Natalie says quietly. And I know I'm losing her, but more than that, I think I'm losing myself. A couple of days ago, I'd have said Dan would save me, that he wouldn't let anything bad happen to me, but now I think he wants me to go, too. I can feel it with every fibre of his being. He wants to push me further and further down into the darkness. But he wouldn't do that if he knew, because there's something swimming in the darkness with me. A shark, I don't know which breed. The special thing about this shark is that it's very docile and it doesn't often bite. But when it does, its jaws lock in place and nothing but death can release you from it. Even after death, it can keep you in its clutches.

I need to keep him onside. I need him to remember the thing he's been trying to forget.

You know why I'm here, don't you, Dan?

'What do you mean?' he asks. He's happy, content. Natalie is leaning her head on his shoulder as they walk arm in arm along the street.

The thing you've been trying to forget, I say cruelly. *The thing you're hiding from me.*

'I don't understand,' he says internally. He almost never speaks to me out loud anymore. He knows Natalie doesn't like it and she's now more important than me, apparently.

The accident, I say. *You keep telling Natalie you don't remember it, but you've always remembered.*

'What are you saying?' He stops dead in the street, frowning. Natalie looks at him, her hand still resting on his forearm, a questioning look on her face.

You know exactly what I'm saying, Dan.

He's fighting it, but I know I'm right. Against his will, images from that day are flitting into his head.

There he is, homeless and staggering along the street, gripped with the strongest feeling of being outside his own body he's experienced since his grandmother was taken away. But it's different than before, he's getting other feelings, other voices in his head, he has been for weeks, ever since he stopped taking his medication. He's been trying to hide away, under the pier, in the park, tucked away from normal people, for their sake as much as his own. He's scared, worried he's losing his mind. He's cold and itchy and somehow he's on West Street and it's busy, too busy. There are too many people; he doesn't know why he's here. He wants to get into an alleyway at least, somewhere he can curl up and cover his ears and...

There's an old couple in front of him and the woman glances back at him and he can see she's scared; she's terrified. She grabs her husband's arm tightly, looking away. He doesn't want to scare her; he doesn't want that at all, so he darts off the pavement and into the road to overtake her... Then, he hears screeching. A car has swerved to avoid hitting him, and now other cars are swerving to avoid hitting that car. It's like a domino effect, chaos, and he's a moment of calm at the centre of a hurricane of crushing metal and flesh and bone. But it's not his flesh. It's not his bones.

It's mine.

'I didn't know. I didn't remember...' Dan stutters.

It's your fault I'm dead, I spit. *You killed me, Dan.*

PART IV: NATALIE

'That wasn't why you were crying, Joe.'

CHAPTER 13

When she was eighteen, Natalie went to an event for Fresher's Week at university. She stood by the bar watching her friend Olyvia 'dance', a term that Natalie would have used loosely, since Olyvia had been drinking triple vodkas for a pound. Natalie noticed a guy looking at her. He was okay looking, if a little short, and while he wasn't her usual type she held her nose and knocked back a vodka, thinking, *why not?* as he stumbled toward her. The guy Olyvia was dancing with was the kind of guy you'd call a ladies' man—or a slag if he'd been a woman. They were only a few weeks into Fresher's, and both Olyvia and Natalie already had this guy's number, metaphorically speaking. He'd been through about five of the girls in her halls already. That didn't stop Olyvia from fancying him, though; it didn't stop her giddily laughing and running her fingers over her open neckline, gently brushing them down to her cleavage as he came over to talk to her.

'Fuck it!' she shouted as she tottered off to the dance floor, unstable in the heels she wasn't used to wearing. Natalie leant on the bar, wondering where the others from her hall flat had disappeared to. They'd been eight strong when they'd left for the evening, each downing a couple of glasses of wine before heading out, to save money.

The music was loud, too loud, and not Natalie's type of thing. But she didn't mind; it was all part of the mad freedom she was now experiencing, away from home, from her parents, for the first time. Slowly, the okay-looking short guy made his way over to her and she smiled in spite of herself. As he drew near, she didn't look away. She wanted to appear confident and in control, so she met him, eye to eye.

'You're beau—' he started, before his head bowed and he started heaving all over her lower legs and shoes. She pushed him backward, trying to sidestep the biblical flood of vomit. He collapsed on the floor, turning over onto his side and continuing to be sick.

'What the fuck, Sam?' a guy said, bending down and rolling the guy over to check that he was okay.

'I'm aohky,' the vomiting guy tried to say.

His friend put his hands under the guy's arms and dragged him off, propping his back up against the bar so that he was sitting, legs spread, head dangling limply. A barman had come around and was ushering them away from the pool of sick so he could clean it up, but otherwise the rest of the bar carried on as normal, music pumping, drunk students dancing and drinking.

Natalie stood staring down at her sick-covered legs and shoes, then felt someone gently touch her arm.

'Sorry about him,' a voice said.

Looking up from her shoes, she saw him smiling apologetically at her. It was a warm smile, caring.

'Look,' he said. 'Why don't you go and clean yourself up, and I'll get you a cab home?'

She nodded silently, not sure what else to say, her nostrils filled with the acrid smell of sick.

'I've got to get him home anyway,' he said, motioning towards his friend, Sam. 'He's a liability, this one. Always throwing up on people.'

He laughed. Despite herself, despite the burning sensation from the sick on her legs and the fact her shoes were probably ruined and would need to go in the toilet bin, Natalie smiled back. He seemed nice. Handsome, too, with dark hair and a tiny bit of stubble. This one was much more her type than Sam would have been.

Fifteen minutes later, they managed to convince a taxi driver to take them. Natalie sat by the window, her bare feet having been washed in the sink of the student union bar; her shoes had been unsalvageable.

Sam was lolloping, half-conscious in the seat between her and his good-looking friend. For a while, neither of them spoke. They exchanged glances, catching each other's eyes and smiling. Eventually, he leant over, placing his hand on her thigh and pushing it lightly up her dress. She let him. Awkwardly, with Sam semiconscious between them, they leant in for a kiss and his hand pushed farther up her leg to her knickers, exploring their warmth.

She liked him, but she wouldn't normally have instigated anything while his friend was in between them. Sensing this, he took his hand away and sat back, breaking their kiss and their intimacy. For a second she thought he was stopping; she felt partly disappointed and partly relieved. Then, not even caring about the cab driver flicking them furtive glances in the rearview mirror, he sat back and unbuttoned his flies, grinning at her.

'Don't worry,' he said quietly, leaning over Sam and grasping her hand. 'He won't wake up.'

He wrapped her hand around his penis. As she started to move her hand up and down furiously, she began to feel a little bit sick herself, a combination of the car's movement and the drink.

'My name's Joe, by the way,' he said, letting his head fall back on the seat and closing his eyes.

'Natalie,' she said, hoping he was going to come quickly because her arm was already aching.

* * *

The morning after Dan arrived, Natalie woke with a slight hangover. It was nothing she couldn't handle, but as she sat on the edge of her bed staring at her locked bedroom door, she gently massaged her eyebrows, rubbing them from the bridge of her nose outward, to calm herself down. She could hear the shower running. He was already up and getting ready. He'd been without a shower for a long time, she supposed, she couldn't blame him for wanting to use it. She grabbed a pair of jeans and a sweatshirt. Walking out onto the landing, she approached the closed bathroom door and knocked on it.

'I'm just going to get some milk,' she shouted through the door. 'Won't be long.'

'Not on my account,' he shouted back, sounding happy and relaxed.

That was good. Reassuring, even.

As she walked around the corner to the local shop, Natalie shoved her hands in her pockets and tried to make sense of what she was doing. People didn't invite strangers into their homes like this. People didn't...

Who were these 'people', anyway? She'd had enough of expectations, of norms and rules and obligations. As she rounded the corner, she could hear a woman singing at the top of her lungs, not tuneful, but not awful.

'Are you okay?' the woman asked, stopping her singing and pushing a pair of massive black sunglasses up her nose. The woman was staring directly at her, and for a moment, Natalie couldn't work out where she'd seen her before, then she realised it was the weird lady from the pub the night before, the one who'd told her and Dan they made a good couple before running out the door, singing.

'Yeah, I'm fine,' Natalie replied, not sure if she was irritated or uncomfortable. The woman was barring her entrance into the strangely named local shop 'Happy Planet'.

'Could I?' Natalie indicated the door behind the woman, who tightened her long, espionage-style rain mac around her waist, but didn't move.

'It might help to talk,' the woman said.

'Seriously?' Natalie said, surprising herself. 'Do I look like I need more crazy?'

With that, she gently edged the woman aside and walked into

the shop to get her milk, feeling slightly unnerved.

* * *

On her second date with Joe, they went to see a band. They were okay, not Natalie's type of thing, but she loved the thrill of live music, the immediacy, the intimacy. Afterward, they carried on drinking and chatting for hours. It felt so natural, like it was meant to be. Then, as the drink took hold, in a dark corner of some club or other, she asked about his family. He darkened, breaking eye contact with her.

'I don't talk about them.'

'I'm sorry...' Natalie started, realising she'd made a faux pas. But already something was peaking her interest. There was a story there. Until that point, he'd seemed so controlled, but there was baggage, and now she could feel it.

'No, it's okay. It's just...'

He paused, as if deciding whether to open up to her or shut down. Her experience of boys and men to date told her that he'd close down, that he'd brush it off and move on. Instead, he said quietly, 'One of my earliest memories is Dad pinning my mum against the kitchen wall with a bread knife to her throat...'cos she'd cooked him chicken instead of beef.'

'Oh, Joe.' Natalie reached over for his hand and he let her take it, but he was still refusing eye contact.

'I was only six. I got out of bed and stood there, piss wet in my pajama bottoms. I didn't know what to do.'

'Oh, Joe,' she said again, gripping his hand tighter still. 'That's terrible.'

'No, it's okay,' he replied, finally looking up at her, tears filling his beautiful brown eyes. 'We all have shit in our childhood, right?'

But Natalie didn't. Her parents had always been incredibly supportive of her. They had taught her and her brother to face life head on, to grab hold of reality, not shrink from it. She'd had a wonderful childhood. Staring across the club table, she felt immediately like Joe needed her, that he could open up and be vulnerable with her. And to Natalie, that felt like the most powerful thing a woman ever could offer a man.

As their relationship progressed, she made it her mission to help him, to explore his childhood traumas and release his demons.

'I left my M&Ms at the counter once,' Joe said, putting his arms around her and hugging her. 'Dad went absolutely mad.'

'What?' Natalie asked. 'Why?'

'I'd got the tin of beans and spaghetti hoops and a white sliced loaf and Pot Noodle he'd asked for, but when I looked in the bag, there were no M&Ms. Dad wasn't even looking at me, he was staring out of the window at a young trolley girl, bent over in her tight nylon skirt.'

'What did he do?' Natalie asked, stroking his skin lightly, wanting to take all the pain away.

'Nothing. Well, he didn't hit me or anything.' Joe tapped his head. 'It was all up here, see? He terrified me, that man. Still does...' Joe swallowed dryly, wincing, as if the lining of his throat had little cuts in it. 'Funny, the things you remember, isn't it? I was sitting there in the car next to him, my fingers pressed into the carrier bag, pushing and stretching until each one broke through to become locked into its own little noose of white plastic.'

'Oh, Joe,' Natalie said again. She wished something more useful would come out of her mouth, but she just kept saying the same thing over and over, as if it would help him, as if anything could take his pain away.

'Dad said, "Look, you little faggot, you paid for them. Go and get them," and I started crying. Can you believe it? Twelve years old and I started crying 'cos he asked me to go back in the shop.'

'That wasn't why you were crying, Joe...' Natalie started, but

Joe was still speaking, lost in his memories.

'"I mean it, you little pussy. Go and get them,"' Joe continued, mirroring his dad's voice.

'Oh Joe, that's awful,' Natalie said.

She wanted to hold him forever, to tell him it was okay, that she was there now. She wanted to tell him how wrong his father had been and that it wasn't Joe's fault.

'Will you marry me?' he asked out of nowhere. 'You and me. Let's run away and do it. What do you say?'

'Yes,' she replied giddily. 'Yes, yes, yes.'

* * *

Natalie slammed the front door behind her, as she returned from the shop, lost in memories of Joe. Clutching the milk in her hand, she braced herself. How could she play this out?

'Dan?' she called up the stairs.

'In here,' he shouted back from the living room. As she peered in through the door, he was sitting on the armchair, legs slung over the end, a book in his hand, reading.

'It's been months since I've been able to read a book. God, I've missed them. I didn't realise how much.'

Despite herself, she smiled widely. For a moment, she didn't move, she just leant on the doorframe and watched him read, her heart slowing down to a comfortable rhythm.

'I'll make us a coffee,' she said eventually.

'Okay, thanks,' he said, without looking up from his book. 'I've boiled the kettle and the cups are out on the side.'

* * *

Agreeing to elope with Joe and breaking her parents' hearts had been one of Natalie's first mistakes, and her biggest regret. But the mistakes and regrets had come thick and fast from then on.

After the wedding, she met Joe's parents and realised not everything he told her added up. They seemed so committed, loving and supportive, nothing like the people Joe had described. At first, she thought it must have been a front on their part. Monsters don't look like monsters to the outside world, after all. Then one day she realised the truth.

'What are you trying to say?' Joe snapped when she mentioned how lovely his parents seemed. 'You saying I made it all up?'

'No, of course not,' Natalie said, shrinking back from his anger slightly. 'I was saying...'

'What would that make me?' he shouted, coming close to her face, flushed with anger. 'If I made shit like that up?'

The trouble was, newly married Natalie already knew what it made him. The morning after their private, secret wedding, she had woken up as Joe had entered her roughly from behind, pinning her shoulder down as he'd fucked her.

'Joe...' she'd said, as he'd grunted, speeding up and pushing her farther onto her front so that his body weight held her in position as he thrusted.

Olyvia had always said she loved morning sex, that she loved to be woken up by her boyfriend's advances.

'Have you ever woken up to find he's already started?' Natalie had asked her once, trying to sound nonchalant.

'Kind of, I suppose. Not sure I've ever been fast asleep when he's...' She wrinkled her nose up and smiled, too prudish to say the words. 'Well, when he's...you know.'

'Right,' Natalie said, nodding and smiling the most natural smile she could muster, all the while thinking about her experience with her new husband. He'd woken her up with sexual advances before, but this time it hadn't felt gentle or loving. She couldn't allow herself to think the word, but allowed or not, there it was, floating about inside her mind, clattering its sharp edges against the confines of her skull: consensual. Her honeymoon morning experience with Joe hadn't felt consensual at all. But consent was a more difficult concept than she was willing to acknowledge when it came to her own body.

* * *

After Dan moved in with her, days turned into weeks and something curious began to happen. Natalie realised that she was enjoying his company, his stories, and his attention. Each day she planned to tell him to leave and each day she extended the arrangement by just one more day. He did his share of the cleaning and tidying; he washed his own clothes, all things she wasn't used to. He was fun to be around and, curiously, sometimes he spent days where Joe didn't manifest at all. There were days when Natalie could forget all the bad stuff and when Dan was Dan, with no trace of Joe or the south-London accent, she felt content, like things were going to be okay again.

She quickly worked out his trigger points. She knew that Joe came to the forefront when Dan got stressed or upset. If something was out of his comfort zone, Joe would take full charge, sometimes for hours. Those were the days Natalie found most stressful, the ones where she thought she was making a huge mistake. But the times with Dan made up for it. On those days, she glimpsed a life she'd barely dreamed possible. It was an ordinary life, stunning in its simplicity. Two people falling in love, side by side, enjoying each other and everything life had to offer them: Brighton, vibrant and exciting, the seafront and its crashing waves and pebbles, and the Sussex Downs, stunning views and green as far as the eye could see. At one point, in the middle of Devil's Dyke, you couldn't see anything man-made, no roads, no railways, no buildings. Dan always joked that it was like they'd time travelled, that they could be in any point in history. And she realised that if she was with him, it wouldn't have mattered. She'd have gone anywhere—or any when—with him.

Then, Joe would come back, with a cockney comment or a sly dig. The longer he'd been away, the more bitter he'd be when he returned. Sometimes he scared her. Not like *her* Joe had done, never like that. But he was a part of Dan she couldn't penetrate and couldn't understand. She knew she had to convince him to get professional help, but didn't know where to start. And she didn't want to ruin things. The two of them were happy. It didn't make sense, and it wasn't perfect, but what relationship was?

* * *

A few years after they were married, Joe got a job in Brighton, so they moved. Natalie wasn't keen at first; her family and friends were in the Midlands or the north. Living on the south coast wasn't in her plans. But she made it work and got a job with a local company, moving up the ranks and eventually becoming their finance director. And life wasn't all bad. When Joe had her to himself, without distraction, when his job was going well and he felt confident, they had fun. Time passed and life wasn't terrible, but neither was it what she'd dreamed of.

One day, Joe came home with a gift. Excitedly, she pulled the wrapping paper off to find an Ann Summer's dildo, the kind with a sucker on it could stick to a door or window.

'Thought we could spice things up a bit?' Joe said, leaning over and kissing her. She laughed nervously and nodded. Later, standing in the back garden in just her bra and knickers, cold and ashamed, she stuck the dildo on the kitchen window at head height and began fellating it. Joe was watching her through the window, pulling himself off as he shouted instructions to her.

'That's it, get it right down until you choke.'

She was freezing and uncomfortable, terrified that the neighbours would see her or hear Joe shouting. She wanted to make him happy, and she didn't want to come across like a prude, but...

'Keep going, that's it. When you're done, you can come in and scrub the floor, you dirty bitch.'

When he was finished, he didn't speak to her, he just left the kitchen to go upstairs and clean himself up. She pulled the dildo off the window and came inside, picking her clothes up off the kitchen floor and pulling them on over her shivering frame. Nothing about the experience had been enjoyable. Far from spicing things up, it had made her feel degraded and abused. When he came back downstairs, he walked into the kitchen.

'Want a cup of tea?' he said, as if nothing had happened.

'I didn't enjoy that,' she said firmly.

'Oh for fuck's sake, Nat. It was just a bit of role-play. Do you have to make such a big deal of everything?'

* * *

A week later, Joe lost his job. Staff cutbacks, they said; but Natalie couldn't help noticing they started recruiting again only weeks after Joe left. Unable to prevent Natalie from working because they relied on her income, Joe settled for undermining her. He told her that her bosses were taking advantage of her, and she should cut down her hours.

'They're using you, Natalie,' he said if she'd had a hard day.

Natalie partly believed him. He'd played with her emotions for years by that point, subtly making her question everything she thought and felt. But *how* were they using her? By paying her a high salary? By promoting her to be a director of the company? Her job challenged her and sometimes she did have shitty days, but she'd always *liked* to be challenged and she'd always loved her job. Still, Joe's negativity chipped away at her, making her doubt herself.

'You don't have to carry on working there,' he'd say, without conviction, usually when she'd asked how his job hunt was going. 'Not when they take advantage the way they do. We could manage.'

'Not now that you're not working,' she'd reply.

'Oh, here we go again,' Joe would say. 'I'm doing my best.'

'I didn't mean that, Joe. I'm sorry, I...'

He wasn't violent. Even the sex wasn't... Well, it wasn't like he forced himself on her, not really. Could it be considered force if she let it happen? Because he didn't mind if she didn't want to do it? She assumed that was a normal part of any relationship.

Once upon a time, at the very beginning, she had enjoyed sex with him. When it was based on mutual understanding, she'd liked how he objectified her, how he'd used her for his own ends. But how quickly and easily something mutual had turned into something darker, something no longer acceptable. She'd stopped bothering to tell him to stop if she wasn't into it. It was easier that way.

Sometimes, she felt that sex was the only thing that stopped him going about the business of unpicking her emotionally, piece by piece. If she was lucky, it meant he would go to sleep early and she would get some of her evening alone. That alone time became the most precious thing in her world.

'I'll never leave you alone,' Joe said one day, like he was mulling something over inside his head. It wasn't reassuring. It wasn't talk of an endless, undying love. It was a threat.

'Don't talk like that,' Natalie replied, trying to stand up, desperate to be away from him.

'Sit back down,' he snapped.

'I wanted to go and start dinner,' she stuttered.

'Did I say I wanted you to start dinner?'

* * *

Natalie understands everything now, how she turned from a happy, confident little girl into a self-doubting, insecure wife. The hatred she feels for Joe is only secondary to the hatred she feels for herself in allowing it to happen. Until Dan turned up on her doorstep, she hadn't realised the full extent of the damage, how filled with fury she was. Then this gentle, insane man showed up on her doorstep and turned everything on its head. He gave her a purpose, something else to concentrate on. But what started out as a project soon became something else. She never expected to fall in love, not after Joe, not after everything. Yet there she was.

She hasn't fixed Dan yet, not by a long shot. But something else has happened, something totally unexpected. He's fixing her. And the magic of him is that he's doing it without even trying.

CHAPTER 14

When Dan moved in, Natalie swore to herself she'd never sleep with him. Her relationship with him—and that's what it had become—wasn't about sex. She wasn't sure what it *was* about, but she loved spending time with him, being around him. It wasn't just the invented stories about her past, either. She liked his take on the world, his way of looking at things. There was no judgement in Dan; he wasn't ever looking to change people.

Of course, her resolution didn't last. She could blame the wine, one too many glasses while she made dinner and another while they lay on the sofa together watching television.

'I want to tell you everything.' Dan flicked the television off, staring straight at her, his beautifully mismatched eyes sparkling. What was it about him that made her feel so...teenage?

'About my past and my condition.'

'Okay,' Natalie said cautiously, not sure she wanted to know. 'You don't have to, only if you want to.'

'I do want to. I hid everything from Debbie and that was wrong. Well, not wrong, not with her, because she was... Well, she wasn't you. But you need to understand how this happened to me, how Joe...'

'It's okay,' Natalie touched his wrist lightly, surprised at the unfamiliar tingle she got when her skin touched the skin of someone she fancied. Loved, even. Christ, was she falling in love? This wasn't in her plan; this wasn't supposed to happen.

'Am I babbling again?' Dan said, his infectious smile lighting up his features again.

'Little bit,' Natalie held her hand up and pinched her fingers together, smiling in spite of her beating heart and the sick feeling rising in her stomach.

'Okay,' Dan nodded his head. 'I don't know where to start. My mum I suppose. She died giving birth...'

* * *

His story was long and disjointed, dead allergic mothers, grandmothers with dementia, detachment disorders and Babalaway Clinics, therapists and drug treatment, bulimia and vomiting. He was a man who looked in the mirror and saw someone else looking back. As he spoke, she didn't interrupt, didn't offer an opinion or a solution; she simply listened. Nodded. Drank wine. Finally, she held him tightly as he wept. And she knew without question that this was love. This strange, broken man had come to her for a reason. He was ill. Yes, he was troubled. But he was also completely without artifice, totally open and honest. If she could fix him, she would, but it wasn't one-sided. Somehow, she knew he could fix her too, without even trying. Wasn't that love? A perfect symmetry of two people who shouldn't fit together, but who somehow slotted into place as if they were meant to be?

At bedtime, she lingered on the landing upstairs and kissed him lightly on the cheek as he went off to the spare room again. Standing on the landing, indecisive, she walked slowly to her bed, heart pounding, hoping he was going to come back out after her and twirl her around, kissing her passionately and telling her he loved her.

She slipped under her covers, but couldn't settle, and she knew she'd never settle. Back on the landing, she crept gently into his bedroom and slipped under his covers, her fingers gently spidering their way down his body.

* * *

After, Dan hadn't rolled over and slept like Joe used to. He'd stroked her warm skin and lifted her hand to his mouth to kiss it.

'You didn't run, Natalie. When I arrived on your doorstep. Why not?' he said, leaning up on one elbow and reaching over to kiss her lips.

'Because I'm her husband, Dan,' he spat, south-London accent full throttle.

Natalie physically jerked away, shocked. Joe hadn't made an appearance for ages and Natalie had been telling herself Dan was getting better, that maybe she wouldn't need to make him get help after all. But here he was, full force.

'We made a promise to each other, didn't we, Natalie?' he continued, his voice filled with hate.

'Till death us do part, Joe,' Natalie said, rolling over in bed so she didn't have to look at him. Her heart was thumping loudly.

'I'm sorry if that wasn't very good,' Dan said in his soft, gentle voice. Natalie wondered if he was even aware of his alter ego sometimes. Did he know he'd just shouted at her?

'What do you mean?' Natalie asked quietly, rolling back over so she could see his face. He was staring at her with concern in his eyes, like he was worried about something. She rested her head on his chest and gently ran her fingers over his stomach.

'The sex. I'm not very experienced, that's all,' Dan carried on. 'I've only slept with one person before.'

'You're shitting me,' Natalie sat upright, her hair dangling over his face slightly, tickling his nose. 'One person? But you're thirty...'

'All right.' Dan squirmed, brushing her hair off him and looking over her shoulder rather than directly at her.

'Sorry, I didn't mean... I just. Wow. One person.'

'Debbie. I lived with her, before...'

'It was good... I mean, you know it was good,' Natalie said, trying to keep him calm. She didn't want him to get stressed out—that was when Joe would come out.

'When we first got together, me and Debbie I mean, I didn't know anything. She taught me, I suppose.'

'Did you love her?'

'Debbie?' Dan said quietly. 'No. I'm not sure I even liked her.

Don't get me wrong, I mean… We lived together. I was with her for years. But I was never *with* her, if you know what I mean. She was barely even real for me.'

'Why did you stay with her?' Natalie asked, trying to work out what she was feeling. Jealousy. She felt jealous of this nameless woman from Dan's past. For some reason, it hadn't occurred to her that he'd had a real life before he'd arrived. He'd turned up, homeless and mentally unbalanced, a blank slate for her to write on. But he'd had a life before her, of course he had. Before he'd invented another personality, before living on the streets, he'd been someone. And that someone had a girlfriend called Debbie.

* * *

The next morning, Natalie had work. After her shower, she went back to her own room to get dressed and found Dan lying in his boxer shorts on her bed. He lay watching her get ready, not moving, not speaking, just devouring her visually, watching her drop her towel and walk naked to her chest of drawers as she chose her knickers and bra.

Her heart was thumping, and the excitement of a teenager flooded through every vein. The fire within was quenched only by the coolness of her flesh as she slowly pulled her underwear on and chose a small charcoal grey skirt she knew accentuated her figure. She coupled it with a new French Connection blouse and when she was finally ready, she took a pair of low heels from her wardrobe and sat with her back to Dan on the edge of the bed to put them on. He exhaled a long, deliberate breath before she felt his hands on her again, starting at her waist, moving up. She turned around, laughing and half-heartedly batting him off.

'I've got work.'

'You can be late…' he persevered, kissing her on the lips.

'One of us has to earn a living, Dan,' she said.

At that, he shrank back, letting her go.

She hadn't meant it like that; she hadn't meant to make him feel bad. It was just something she was used to saying, something she used to say to Joe. Except that with Joe, she'd said it out of spite, and she'd meant it to hurt. But it wasn't the same with Dan.

'Of course,' Dan said. 'I wasn't thinking.'

With that, he pushed himself off the bed and left the bedroom, leaving her feeling anxious.

* * *

'You drink too much,' Joe said once as he dropped down into the armchair in the living room, picking up his bottle of beer and taking a sip. 'You're going to end up like one of those middle-class alcoholics, downing a bottle of wine every night.'

'You drink beer every night,' Natalie countered, knocking the last of her wine down in one gulp and walking to the kitchen to refill it.

'I'm serious,' Joe said, following her into the kitchen, beer bottle in hand. 'Every night you get home from work and you start knocking back the wine. If your job makes you that stressed, leave.'

He was still using his reasonable tone, the one that could still fool her into thinking he was a reasonable human being. She still fell for it, every time. How could she not have seen it was a ruse, the lead-in to him manipulating and controlling her?

'It doesn't stress me. Not more than it should, anyway. It's...' she said, stopping herself before the word came out, but they both knew what she was about to say: *You. It's you.*

'Oh, I knew it would be *my* fault. I didn't ask to be made redundant, Nat.'

'You're not doing much about it either, are you?' she said, opening the fridge to get the half-empty bottle of white out.

'Saint Natalie,' he spat. 'The breadwinner. The functioning

alcoholic.' He raised his beer to her and walked out of the room and back into the living room to watch whatever mindless television show he was into.

The problem was, Natalie knew he was right. She was drinking to compensate, not because of her job but because she was unhappy. Because she hated her husband. Months passed before she even contemplated doing anything about it, but after a Christmas spent alone with Joe—'It'll be nice, Nat. Just the two of us. Nobody else to cause friction'—she decided to take control.

'I'm doing the dryathlon,' she said to Joe, proudly.

'Why?' he said, not looking up from his iPhone as he lounged on the sofa.

'I won't drink for the whole of January, then I'll be more moderate when I start again.'

'They're a waste of time, those things. It's like dieting, you'll just fall back off the wagon harder afterward.'

'Then what do you suggest?' she asked, exasperated.

He shrugged, still not looking at her. In the end, she'd gone into the kitchen and poured herself a glass of wine. It was the only protest she had the energy to muster.

* * *

Things were different with Dan. She didn't drink to escape him; she drank to escape Joe, but this time it was Dan's Joe, not hers. Would she ever be free of Joes?

Dan himself, however, was full of surprises. He'd returned home, all smiles, cooking her dinner and telling her he'd got his old job back. Just like that. She'd only made one comment that morning, but he'd been perceptive and committed enough to just go and sort it out. He was more capable than she'd given him credit for. She'd assumed because he'd been homeless, because he had clear mental health issues, that he couldn't look after himself, but that wasn't true. And if he was capable of that, what else was he capable of? She didn't want to push him too far, too fast, and she could come up with a million reasons not to risk the status quo.

But the elephant in the room was fed up with being ignored. He'd learnt to tap dance in the shadows and the sound had become deafening. Natalie couldn't keep ignoring it. After all, if she loved Dan, she had to do the right thing by him, like he was doing by her. He'd got his job back so he could pay his way. Now she had to do her bit. She had to be honest with him. She had to tell him she'd lied, that Joe wasn't Joe and he was... What? What was he? She couldn't answer that; she'd never be able to answer it. But someone could. Joe's dad, maybe? His doctor? She went over and over these thoughts, day in and day out with no resolution, no clarity. Yet each day, she would finish work and meet Dan and they'd go out for dinner or they'd go to the cinema or they'd eat a takeaway and have a glass of wine, and things would seem okay; they would seem *normal*. So, she let it slide. Just one more day wouldn't hurt, would it?

* * *

'Don't you think it's selfish?' Joe snapped at her once. 'You've been at work all day and now you want to sit on the phone to your mum. What about me? Don't you think *I* want to talk?'

For a while after they moved to Brighton, Natalie tried to stay in contact with her friends and family, even if it was by phone. But Joe would get angry with her. He'd tell her she was selfish, that she only thought of herself and never of him. He'd listen in on the conversations and always find something she'd said that he objected to—either that or he felt she should have been doing something else at the time of the call, something she was neglecting. After a while, she stopped calling people because it wasn't worth the hassle. And somewhere inside, she believed him. She was selfish.

Social media and texting were no more available to her. Joe told her they should have a joint Facebook account—NatandJoe Best. When she argued that none of her friends did this, that they could both have their own separate accounts, he accused her of hiding something. Why wouldn't she want a joint one? What didn't she want him to see? So, Facebook became a place she could view other people's lives from afar, see the photos and stories and exploits of friends and family, perfect lives lived through a screen. They were untouchable and, ultimately, depressing.

For a while, she'd kept up email contact with her friends and parents. She'd sent emails and then immediately deleted them. She'd read the responses at work and then immediately deleted them. Then, one day she found him sitting with her laptop closed on his lap in the living room.

'Do you want to tell me what you've been saying about me?'

'What?' she replied, nervously fingering the zip on her shoulder bag.

'Don't lie to me, Nat. I installed spyware on your laptop. I've been recording all your keystrokes. I know who you've been emailing.'

* * *

Life sank further into the abyss. At home, Natalie was expected to be well groomed but not sexy; she had to keep on top of shaving her legs and wearing makeup and nice clothes, otherwise she was 'letting herself go'.

'What would that say about our marriage?' he'd say. 'What would it say about how you feel about me? Do you love me so little that you can't even be bothered to shave your legs?'

On the other hand, if she didn't dress modestly, erring on the side of prudish, at work, she was being slutty or was having an affair. Joe chose her makeup for home but told her not to wear it to work at all. He told her how he liked the towels folded in the bathroom and how the magazines should be arranged. He told her how the books should be placed on the living room shelves and how often the carpet should be vacuumed.

This didn't all happen at once. If it had, Natalie feels sure she would have known it was unreasonable and would have fought back. But these things were drip-fed over years of marriage. At first, they were imperceptible, small foibles she could ignore or pretend weren't important. Over time, she accepted things, bit by bit, until she wasn't even sure what she thought anymore. She didn't trust her own judgement, couldn't tell what was appropriate and what wasn't. Every interaction with him cemented the feeling that these things were her fault, not his. She wasn't good enough, she overthought things, she was too sensitive.

'I think you're a miserable person,' Joe said to her one day. 'Always making problems where they don't exist.'

Somewhere along the way, she still doesn't know when, she began to see his demands as 'normal'. There's that word again: *normal*. It's hateful to her now, so filled with venom.

By the time she was thirty, she'd been married to Joe for six years and everything she thought, felt and experienced was filtered through Joe's prism. From the outside, she was a strong, capable woman with a good career and a loving husband. On the inside, her world didn't exist, only Joe's version of it. She was isolated, controlled—not that she understood that then. Looking back, she doesn't recognise herself. On some level, she thinks she knew somewhere inside there was a fierce and capable little girl, filled with life and potential. But Joe had buried her under choking mounds of earth—and she'd helped him do it.

She'd always imagined depression was a sudden thing, based on a big event, caused by a bereavement or a tragedy or a terrible childhood. Something tangible, a visible building block a therapist could trace a person's problems back to. She thought the depressed knew they were depressed. The thing was, her growing depression was gradual, something she couldn't see coming, couldn't touch or taste. Some days, she'd let her head slip under the bathwater and she'd stay there, a little too long, thinking if she just opened her mouth, just breathed in and in and in, it would all be over. She wouldn't have to feel the way she did anymore. Of course, she never did it. As her lungs began to beat, she pushed back out of the water, she inhaled, hating herself just a little bit more for her inability to do it. It never progressed from there, she never planned to take pills or throw herself from the end of the pier or anything else. She could barely even communicate to herself what she was feeling. She was dissatisfied, she told herself. If she could just pull herself together, she'd be okay. The most important thing was to make sure Joe didn't know she felt like this. She didn't want him thinking she was mad along with everything else. She'd find a way to show Joe she wasn't a miserable person, she wasn't always creating problems.

If she recognised her feelings as anything, it was self-hatred. She's didn't even lay the blame at Joe's door, not consciously. Her insecurities had grown to such proportions that all she could see were her own shortcomings. She was disconnected from everyone: her parents, her brother, her friends. Her work colleagues were just that, colleagues. She had developed a 'work' version of herself, and at home, she had another version, still hidden, still mute, no more herself than a mannequin. Deep inside, she was burning, screaming. Outside, she was normal. She smiled at the neighbours and made small talk. She talked to Lucy at the office about TV shows she hadn't even watched and laughed with the short jovial woman in the newsagent around the corner.

A week before Joe died, Natalie stood by Brighton's clock tower, opposite Waterstones and contemplated stepping into the road in front of a bus. The thought wasn't shocking to her, it was mundane. She knew she felt empty. End this. One tiny moment and it would all be over.

She stood, staring at the buses and cars whiz past, her low-heeled work shoes edging closer and closer to the pavement edge. A thought occurred to her: Why had she fallen in love with Joe in the first place? She couldn't even remember what she'd ever loved about him. When she thought about him, that damaged but charming man she met all those years ago, she couldn't remember the moment, couldn't recall anything about him that gave her any warmth. She shouldn't have tried to fix him. Some people were just broken and if you hung around them long enough, they would break you, too.

It was the first moment she'd truly realised what he'd done: he'd broken her. All these years, telling her she was neurotic, overthinking things, selfish, thoughtless...whatever he needed to say to keep her in check, keep her under his control.

A bus flew past her, so close to the curb where she stood she could feel the breeze on her face. And just like that, the emptiness, the deadness inside her formed butterflies. Black, scorched and feeble butterflies, but butterflies none the less, fluttering and trying to fly.

One tiny moment and it would all be over.

She wasn't sure which emotion was more powerful—the need to silence her thoughts, the knowledge of what she'd let him do to her, or the feeling of empowerment. She could control it; she could end this. She squeezed her eyes shut, chest burning, willing herself to step forward, to do it, to own her feelings, her life, if only for a moment.

She doesn't know how long she stood there, unmoving, but at some point an old man tapped her on the shoulder and asked, 'Can you help me across the road?' and linked arms with her. So, she smiled and said, 'of course,' and waited for the road to clear and stepped into it, guiding him to the other side safely.

As he thanked her and ambled away, she walked slowly into the bookstore, heart pumping loudly.

She glanced down at the piles of novels before her, wandering around, running her fingers over the tops of the books, table to table to table. Then, near the back of the store on the local author table, there was a solitary book lying at an angle, out of place, like it was in the wrong section. *Reasons to Stay Alive* by Matt Haig. She brushed the front cover with her finger lightly and the butterflies in her stomach managed to flutter into the air, just a fraction.

She bought the book that day, hiding it from Joe under her side of the mattress, feeding from it whenever she had the chance, devouring its words and letting them enter her and change her.

* * *

Then came the day of the accident. As she and Joe were leaving the house to walk into town, Joe turned to her and smiled, reaching out and tucking her hair behind her ear.

'Let's have a baby,' he said excitedly.

The steel casing she'd grown around her heart constricted, an iron maiden closing around it, spikes thrusting easily into its grey-pink flesh.

'Let's have a baby,' he repeated, grabbing her by the shoulders and hugging her tightly.

As the blood flooded out of Natalie's punctured heart, something curious happened. She understood everything. Who he was, what he'd done to her. A calm reality descended. She'd never have a child with this man; she'd never allow him to make another human being feel the way he made her feel. Something had to change.

* * *

214

Natalie has taken the afternoon off work and she's sitting in the back garden again, staring at the ivy as it strangles everything in its path. It's been a few weeks since Dan came home, bursting with excitement at the news of his job. And he's settled in well, much to her surprise. He's so happy, so content with their life that she can't bear to burst his bubble. His bitter alter ego is showing his face less and less frequently. Maybe one day he'll disappear forever? Maybe she doesn't have to do anything at all? She sips her wine. It's 4 p.m., so it's okay. It helps her think. Something like that, anyway.

She is closing her eyes and letting the warm breeze caress her face when the telephone rings. Her parents are the only people who ring the home phone, at least they had been before they'd stopped calling. It's like a relic from another time, a strange object sat on the side, out of place, shouting for attention. She wanders into the house, twirling her glass in her fingers and in no great hurry. As she picks up the phone, she fully expects to hear a five- or ten-second pause as the line connects with India and someone asks her if she's settled her PPI claims yet. Instead, she hears a man's voice, wavering, like he's nervous.

'Hello?'

'Hello,' Natalie replies. She never speaks first when she answers the home telephone; she doesn't want to give the cold callers the satisfaction.

'I'm sorry to bother you,' the man says. 'My name's Bob. I'm looking for my son.'

'Your son?' she says, her heart speeding up a little. She puts her glass down on the side and sits in the seat beside the telephone table. As her bottom perches on the small green cushion, she realises she's never even sat in this seat before. People usually ring her mobile, so when she's chatting she paces up and down or curls up on the sofa. She never sits in this strange wicker chair with a plump green cushion.

'Yes. He's been missing. But I had a call from one of his old work colleagues and... Well, I don't want to get him into trouble, not if he has his job back.'

'Trouble?' Natalie says quietly.

'Yes. He's a missing person, you see.'

'The police?' Natalie replies, her heart jabbing the walls of her chest. 'Has he done something?'

'No, no. Nothing like that. At least, I don't think...' The man trails off.

Natalie recognises his voice, the accent, the inflection.

'His name is Dan,' he says, as if it's necessary. 'His work friend gave me your number, said I should contact you.'

Natalie sits quietly on her plump green cushion, pushing the phone handset into her ear harder, and harder still.

'He's here,' she says eventually, and she can feel the relief flooding through the handset; she can almost see him collapsing back into his own telephone chair, perhaps with a plump little crimson cushion with gold stitching around the edges.

'And is he...' He pauses, like he's trying to find the words. 'Is he okay?'

'He's okay... Well, no. No, he's not. He's not well. In his head, I mean. Physically, he's fine, but...'

'Is he making himself sick again?' his dad asks.

'Sick?' She realises she hasn't considered this. Dan told her about his bulimia, but there had been so many other factors at play, she'd almost forgotten about it.

'Dr Alabi says that's one of the first signs that he's disassociating again.'

'Disassociating?'

'Yes, like... It's difficult to explain. He gets this feeling... Like he doesn't think he exists. He's been well for years, but then his gran...'

'I don't think it's that,' Natalie says. 'He's...' She has no idea how to say it. How can she tell Dan's father what she's done? That she's lied to Dan and made him believe the fantasy he's created? That not only has she let him believe he is possessed by her dead husband, but she has actively encouraged that delusion. She hasn't been making him better; she's been prolonging his illness. She's been making him worse.

I'm a selfish bitch, she thinks. *Joe was right all along.*

She knows she must acknowledge the thing she's been avoiding. Things can't carry on like this, in limbo. She can't keep pretending that everything is okay.

She doesn't tell Dan's dad the full extent of his son's delusion because she doesn't know how to. It would expose her own selfishness. It would lay bare her part in the whole mess. She can't tell his father the truth; but she can tell him Dan's struggling. Maybe she should tell him the depersonalisation disorder has returned. In a way, it has, hasn't it? Dan isn't himself...

'Please, try to get him to see his doctor,' Mr Garrison says. 'I'll give you his number. Dr Alabi. He helped him when he was younger and...'

'Okay, Mr Garrison,' Natalie says, fumbling for a biro and a scrap of paper to write the number down with. 'Go ahead.'

After she's taken the number down, she says, 'I promise I'll get him to come and visit you, but don't send the police. He's back on his feet. He's okay.'

'I'll have to call them. I'll have to...'

'We'll visit this week, okay? Wait a few days at least?' she says hurriedly.

'Okay,' he agrees, finally.

'And Mr Garrison, don't tell him you've spoken to me. It needs to be his decision, okay?'

'Okay,' he says again. Then, 'What's your name, by the way?'

'Natalie.'

'Okay, Natalie. I'm Bob,' he says, before a long, drawn-out pause. 'I'll see you this week, then?'

For what seems like an age, Natalie sits silently in the uncomfortable wicker telephone seat, scribbled telephone number in hand, unsure what to do. She should tell Dan, be honest with him. That's what she'd expect if it were the other way around. But she also has a duty of care toward him. She has to do what's right for him, to give him the best chance of getting back on his feet. Picking up the telephone again, rather than her mobile, she makes a decision. She's going to call his doctor. She can't handle this on her own, not anymore. She needs to help Dan, and to do that, she needs outside help.

'I need to speak to Dr Alabi,' she says quickly, before her nerves get the better of her and make her slam the phone down. 'It's about one of his patients, Dan Garrison.'

* * *

After the telephone call, she busies herself with anything she can, trying to keep her mind off it. She messages Dan, asking him to pick some things up from the Co-op at the end of the road on his way home from work, like Dr Alabi suggested. Bumping into him in an informal setting would help him gauge how Dan was getting on, he'd said, so he would make sure he was there. Perhaps by bumping into him, he'd be able to convince him to drop by the clinic for a session.

Natalie doesn't know if she's done the right thing or not. It certainly doesn't feel like it. She feels like she's betrayed Dan, like she's thrown him to the wolves. But she's trying to help him, he'll have to see that, even if he doesn't realise it straight away. Somewhere deep inside the scars of her heart she knows she's going to lose him, that this decision is going to be the needle that unpicks their love, allowing it to unravel as quickly as it arrived. Yet she knows their love can't survive any other way. He should face reality. Somehow, she'll have to tell him the truth, that Joe isn't inside him.

And what of the darker truth, the one she won't even acknowledge to herself? Will she have to tell him that as well?

Does his mental health hinge on absolutely honesty? Where should the line be drawn? She shudders, grabbing her thin grey cardigan from the back of the kitchen chair and throwing it on, busying herself to prepare chicken in breadcrumbs for dinner. He likes that because his dad always cooked it. And she wants to do something nice for him, something to offset the betrayal.

She can barely contain herself when Dan replies to her text telling her he'll pick up the things for dinner. How will he react? Will he know she's the one who called Dr Alabi? How will he feel about it? Maybe he'll be happy. Maybe he knows he needs help and he'll thank her for it. When she finally hears the front door open, she holds her breath, steadying her nerves.

'You're home,' Natalie says, trying to sound nonchalant. 'Did you remember to get pudding?'

Silence. He's not even moving; she can't hear any footsteps.

Grabbing a tea towel to wipe her hands on, she walks into the hallway. He's standing behind the front door, leaning back against it and rubbing his hands against the grain, back and forth, back and forth.

'Hey,' Natalie says, trying to smile. 'What's up?'

'Hey,' Dan says, grinning unconvincingly and walking over to give her a hug. 'Nothing, love. Tough day, that's all.'

He's seen the doctor. She knows he has. She can tell by his demeanour.

'Want to talk about it?' she asks.

'No, no. It's fine. Work stuff, you know?' Dan says.

She stands still for a moment, holding eye contact for longer than he feels comfortable with. He's not going to open up to her. He's not going to tell her anything. Will Dr Alabi be able to tell her? Is it be bound by doctor-patient privilege?

'Come and chat with me while I finish dinner,' she says, turning her back on him, heart beating superfast, threatening to make her vomit.

'What are you cooking?' Dan asks, wandering in behind her

and sitting down at the kitchen table.

'Chicken in breadcrumbs,' Natalie says. 'You said you liked it the other day, so I thought I'd cook it for you.'

'I said my dad cooked it for me a lot,' he snaps, all south-London accent. 'I never said I liked it.'

Dan must be stressed out; he's bringing Joe out. Natalie turns back to him, trying to think of something calming to say when the doorbell rings.

Shit. Is it him? Has Dr Alabi decided to do a house call? Or Dan's dad? Shit, all the lies, all the half-truths, they're all going to come flooding out.

She has to make him understand she's doing it for him, that she wants to help him.

'Watch that while I go and see who this is, will you?' she says, nodding toward the pan on the stove.

'You're not even cooking it yet,' Dan replies. 'What's to watch?'

Natalie barely hears him as she walks down the hallway, which seems to stretch on and on like a horror movie corridor, elongating with every step. She can't remember the last time reality was...well, reality.

She stands behind the front door and braces herself, knowing that once one lie comes out, the rest must all follow. *So be it*, she thinks, pulling the door open.

'Natalie!' Joe's mother says shrilly. 'I've been trying to get hold of you for weeks. Have you been avoiding me?'

'Valerie,' Natalie says, expelling all the air from her lungs in one breathy word, as if her mother-in-law has physically punched her.

From behind, she hears a body collapsing. Spinning around, she sees Dan tumble to his knees, falling with a thud onto the hallway rug.

'Natalie, what on Earth is going on?' Valerie asks, pushing her way into the house and standing next to Natalie, staring at

Dan's prone body.

'It's a long story,' Natalie says quietly.

'Then you'd better start talking, hadn't you?' Valerie says.

CHAPTER 15

Natalie and Valerie stand still for a moment, each unsure of what to do, but for different reasons. Dan is moaning, pushing himself back to his feet, squinting in their direction.

'He wants to talk to her,' he mumbles.

Natalie rushes over to him and lets him lean on her, whispering 'quiet' in his ear as he does so.

'He?' Valerie asks, still not moving. 'Natalie, who is this? What's going on?'

'I'll explain, Val, I promise. Let me get him upstairs to lie down,' Natalie says, leading Dan to the bottom of the stairs.

'Joe wants to see her,' Dan says again as she manoeuvres him upstairs and into the spare room.

What does he think Valerie is going to do? Grab him with open arms, wailing in ecstasy that her dead son has been returned to her in a new body?

'I think he's gone into shock. I can't feel him,' Dan moans, and for a moment, he seems terrified at the prospect.

'Dan,' Natalie says sternly, grabbing him by both shoulders as they stand next to the made-up bed. 'Pull yourself together. You can't see Valerie.' She stares into his eyes, waiting for him to return her gaze. 'Do you understand?'

He nods quietly, sitting down on the side of the bed.

'I think Joe's unconscious. I can't feel him. Fuck, I can't feel him, Natalie.'

'Just get some sleep,' she says, trying not to snap. 'Let me get rid of her.'

Natalie edges back out of the room, conscious of Valerie standing in the hallway downstairs, filled with question after question about Dan.

'You okay?' she asks gently before she shuts the door.

He doesn't answer, but she can't wait around. She's got her

mother-in-law to deal with.

* * *

Back downstairs, Natalie does the only thing she can think of, grabbing Valerie and ushering her out of the front door again, saying, 'Let's get a coffee, shall we?'

Walking down the hill to one of her local cafés, Natalie shoves her hands in her pockets and smiles thinly at her mother-in-law, who is walking silently beside her. She's processing things, Natalie can tell. The silence is unnerving, so much so that it's almost a relief when a woman barges past them, arms laden with bags as she overtakes them and knocks into a *Big Issue* seller at the side of the pavement.

'*Big Issue*, madam?' the man asks.

The woman flinches slightly, taking a step back and treading on Natalie's foot as she does so. Without apologising or even acknowledging Natalie, the woman lifts her bags in the air towards the *Big Issue* seller.

'I've spent all my money,' she says.

Natalie and Valerie continue down the hill, ignoring an armada of bubbles floating down the street past them, part of a promotion to celebrate the re-opening of the café.

Natalie had only been in the café once or twice before it was refurbished. It had been nothing more than a greasy spoon really, but it had always been busy. Now it had been revamped, making it more modern. More *Brighton,* Natalie supposes. As Natalie and Valerie enter, she sees it is now filled with books, and where there had once been plastic chairs and grey tables, there are now wooden tables and beautiful padded seats. Each wall is lined with shelves and books, the lowest levels filled with children's titles, the higher ones with adult novels and literature. The entire café now breathes in a way it didn't before. Natalie stands in the doorway, stunned into silence for a moment, unintentionally barring Valerie from getting past her.

'Louise!'

The woman with the bags is also in the café, striding toward the woman behind the counter with purpose.

'You won't believe what Gavin's done now. He's cut my credit cards off...'

'Just a minute, Imogen,' the woman behind the counter says. She looks familiar, somehow, like Natalie has seen her somewhere before, but she can't quite place her.

'Louise, I'm in turmoil here...' the woman with the bags says dramatically.

'In a *minute,* Imogen,' the café owner hisses, turning back toward Natalie and Valerie, motioning them to sit down at one of the tables.

'Natalie, right?' the woman says gently, walking over to them. 'We met at the bereavement group.'

That's right, she'd been at the group. She lost her own husband last year.

'You went to that?' Valerie says, a mixture of surprise and... Well, Natalie could swear she sounds pleased.

'Look, I'll leave you to it,' Louise says kindly, touching Natalie lightly on the arm, then glancing at Valerie and smiling.

Natalie nods, feeling strangely comforted, like she isn't alone with Valerie anymore; she has someone in her corner, even if it is a near-stranger.

'What would you like to drink?' Louise asks. 'I'll bring it over.'

'I'll have a skinny latte please,' Natalie says, looking at Valerie to ascertain her order.

'Earl Grey please. Is it strong? I hate it weak,' Valerie says curtly.

Louise nods and walks back behind the counter, leaving Natalie and Valerie sitting quietly at the table in the window.

'I know things weren't perfect with you and Joe, Natalie,'

Valerie says, every syllable pronounced with the utmost delicacy and precision. 'But to move on so quickly?'

'It's complicated,' Natalie replies.

'I always knew you were flighty.'

Flighty? Natalie's heart beats a little faster. She wants to run out of the café, away from her mother-in-law and her incessant... mother-in-law-ness. Instead, she plasters on her best smile and reaches a hand over to Valerie.

'Please, Val, don't be like that.'

Natalie is struggling to remain confident, to remain in control. But she'll be damned if she'll give this woman any kind of emotion, she hasn't earned that. She'll never let her see a chink in her armour. Never. She knows what her son was like; she has to know. Maybe she even caused it. Natalie has no idea how much of what Joe said was true and what wasn't. Either way, this woman was nothing to her, an inconvenience at best.

'It's Valerie, not Val,' Joe's mother says sternly. 'And don't change the subject. He's not even cold in his grave yet.'

Natalie withdraws her hand and settles for tapping the tabletop lightly with her nails, not long, not short. Unpainted. Tap, tap. Tap, tap.

'Don't do that, Natalie. It's very annoying.'

Your voice is annoying, Natalie thinks but doesn't say.

They drift into silence again. Natalie knows she is going to have to talk to Valerie about Dan at some point, but she is happy to delay it as long as possible. How is she supposed to explain it, anyway? She isn't sure she understands it all herself.

'I never liked him much,' Valerie says eventually, picking up a packet of sweetener and shaking it before putting it back into the small white china bowl in the middle of the table.

'Who?' Natalie replies, slightly confused.

'Joe,' Valerie says. Natalie clearly can't hide the expression on her face because Valerie continues, 'Oh, I know he was my son. And I'm not saying I didn't love him. Of course I did. But he was such an objectionable child and I never took to him. Always wailing and crying about something or other. Always wanting his own way. And then, as an adult… Well, you know what he was like.'

Natalie nods, wondering again if his mum did know what he was like after all. Had she seen the full extent of her son's character?

'Earl Grey with a slice of lemon,' Louise says, appearing with perfect timing and putting a cup down in front of Valerie and smiling. 'And a latte, Natalie.'

'Thanks, Louise,' Natalie says, smiling and watching Louise walk back behind the counter.

She's been through all of this already, Natalie thinks. *The in-laws, the loss.*

'But now Joe's gone,' Valerie continues, jolting Natalie from her thoughts. 'Now I can't see him again, and I miss him. I've spent my entire life as a mother wondering why I couldn't take to him and now he's gone. I find myself lost.'

Valerie inhales deeply. Public displays of emotion aren't part of her repertoire, Natalie knows. Everything is about appearances, about respectability and façade. Until this moment, Natalie wondered if she ever felt anything at all. Even after Joe's death, it was as if she went into organisational mode, planning and sorting and arranging. As long as she was doing something, Natalie supposed she could keep the demons at bay. But nobody could do that forever. She's lost a son and seeing her façade drop for a moment, Natalie is overcome with emotion for her.

'Excuse me,' Valerie shouts over to Louise, who is leaning against the counter, half listening to Imogen and half listening in on Natalie's conversation.

'I did ask if the Earl Grey was strong when I ordered it,' Valerie continues.

'Sorry?' Louise says.

'It's very weak.'

'It should be quite strong.' Louise fumbles, standing upright.

'It's not,' Valerie says, standing up and walking over to her, putting the cup down in front of her heavily, sloshing it over onto the worktop.

'Maybe it needs a stir?' Louise continues valiantly and Natalie doesn't know whether to laugh or cringe.

'I've already stirred it,' Valerie says sternly. 'Put another teabag in it and I'll make do.'

Natalie sits back in her chair and squeezes her eyes shut, listening for a moment to the clattering cups and other conversations in the café. She listens to the people chatting about work or school entry requirements, not about dead sons and husbands.

'I didn't plan it,' Natalie says as Valerie sits back down in front of her, dipping her new teabag over and over again. She gives Natalie a steely gaze.

'Dan, I mean. I wasn't looking for someone; it just happened.'

'Nothing just happens,' Valerie says coldly. 'What will people think? They'll assume you didn't love Joe.'

'Like you, you mean?' Natalie says, unable to help herself.

A wave of darkness washes over Valerie's face, but is replaced almost immediately with a confident, statue-like expression.

'I'm sorry,' Natalie follows up immediately. 'I didn't mean that.'

'Yes, you did,' Valerie says, finally removing her teabag and placing it onto the saucer beside her cup.

'I can't help what people think,' Natalie says, before repeating: 'I didn't plan it.'

'What will I tell Joe's father?' Valerie says, lifting her cup and sipping her tea before grimacing, placing it back on its saucer and pushing it into the middle of the table.

'Tell him I've met someone,' Natalie says. 'Can't you be happy for me?'

'*Happy* for you?' Valerie says. 'I buried my son less than six months ago and his wife has already moved someone else into his home, into his bed. Who in the world is going to be *happy* for you? What was it? Couldn't you bear to take care of yourself, Natalie? Did you need another man to control you, to look after you like Joe did? Don't think I don't know how much you relied on him, how he had to make every decision for you. I don't know how he put up with it.'

'Valerie, please.' Natalie is doing everything in her power to remain calm, to ignore the blood surging in her veins, to stop herself from shouting that she doesn't give a fuck what Valerie thinks. Who the hell does she think she is, anyway? Coming here and spouting misinformation as if it's fact, as if her version of Natalie's marriage was anything like the reality? Instead, as calmly as she can manage, she continues, 'I fell in love, that's all. You should try it.'

Natalie is aware of the other people in the café listening to their conversation. Half of them are speaking in hushed tones so they can listen to what is said next.

'We don't all need to display our feelings quite as brazenly as you, Natalie,' Valerie continues. 'How do you think most of us get through the day? We control how we feel. We keep our emotions in order, in check. That's how life works. We don't all go around *feeling* everything we want to. Emotions have *consequences.*'

'So does *not* feeling,' Natalie butts in. 'I'm not like you.'

'Clearly,' Valerie finishes.

Silence.

They sit defiantly opposite one another, Valerie still refusing to sip her tea, while Natalie gulps her coffee, finishing it as quickly as she can.

'And he's moved in?'

'Yes.'

'I can't tell Harry. It would kill him. Knowing you thought so little of Joe that you could replace him so quickly. It would kill him, Natalie.'

'Poor choice of words, Valerie,' Natalie says quietly.

The clock on the wall ticks. Murmured conversations filter in and out from the other tables, and from Louise and Imogen at the counter.

'Do you know what he used to say about you, Valerie?' Natalie says, eventually.

'Who, Joe?' Valerie asks.

'He used to tell people you neglected him. That Harry was abusive toward him.'

'Harry? Oh, don't be ridiculous, Natalie.'

If someone had told Natalie something like that, she'd have been shocked. Horrified, even. But there's not a flicker of emotion on Valerie's face, not even a hint of surprise. She simply stirs her Earl Grey over and over, before picking it up and taking another sip, and placing it down so carefully that Natalie can barely hear the china chink against the saucer.

'When Joe was young, he was a very willful child. I spent most of my time telling him not to answer back. He always had an answer for everything, and I used to tell him nobody was interested, that nobody wanted to hear his opinion all the time. But would he listen?' Valerie sighs heavily. 'I know he was my son, but he was so hard to take to. I was always amazed that you fell in love with him.'

Natalie doesn't speak. She isn't sure what merit there would be in saying what she wants to say. What would be the point in telling Valerie that in her opinion, this sounded like terrible parenting. Constantly telling a child that his opinion isn't worthwhile, that nobody is interested in them. No wonder Joe grew up like he did. Except, Natalie doesn't buy that either. People aren't only a product of their upbringing, surely? Some people suffer terrible childhoods and grow up to be wonderful, caring people who bring goodness and light into the world. So what if Joe had neglectful, even verbally abusive parents? So what if his dad had been as aggressive as Joe made him out to be? That didn't mean he had to behave the way he did. He had a choice, surely?

'If that's how you feel, then why are you seeing a counsellor?' Natalie says eventually. 'If you disliked him that much, surely...'

'He was my son,' Valerie interrupts, and Natalie's voice dies in her throat.

They sit in silence for another minute, sipping their drinks.

'What's wrong with him?' Valerie asks.

'Who?' Natalie says, frowning.

'Your new *boyfriend*,' she spits out the word. 'He collapsed. Is he ill?'

Natalie is gripping her tall latte glass so firmly that she feels like the skin of her palm might just slip off her hand, leaving a bloody red stain in its wake.

'He's okay,' she lies. 'He banged his head before you arrived, that's all. He needed a lie down.'

Valerie nods slowly and Natalie can't tell if she believes her. Maybe she simply doesn't care.

'Where did you meet him?'

'Does it matter?'

'Yes, it matters,' Valerie barks. 'Were you *looking* for someone? Couldn't you bear to be alone for a moment?'

'Oh for fuck's sake, Val,' Natalie snaps, and her mother in-law is visibly taken aback. 'I wasn't looking. It just happened okay?' Natalie leans forward, looking directly into Valerie's face, measuring her words out carefully. 'You *knew* what Joe was like, didn't you?'

Valerie moves back in her seat slightly, averting her gaze from Natalie as she does so, not wanting to make eye contact.

'I have no idea how much of what Joe told me about you and Harry was true,' Natalie continues, liberated from protocol, from polite chatter. 'Probably not much, knowing him. But I don't believe you didn't know what Joe was like, not for a second.'

Valerie's silence and refusal to look at Natalie answers for her. Natalie doesn't move, doesn't lean back. She's not willing to let go of her aggressive stance yet.

'So, no, *Val*,' she says, emphasising the Val—not Valerie—to annoy her. 'I didn't go looking for someone else. After Joe, I didn't want anyone, not ever again. Your son was a monster.'

'He wasn't a...' Valerie starts, but seeing Natalie's red, fury-filled face seems to snap her jaws shut again.

'I'm glad he's dead, Val. I know he's your son. I know that hurts, but that's the truth. But I wasn't looking to replace him. It just happened.'

'Nothing just happens,' Valerie says quietly.

She has no fight left in her, Natalie can tell. Maybe it's all been knocked out of her. All she has left is pretence, an outward persona. But now, Natalie has roughly peeled it away, bloody chip by bloody chip, and the woman sitting opposite her is fresh and pulped and bleeding.

'I know what you think of me, Natalie,' Valerie says, looking down at the table and fingering her Earl Grey. 'That I'm cold, unfeeling.'

'I don't think that...' Natalie starts, feeling ashamed of her outburst.

'Yes, you do. And you're right. Maybe I am. And maybe I did look the other way.'

Both women exhale, the weight of all the previously unspoken words falling off their shoulders, brick by brick.

'But he was *my son*, Natalie. You don't understand what it feels like. I could see what he'd turned into, of course I could. But I couldn't admit it. What would it say about me if I did?'

Natalie isn't sure how she's feeling. Angry, yes, but relieved as well. For so long, the private Joe was just that: private. The real him was a version that he saved only for her. The external him was all smiles and charm. For a long time, Natalie had believed that it was all her fault. If everyone else liked him so much, maybe it *was* her. Maybe she made him act like he did, just like he said. Hearing his own mother acknowledge that it was something else, that Joe was who he was irrespective of Natalie felt like a release, a freedom she hadn't known she needed.

'Look, Valerie. I'm sorry, I shouldn't have said those things,' she says, reaching her hand across the table.

'Yes, you should have,' Valerie says, looking down at the hand being offered to her but not taking it. She breathes in deeply, resetting her shoulders, square and firm.

'I'm glad you went to the bereavement group.' She stands up, lowering her voice slightly. 'I'm not completely cold. I want you to have someone to talk to about it, but it's not me. I'm sorry, it can't be me.'

I never asked you, Natalie thinks, coming to her feet.

She's surprised to find that she wants nothing more than to grab Valerie and hug her, to hold her tight and tell her everything will be okay. Instead, she remains motionless, nodding her head and saying, 'I know.'

'Goodbye, Natalie.'

For the briefest moment, Valerie reaches out and squeezes Natalie's hand, pursing her lips in a sad smile. Then the mask is back, the shoulders straighten again and she hooks her bag over her shoulder.

'I'm off home to Harry,' she says, turning her back and walking to the café door. Just as she's about to leave, she turns back and says, 'Be happy, Natalie.'

With that, she's gone.

Natalie stands motionless, realising it's a final goodbye. Valerie won't be back. She doesn't want to know the things Natalie can tell her about Joe. Perhaps no mother needs to know those things.

* * *

Natalie sits back down at the café table, alone, thinking of Dan at home in bed or, more significantly, thinking of Joe rearing his ugly head, given how stressed Dan seemed when he got home after his 'run in' with Dr Alabi. She shuts her eyes. She can't think about Dan or what she's done. There is only so much she can take in one evening without having a breakdown of her own. Instead, she glances over to the café counter where Louise and her friend Imogen seem to be arguing.

'Louise, did you even hear me?' Imogen shouts at the counter behind Natalie, her clothes bags in a heap by her feet. 'Gavin's cut me off.'

Natalie turns around to see Louise raise her eyebrows and smirk, indicating all the bags and saying, 'You don't look very cut off, Imogen.'

'Thanks for your support,' Imogen says, grabbing the bags and strutting past Natalie and out the door. Louise smiles at Natalie, who surprises herself and smiles back.

'Another coffee?' Louise asks, walking over toward her.

'Yeah, why not?' Natalie says hesitantly.

* * *

Five minutes later and the other café patrons are filtering out, leaving Natalie alone with Louise.

'Mind if I join you?' she asks, putting Natalie's coffee down in front of her and holding her own steaming mug. 'I'm working late to avoid my kids,' she continues, candidly, sitting down next to Natalie rather than opposite her. 'I want to make sure they're asleep before I relieve the babysitter. That's an awful thing to say, isn't it? But it's true.'

Louise pauses, running her fingernail around the rim of her coffee cup before looking at Natalie. Louise's green eyes are tearing up a little, and Natalie can see that the pain is still present for her, as raw as the day her husband died.

'I treated my husband badly,' Louise says. 'I treated my kids badly. But I'm trying. I'm trying to be a good mum now. But some days, I just...' She pauses, nodding her head, as if Natalie knows exactly what she's trying to say.

Natalie doesn't speak. Louise is a widow, and she thinks they share a bond, a common loss. Natalie knows she means well, but she wishes that one person, just one, would tell her that it's okay to feel liberated and not devastated. This woman, grieving and trying to find a way to move on, isn't going to be that person. She's going to make Natalie feel worse—guiltier.

'It makes you see things a little more clearly, doesn't it?' Louise continues. 'Their death, I mean. I can't bring Adam back, but I can change. At least I can try to.'

'Don't be hard on yourself...' Natalie starts, mentally trying to find a way out of the conversation. Her mind is starting to scream a little, and it's as if her entire world is imploding and if she doesn't escape, she'll be trapped, screaming internally forever.

'I've spent my life making excuses.' Louise pauses again, lost in thought. 'No more. Take Imogen... She does my head in, but her husband is going off the rails and she hasn't got anyone, not really. You can see why...' She pauses, laughing a little. 'And she can be such a nightmare... The old me would tell to her fuck off, that I've got enough of my own shit to deal with. But underneath it all she's scared, you know? So I'm trying to be there for her, trying not to push her away even though every part of me wants to scream in her face.'

Trying not to push her away though every part of me wants to scream in her face. Natalie focuses on this. Does Louise know that this is how Natalie feels about her at this precise moment?

'We've all got friends like that, the ones the world revolves around,' Natalie says, forcing a fake laugh, trying her best to be a fellow widow, comparing war wounds. Then it hits her. She *hasn't* got friends like that. She hasn't got any friends at all. Joe had made sure of that, and she still hasn't rectified it.

'Yeah, I suppose so,' Louise says thoughtfully. 'What I'm trying to say is, find something positive to hold on to. Whatever you need to get through the day. I'm focusing on the kids, on being a better mother, a better friend. Whatever your thing is... find it. Cling to it.'

But Natalie doesn't have a thing. Except Dan, maybe. Perhaps he *is* her thing.

'Do you feel guilty?' Natalie asks Louise.

'For how I treated Adam?' Louise replies. 'Every day.'

'And how do you deal with that?' Natalie says.

'Day by day,' Louise says. 'And you?'

'I try not to think about it,' Natalie says, truthfully.

'You can't rewind, Natalie. But keep hold of the fact your husband loved you.'

'He said he'd never leave me,' Natalie replies, quietly.

Louise leans over and squeezes her hand, mistaking the comment for one of regret instead of fear and anger.

'You haven't got children, have you?' Louise asks, leaning back into her seat.

Natalie shakes her head.

'Not that that makes it any easier for you,' Louise adds quickly. 'But mine... They still blame me, I think. They miss him so much. He was their world. I'm trying to build a relationship with them, but it's hard. And his bloody parents barely give me a second's peace...'

'Oh, don't talk to me about in-laws,' Natalie laughs.

'Oh, thank God I'm not the only one,' Louise chuckles.

They sit in silence for a little while, Natalie glances around the café, at the wooden bookshelves and books on the walls, the warm amber lighting and comforting décor.

'How did Joe die? If you don't mind me asking,' Louise says eventually.

Natalie's heart stops beating.

Stops beating.

Stops beating.

'A car hit him.' She exhales, and it starts beating again, slowly, slowly. Then, a little faster. 'On Western Road. You probably read about it.'

* * *

By the time Natalie gets back home from Louise's café, it's late. Dan is still upstairs, fast asleep, she assumes. She can't bear the idea of checking on him, of having to have a conversation with him or Joe. Instead, she pours herself some sparkling water and sits down in front of the television, trying anything to quiet her mind, to stop it whirring and thinking and feeling. At some point, she doesn't know when, she goes upstairs to bed, avoiding the spare bedroom, not wanting to see him or be close to him. Not tonight. She needs some space; she needs the darkness to take her, to make reality go away, just for a little while.

* * *

The next morning, Natalie is up early. She showers and dresses and goes downstairs to the kitchen. Dan is still asleep and for a second she worries that something has happened to him, that he really did pass out after all and she just left him to sleep it off. What if something was wrong? She pours herself a glass of coconut water, mild panic rising again.

Is he okay up there?

Then she hears him. He doesn't speak; he's leaning in the kitchen doorway, wet hair combed back, fully dressed in Joe's clothes. Not smiling, no scowling, just staring at her. It's a little unsettling.

'Hey,' she says softly. 'How you feeling? You were asleep when I got back, I didn't want to wake you.'

Dan nods but doesn't say anything.

'You must be starving,' she says, waving her arm over to the chicken in breadcrumbs, still sitting raw on the side. 'I never even cooked.'

'How do you know I was asleep?' he asks quietly.

'I don't... What do you mean?' she stutters. Had he been awake when she came back? Did he know she didn't want to see him, that she needed some space? And so what if she did? She'll never have a relationship like that again, where needing some space is somehow an indictment of her love, her commitment. He isn't the only one who is having a hard time. Fuck him if he wants to make her feel guilty for wanting some space.

'You didn't come and check on me when you got back. I was awake, but you didn't come to see how I was. You watched telly.'

He walks over to the kettle and picks it up, shaking it to check if there's any water inside.

'Don't, Joe,' she says, aware of the accent. 'I thought you wanted some space.'

He's angry, he must be angry because he's letting Joe out, letting him do the talking. She hates this Joe as much as she hated her own, and she wants him gone.

'I can't imagine how hard that was for you,' Natalie says, addressing Dan's Joe directly and turning her back. She's glad she called Dr Alabi. She's glad Dan's dad called. He must sort himself out, once and for all. She wants Dan; she loves him. But she can't have Joe in her life. Not the ghost of her own dead husband and not Dan's version of him.

'Or for you,' Dan says.

She's relieved to hear his voice and not Joe's. She wants him to hold her, to tell her it's okay. She just wants a moment of comfort.

He walks over to her and crouches down next to her seat, putting his hand on her knee. 'Did it go okay?'

He's smiling sympathetically. This is the man she loves. Not his fucked-up alter ego.

'She was upset,' Natalie says, squeezing Dan's hand. 'Of course she was. She thinks I've shacked up with another man so soon after Joe's death. She thinks I've moved on.'

'For fuck's sake, Joe. Will you shut up?' Dan shouts, making Natalie jolt backward, letting go of his hand. For the first time since she met him, she's actually scared. More than scared, she's terrified.

'Oh, shit. Sorry, Nat. I didn't mean to say that out loud. It's just Joe won't shut up moaning and…'

Natalie sits in silence, breathing deeply and trying to calm herself as Dan begins busying himself making coffee, as if everything is ordinary and this is an average weekend morning in an average house and…

'Fuck this,' Dan says, spinning around and smiling unconvincingly. 'I'm starving. Let's go to the café and get breakfast, shall we?'

Natalie doesn't answer. She stares at Dan, her mind whirring. She has to take him to his dad; she has to move things forward. He hasn't even mentioned Dr Alabi in the supermarket last night; he's pretending it didn't happen. But it did happen. It *has* to happen. Things have got to change.

'Okay,' she says, as they silently pull on their jackets and leave the house, walking down the road toward Louise's café.

* * *

'I know the woman who runs this place,' Natalie says, pushing the door half open, not quite tinkling the bell.

'You said,' Dan replies, giving her a tiny smile. As they walk in, Natalie sees Imogen sitting at the café counter again, talking earnestly with Louise.

'And you're seriously considering it?' she says.

'I have to at least think about it…' Louise replies.

'No, you don't. Look at all the grief he caused you. I can't believe you're even...'

'It's complicated. You don't know the full story.'

'And besides, how are you ever going to meet someone new if you...' Imogen trails off as she hears the bell above the café door tinkle as Natalie pushes it open wider.

'Natalie, hi,' Louise says breathily, glancing at Imogen with a 'shut up now' face. 'Imogen, you remember Natalie, don't you? I met her at the bereavement group after Adam...' She trails off.

'Of course I remember Natalie,' Imogen says with an 'it was only last night' roll of her eyes.

'I'm Louise, by the way,' Louise holds her hand out to shake Dan's hand.

'Oh, hi.' Dan's awkward, fidgeting. 'I'm Dan.'

Natalie takes his arm, leading him away from the women.

'Latte?' Louise asks as they walk over to a table.

'Yes, please,' Natalie answers. 'And a black Americano.'

She and Dan sit at a table by the window, away from Louise and Imogen. For a while, Natalie doesn't speak and Dan seems lost in his own thoughts—or Joe's. Natalie kicks her trainers off and crosses her legs in her lap, trying to think of the best way to start the conversation.

'Did you ever get help?' Natalie asks.

Dan frowns at her, clearly unsure what she means.

'When you were homeless, I mean,' she continues.

'Help?'

'You were on the street for a few months, you said. Didn't you go back to your dad?'

'No,' he says frostily. 'I couldn't.'

'Okay, but what about hostels or the council? Weren't there people who could...' She wishes she hadn't started this conversation. She thought it would be a good route into talking about his dad, a way to suggest getting in contact, but the way he's reacting suggests it isn't going to be that easy.

'There are places that help, people that care,' he says, surprising her. He's looking over her shoulder, lost in his own thoughts. 'Hostels and project workers, people trained to help. But it's hard. A lot of people are on heroin or benzodiazepine, or they drink all the time, anything to numb the pain and take them away from themselves.'

'You found another way,' Natalie says quietly.

He wasn't a substance abuser. He barely even drank. But maybe he'd found another way to cope; maybe his mental illness was a manifestation of his need to shut down his thoughts and feelings. Maybe that's where Joe had come from.

'What do you mean?' Dan sounds anxious, which is something she doesn't want.

'Nothing... Nothing. Sorry. Go on.'

'So, why didn't you get help? If there were people willing to do something, if—'

'It's not that easy, Natalie,' he says, sounding irritated with her, bordering on angry. She doesn't want Joe to come out. She doesn't want a conversation with him. She wants to hear Dan's thoughts and feelings, not those of his alter ego.

'It's hard to accept help when you hate yourself, when you're ashamed of what you've become. You start to think you'll die in a doorway or in a car park or on a park bench. And you're okay with that; you just accept it. Life is so tough some days that you even hope for it. You think to yourself, maybe I won't wake up, and that'll be a good thing. Nobody will miss me.'

* * *

He's still talking in his own voice, calming down, managing his emotions. He does this more and more nowadays. Natalie wants to speak, wants to ask more, but she also doesn't want to push it too far, so she opts to remain silent, pursing her lips and nodding.

'There was one guy who kept coming out at night, delivering soup and food, that type of thing. He was with one of the charities, I think. Red Cross or something, I don't know. He used to try and talk to me, try and get me to get shelter. But I made it so hard for him, I was so wary of everyone. I was scared to be around people.'

He stops speaking for a moment, a distant look coming over him. In the background, Natalie can hear Louise and Imogen chatting quietly to one another, and other café patrons having their own conversations about life.

'I was experiencing some weird things, mentally,' he says at last.

'Weirder than Joe?' she says, before she can stop herself.

Luckily, he laughs.

'Yes, weirder than Joe. Like, sometimes, I thought I was leaving my body and going inside other people. I know it sounds crazy.'

'No crazier than being possessed by my dead husband,' Natalie says.

Neither of them smile this time, as the reality of their situation comes into focus. *Shit*, she thinks. *I'm going to have to bite the bullet and come out with it. No point dancing around the edges, go for the jugular.*

'You have to visit your father,' she says. 'He probably thinks you're missing.'

'Are you serious?' Joe says, back in control of Dan with a vengeance. 'You've stopped me from speaking to my mum and you want him to patch it up with daddy?'

'Dan?' Natalie says, reaching over and grabbing his hand. 'I'm talking to you, not Joe. If you're going to move forward, you have to patch things up with your dad.'

Her heart beats furiously in her chest. She's never done this before, directly addressed Dan when Joe is talking. She's never told him to shut up, that she wants Dan, not him. But she has to get through to him, has to try.

'I don't think I can, Natalie,' Dan says, his soft voice back. 'And it wouldn't be fair on Joe, either. We stopped him talking to his mum. Do you know how that felt? He's gutted.'

'He'll be fine, Dan,' Natalie says, moving her arm away. 'It's you I'm worried about.'

'Don't say that...'

'You need to get your shit together,' Natalie snaps. 'You've got a job and that's great. But it's time you started sorting yourself out. You can't keep running from him. He'll be worried about you.'

'What would you know?' Joe spits, a sneer crossing Dan's face.

'I'm talking to Dan,' Natalie says again, firmly, her heart pounding, pounding, pounding. She glances over her shoulder at Louise and Imogen, feeling strangely bolstered by their presence, even though she barely knows them. 'I'm sorry about your mum, Joe. I am. But you know why you can't see her. Deep down, you know.'

He doesn't respond.

'Dan,' she continues. 'You've got to move forward. You've done the running away thing; you've done the hiding out on the streets thing. Now you've got to stand up and face things. Nobody else is going to fix your life for you. Not me, and not Joe.'

'I don't need...'

'Yes, you do!' she shouts, anger rising. She's doing it now. It's happening. There's no going back. 'If we're going to make this work, you can't keep running, you've got to meet things head on.'

'Make this work?' Dan says quietly.

'Yes, maybe. But I've got to know I can trust you. I've got to know you mean it when you say you're going to sort yourself out.'

'Yes, yes, okay. We can make this work,' Dan says desperately, like he realises that he might lose her if he doesn't. 'I know we can.'

'And your dad?' Natalie presses.

'Okay.' Dan nods and squeezes his eyes shut. Natalie sighs in relief, unfolding her legs and slipping them back into her trainers on the floor. She knows how hard this is for Dan and part of her feels guilty, for pushing him into seeing his father, for arranging for Dr Alabi to 'bump into' him. But until now she's been doing the wrong thing by him; she's been selfish. But she loves him. And it's a painful, bigger love than anything she's felt before, gnawing away at everything she thought she knew or wanted. She has to help him, even if he hates her for it.

The noise from the café is background, comforting somehow. Things are going to be okay, one way or another. She's going to make sure of it. As she stares across at Dan, nervously sipping his coffee, all jitters and mannerisms, she is struck by a strange sense of calm and contentment. She's in control of this and she's going to fix him. In the process, she might even fix herself.

CHAPTER 16

As they walk down the road toward Dan's dad's house, Natalie feels more positive than she has done in years. He opened up to her in the café, talked about his parents and his gran, his mental health problems. She feels like they're making progress, like there's a light at the end of the tunnel for them.

His memories have made her think about her own parents. After Joe died, Natalie didn't know where to begin repairing things with them. So, instead, she retreated into herself, painting on a smiling phone voice whenever they phoned her. If they'd seen the smile, they'd have known it was fake. They'd have seen it quivering when she held it that little bit too long.

'Typical man,' her mother said once, when Joe was still alive.

In a rare moment of clarity, Natalie had realised how isolated she was becoming. She'd known she needed her mum's help. But it had come out all wrong, like Joe was just a bit blokey instead of worryingly controlling.

'They all hide their feelings,' her mum had continued. 'Your father's the same. It's their way, love.'

'He's nothing like dad,' Natalie had said curtly, pressing the warm mobile phone harder into her ear as she stared out of her kitchen window.

'What have I done wrong, Natalie?' her mum had implored on one call, as their phone contact grew less and less frequent.

'Nothing, Mum. Things are manic here. I've got a promotion, I'm Finance Director now. It's full-on. And Joe...' She'd trailed off. What could she say about Joe, especially as he was standing over her shoulder, his eyes boring into her skull?

'Joe what?' he'd whispered in her ear.

'Nothing, It's nothing, Mum. Look, I've got to go,' she'd said, hanging up quickly and turning back to Joe, trying on her best smile and putting her arms around his waist.

'It's always the same, isn't it?' he'd said darkly.

'What?' Natalie had fumbled. 'I...'

'She's always trying to drive a wedge between us, isn't she? Always sticking the knife in. I've told you, I don't like you talking to her.'

'She's my mum, Joe...' Natalie had said desperately, watching him walk away down the hallway and into the kitchen.

'And I'm your husband, Nat,' he'd said, simply.

After his death, Natalie realised something awful. Her relationship with her parents was forever changed. Like an invisible wall had been built, one she'd constructed under Joe's instruction. After his death, when she'd needed them most, when she'd wanted them to clamber over the wall and hug her, they couldn't. They were too old, too exhausted and bewildered for the climb.

The guilt was enormous. She'd dumped her parents, the two people who loved her most in the world, who'd always put her first, no matter what. She'd chosen Joe over them. She couldn't reconcile the woman she'd become to the woman they'd brought up. It was like he'd scooped out her insides and attached her entrails to marionette batons, making a puppet of her. In the end, she existed only to appease him, to make him feel better. Because if he felt okay, then he didn't undermine her or make her feel bad.

Is she making the same mistakes again?

Here she is, marching Dan to reconcile with his father, hoping it will mend him, make him whole again so they might have a chance together. Yet, she can't even fix her relationship with her own parents. Not only that, she can't talk to the man she loves about it because she's terrified of overwhelming him. He has enough problems of his own without her heaping more on top of them. But maybe if she can help Dan turn things around with his dad, she'll be brave enough to do the same with her own parents. Redemption is waving in the distance, out of reach. She wants to reach it. She wants to grab it and squeeze it tight and never let it go.

* * *

Dan's dad lives on a street on the other side of Brighton, up the long hill from The Level, in one of the narrow streets with barely any space to drive down, where cars park either side leaving no space to drive. It's not what Natalie expected. She thought he'd live somewhere out in Hove, or even farther into the suburbs. This is where the students live, or the young professionals in their first homes after university. She doesn't expect people's dads to live here, for some reason. As they arrive at the front door, Natalie smiles, unconvincingly she's sure, and squeezes Dan's arm.

'You okay?' she asks, already knowing the answer. He's rubbing his fingers together furiously, brow furrowed.

'I don't think I can do this,' he says, taking a step backward.

'Of course you can. If you want to move forward, you have to,' Natalie says firmly. 'You'll be fine, Dan. I'm right here with you. You're not alone.'

He nods, pressing the doorbell.

It's a while before the door opens, before Natalie sees an older version of Dan in jeans and a grey T-shirt standing in the doorway, looking so overcome with emotion she thinks he might cry.

'Danny!' the man says, stepping forward and pulling Dan into a strong embrace. 'Oh my God. Where have you been, Danny?'

'Don't call me that,' Dan snaps. He's stressed, which is always a danger point. Natalie doesn't want Joe to take over and start speaking. She didn't mention Dan's alter ego to his dad; she hadn't wanted to worry him.

'Dan,' Natalie starts, her fingers reaching out to find his hand again, to try and steady him.

'Please, Daniel,' his father says, stepping back slightly and dropping his arms back by his sides. 'Let's not fight.'

'I...I need my things, Dad. My P45, some of my clothes. I'm trying to sort myself out, trying to...' He trails off, looking at the floor.

'But where have you been, Daniel?' his father implores him. 'You've been gone for months. I've been *worried.*'

'I'm sorry, Dad,' he says, quietly. 'I didn't think. I didn't...'

'I'm Natalie, by the way,' Natalie interrupts, stepping forward and taking Dan's dad by the hand, giving him a look that she hopes says, 'I haven't told him I spoke to you.'

'And I'm dying for a wee,' she continues, squeezing his hand tightly. Dan's dad smiles at that, a broad grin. It's charming, just like his son's.

'First on the right,' he says, nodding toward the stairs as they all step inside.

'Thanks,' Natalie says, slipping off her trainers and heading upstairs to the toilet. She wasn't desperate for a wee at all, but has one anyway. She stares at herself in the bathroom mirror as she washes her hands, trying to convince herself she's doing the right thing. When she walks back downstairs, she hears Dan and his dad talking in the kitchen.

'You're a *missing person,* Daniel.'

'Fuck,' Dan says, like he's shocked, like it hadn't occurred to him.

'What the fuck did you think, Daniel? That I'd forget about you and move on? You're my *son.*'

Natalie walks into the kitchen, smiling reassuringly at Dan and saying: 'He's been dealing with some things, Mr Garrison. I'm sure he didn't mean to...'

'I *know* my own son,' Dan's father snaps. 'I'm aware how self-absorbed he can be.'

'Jesus, Dad. Come on...'

'I lost my mother, Daniel. Then I lost my son. You disappeared.'

'I didn't think...' Dan says. 'I'm sorry. I'm an arsehole, I'm...'

'Don't, Daniel.' His father rounds on him angrily, walking toward him, finger in the air, pointing. 'Don't do the self-pity thing. I'm not going to make you feel better, not this time. You *are* an arsehole, is that what you want to hear? You're selfish. You're a prick. All of those things. But you're my *son*, Daniel,' his father's tone softens again. 'None of it matters. I'm glad you're safe.'

Natalie feels like a spare part as Dan and his father embrace again, holding each other tightly.

'I'm glad you're home,' Dan's dad says.

'I'm not home, Dad,' Dan says softly. 'I can't come home, but it's not you. I need to sort myself out, okay? I can't rely on you.'

'Whatever you do, I'll have to ring the police in a minute,' his dad says, glancing at Natalie and nodding almost imperceptibly. She knew this was coming; knew he'd have to do it. His dad, the police, Dr Alabi, it all had to happen. It's better to get it all over with quickly, to rip the plaster off. Then they'll be able to start moving forward. Building a life together with Dan getting the help he needs.

'Tell them you're not missing...' Dan's dad continues. 'They'll probably want a statement.'

* * *

Dan and his dad, Bob, sit awkwardly next to each other on the living room sofa, and Natalie sits on the two-seater at a right angle to them. His dad doesn't ask much, doesn't push him for answers. Natalie likes him for this. He's a gentle, loving man; she can tell. That's probably where Dan gets it from.

'The police said they'll send someone here,' Bob says.

Dan shifts uncomfortably in his seat, chewing on his fingers but not replying.

'I don't know what the normal protocol is in situations like this,' Bob continues. 'I explained that you've been living rough, that you're home now…'

'I'm not home, Dad,' Dan says again. 'I've told you.'

Bob nods, closing his eyes. Natalie can see he hasn't quite absorbed this yet. He's still thinking he can talk Dan—or Natalie—around.

'Are you still taking your meds?' he asks quietly.

Dan looks away from him, staring intently at the carpet.

'He's not,' Natalie answers decisively.

'Natalie, don't…' Dan starts, but as he makes eye contact with her, he stops speaking. Perhaps he sees something in her eyes; perhaps he realises she's trying to help him.

'He's not been taking anything since he moved in with me, at least. And that was going on three months ago,' she continues.

'For Christ's sake, Dan,' Bob says. 'You know…'

'Dad, I'm fine,' Dan snaps. 'I'm dealing with things, okay?'

Bob is about to answer when the front doorbell rings, taking the wind out of both father and son. Natalie tucks her leg under her uncomfortably, wondering for a moment if she should be the one to go and answer the door.

'You ready?' Bob asks, standing up.

Dan nods quietly as his father walks slowly out of the living room. Natalie goes over to Dan, sitting down beside him and squeezing his hand, kissing him on the lips.

'Be strong, Dan. I'll be right here if you need me.'

'I love you,' he says, staring directly into her eyes.

She wants to grab him and run, to drag him out of the house and protect him, to stop him from having to go through the police questioning and the stress of getting things back in balance. But she knows he has to do it. Somehow, she can see he's getting better, that he's battling his demons. Joe rears his head less and less frequently now. Sometimes, he goes for days or even a week at a time without appearing at all.

When Bob shows the police to the living room, Natalie takes

the opportunity to get Dan's dad on his own.

'Why don't you come in the other room with me, Mr Garrison? Let the police finish up with Dan,' Natalie says, touching Bob's arm gently. 'Come on, I'll make more tea.'

'It's Bob, call me Bob,' he says as she leads him out. She shuts the living room door after them, giving Dan a reassuring smile on the way out.

* * *

'Thank you for bringing him,' Bob says as he puts the kettle on. 'Tea?'

'Yeah, why not?' she says. 'Black, please.'

'Like Dan,' Bob says.

'Yeah,' she replies. They lapse into silence for a while, before she asks, 'What you said about his meds…'

She isn't sure how to broach the subject, how to tell his dad what Dan's been going through.

'He's not taking anything. I'm worried he's…' She trails off. She's so complicit in this, she's been lying to Dan all this time, letting him believe he's possessed by someone else's spirit. How can she tell Bob that?

'Depersonalisation disorder, they call it,' Bob says, his back to her, his voice flat. 'I could never get my head around it, really. He says it's like he's not connected to his own body, like when he looks in the mirror, he thinks he's someone else.'

'I don't think…'

'And bulimia,' Bob continues. 'Self-harming is quite common with this condition, apparently. So, I suppose I should be grateful he's never cut himself… Not to my knowledge anyway.'

'It's more than that…' Natalie stammers, her mind racing.

Dan doesn't have any scars on his body; she doesn't think he's ever self-harmed. Although bulimia is a form of self-harm, she supposes.

'Is he making himself sick again?' Bob asks, turning around and staring at her desperately, wanting to hear good news, wanting to know his son is okay.

'No,' Natalie says. 'At least, I don't think so. I'm pretty sure he isn't...'

But the truth is, she isn't sure of anything. Perhaps he nips off and makes himself sick after meals. Maybe he has a stash of binge food hidden away. She doesn't know. It's dawning on her how little she *does* know.

'When did you first know about the...' She pauses. 'What did you call it?'

'Depersonalisation disorder,' Bob answers, walking over to the shelves to pick up a photo album. 'When he was a teenager. Took us a while to get a diagnosis, mind. He didn't cope with his gran going into a home very well. He took her loss badly. I think that's what kicked it off... But when I think about it, he was always... I don't know. Sensitive, I suppose.'

Natalie nods, but doesn't answer, trying to work out how to tell him that things have changed. Progressed, even. How can she tell him he now thinks he's possessed by someone else?

'It took a while, therapy, medication. But he got there, you know. He got back on track. Then Mum died...'

'Mum?' Natalie asks.

'My mum, his gran,' Bob says.

'What happened?'

'He disappeared. Left his girlfriend, left his job. His friend Stuart told me Dan stayed with him for a few nights and then left there to come home to me. Then, nothing... He vanished.'

'I'm so sorry,' Natalie says, shame burning through every pore of her skin. She's sure her face must be beetroot, a beacon of guilt, guiding Bob to the truth inside her. 'I should have made him come sooner. I should have...'

'No,' Bob says. 'It's not your fault. You couldn't have known.'

'He was homeless,' Natalie says, reaching out and touching

Bob's arm. 'When I met him, I mean. And I didn't think. I should have questioned him about his family, about...'

She drops her arm and looks away from him, staring at the fish tank at the back of the room. Bob sits down, putting the photo album he picked from the shelf on the table in front of him.

'You're here now,' he says quietly. 'He's here now.'

They're silent again. Natalie picks up her mug of tea from the corner of the table as Bob opens the album in front of him, a small smile crossing his lips. She feels a little like she's intruding on his memories, so she turns her back.

'I like your fish,' she says, walking over to the tank and putting a single fingertip against the glass, trying to entice one of the black moor goldfish over to inspect it. The glass is clean and well kept, not like when she'd had fish at eleven years old and couldn't be bothered to clean the tank. The weeds sway as the pump exhales a beautiful stream of bubbles. Outside, a seagull stands on a ledge, pecking at the glass. It can see the fish in the tank and it's trying to work out a way to get to them.

'Come and sit with me,' Bob says.

Natalie refocuses on him, taking a deep breath.

All of this, the whole mess...she's dealing with it. She's dealing with Joe, with Dan and his mental health. Not perfectly, she's sure, but she's dealing with it; she's getting through it. Maybe that's all anyone is doing, getting through life in whatever way they can, dealing with the shit that's thrown at them. Perhaps she is her parents' strong, independent daughter after all. She lost her way for a while. Joe took her off her path, playing wolf to her Little Red Riding Hood. But that's okay. People lose their way all the time, it's part of living. As long as you find your way back... Because that's the key, she now understands: realising you're lost and navigating back to the right track, no matter how difficult it seems. That's what she's helping Dan to do, even if he doesn't realise it. And, really, he's doing most of the work.

He got his old job back by himself, with no help from her. He stayed with her; he didn't go running back to the streets, hiding out there in plain sight. And he's here now, talking to the police, repairing his relationship with his father. He's doing all these things by himself; she's not doing it for him.

Like an electric shock from a faulty wire, the knowledge burns through her: she isn't fixing him, and he isn't fixing her. They're fixing each other, supporting each other. That concept is so alien to her, so removed from her marriage to Joe, she hasn't been able to recognise it until this moment. Yet it's the truth, and it's glorious.

Grinning madly, she sits down next to Bob, glancing at the open photo album in front of him. Inside, there's an old photo. It looks from the clothes to be from the 1970s. A woman with long red hair blowing in the breeze is standing on Brighton beachfront. West Pier, already derelict—but not collapsed and burned out like it is now—is perched in the sea behind her.

'That's Dan's mum,' Bob says quietly.

'She's beautiful,' Natalie says, pursing her lips together as she glances at Bob.

It still hurts him; she can see it. All these years later and he still loves her, still misses her.

'The most beautiful woman in the world,' he says. 'I met her while I was still at school. I remember our first date like it was yesterday. We'd arranged to meet at the train station. It was boiling hot, and I was overdressed, wearing these skin-tight beige bell-bottom jeans and a thick denim shirt.'

Bob pauses, lost in the memory. But Natalie realises that she's heard this story before. It's the story Dan told her when he described her first date with Joe. The stories Dan's been telling her, the memories he's been spinning of her life with Joe, they're real. They aren't an invention. They're his father's stories about meeting his mother. He's been creating a history from his own family's history, from his own loss.

'Boiling hot, it was,' Bob repeats. 'I was worried she wasn't going to turn up, but of course she did. Late. She was always late, that one.'

He stops speaking, stroking the photo in front of him sadly.

'She'd have been so proud of him. It's not been easy; he's not like other boys. Other men,' he says, correcting himself. 'Silly, I still think he's too young to look after himself, to cope. He's had so many problems. I can't let him go, I suppose.'

'I'll look after him,' Natalie says quietly. 'I promise.'

He stares at her intently for what seems like minutes.

'I know you will, Natalie. I'm glad he's found you.'

'They're beautiful stories,' Natalie says, as Bob looks back at his wife's picture, leaning back in her chair. 'I'm glad they're real.'

'Real?' Bob says, frowning. Natalie doesn't reply for a moment. Then, as she's about to tell Bob everything about Joe, about the stories, Dan opens the door.

'They're gone,' he says.

'Your dad was showing me some pictures of your mum. She's beautiful,' Natalie bursts out, feeling guilty somehow, like she and Bob were talking about things they shouldn't have been. Old habits. Dan isn't Joe. She could tell him. She could tell him anything and everything and they'd work it out.

'And some of you as a baby. Couldn't help myself,' Bob says, smiling and indicating a chubby baby picture on the next page of the album.

'You were a *weird*-looking baby,' Natalie exclaims.

'Yeah, he was an ugly thing wasn't he?' Bob grins, joining in with the teasing. 'But look how cute he got...' Bob pauses, flicking through the album before jabbing his finger toward a picture. 'There. Look at him at four. Cutest little boy that ever lived.'

'Oh, my God. You were *adorable*,' Natalie says, beckoning Dan over.

'Oh, you wait until you see him on his fifth birthday. Do you remember, Danny, you found the poster paints before me and gran woke up? You were covered head to foot in blue paint, so was the carpet...'

'Oh, God. Yeah, I remember. You were livid. I thought that vein in your forehead was going to burst. Even grandma lost her temper and shouted at me...'

* * *

It's gone five when they finally leave Dan's dad's house.

'Thanks for bringing him back to me,' Bob says as they leave. Tears well up in Natalie's eyes, so much so that she turns away so he doesn't see them.

'I didn't bring him, Mr Garrison. He wanted to come.'

As they walk down the street together, Natalie feels another wave of contentment washing over her. Things are going to be okay, she knows they are.

'Don't you miss me at all, Nat?' Dan shouts in his Joe voice, all cockney geezer, anger and resentment and bitterness.

'Hi, Joe,' she says, wearily. Then, feeling angry, wanting to keep this moment with Dan pure, she snaps back, 'Do you remember our first argument, Joe? You keep telling me about all of our good times, but what about our first row? It wasn't all good, you and me. Don't you remember? Nothing is.'

'We never had any proper arguments, though, did we Nat? Just silly stuff.' Dan's Joe voice fumbles and stutters. He tries to smile and fails, linking arms with her as they carry on walking. He doesn't want to hear anything bad, she realises. He won't hear anything that will burst the bubble she's helped him create.

'That's not how I remember it, Joe,' Natalie says quietly.

'Well, how do you remember it?' he asks, almost sneering.

'Not here,' she says, realising what she must do. He's not getting better on his own. He'll never get better on his own. 'Wait till we get home, eh?' she blinks back tears. 'Then we'll talk. But Dan...everything is going to be okay. You believe that, right?'

* * *

When they finally get back home, Dan runs straight upstairs to go to the toilet.

'Cold air,' he says. 'Always makes me want to wee.' He pauses on the stairs, staring down at her. 'Is that a bloke thing or does it make girls want to wee too?'

'Yeah, us too,' she says.

Then, as he disappears upstairs, she sits by the telephone table and dials Bob.

'I lied earlier. He's not well,' she says quietly. 'You need to come. You need to bring his doctor.'

After, she sits cradling the telephone in her lap, crying. As the toilet flushes and the sink runs upstairs, she pushes herself to her feet and wipes her eyes. When he comes back down, he seems filled with a new optimism.

'It feels like things are coming together, though,' he says, coming over and cuddling her, holding her tight. 'I've got a job, my dad's okay. I've got you.'

He squeezes her tightly and kisses her. She wishes things could be like this always, her and Dan, an ordinary couple in love. And maybe they can be, if she pushes through this, if she makes this happen.

'You're right,' she says. 'It's going to work out. And I'll always be here, I promise.'

He releases her from their embrace and holds her at arm's length, looking into her eyes.

'You're being weird, Natalie,' Dan says. 'You all right?'

'Yeah, of course I am,' she says. She's used to lying to her partner. It's a skill she had to learn early with Joe or she'd never have survived. But she doesn't want things to be like that with

Dan, she wants honesty and openness. Except everything they are is based on a lie. She let him into her home, believing that he was possessed by her dead husband. She let him carry on believing that, rather than seeking help. When he finds out, she's not sure he'll ever forgive her. Because he's never lied to her, not really. Despite his mental health, he's never been anything but honest. He's not a liar, but she is. She needs to tell him the truth before the shit hits the fan.

She turns away and kicks her shoes off, walking into the kitchen. She loiters in the doorway for a moment before turning around, chewing on her finger.

'Dan? Everything is going to be okay,' she says, trying to convince herself more than him. 'But there are some things you need to know. I haven't been honest with you, not from the start.'

'What do you mean?' he asks, following her into the kitchen, a worried frown on his face.

A chill runs through her, solidifying as it travels down her body, making her feel like a statue, something not quite living. Her body feels so tight around her that her breathing is constricted as she tries to form the words. *Best start with the biggest lie, the thing that kicked everything off*, she thinks.

'I killed him, Dan,' she says, clutching the kitchen side, a wave of nausea coming over her so strongly that she thinks she might throw up. 'You think it was your fault, but it wasn't. I did it. I killed Joe.'

* * *

Her kitchen seems colder than before, greyer, like the colour is draining from the cabinets and walls, wet paint in the rain. Natalie leans back against the work surface as Dan stands in the doorway, frowning.

'What are you talking about?' he says quietly.

At least it's still Dan speaking, Natalie thinks. *At least Joe isn't taking over. Yet.*

She draws a deep breath, holding it for a moment before speaking.

'I lied to you, Dan. About everything.'

'No. No, you didn't,' Dan says, desperation making his voice waver.

'I did, Dan,' she nods her head. 'And deep down, you know it. You do.'

'Natalie, don't do this, don't spoil...' he starts.

'You saw it, Dan. You saw everything,' Natalie says, and Dan buckles slightly at this, steadying himself against the side.

'Joe isn't the man you think he is.' Natalie pauses, considering walking toward him, taking him in her arms, offering support. But she can't do that. She's the last person alive who can do that now.

'I don't know what you're talking about,' Dan starts. 'You didn't...'

'All the stories you told, about how Joe and I met, our holidays, our life together. I started to enjoy it, to like how you were rewriting my past, erasing the old one, the real one I wanted to forget...'

'Stop this!' Dan shouts, his Joe voice back, full-on cockney geezer.

'For fuck's sake, Dan. Joe wasn't even from London!' Natalie shouts, the emotions she's been trying to supress flooding out of her in full force. 'He was born in Brighton. His parents are from Brighton. That weird cockney accent you use for him isn't real. None if it is real.'

'Please, stop this,' Dan says quietly.

Natalie wants to cry, wants to scream. She's already broken him and he doesn't even know the half of it yet.

'Please listen, Dan. You have to understand, I didn't mean for any of this to happen. I didn't want it to go this far but...'

'You told me it was true,' Dan says.

'I know, and I can explain, I can...'

'Why would you do that?' He's angry now, and it's the first time she's seen Dan get angry. Until now, he's always flipped into Joe mode when he's lost his temper, but this time he's tempering it; he's got control back.

'It's a long story. Please. Let me explain,' Natalie says, holding her hands out, palms upward, staring at his hurt face. She'd do anything to take the pain away from him, the pain she's causing him. But in order to get better he has to face some things. So does she.

'Joe, the real Joe, was nothing like yours. Yours is gentle really, even when he's angry. He's interested and loving and kind. Because he's you, Dan. Do you understand? He's you.'

'You need to stop talking now,' Dan says, looking at the floor. He moves his hands up to cover his ears for a second, then starts pacing. 'You need to stop.'

'My Joe was abusive. Controlling. He was nothing like you, Dan. I never loved him like I love you. Please believe me.'

'Love me? It's all a lie? Everything we are is based on lies,' Dan says. He's pacing now and he won't stop, won't stop staring at the floor.

'You *killed* me?' he snaps, Joe voice at full throttle, making angry eye contact.

'I didn't plan it. I didn't. You've got to believe me. If I'd have thought about it, I'd have been too scared to do it. But the opportunity was there. I heard the car skidding, avoiding you as you staggered into the street. I saw it coming toward us and Joe had grabbed me. He was hurting me, so I pushed him off me as hard as I could. But he fell into the road and the car hit him. God, it hit him so hard...' Natalie pauses, squeezing her eyes shut. 'I still see his face at night when I close my eyes.'

Silence.

All she can hear is her own breathing. The kitchen, Dan, everything in greyscale, a world on pause, poised for something, an action that might never come. She closes her eyes again, her mind's eye taking her back to that day, walking along Western Road with Joe.

* * *

'I know you think she wants to be your friend,' Joe said, glancing across the street, not paying much attention to Natalie. Crossing by Waitrose, Natalie tried to zone out as Joe tried to tell her that she was too sensitive, that he was sure her new friend hadn't meant anything by it. Except... Well, maybe he was reading too much into it. Of course she hadn't meant it. Except... Maybe it would be a good thing if Natalie saw less of her, just to be safe. Did she really need a new friend anyway?

Natalie had been simmering, bubbling away, listening to the sound of the traffic, to the busking babushka outside the Mad Hatter who'd caught her eye. For a moment, Natalie had been mesmerised by her, with her brightly coloured headscarf, flowing dress and fabric blowing in the wind. Her strange, high-pitched voice was both beautiful and unsettling. Natalie dug into her shoulder bag and grabbed a couple of pound coins, throwing them into the babushka's hat, catching her eye for a moment. The busker winked and smiled, without stopping her song.

'We've got a rainbow,' the busker sang, reaching a loud crescendo.

'Natalie, are you listening to me?' Joe said, grabbing her by the arm, drawing her attention back to him. His fingers were digging into her flesh a little and as she looked at his face, a wave of intense hatred welled up inside her. She wanted him off her, away from her. She pulled her arm free, shoving him as hard as she could.

'Get off me!' she shouted.

She heard the screeching of brakes.

Across the road, a homeless man had darted into the road,

and a car had to swerve to avoid him, coming over onto their side of the road as it did so. In turn, the cars on their side of the road also had to swerve, and as she shoved Joe, he overbalanced into the road. Before she knew what was happening, she heard the thud, the smash of metal and plastic against flesh and bone. Then came the smell, the awful smell of burning rubber, the screaming and shouting. Then came the silence. Running into the road, cradling his head in her lap, she cried for help. But it was too late. She'd killed him.

She doesn't remember much from the moments directly after the accident. At some point, she remembers someone staggering toward her, a homeless man. As she looked up at him, he stopped moving and stood stock-still, staring at her.

'Did you see?' she shouted, her heart beating, beating, beating.

Had he seen her push Joe? Did he know what she'd done?

But, as quickly as he'd arrived, the man was gone.

Police and paramedics were surrounding her, asking questions and crowding everyone and everything else out.

* * *

Back in her kitchen, Natalie stares over at Dan, willing him to say something, anything.

'You were a witness, Dan. That's why I let you in that day. That's why I let you stay. Not because I believed you, not because Joe was in you.' She pauses, too scared to look at Dan, too scared to see the hurt and betrayal she's causing the man she loves. But they can never move forward without honesty. Total, complete honesty, whatever the cost.

PART V: DAN AND NATALIE

'I realise my mistake now.'

CHAPTER 17

'Was it all a lie?' Dan asks, pacing the kitchen and staring down at his palms, rubbing them together, again, again, again. 'Did you ever love me?'

'I still do,' Natalie says, looking scared—or is it horrified? It's hard for Dan to judge when he's flooded with this much emotion. He's used to switching it off, batting the feelings away and externalising them, making them feel like someone else's. But for some reason, he's finding that impossible to do this time, like he's trapped inside himself and can't escape. Is this what it's like for everyone else? Is this how normal people live?

Normal? I spit.

'And Joe?' Dan asks Natalie, desperation filtering into his voice. 'My Joe, I mean.'

My Joe? There's only one of us. You're falling for it, aren't you? This is bollocks, Dan. She's making it up...

'Shut up for a minute, will you?' Dan says internally. 'Please.'

'He's not real, Dan.' Natalie says.

'Stop saying that!' I shout. I want to run over and grab her, but I know Dan won't let me. He's too kind, too gentle.

'If we've got any chance of a normal life, we have to face this...' Natalie starts.

'*Normal?*' I explode. 'Is that something to aspire to? Have you learnt nothing? *We were happy, Natalie.* What's normal got to do with it? That's just someone else's opinion, cramming you into a space that doesn't fit. Who wants *normal?* Let us be happy.'

'We're living a lie,' Natalie shouts back.

'Clearly!' I scream.

'You're not him, Dan,' she says, her anger turning into exasperation as her voice softens again. 'You're not Joe. He's not inside you. Stop using that bloody accent.'

Silence.

Natalie, the woman we love, or at least *used* to love, stands on one side of the kitchen. We stand on the other. United. Always united.

She killed me, Dan. Remember that.

'I said shut up,' he says firmly.

Something is shifting in him, changing. He's scaring me. I think the darkness is coming and he's not going to stop it.

You promised, I say. *Remember? You promised you'd never do this.*

'You think it's simple,' Dan says to Natalie.

I know what he's trying to do. He wants to convince her, to talk her around. If he can do that, then he can convince himself. He needs convincing; he's starting to waver.

She killed me, Dan. I want to punch him. He thinks I can't tell; he thinks I don't know what he's thinking, where this is going.

'It's not simple,' Natalie says gently. 'But Joe's not real. Deep down you know that. You stopped taking your medication so suddenly... It—'

How does she know that, Dan? Think. Come on. Who has she been talking to?

'I know I didn't remember everything about his life, but that doesn't mean...' Dan stutters, like he's scared, desperate even.

You weak-willed piece of shit.

'You stopped your meds,' Natalie says, and I can tell she's measuring every word as carefully as she can. 'On top of that, you witnessed a terrible car accident. You saw someone die.'

Dan doesn't answer, and he won't let me speak. He's clamping down, nailing the lid on my coffin with every sharp inhalation of breath.

'No wonder you had to compensate...' Natalie continues.

She phoned Alabi, Dan. That's why he was in the supermarket. Why won't you listen to me?

'I'll never forgive myself for lying to you,' Natalie continues. 'For making you think it was real.' She sounds almost like she means it, like her emotion is real, but I know her better, I've always known her better. She always gets what she wants in the end. It's happening all over again.

'I know I made stuff up,' Dan says. 'But, think about it. If Joe's spirit did move into me, he wouldn't remember things, would he? He wouldn't have his own body, so how could he remember things?'

'Dan, stop...' Natalie starts.

'No, listen to me,' Dan says, lowering his voice and holding his hands up, palms outward, bowing his head slightly at the same time and pursing his lips. His favourite, non-threatening stance.

You fucking lightweight. You should be a threat. Make her listen.

'Dan, I want the best for you,' Natalie starts. 'You have to believe me. I want you to get better.'

'Stop calling me Dan!' I manage to shout. 'You're talking to me, your husband.'

'You aren't my husband!' she shouts back. 'Don't you get it? You've never been my husband!' She's screaming now, spittle flying from the corners of her mouth, and for the first time in memory, she looks ugly to me, like a banshee, a liar, a witch.

'How do you know?' I stand upright, aware that Dan wants to speak, but he's in shock. It's like he's processing something I don't want him to, something I've been keeping from him.

'Do you know why men give a purse-lipped smile and bow their heads when they pass women in the street?' Natalie says. 'Like you were doing a minute ago?'

'What?' Dan says, taking control of his body again. 'I...'

'Because in primates, baring your teeth and making eye contact is considered aggressive. Not doing that is an unconscious way of telling someone you aren't a threat.'

'So?'

'You were doing it again a minute ago, Dan. Pursing your lips. Bowing your head.'

'So?' Dan says quietly, looking at the floor. 'I don't know

what you're...'

'You aren't Joe. He would never have done that, not ever. He was a bully. He was aggressive, a control freak. He was always upright, always baring his teeth. And I love *you*, Dan. Do you understand? I'm doing this because I love *you*. I want *you* to get better. Fuck Joe. Both of them.'

'Both of them?'

'Yours and mine. Fuck them. Me and you, that's what matters. Don't you get it?' Natalie says, stepping toward us.

Our head is spinning and I feel dizzy. Reality is swirling around me, trying to nick me and cut me and make me bleed.

'I think his memories were stored in his body,' Dan carries on desperately. 'Don't you see? But Joe, the essence of him, that's what moved over to me... He wasn't always like you describe him...'

'Joe chose to behave like he did, Dan, same as everybody else. There was always something or someone else to blame. He used to say it was my fault he lost his temper. If I'd only put the things in the dishwasher in the right order. If only I hadn't put the pans on the top shelf where they don't wash properly. If only I hadn't forgotten to wash his rugby kit before the match on Sunday. Always another 'if only'. Always my fault, never his!'

Natalie is shouting again and I feel something like hatred welling up inside for her. I don't remember being the man she's talking about, but if she acted like she's acting now maybe I was...

'What if—?' Dan starts internally.

No, Dan. Not you, too.

'What if she's right? You could be anyone.'

Who else died when I arrived in you?

'The driver of one of the cars? I don't know...'

You're grasping at straws, Dan...

'Yeah, I am,' he says, and I can hear the resignation seeping into his thoughts. I need to kick him into shape, to make him realise what she's saying isn't true.

'You said going for a walk would make me feel better,' I shout bitterly, taking control again. 'The day I died, you suggested we should go for a walk, didn't you? I remember that.'

'You know Joe and I were walking together. You saw us. You saw the accident, you…' Natalie says, stopping herself before she finishes the sentence. I know what she's going to say, I'm getting flashes of memories from Dan's mind, invading me again, trying to get inside my own mind, to influence me.

I believed Dan caused it, that he was the one who killed me, not Natalie. But now I know. She killed me, too. Dan's been hiding that from me, not letting me see the truth.

'It didn't make him feel better,' Natalie snaps. She's no longer at the kitchen table. She's beside me, a sneer on her face. 'He was angry,' she continues. 'He was threatening me, subtly, like he always did. I can't even remember what he was angry about now. You'd think I'd remember but I don't, because he was always mad about something, always *picking* away at me.' She says 'picking' like she has to spit the word out, hocking phlegm onto the floor.

'I killed him,' Dan says, taking control of his body again. 'I stepped into the road. I made the cars swerve. It was my fault, not yours…'

He's desperate, whimpering, weak. I hate him, everything about his simpering, disgusting lack of self-worth makes me want to smash his face in.

'No!' Natalie snaps.

She grabs his hand and tries to squeeze Dan's fingers tightly. He allows the contact, of course he does. I want to slap her off, to shove her across the kitchen and into the table. But Dan, he's letting her hold his hand; he's making eye contact with her, letting out tiny murmurs, like a wounded child.

Were you always this spineless?

Dan is shaking as Natalie clutches him near her chest. She

holds him like a lover, not like a mother would her son, even though he's acting like a baby. I can't tell if he's crying or if it's her. Maybe they both are. After a while, I realise Natalie is speaking again, but I can't hear her. I am alone in a film scene where the music has stopped and only the actor's breathing can be heard. It is rasping and cold and mechanical, and for a second, I wonder if the actor is alive at all. But I am the actor, so I must be. Mustn't I?

'It wasn't you,' Natalie says gently as I zone back in. 'Think harder, Dan. You're not remembering everything clearly. I think you've blocked it out. But if you're going to get better, you have to remember everything.'

She's lying, Dan. I don't know why, but she's lying.

'You knew, didn't you?' he asks me. 'You knew she'd pushed him, but you let me think it was me. You used me.'

No. She used you, Dan. Not me, not...

'You both used me,' Dan says, reality hitting him hard, knocking the air out of him.

Joe and Natalie have been protecting themselves, looking after themselves. Maybe it was time he started doing the same. He stares over at Natalie, his anger and fear giving way to another emotion as he hears the doorbell ring.

'Who's at the door?' Dan asks, working it out a few milliseconds before I do. 'Who's at the door, Natalie?' His low voice is dry, constricted.

'I'm sorry, Dan. It's for your own good,' she says, darting past us into the hallway and toward the front entrance as Dan runs after her, stopping dead in the middle of the hall as she reaches the door. She glances back, and for a second I see her pain, her regret. Then she flings it open to reveal Dr Alabi and Dan's father. Natalie looks back over her shoulder, shame colouring her face as she lets her hair fall over it, giving her somewhere to hide.

'Now who's bowing their head?' Dan says quietly. 'It's not

always non-threatening, is it? Sometimes it's shame.'

As his father and Dr Alabi step over the threshold, Dan doesn't move, doesn't speak. Resignation is sinking in, terrible resignation that can only mean one thing.

'I'm sorry, Joe,' Dan says internally, walking into the living room without acknowledging his father or his therapist. They both follow him, and Natalie shuts the front door behind them. As they make themselves at home in Natalie's living room, neither one speaks. This strikes me as odd. People are only silent when they don't know how to begin.

Are they going to have us committed?

'Probably.'

* * *

As they begin to speak, Dan stands by the bookshelves, staring at Natalie's books, just like he did on the day he arrived. Everything about that wretched, broken man feels like a lifetime ago. He's different now. Changed. But who changed him? Natalie? Joe? Or had he done it himself? He doesn't know, but as he stands with his back to them—his accusers, his saviours or whatever they think they are—he realises it doesn't matter. What matters is that he *is* different. He *is* changed. And yet, none of them are acknowledging this. He leans forward and picks up a book— the same one he picked up the day he followed Natalie from the park, clutching her discarded envelope in his hand with her address on it. Because that's how he found her, isn't it? He heard the police officers use her name at the accident. He found a discarded envelope with her address on it in the park. Nothing mystical, nothing magical. Just a mentally unstable homeless man chasing a woman back to her home.

Dan, it wasn't like that. It...

'Shut up,' he says firmly, glancing down at the book he's clutching tightly in his palm. He hadn't paid much attention to it the day he arrived, it had just been something to hold, something to cling on to and rub and self-calm with.

Reasons to Stay Alive by Matt Haig.

Jesus. Had Natalie suffered from depression? Had Joe? Her Joe, not his. He glances from the book across to Natalie, sitting small and hunched, knees to her chest on the chair. He realises he's always assumed she was strong and didn't need support. But that's a lie. Everybody needs support. He has no real idea where she's been, what she's been through. She's supported him. Loved him. But she'd had her own traumas, ones he'd never asked about.

'Dan?' His father's voice penetrates the freeze-frame Dan's placed himself in. For a second, he glances back at the book. *Reasons to Stay Alive...*

The voices in the room are picking up speed, mixing and mingling, creating mild background noise. Dan turns around, holding the book. He's not squeezing it, not clutching desperately like he once might have; he's just holding it. It's something to anchor him, something to run his fingers gently against for comfort if he needs it. His father, his girlfriend and his therapist, all with concerned smiles, are filtering in from another reality. Natalie isn't speaking, isn't joining in with the others. Her Judas moment has now passed, and she seems broken. In the corner of his eye, he can see her shrinking into the armchair.

Dan tries to recall the feeling of detachment, so ever-present in his younger years. He wants that emptiness to engulf him now. He wants to be outside of himself and the new mess he's made of his life.

'Stopping your medication like that,' Dr Alabi says, his voice as silken as ever. 'It was dangerous, Dan. There are side effects.'

'You're supposed to withdraw gradually, you know that,' his father butts in. He's stressed out, upset.

'But it's rare that someone goes through the psychosis Natalie has described based on withdrawal from medication alone,' Dr

Alabi continues. 'Has he experienced any other trauma, Natalie?'

There he goes again. Never addressing you personally, Dan. It's like you don't exist, like it always was.

'No,' Dan says. 'It's not.'

They are trying to help him. Dan understands that. He's almost sympathetic. But they don't understand that he's changed. He's not dulled by medication anymore. He spent years existing in an equilibrium that he now knows wasn't life. It was an existence. He doesn't want that again. No matter how fucked up it was to start with, he's been building something with Natalie. It's not conventional, but it's a life. It is *real*, more real than his previous reality, even with Joe.

Even with Joe? With me, you mean? Me! Don't do this, Dan. You were happy.

'What?'

With me. With Natalie. You were happy. Don't do this.

'Don't do what?'

Go with them. They'll pump you full of drugs and purge me from your system. Is that what you want?

'It's not that simple, Joe.'

You don't have to let it happen, Dan. You're so much stronger now than you used to be. You can take control of your own life. Own it.

'You're right,' he says simply, and I realise in a wave of hormones, an orgasm of truth, that I've been misreading him. He *is* in control, and he has no intention of going with them or letting them medicate him.

'I'm sorry,' he says.

Why? I ask, not willing to acknowledge his decision, not able to let it in.

'Because you have to die twice.'

And there it is, the truth he's been hiding from me, the one he's known for a long time. Not content with killing me once on the street, he's going to do it all over again. As he stands, staring defiantly at his father and his psychiatrist, I can feel him pushing me down, placing my head in a black hood, pushing it underwater, down and down and down.

'Stop talking,' he says out loud. 'I'm so sick of listening to other people talk, making decisions for me, about me. It's time you listened.'

I've never heard him sound so strong, so in control. I'd congratulate him, tell him I'm proud of him if my head weren't so heavy. I want to slip down into the water and close my eyes. I'm tired, so very tired. I've been swimming against the tide for a long time.

You're cloudy. I can't feel you anymore.

He doesn't answer me, he's busy talking, telling the people who love him what's what and I'm just a spot, a wormhole in the darkness, expanding away from him as he opens himself up to the light.

'I'm not coming with you,' he says.

Dan's father half stands up from his armchair, about to speak, but Dan holds his hand up.

'Not you, Dad. You, Dr Alabi.'

'Dan, you're not well,' comes Alabi's silky voice again, with the deep, reassuring tones that could convince anyone of anything. 'We need to treat you. Things have progressed and...'

'I said, stop talking,' Dan says quietly, but firmly.

He's not angry; he's not arguing. He's telling them how it's going to be. His dad has frozen in a half crouch position, like he's about to shit on the armchair.

'Okay, go on,' his dad says, like Dan needs his permission.

Dan pauses, rubbing his thumb along the grain of the book cover. It makes a gentle scratching sound, like a whisper. He focuses on that for a while, centring himself.

'I'm not right. Up here,' he says, tapping his head. 'I get it. I do. But I'm going to *be* all right.'

His father opens his mouth, about to speak, but Dr Alabi reaches over and touches his arm gently to stop him, nodding at

Dan to continue.

'I don't know what's been going on with me. Maybe I don't cope well with things, with loss. Or maybe there's something else going on with my chemical makeup. But I'm not going back, Dr Alabi.'

'But you can't live like this,' Natalie bursts out.

Dan holds his hand up to her, stopping her words in their tracks.

'There have to be changes. I get that, I do,' he says, looking at Natalie as a wave of compassion floods through him. He wants to grab her and hold her, to tell her it'll be okay. But he can't do that. He's not the man who can do that at this moment in time. She needs someone else, someone who loves her and can take care of her while he sorts his head out.

'I don't blame you, Natalie.'

She covers her face, and he's not sure if she's hiding from him or simply covering her tears.

'Do you think I haven't noticed how *small* your world is, Natalie?' Dan walks over and kneels in front of her armchair, taking her hand. 'You go to work, you come home, you don't socialise with anyone. You don't call anyone, not your parents, not your brother. At first, I thought it was grief... But it's not, is it? What did he do to you?'

She squeezes his hand with something like panic in her eyes. He realises that he's let her down. He should have noticed these things sooner. He was so caught up in his problems, in Joe, that he didn't realise she was still in freefall.

Joe? You mean me.

'No, you're not real.'

Please, Dan...

'I should have noticed earlier,' Dan continues. 'You've been focusing all your attention on me.'

'That's not true, I...'

'It is, Natalie,' Dan says firmly. 'But you've got your own

damage, your own wounds to heal.'

Natalie flicks a glance across at Dan's dad and Dr Alabi, clearly worried Dan is going to tell them everything.

'I'm going with my dad. For your own good as much as mine.'

'You don't have to,' she says, but the desperation has left her voice.

Dan knows she understands what he's trying to tell her.

'Natalie, the closest I've seen you to having a friend is that woman in the café. If you can't call your parents, at least pop in there. See if she wants to go for a drink.'

'This is about *you*, Daniel,' his dad says. 'Don't deflect things onto Natalie.'

'I'm not, Dad. Really I'm not.'

Standing back up, Dan walks back over the bookshelves, bracing himself.

'So, we are clear. I'm not going anywhere with you, Dr Alabi.'

'Babatunde, Dan. You can call me…'

'Dr Alabi. You're not my friend, you're my therapist.'

'Dan, don't be…' his father starts.

'Stop telling me what to be, Dad. I'm thirty years old. I can decide how to behave and how to speak.'

'That's just it, Dan. You can't. Look at the state of you…' his dad says, a mix of hurt and anger in his voice.

'Yes,' Dan says, holding his arms out wide. 'Look at me. Actually look at me.'

The room descends into a deep, uncomfortable silence.

'You think you're possessed by a dead soul, Dan,' Dr Alabi says eventually. 'However healthy and happy you look—and you do—we can't ignore that.'

I told you.

'Shut the fuck up.'

'I'm not saying I don't need help. Clearly, I need help. But let's start from where I am, not where you think I am. I'm sorting myself out. If you want to support me with that, then I'm all ears. If you want to tell me what's wrong with me, if you want to medicate me and shut me down, I'll find a way to fight you.'

'Daniel, you've got to...'

'No, Mr Garrison. He's right,' Dr Alabi says, that soothing mediator voice washing over the room, a soporific drug of a voice. 'Keep talking, Dan.'

'I'll come back with you, Dad. I'll move home,' Dan says.

Natalie whimpers slightly at this, like it hadn't occurred to her this was the outcome of her actions.

'I'll keep my job, though,' he continues. 'I've been building a life and I can't let that go.'

'What else, Dan?' Dr Alabi asks gently.

'I won't take any medication unless it looks like I absolutely have to. But I will start up my sessions with you again.'

'We'll need to do a full assessment of you, Dan. We can't take your word for it, not given how things are.'

Dan nods.

'Okay. Do your tests. But work with me to find a way I can live fully.'

'You don't have to go,' Natalie says, wiping her eyes. 'You can stay here with me. We can fight this together.'

Dan looks at her, clenching his jaw tightly shut and shaking his head.

'No, Natalie. We can't,' Dan says, and turns to his dad. 'Let's go. Now. Let's do it. Move on, and start getting things sorted.'

'What about your things?' Natalie asks. 'You can't go without your things.'

Dan can tell she's barely keeping it together. But this isn't about her; he's got a lot to process, a lot to think through. The fact that she pushed her husband into the road and killed him, for a start. The fact she'd let him believe his psychosis was real for another. He can't be around her. He can't stay here *and* get better.

'What things? *I* don't have any things here. They're all Joe's.

The clothes, the razor, everything. You let me slot into his space, Natalie. Don't you see? I don't have anything here to take with me.'

'But I love you,' she implores.

'I love you, too,' Dan replies. 'But life doesn't care about that. It never has.'

'Please, Dan. I didn't...'

'It's okay. Honestly.'

Dan wants to grab her and tell her it'll work out. He's hurting for her as much as for himself, imagining how alone she'll be when they shut the door behind them. She has nobody, he realises. No friends, no family even. It was only the two of them.

'Call your parents, Natalie,' he says. 'You need someone to take care of you. There's no shame in that.'

With that, he hands her the book in his hand and takes a deep breath, looking away from her and toward his father and his therapist.

'Shall we?' he says, hoping his dad agrees, that he'll stand and they can walk out the door side by side, because the strength it's taking him to hold it together, to push me down and hold my head underwater, has been immense. At any moment, he could crumble and I could grab hold, take my opportunity. But he knows that. And he knows how important it is that he keeps me in check.

You can't keep me trapped forever! I shout.

But he's stopped listening. He's hugging his father, a tight embrace filled with love and emotion. He's shaking Dr Alabi's hand. He's kissing Natalie and telling her that he doesn't blame her, but that he can't be with her, for both their sakes.

CHAPTER 18

Natalie tries to remain strong. She tries to do all the things the world demands. She paints her face and makes sure she looks presentable for work. She smiles and chats with the neighbours when they stop and talk to her in the street, asking where the handsome man she had living with her has disappeared to. As they smile inquisitively at her, their eyes scream, 'Slut! Your husband isn't cold in the ground and you moved another man in. I'm glad he left. You deserve to be alone.' Then they touch her arm gently, nodding empathetically as they probe her for more gossip, more information on the mysterious Dan.

Her house feels empty in a way it never did after Joe. When he died, it was like a veil being lifted, like every room was more brightly coloured, more able to breathe. It felt bigger somehow, like she could skip and dance naked from room to room without anything encroaching on her space. Once she'd gotten the funeral out of the way, she'd enjoyed those first weeks alone. The solitude had been comforting, a soft blanket to wrap around her newly liberated frame, protecting her from the past—and from her own guilt.

With Dan gone, things are quite different. She feels bereft in a way she never did with Joe. She's realising what lonely means for the first time, how all-encompassing it can be. Before Dan arrived, she liked the solitude so much, she hadn't been fully aware of how isolated Joe had made her. He'd cut her off from her old friends, Olyvia and Kelly, and he'd made sure she made no new ones in Brighton. Worst of all, he'd gradually convinced her to cut contact with her family. She is estranged from everyone.

She calls Dan every day, even though he won't speak to her. It comforts her to talk to his dad, at least. To know Dan's okay...as okay as he can be. Her daily phone calls with Bob have become the thing she looks forward to, the thing that gets her through each day. They keep her connected to Dan while she has them; and they mean that she hasn't severed all ties. There's hope. Deep down she knows what she's done and doesn't blame him for blanking her. He was honest with her, in his way. He laid himself bare, mental health and all. In return, she lied to him, made his fantasy a reality. Who knows what mental damage she did to him, how entertaining his psychosis prolonged or exacerbated it. She was thoughtless. Selfish. She can't forgive herself, except...

They do love each other. No matter how fucked up everything is, that part is real, she's sure of it. And that must mean something, mustn't it? After everything they've been through, separately and together, it must mean something, or else what's the point?

After Dan left, she settled into calling in sick and drinking too much wine to counteract her feelings, knocking it back, self-medicating the only way she knew how. But she realised that was the first thing that had to change. She was functioning; of course, she was. But she drank too much, and for the wrong reasons. She had to remain clear-headed if she was going to get him back.

She settled for throwing herself into work, into exercise and into the daily phone calls with Bob. And day by day, she mustered up the courage to do what she knew she needed to do: re-engage with her friends and family.

In many ways, Dan had been an inspiration. He'd been terrified of going to see his father and confronting his past. He'd been ashamed, she now realises. Ashamed of falling off the wagon and making himself sick, ashamed of stopping his medication, but, most of all, ashamed of 'losing' his mental health again, as if he was somehow culpable.

Is mental health something you 'lose'? Isn't it just a moving target, a pendulum swinging back and forth? Sometimes it's in time with everyone else, sometimes it isn't. People treat mental health like something to be hidden, something terrifying that shouldn't be confronted. But doesn't everyone suffer 'mental illness' at one time or another? There are degrees of physical health problems, after all. A grazed knee isn't the same as having a limb amputated. Someone having a bad day and feeling low isn't the same as someone who is so depressed they can't see any light in the world. Natalie suspects most people's pendulums are suspended by the thinnest of threads that could break at any moment given the right—or wrong—circumstances.

What if Natalie had been that circumstance for Dan? Dr Alabi said his psychosis was a side effect of not withdrawing from his medication in a controlled manner. What if, without her, he'd have righted himself in a few more days and gone home to his dad?

Whatever the reason, mental illness felt like a failure to Dan, a weakness. But even so, when she'd pressed him to visit his father, he'd agreed immediately. No battle, no fight. He'd trusted her judgement and she'd betrayed him.

* * *

Natalie has nobody to talk through her feelings with. She'll never go back to the Afghan hound, but still wishes she had a sounding board, somebody to help her understand what is real and what is just the guilt talking.

Dan's absence has brought her loneliness into focus. Gripping her mobile, she stares at Olyvia's number, open in her contacts. She's been staring at it for days, not daring to call, scared of what her oldest friend would say—if she'd say anything at all. Her finger hovers over the button for a moment before she decides against it for the hundredth time. Grabbing her jacket from the banister, she heads out of the door. She knows where to go: Louise's café. While Louise isn't her friend—far from it, she barely knows her—she is a friendly face. She is someone who has expressed an interest in Natalie, someone she can try to talk to, to make sense of things with.

When she arrives at the café, she isn't even sure how to greet Louise. Maybe Louise won't even remember her, she thinks; or maybe she'll just think it's weird that Natalie wants to talk to her.

'Natalie!' Louise says warmly, standing behind the counter, a soft glow coming from the candles on the tables.

'Hey, Louise,' Natalie says, a genuine smile crossing her features.

'Latte?'

Natalie nods, calm descending over her as she takes a table in the corner, next to one of the bookshelves. She sits down, pulling down a book and turning it over to read the back cover. She flips it back over to read the title: *It Feels Like I Can Still Smile.*

'My husband wrote it,' Louise says, placing a tall latte glass in front of Natalie.

'Oh, wow. I didn't know,' Natalie says. She's not sure whether to be embarrassed or impressed.

'No reason you would,' Louise says, a darkness flashing over her features for a moment before she smiles again sadly. 'Turns out he couldn't.'

'What?'

'Still smile.'

The coffee Louise is holding trembles.

'May I?' she says, nodding to the chair next to Natalie, who nods in agreement. 'Now,' she continues in a lighter tone. 'Who was that guy I saw you with the other week? I want *all* the gossip.'

* * *

As Louise sits down, Natalie prepares herself, mustering everything she has inside to tell her story. Not about the homelessness, not the fact that Dan thought he was possessed by Joe. Part of her feels she should be open and honest. Dan is ill, nothing more, nothing less. Why should she hide it? But a bigger part of her knows that it isn't her story to tell, it's his. If he wants to tell people about it, he can—but she has no right to do it for him. Natalie tells Louise the basics, how she met someone else and fell for him. Then she lies, tells her she felt guilty, it was so soon after Joe, so she's pushed Dan away because of it.

'Go after him,' Louise says, reaching over and squeezing her hand. 'Don't leave it too late like I did.'

For a moment, Natalie stares at Louise's green eyes, and they're distant, like she's reliving some past horror nobody else is party to.

'He won't speak to me, he...' Natalie drifts off. 'I know I haven't explained properly, I...'

'You don't need to explain to me of all people,' Louise says, smiling sadly. 'I jumped straight into another relationship after my boyfriend died.'

'Your boyfriend? I thought you and Adam were married?' Natalie starts.

'We were. I meant before him. It's a long story. The point is, I let guilt get in the way of my marriage. Not just guilt, a lot of baggage.' Louise pauses, still not looking at Natalie. In fact, Natalie isn't sure she's talking to her at all; it's more like she's talking to herself.

'Natalie,' she continues earnestly. 'It was pointless, all the introspection, all the self-indulgence. It was self-destructive in the end.'

'I'm not being introspective...' Natalie starts.

As they drift into silence, she realises that this was probably a mistake. She and Louise are different, very different. Just because they both lost their husbands doesn't mean they'll become friends. It doesn't mean they can help each other.

'Look,' Natalie says. 'I'd better go, I think I'll...'

'Don't let him go, Natalie,' Louise says. 'Okay? Just don't let him go.'

'I won't, Louise. But I need to give him space.'

Louise nods.

'Not too much, though, okay? If I'd chosen to find Adam a few hours earlier, I could have saved him.'

'Dan isn't Adam,' Natalie says before she can stop herself.

'No. No he isn't. And you're not me, thank God.' Louise surprises Natalie by smiling. 'You're strong. I can see that. Trust yourself. You'll find a way through it.'

For some reason, a warm chill runs through Natalie as Louise says those words. It's been a long time since anybody has said that to her. Certainly while she was married to Joe she never heard those words. *Trust yourself.* She stands up, her coffee only half finished, and puts her jacket on.

'Thanks, Louise,' she says, surprised to find that she means it. 'You've really helped.'

'Nat,' Louise says. Natalie tenses up a little at the diminutive but says nothing. 'Why don't you come around for dinner? Not now, I know you've got stuff going on. But next month, maybe? Me and my friends, we do these dinner parties, alternate months. We've just had Alice's and next month it's Imogen's turn.' She pauses, shaking her head lightly. 'Why don't you come along?'

'Thanks, Louise,' Natalie says, hugging Louise and moving toward the café door. 'I'm not sure I can, but...'

'I insist,' Louise says firmly. 'Please come. You'll like everyone. Well, you'll like Alice, at least. Bring Dan if you can?'

Natalie opens the café door and smiles back at Louise, nodding.

'We'll see,' she says, walking out onto the street and rummaging in her pocket for her phone. A few more steps and she holds it to her ear, walking quickly up the hill, listening to it ring, heart thumping.

'Natalie?' The voice at the other end sounds surprised, nervous even, but not unhappy, not angry.

'Olyvia?' Natalie says. 'It's me. I'm so sorry.'

Back at home, Natalie feels strong. Within moments it had been like old times with Olyvia, apologies had flowed from both sides.

'I should never have cut you off.'

'No, I should have realised something was wrong. I'm your best friend, I should have...'

'There was nothing you could do, Olyvia. Don't blame yourself, blame me.'

Natalie curls up on the couch, staring at the mobile in her hand and smiling. Olyvia is going to come down and visit next month, and Natalie has the strangest feeling that the inkblot mess of her life is starting to pulsate and coalesce. It's forming a picture. A beautiful, complex picture where before were only stains and spillage.

The next phone call is going to be more difficult, she knows. She wishes Dan was with her. She'd give anything to have him holding her hand as she dials her parents' number. She treated them so badly; how can she make it up to them? Besides, her mother sees right through her, always has done. She'll know what she's done. She'll know she's a murderer.

No, it was an accident. She hadn't meant for Joe to die. She's not a murderer; she can't think like that. If she does, she's marking herself for self-doubt again, for self-hatred. And he'll win. If that's the legacy Joe leaves, he'll win and she won't allow that. She won't give him anything, not even her guilt. She sits on the sofa with her mobile loosely in her palm, staring at her contacts page. *Mum and Dad.* The last conversation she had with them wasn't a good one. She hadn't even rung them to tell them Joe was dead until after the funeral. That hadn't gone down well with her mum.

'What will his parents think, Natalie?' her mother had implored. 'Do they think we couldn't be bothered to come to our own son-in-law's funeral? I don't understand you, I don't understand one little bit.'

'I'm sorry, Mum. It's all been... I'm not thinking straight.'

'I'll have to call Valerie and Harry, give them my condolences. What will I tell her, though?'

'Mum, please. It was a small service, anyway. Only a few close family members there...'

'We weren't close family? Is that what you're saying?'

'No, I just—'

Natalie had slammed the phone down in a fury, muttering 'forget it' under her breath as she did so. She couldn't cope with other people's drama, not even her mother's. After that, Natalie had started screening her mum's calls. She'd drifted so far from her while she'd been married to Joe that she couldn't see a way back from it. She'd treated them so badly; she wondered if they even cared anymore.

She steels herself and pushes her thumb down on the green dial button, watching as the phone beeps and dials her parents' number. Pulling the sleeves of her jumper down over her hands for comfort, she puts the phone to her ear.

'Hi, Mum. It's me,' she says nervously, chewing her lower lip.

'Oh, Natalie. Thank God. Are you okay?' her mum says, her voice filled with worry and love.

'Mum,' Natalie says again, her voice breaking as the tears start to fall, 'I'm so sorry.' Before she can get another word out, her mum is shushing her, telling her that it's all right and she has nothing to be sorry for.

'I'm your mum, silly,' she says, instantly transforming Natalie into a seven-year-old girl running into her arms. 'I'm always here, no matter what.'

Natalie realises her parents are a constant. As long as they live, they'll take anything she throws at them and come back for more. She's pushed them away, ignored them, stopped answering their calls. She's shut them out of her life, hidden Joe's true nature from them and even not invited them to their son-in-law's funeral. They have every right to hate her, yet all her mum says is 'I'm here, no matter what.' This makes Natalie cry more than anything, and once she's allowed the sobs to come, she can't stop them, her body is attacking her from within, mini-grenades of grief exploding and causing her to gasp and grab for air. Wiping her snotty nose on her jumper, she tries to speak, to tell her mum something, anything. But she doesn't have to. Her mother is saying her name over and over, trying to get her attention.

'Sorry,' Natalie manages to say into the handset.

'Your dad is coming to get you,' her mum says simply. 'He'll drive down today. You're coming to stay for a few days.'

'Okay,' Natalie says without hesitation. She's in her mid-thirties, but the only thing she wants in the world is a hug from her mum and dad, and to hear them tell her everything is going to be okay.

* * *

It takes Natalie four days before she can even begin to come clean to her mum and dad. She feels so ashamed of her marriage to Joe, of the person she became, the person she let herself become. She let them down. They'd raised her to be independent and strong, to never let anyone define her, and look what she became.

'It's not your fault,' her mother said immediately, grabbing her and holding her close. Then she held her at arm's length and stared into her eyes. 'How he treated you, how he made you feel. That's not you.'

Natalie doesn't think she's cried so much in her entire life. The past ten years have been pushed painfully down into the deepest crevices of her soul, but cracks are finally appearing. They're spreading. The crevices are crumbling, letting the gaseous emotions she's kept at bay flood into her system, overpowering her.

'I'm sorry,' she says to her mum. 'I don't mean to keep crying

286

it's just…'

'Don't ever say you're sorry,' her mum says, stroking her hair. 'It's me who should be sorry. I didn't protect you. I should have seen what he was doing.'

Days turn into a week, which turns into two weeks. Her mum and dad look after her, bring her tea in bed, feed her and listen to her. Some days, she doesn't even get dressed, regressing—as all adults do in the company of their parents—into being a child-like version of herself, ready to be waited on and looked after.

'I'm so proud of you,' her dad says one day.

'Proud? Are you joking?' Natalie replies. 'Didn't you hear me on the phone a minute ago? I'll be lucky if I have a job to go back to if I don't go in next week.'

'I don't care about your job, Natalie,' he says. 'I'm proud of *you*. Of who *you* are.'

'I don't understand,' Natalie says, confused.

'Do you think being strong means never getting into trouble? Do you think it means never making mistakes or going down the wrong path?'

He steps forward and hugs her close, squeezing her to him and holding her there for a moment.

'That's not strength,' he continues, releasing her and looking into her eyes. 'Strength is coming through the other side. Recognising a problem and dealing with it.'

Then it hits her. All this time she thought Dan needed fixing or protecting. She thought he was weak. He wasn't. He didn't need her strength or anyone else's. He was already strong. Just look at what he was dealing with. Bereavement and mental health problems, homelessness, bulimia and God knows what else. Difficult things were happening to him and he'd found a way to cope, a way to deal with it, however strange his methods were. He'd found a way to cope by creating Joe. And bit by bit, he'd pulled himself back from the brink. He'd done that all on his own. Maybe, she thinks, he's one of the strongest men she's ever met.

'I've got to go home, Dad.' she says, decisively.

'Don't worry about your job,' he started. 'You need to look after yourself, they'll understand.'

'It's not my job, Dad. It's my boyfriend,' she said, running from the living room and mounting the stairs in twos. As she began throwing her clothes into her suitcase, her father called up the stairs after her.

'Your boyfriend?'

'Yes!' Natalie shouted down to him. 'I'll explain, I promise I will. But right now, I need you to drive me back to Brighton. I have to see him. I have to make things okay.'

CHAPTER 19

Weeks pass and Dan settles into a new routine, a little bit emptier than before. But it's a road he's travelling. He knows that now. It'll lead somewhere better. Natalie phones most days, and speaks to his father, but Dan refuses to speak to her. Not because he hates her, not even because he's angry. She took him in and while she lied, she also cared for him. How could he be angry with her? But he also recognised that last day just how much she was channelling into him at her own expense. He refuses to allow that to continue.

Having his old job helps, gives him routine and structure. Even being at home with his dad isn't as annoying as it might once have been. He loves him, and now that the clouds are clearing, he can see how much his father needs him. He's lonely and God knows how much stress Dan's put him through. It's good to be with him, to listen to him and give something back. His sessions with Dr Alabi are helping, giving him new coping mechanisms, new ways of dealing with things. The detachment side of things is almost like a memory. He'd be lying if he said the bulimia was completely under control, but it's managed. It's still his go-to when he's stressed, so he's working on managing that in other ways, with exercise and mindfulness. Things aren't perfect, but they're getting there.

* * *

Then there's Joe, the voice inside his head that won't go away, won't shut up.

'I think your approach is a good one,' Dr Alabi said during their first session.

'My approach?' Dan asked, frowning.

'Not giving him airtime, not engaging with him or responding to him.'

'It's hard,' Dan said. 'He makes me feel guilty.'

Before coming, he'd decided that honesty was the only way forward, the only way this could work. 'Sometimes he's agitated, almost aggressive.'

'Wouldn't you be?' Dr Alabi said.

Dan settled back into life. He was monitored. He had regular meetings and therapy sessions. He went to work and avoided alcohol and too much caffeine. He ignored Joe when he tried to engage him. After a few weeks, his dad seemed to relax a little, seemed to realise his son wasn't a homicidal maniac waiting to pounce.

Life has become as everyday as possible. But something is missing. Natalie.

* * *

Then, one nondescript Saturday morning, the doorbell rings.

'You answer it,' his dad says, and Dan knows instantly who it is.

'Go on,' his dad encourages.

Slowly, he does. He feels the cold metal on his fingertips as he pulls the door latch down and swings the door open. And there she is.

'I was wrong,' she says, standing on the doorstep, refusing to make eye contact, refusing to look at him clearly. Her long hair is hanging loose, covering her face as she stares at the floor. 'Thing is, even though I knew he wasn't real, all I could see was *my* Joe. I couldn't help hating him. But your version was nothing like my husband. The stories he told, his version of our relationship, of our marriage... It was beautiful Dan.'

She steps forward, tucking her hair behind her ear and taking his hand.

'And that was *you*, Dan,' she continues. '*You* told those stories.

You had that beauty in your heart. He was always you, wasn't he?'

Dan cuts her off. 'No, Natalie, he wasn't. We can't start like that. I thought your dead husband was possessing me.'

She takes a deep breath, clearly not sure what to say.

'We can't act like everything was normal,' Dan continues. 'We can't rebuild based on that.'

'But can we rebuild?' she asks hopefully.

Such a strange place I find myself in. Non-existent, really. Maybe I was never Joe, but I'm not Dan either. And now he's letting me go. He's been letting me go for a long time, even before Natalie shopped him to Dr Alabi. He needs me less and less, no longer relies on me to step in for him, to take charge. He's taken control back, probably for the first time since he was a teenager, since his grandmother was taken into the home. And I'm pleased for him; I am. But that doesn't mean I'm not scared. Of course I'm scared. Who wouldn't be in my position? What's going to happen to me now? Will I cease to exist, like a memory that doesn't get accessed anymore, retreating deeper into the shadows of the mind, until one day the darkness envelops it fully? If that is my fate, I need to do one last thing for him, one final act of kindness—because despite everything, he's been kind to me. I owe him something.

Before you kill me again, I need you to remember something, I say desperately, knowing he won't acknowledge me. *Remember who you are. This self-hatred, this need to purge yourself, channel it into me. Your mum didn't leave you, she died. Your gran didn't leave you, she got sick. None of it was ever about you.*

'I know.'

Shit! He's talking to me again.

Don't turn Natalie away. She's special. She wants you even though you're loony tunes.

He starts laughing out loud at that, a wide grin crossing his face as he leans back against the doorframe and waves Natalie into the house.

'Was that him again?' Natalie asks, frowning as she steps over the threshold.

'I'm okay, Natalie. You've got to trust me,' Dan says, shutting the door behind us. 'I'm going to be okay.'

'And Joe? *My* Joe, I mean. Are you going to tell anyone?' Natalie asks, standing awkwardly in the hallway.

'Is that why you're here?' Dan replies, but I can barely hear him, everything is distant.

'I won't tell anyone,' Dan says. 'You don't even know if it was your fault. That car might have hit him anyway. I'm as much to blame, I made it swerve in the first place.'

'I know, but...'

'It's time to let go, Natalie. For both of us. Joe's dead. We're alive.'

* * *

He feels alive. His blood is pumping, his nerves are tingling, and the woman he loves is standing opposite him. There are no more lies. They have a million things to learn about one another, but the lies are gone. They are unified. He can't imagine a better feeling.

'Do you think we can start again?' Natalie asks, hopefully. Dan stares at her, drinking her in. They stand quietly in the hallway, not speaking, not needing to. Eventually, Dan asks the question he most needs an answer to.

'Why did you go along with it, Natalie? The whole Joe thing. Was it just to find out if I'd seen you push him?'

He releases their embrace and puts a hand on each of her arms, looking directly into her eyes.

'At first, yeah.'

'Weren't you scared of me, though?'

'It's complicated,' she says. 'I was scared. I was all over the place. Feeling guilty, feeling alone. Maybe I'm not the full ticket myself.'

'Do you want a drink?' a voice interrupts.

Dan looks over his shoulder to see his dad loitering in the hallway, listening to every word. Shaking his head, Dan takes Natalie's hand, leading her upstairs and away from his father's prying ears.

'I don't miss him,' Natalie says as they walk into his bedroom. 'Joe, I mean. I never missed him, not even a little bit. Does that make me a terrible person?'

'Will you tell me about him one day? What he did to you?' Dan said, sitting down on the corner of the bed.

Natalie nods. 'I'd like that. I don't think it was all his fault, I'm sure I was—'

'No, Natalie. You can't carry on like that. I know I don't know the full story, but I do know you. If he was an arsehole, you need to stop taking responsibility.'

'He was just fucked up, I think.' She hesitates, as if she's wrestling with her conscience.

'Aren't we all? But it's not an excuse. He damaged you, didn't he. He took something from you, some spark—'

'He never killed anyone, though, did he?' Natalie is quiet, almost mumbling. 'Not like we did. I'm not sure I can get past that, Dan.'

'We didn't kill him, Natalie. It was an accident. You pushed him off you; I didn't look before stepping into the road. It wasn't premeditated. We aren't killers.'

'Since when did you get to be the voice of reason?' Natalie smiles a little, but it's too nervous to have any humour.

'We killed him,' she continues, sitting down on the bed next to him. Dan reaches over and puts his hand on her back, rubbing it gently.

'We *didn't*. If we're going to move forward, you have to accept that.'

She sits silently for what seems like minutes, not weeping, just breathing in, out, in, out.

'I lied to the police,' she says eventually. 'I didn't tell them I'd pushed him. The driver of the car said he'd swerved to avoid someone, but that he didn't remember what he looked like. All those witnesses and nobody really saw what happened.' She looks at Dan, imploring him, wanting something from him he doesn't think he can give her. 'The police ruled it as an accident, the drivers weren't charged. Nobody else was seriously injured and life just...moved on. For everyone except Joe...'

'Natalie, it wasn't your fault. I've made peace with my part in it.' Dan says before stopping for a moment, weighing up whether to be totally honest or not but knowing he has to. 'Joe and I talked and...'

'Joe again?' Natalie sounds on the verge of tears, so full of nightmares that one more thing will push her into a deep pit. 'It was never Joe. I thought...'

'Yes, okay.' Dan raises his voice slightly, not irritated, but not calm either. 'I know he wasn't the real Joe. I know that. He was a construct; I get it. But he helped me through it. And I'm climbing out the other side. I won't go back, Natalie... But it's not like flicking a switch.'

She frowns at him, unsure what he means.

'I'm sorting myself out. But you need to find a way to forgive yourself, to move on,' Dan says. 'If you can't, we've got no chance.'

'Maybe we should go to the police, tell them what happened,' Natalie says. 'Then I could move past this, I could...'

'If you need to,' Dan says calmly. 'But you don't have to do it for me. It wasn't premeditated. You're not a murderer.' Dan pauses, reaching over to take her hand. 'We aren't killers. It was an accident.'

'But I... God, I don't even know what I think. I don't know my own mind anymore.'

Dan chuckles, making her squirm.

'Oh shit. I'm sorry, I didn't mean...'

'It's fine... I don't want you walking on eggshells around me.' Dan lowers his voice slightly. 'Look, whatever it looks like, I started the process of healing a long time ago. Joe, the whole thing, was me finding my way out of the fog. I'm not out yet, but I'm getting there. Things are clearer for me. But you...you're at the very beginning. You barely started to heal, I see that now.'

'Most of the time I'm fine,' she starts.

'You're not fine.' Dan forces her to make eye contact and hold it. 'It's going to take you a while to find yourself again.'

'I thought it was me. Joe made me think it was me. Oversensitive, neurotic, even...'

'It wasn't.' Dan squeezes her hand lightly. 'It isn't. And I'm here. When you want to talk, to pick through it all, to start healing.'

'But I don't want to burden you, I don't...'

'Shhh. Stop that. I'm sorry it's taken me this long to realise you needed me, too. We're a unit, a team. You help me, I help you. It's a balance.'

She's silent, gently banging the tips of her fingers on her forehead, rhythmically, thoughtfully.

'Do you think we'll make it? We're both such a mess. We can't be good for each other.'

'Honestly? I don't know,' Dan says. 'But who does? We can give it a try, can't we? That's all anyone can do.'

They both sit silently on the edge of Dan's bed, staring not at each other but at the plain, cream-coloured, picture-less walls.

'No more hiding, then?' she says, reaching over and squeezing his hand.

'No more hiding,' he repeats.

'But we do it together, yeah?' she says. 'Whatever we do, can we do it together? I don't think I can do it without you.'

'Of course you can,' Dan replies. 'But that doesn't mean you have to.'

They sit silently, their breathing synchronised.

'I love you, Dan.'

'I love you, too, Natalie. But you've got to know what you're taking on. I'm not wired the same as most people, you know that. It's not going to disappear overnight. Whatever you want to label it as... It's part of me. It'll probably always be there.'

'Nobody's perfect,' she starts, a nervous smile on her face.

'Listen, Natalie,' he says. 'You should care; you *should*. It's not going to be easy. I know from last time how long it took to get back on my feet, to be *normal* again.'

'Will you stop using that word. Normal. I hate it, it's so... judgmental. Like you've deviated from a path somehow.'

Dan laughs at that, smiling.

'Ordinary, then,' he says.

'Now that I can get on board with,' Natalie says. 'Ordinary. I like the sound of that.'

'Yeah,' he sighs, flopping back onto the bed. 'Me, too.'

'It's there, Dan,' Natalie says, lying back horizontally across the bed next to him. 'Ordinary. Giving us a wave in the distance. All we have to do is wave back.'

They lie side by side on his bed, feet planted firmly on the floor. Natalie reaches over and brushes her fingers against Dan's as they turn their heads to look at each other, staying flat on the bed as they do so.

'Ordinary it is, then.'

EPILOGUE

I keep seeing a shark, swimming alongside me in the murky no-man's land of Dan's subconscious. All this time, I thought it wanted Dan, I worried it would bite him. I wanted to protect him from it. I realise my mistake now. It never existed, it was an apparition, a manifestation of Dan's fear of me, what he thought I could become. He should have known I'd never hurt him, though. I only wanted to help. Instead of letting me, he dragged me down into the depths where nobody will ever find me. And now it's engulfed me. I am the shark. He's turned me into the thing he feared, the thing everyone fears, alone in the darkness, swimming, swimming, swimming. Dan knows what he's done to me. He knows where he banished me to.

Don't you, Dan? I shout. *You can still hear me.*

He doesn't care. It's an echo chamber now, a watery cavern filled with shimmering darkness. He refuses to acknowledge me, won't engage me in conversation. Lonely is such an inadequate word. What did I do to him to deserve this? I still get glimpses of his life, beacons of light down here. I can hear him laughing, see Natalie smiling back at him, leaning in to kiss him or hold his hand. I catch moments of their lives being lived, day after glorious sun-filled day. Their happiness erodes me, piece by piece. I have no form anymore, no free will. Sometimes I wonder if I exist at all. Maybe I never did. It's such a strange notion, the *self*. I was certain I had one. Can I possibly be just a trick of the mind, an invention of neurons and chemical imbalances and hormones?

'Maybe that's all any of us are,' Dan whispers, so quietly I'm not sure he even said it.

Dan, is that you?

Silence. It wasn't him. He doesn't need me now. I don't think he'll ever need me again. He has Natalie. And I'm happy for him.

I served my purpose. I've been discarded. I'm the shark. Alone in the darkness.

More from this author

The Pursuit of Ordinary is Nigel's second novel. His debut, *Beat the Rain*, was the bestselling JHP Fiction title of 2016 and was a semi-finalist in the Best Debut Author category for the Goodreads Choice Awards in the same year.

You may recognise one of *Beat the Rain*'s main characters, Louise, as the café owner Natalie bumps into at the bereavement group in *The Pursuit of Ordinary*.

Can Louise move on from the loss of her lover Tom? Can she and Tom's twin brother, Adam, really find a way to love one another? Or are they trapped on a path of self-destruction, moving toward a tragedy neither can avoid?

Beat the Rain *is a moving and vulnerable depiction of a relationship in decline. At times humorous, at times heart-breaking, it explores what it means to live, to love and to lose.*

Beat the Rain is available from Amazon, Waterstones, Barnes & Noble and other booksellers.

About the Author

The Pursuit of Ordinary is Nigel's second novel. He lives in Brighton with his partner, their two children and their greying ginger dog Luka. Previously, he co-founded digital marketing agency Qube Media (Qubist) and was a writer and editor for Channel 4 Television in the UK. Find out more about Nigel on his website and social-media pages:

Website: www.nigeljaycooper.com
Facebook: www.facebook.com/nigeljaycooper
Twitter: www.twitter.com/nijay

If you enjoyed *The Pursuit of Ordinary*, please recommend it to a friend and review it on Amazon.

An excerpt from

Beat the Rain

Chapter One

Louise does all of the things the bereaved are supposed to do; she's had enough practice. She gracefully accepts well-meant platitudes from people she can't stand; she smiles in the right places and pretends she's still able to care. Everything she's become is now an invention, a persona created to make other people feel better.

If she could, she'd never leave the flat again, she'd switch off her mobile, stop answering the door and lie in bed, endlessly staring at the ceiling. This morning she slept through the postman knocking as she dreamt of hot narrow lanes and enormous churches. She smiled and pointed out of the window, past the church, past the market stalls in the square, past the sea. She felt Tom's presence behind her, tried to turn around to see him, to kiss him. Then she felt her sheets clinging to her. Morning.

Tom would have heard the postman. He would have jumped out of bed like an excitable ten-year-old.

"A package, Lou," his gleaming eyes would have said.

"You're a grown man, Tom," she would have replied, barely glancing at him as he danced around the bedroom in nothing but his boxer shorts.

"What do you think it is?" he'd have asked.

"Same as every month, Tom," she'd have smiled. "Your books."

She stares at the yellow-white stained walls of their flat. Her flat now, she reminds herself, just hers again. Today is book day again. She has one every month but this one's early. She stubs a cigarette out on the faded mahogany dresser under the hallway mirror. This thing that she is, this woman, barely formed, stares back at her, like an alien, a shadow of someone who used to exist. Is loss something she's supposed to accept in her life, like other people accept doing a job they don't love or avoiding chips and chocolate cake? She checks her eyes in the hallway mirror to make sure they're not too puffy and braces herself before opening the front door, mentally preparing her 'outside' face, the one that can still smile.

Her days are alike, or different. It doesn't matter. None of them contain a version of her that isn't alone. She shuts her front door, looking away from Mr Carmichael, her ever-smiling, ever-gardening neighbour as he potters around in a pair of overalls. Louise has often wondered what he does for a living – he and his wife don't seem to work, they're always at home, gardening or singing in their front room around an enormous piano that seems much too big for the space. She feels lucky her flat is upstairs so at least she doesn't have to listen to them harmonising.

"Louise." He smiles at her with ceaseless hedge-trimmer hands. "How are you feeling today?" She ignores him and shuffles down the street, sinking into her jumper.

The post office is a thirty-minute walk or a five-minute bus ride away. She imagines the jolting, crowded red double-decker full of kids, old bag ladies and men with body odour and decides to walk. For the most part, her journey produces untroubled faces but occasionally, they become familiar. That's when everyone's smiles freeze.

"Louise, you look great," the familiar will say eventually, their frosty hands touching her jacket sleeve in faux concern. Louise will lick her dry lips in preparation.

"Do I?" she'll finally ask, sometimes genuinely. They'll nod as their fingers grip her arm more tightly.

"We were so sorry to hear about..." Then their voices will trail off. They all think she's dealing with it and she has become practiced in keeping her smile on long enough to reassure them they're right. She waits until they've scuttled away before allowing it to crack.

"Tell your fortune," someone says as she rounds the corner by the bank or pub or restaurant. A lucky-heather woman is standing in front of her, a rainbow headscarf and flowing dress billowing in the gentle breeze. With the morning sunlight glinting behind her, she looks somehow otherworldly and for a moment Louise is mesmerised.

"Some change for your fortune?" the woman says again and for the tiniest of moments, Louise thinks to herself, *Why not?*, then she shudders, remembering what her fate is like. She closes her eyes tightly for a second, as if this will help her break free from the spell she's sure the lucky heather woman has put her under.

"No," Louise says loudly, almost shouting and stepping away. Then, as her manners take over, she says quietly, "Thanks anyway," and continues her journey.

* * *

"What would you do if I died?" Tom asked her once, leaning over and smiling. His left hand invaded her top, resting on her breast.

"I wouldn't let you," she replied, thrusting her chest out and grinning.

"But if you couldn't stop it."

Fingers explored, she pulled him closer. "I'd fuck the postman."

Later, smoking cigarettes and shivering: "Promise you'll never leave me," she said. He kissed her, rolled over, slept.

* * *

"It's Louise, isn't it?"

Louise rounds another corner and is confronted by a woman who grabs her and hugs her tightly, as if she has found her long-lost sister. Louise wishes she'd caught the bus, at least people would have left her alone then.

"I haven't seen you for ages."

Louise stands motionless, arms by her side, not returning the embrace.

"It's me, Narinda," the woman says. "From school. You remember? Of course you remember. The old gang?"

"How are you?" Louise forces out eventually. Seeing her is almost as painful as losing Tom. Narinda is someone from an old life, one Louise wants no part of. Just seeing her has given her gooseflesh, reminding her of the person Tom helped her leave behind, someone she no longer recognises.

"Oh it's so good to see you again. How's…oh what was his name? Tom, wasn't it?"

"Dead," Louise says defiantly, cutting her off. Narinda rocks back slightly, clearly unsure what to do or say.

"Oh, I am sorry," she manages eventually.

"Bye, Narinda," Louise says quietly, pushing past her and continuing her journey.

As she enters the post office, the air conditioning dries her eyes. People are littered around, some waiting in the queue, some filling out forms with broken black biros with snapped silver chains hanging from the ends. Louise hugs her jacket to her chest and waits her turn and when she eventually gets to the counter, she looks away from the man and pushes the card under the glass along with a bill and driving licence as proof of address, hoping she's not going to have to have the same conversation as last month and the month before.

"Has Tom Gaddis signed to say you can pick this up for him?"

"He's dead."

A beat. Frozen features, unsure how to respond to her. "We can't release anything to you unless he's signed to say you can pick it up for him, you see."

"Can dead men sign forms?" Steely green eyes, staring unflinchingly through the glass, daring the man to be a jobsworth. "You can see it's my address, you can see we live together..." A pause, reality sinking in for the twentieth time that day. "Lived together."

Luckily, today, the assistant simply looks at the note and says, "Cold, isn't it," and he grins a British yellow-tooth smile. "Sign here." He shunts a form towards Louise. Her fingers do the work and as he hands her the parcel; she clutches it to her chest and steps back out onto the morning high street.

Every month, she receives the company's 'choice' of book for Tom. It was in the small print when he signed for it – if he didn't choose one himself from their catalogue, they would send one of their own recommendations for him to read. She couldn't allow herself to cancel it, to cancel him. It's strange, though, because the books are early this month and the package seems different. She lets her arms fall back slightly to read the label. It's not the normal printed name and address at all. It's a handwritten one. Tom's writing: Lou.

* * *

"Why don't you like Lou?" Tom asked her once, slipping onto the arm of her chair.

"It's not my name."

Eyes smiled. "So?"

"I was christened Louise."

"Lou, Louise. Same name."

"Different name entirely. Different name, different pronounciation,"

"Pronunciation."

"What?"

* * *

She clutches the box tightly, swallowing and swallowing again, sure the spinning in her stomach will cause her to be sick. She drags herself upstairs and sits staring from the window, hugging the parcel so tightly it hurts her small breasts.

Time is suspended as she walks down their street. *Her street.* The parcel is warm in her arms, like it's emitting some sort of heat, some sort of *life.* As she walks into her front gate, Mr Carmichael is still pruning his hedges and deadheading flowers. He smiles and nods. Her fingers are freezing as she hunts for her keys to the flat, avoiding his gaze, pretending she doesn't feel like a madwoman screaming behind alabaster skin.

"They can teach you a lot, you know," he says.

"Sorry," she mumbles, trying to get her keys in the lock to avoid a lengthy discussion with him.

"Plants and flowers. Trees."

"Sorry, Mr Carmichael, I've really got to get in and..." Louise says without looking around, not even caring if she appears rude.

"When leaves die in autumn, the trees don't hold on to them," Mr Carmichael continues regardless. "They let them go, Louise. If they didn't, no new leaves would grow."

"Mr Carmichael, I..." she starts, glancing around at him and pursing her lips.

"And how sad that tree would look when spring arrived. Still bare."

Louise doesn't respond, she simply nods her head as if she's listened and walks into her flat. She mounts the stairs and stares down the end of the hall at her kitchen, swimming in washing up and ready meals. If Tom were alive he'd be angry.

What readers are saying about

Beat The Rain

A spectacular debut novel by Nigel Jay Cooper. This compelling tale of love and loss is deeply moving and wonderfully written. Full of troubled characters, hidden messages and unexpected twists and turns, this book took me on an emotional roller coaster ride and had hooked me from start to finish. I won this novel in a Goodreads giveaway and it's one I won't forget in a hurry.

Lisa, *Goodreads review*

What an incredible writer and incredible novel. The style, the detail, the deeply captivating imagery. The powerful psychological depth that keeps you gripped. Boy, does this male writer know how to write a deeply complex and believable female character. This book deserves to be vastly read by all...buy it and marvel at it, as I did.

Jules, *Goodreads review*

A brilliant read but be prepared for an emotional journey... twists and turns, breath-taking moments and some that we can all relate to at some point of our lives. Hilarious moments too and a fabulous dinner party!

Carrol M, *Goodreads review*

The writing is absolutely compelling. Normally it takes me quite a while before I really get emotionally attached to a book, but this book pulled me in from the first page. The characters are beautifully written and flawed and the plot twists are endless. I finished this book last night and I'm still reeling in my emotions. This has become one of my favourite books of all time.

Charlotte W, *Goodreads review*

Nigel Jay Cooper is an excellent author, getting so deeply into the heads of his characters that he takes the reader along for the dive. Reading this book has been, for me, a totally immersive experience and left me completely enveloped in the deepest recesses of the psyches of the two main characters Adam and Louise. This was at times a breathless ride, through depression, obsession, grief, despair, excitement and anxiety. As a therapist I found the internal portrayal dead on, and it was hard to put the book down. Each plot twist kept me hanging on for more ... now I find myself hanging on for Nigel Jay Cooper's next book, whenever that might be.

Beverley K, *Goodreads review*

It says so much about a book when I read it in one sitting – something I have never done before. Staying awake well beyond my normal time desperate to keep my eyes open to complete this. It grabbed me, pulled me in and I couldn't put it down. A thoroughly, totally un-put-down-able book. A stunning debut.

Nicki M, *Goodreads review*

Wow, I just finished this unique book. It is about love, fractured relationships, deception with a dash of Fatal Attraction thrown in. If you are looking for a story that introduces you to interesting characters and has taken a few steps off the beaten path then this is the one for you. What a wonderful first novel and I'm looking forward to further stories from this author.

Becky N, *Netgalley review*

Such a powerful story that I couldn't put down - so much so that I missed my train stop! The inner emotional histories, guilt and desires of the characters are all stripped back and lain naked for the reader to love, hate, or sometimes relate to. While the characters are ordinary people, the writing is extraordinary, and I was gripped from start to finish. It has been almost a week since

I missed that train, and the book is still lingering in my brain. I look forward to reading more from this amazing author.

Elaine F, *Amazon review*

Roundfire

FICTION

Put simply, we publish great stories. Whether it's literary or popular, a gentle tale or a pulsating thriller, the connecting theme in all Roundfire fiction titles is that once you pick them up you won't want to put them down.

If you have enjoyed this book, why not tell other readers by posting a review on your preferred book site.

Recent bestsellers from Roundfire are:

The Bookseller's Sonnets
Andi Rosenthal

The Bookseller's Sonnets intertwines three love stories with a tale of
religious identity and mystery spanning five hundred years and
three countries.
Paperback: 978-1-84694-342-3 ebook: 978-184694-626-4

Birds of the Nile
An Egyptian Adventure
N.E. David

Ex-diplomat Michael Blake wanted a quiet birding trip up the Nile
– he wasn't expecting a revolution.
Paperback: 978-1-78279-158-4 ebook: 978-1-78279-157-7

Blood Profit$
The Lithium Conspiracy
J. Victor Tomaszek, James N. Patrick, Sr.

The blood of the many for the profits of the few… *Blood Profit$* will
take you into the cigar-smoke-filled room where American policy
and laws are really made.
Paperback: 978-1-78279-483-7 ebook: 978-1-78279-277-2

The Burden
A Family Saga
N.E. David

Frank will do anything to keep his mother and father apart. But
he's carrying baggage – and it might just weigh him down ...
Paperback: 978-1-78279-936-8 ebook: 978-1-78279-937-5

The Cause
Roderick Vincent

The second American Revolution will be a fire lit from an internal spark.
Paperback: 978-1-78279-763-0 ebook: 978-1-78279-762-3

Don't Drink and Fly
The Story of Bernice O'Hanlon: Part One
Cathie Devitt

Bernice is a witch living in Glasgow. She loses her way in her life and wanders off the beaten track looking for the garden of enlightenment.
Paperback: 978-1-78279-016-7 ebook: 978-1-78279-015-0

Gag
Melissa Unger

One rainy afternoon in a Brooklyn diner, Peter Howland punctures an egg with his fork. Repulsed, Peter pushes the plate away and never eats again.
Paperback: 978-1-78279-564-3 ebook: 978-1-78279-563-6

The Master Yeshua
The Undiscovered Gospel of Joseph
Joyce Luck

Jesus is not who you think he is. The year is 75 CE. Joseph ben Jude is frail and ailing, but he has a prophecy to fulfil …
Paperback: 978-1-78279-974-0 ebook: 978-1-78279-975-7

On the Far Side, There's a Boy
Paula Coston

Martine Haslett, a thirty-something 1980s woman, plays hard on the fringes of the London drag club scene until one night which prompts her to sign up to a charity. She writes to a young Sri Lankan boy, with consequences far and long.
Paperback: 978-1-78279-574-2 ebook: 978-1-78279-573-5

Tuareg
Alberto Vazquez-Figueroa

With over 5 million copies sold worldwide, *Tuareg* is a classic adventure story from best-selling author Alberto Vazquez-Figueroa, about honour, revenge and a clash of cultures.
Paperback: 978-1-84694-192-4

Readers of ebooks can buy or view any of these bestsellers by clicking on the live link in the title. Most titles are published in paperback and as an ebook. Paperbacks are available in traditional bookshops. Both print and ebook formats are available online.

Find more titles and sign up to our readers' newsletter at
http://www.johnhuntpublishing.com/fiction

Follow us on Facebook at https://www.facebook.com/JHPfiction
and Twitter at https://twitter.com/JHPFiction